PRAISE FOR
THE DOMINO MEN

"If you only read one black comedy with the brains and labyrinthine twists of Vedantic hair-splitting, make it this one. . . . a gripping yarn." —*Chicago Sun-Times*

"Unmatched life and verve." —*Washington Post Book World*

"A fantastic novel." —*Denver Rocky Mountain News*

"Another remarkable outing, an infectious blend of wit, wonder, and the bizarre presented with remarkable style. This is literary fiction for the genre fiction set, or possibly the other way around . . . genuinely shocking and inventive."
—*San Antonio Express-News*

"Barnes's growth as a writer is evident: His plots are still fresh but smoother, and the final twists are unexpected, yet not jarring. Kudos to Barnes for another winner that is as funny as it is creepy, as thought-provoking as it is entertaining."
—*Colorado Springs Independent*

"Barnes's second novel, a compelling supernatural thriller, shows that his impressive debut, *The Somnambulist*, was no fluke. . . . Thanks to Barnes's evocative prose, readers will easily suspend disbelief. Those who enjoy the grafting of fantasy elements onto contemporary urban landscapes will be more than satisfied."
—*Publish*

Amelia Wallace

ABOUT THE AUTHOR

JONATHAN BARNES is the author of *The Somnambulist* and *The Domino Men*. Educated in Norfolk and at Oxford, he is a regular contributor to *The Times Literary Supplement* and lives a few miles outside of London. He is currently hard at work on his third novel.

ALSO BY JONATHAN BARNES

The Somnambulist

THE
DOMINO
MEN

JONATHAN
BARNES

HARPER

NEW YORK · LONDON · TORONTO · SYDNEY

HARPER

A hardcover edition of this book was published in 2009 by William Morrow, an imprint of HarperCollins Publishers.

HarperCollins books may be purchased for educational, business, or sales promotional use. For information please write: Special Markets Department, HarperCollins Publishers, 10 East 53rd Street, New York, NY 10022.

FIRST HARPER PAPERBACK PUBLISHED 2010.

Designed by Lovedog Studio

Library of Congress Cataloging-in-Publication Data has been applied for.

ISBN 978-0-06-167141-8

10 11 12 13 14   OV/RRD   10 9 8 7 6 5 4 3 2 1

For Amelia

Acknowledgments

In the U.S.—Diana Gill, for her invaluable guidance.

In the U.K.—Simon Spanton for his editing expertise; Bede Rogerson for his indispensable advice; Ben Marsden and Michael Caines for their ongoing encouragement; Thomas Ellis and Christopher Barnes for their assistance with research.

At home—my parents for all their support; Amelia for continuing to change everything.

EDITOR'S NOTE

In preparing this manuscript for publication, I have made only minor adjustments and corrections, principally in matters of spelling and grammar, in the smoothing over of certain infelicities of style and in the division of the text into sympathetic chapters.

The rest may be considered verbatim—even those curious shifts and modulations against whose inclusion my advisers have so strenuously objected, warning of the most appalling damage both to my own reputation and to that of my family.

In all significant respects, *The Domino Men* is just as I found it, waiting for me on my doorstep last summer, on the day that its author disappeared from the face of the earth.

I believe that the pages which follow provide the nearest thing we shall ever be granted to an explanation.

AW

THE DOMINO MEN

CHAPTER 1

I'M HORRIBLY AWARE, AS I SIT AT THE DESK IN THIS room that you've lent me, that time is now very short for me indeed. Outside, the light of day is fading fast; in here, the ticking of the clock sounds close to deafening.

I've come to terms with the fact that I won't have time to write everything that I'd hoped—my definitive history of the war, from its origins in the dreams of the nineteenth century to the grisly skirmishes of my granddad's day to the recent, catastrophic battle in which you and I played modest parts. No, I simply have to hope that there'll be time enough for me to set down my own story, or at least as much of it as I can remember before the thing which sleeps inside me wakes, stirs, flexes its muscles and, with a lazy flick of its gargantuan tail, gives me no alternative but to forget.

I know where I have to start. Of course, I wasn't present in person—wasn't even born then—but I'm sure that it was there, for all intents and purposes, that it began. I can picture it so clearly, as though these events are calling to me across the years, pleading with me to set them down on paper.

It's probably no coincidence that I've been thinking a lot lately about the old flat, the place in Tooting Bec where I lived with Abbey in happier times and which, in a strange sort of way (although I didn't realise it back then), was always at the heart of the business. Our house was built at some point late in the 1860s. I had other things on my mind whilst I lived there and I never looked into its history, but Abbey did once, in an offhand, mildly curious sort of way, spurred on, I think, by some TV show or other. Her findings were faintly disquieting, although she never discovered what I now know about the place. But then, how could she? The Directorate kept those records locked up safe and everyone who was present or who knew anything about them is long dead.

It happened late one night towards the end of April 6, 1967. Years before the house was divided into flats and a decade or so before I came into the world, a long, dark sedan motored to a stop outside the flat in Tooting Bec. Although spring should have been in full bloom, it had felt more like winter for almost a week and everyone had started wearing thick coats, hats and scarves again, shouldering their way to the backs of their wardrobes to tug out winter outfits that they'd hoped not to see again until October.

It had been raining for hours and the streets, lit up by the unforgiving yellow of the lamps, seemed to shine and dully glisten as though they'd been smeared with some grease or unguent. No one was abroad and the only sounds were the distant wail of a baby and the plaintive whinnies of urban foxes, padding through the darkened city, foraging for anything that might prove edible amongst the junk and wreckage so carelessly abandoned by humanity.

The car door opened and a tall man unfolded himself from the driver's seat—middle-aged; sharply, almost dandyishly dressed in a dark blue, single-breasted suit and still handsome, albeit with a cruelly vulpine quality to his features. With him was a woman, about the same age, but already moving like someone much older, a brittle spinster decades before her time. Both wore expressions of stoic professionalism mingled (and I suppose we must consider this to be to their credit) with a kind of distasteful disbelief at the unconscionable demands of their jobs.

They had a passenger with them, lolling in the back seat, apparently drunk almost to the point of insensibility. It was a woman, very young and even then, after all that had been done to her, still extremely beautiful. Most of her hair had been shaved away, although a few scattered, tufty islets remained. Her scalp was marked out with scorings, scars and half-healed incisions, and she seemed only dimly aware of what was happening to her, clinging to the man in the same way in which a child clutches at her father's hand on the way to her first day at school. He pulled her out onto the street and helped her stagger towards the front door of the house, letting her slump and flop against him, an arrangement which lent him the appearance of a shop boy grappling (not a little salaciously) with a storefront dummy.

When they got to the door, the older woman reached into her handbag, first for a key and then for a pair of torches. Once the door was open and the torches were switched on, the man steered the girl over the threshold, whispering declarations of love into her ear, honeyed fictions designed with the sole purpose of keeping her moving, saccharine lies told only to propel her onwards. Inside, the house was stripped and empty. The man dragged the girl down the corridor towards the dining room, the bobbing light of his torch picking out their way. His companion, after surveying the street with baleful eyes, busied herself in locking and bolting the door and ensuring, with the painstaking paranoia of the career professional, that the place was completely free of all listening devices, surveillance equipment and sundry bugs.

In the dining room there was an old white wooden chair, a few unlit candles and a brand-new television set. The floorboards were bare and seemed to have been daubed with strange signs and symbols in what I can only hope and pray was red paint. There was a strange quality of power in the room, of energy crackling in the air, its presence understood in the same distant way in which one might sense the throb of an engine or the humming whine of a generator.

The man helped the girl into the chair. She was moaning a little now, grizzling like a baby in the grip of a bad dream. He patted her head before producing a length of rope and binding her to the chair, winding it so tightly around her wrists and ankles that he drew blood. At this, she started to whimper and complain but the man cooed softly, stroked her lips and ran his fingers along the bridge of her nose in the kind of intimately soothing gesture which only a lover can perform, until she fell silent once again.

They had a moment alone together then. He could have begged for her forgiveness, he could have wept tears of shame and regret, he could, at the very least, have said something to try to make amends. But he didn't. She stared up at him with dull accusation in her eyes and he found himself unable to return her gaze. Head bowed, he walked across to the other side of the room and began, with sacerdotal reverence and intensity, to light the candles. A few minutes later, the woman came into the room, closed the door behind her and suggested, with only the barest tremble in her voice, that they begin.

What they did next sickens me to think of it, no matter how many times I've been vociferously assured of its necessity.

The handsome man stood over the chair and, reaching down to a leather pouch that he kept out of sight and strapped to his flank, produced a knife. Its blade gleamed in the candle-light.

There may have been a ritual of some kind. Who can say? I never understood the specifics. But I feel certain that the older woman would have said a few words, that, in that clear, precise schoolmarm's voice of hers, she would have issued an invitation into the dark.

Once she had finished speaking, the man moved closer to the girl and, in a few swift motions, lifted the knife into the air and brought it slicing down. Just before the blade bit into her flesh, he told her the same thing that, four decades later, he would say to me.

"Trust the Process," he said.

Then again, as though repeating a lie somehow makes it true: "Trust the Process."

I don't want to imagine what came next but I find it almost impossible not to—the cutting of her wrists, the animal screams of pain, the awful, unstaunchable flow of blood.

Once the bleeding had stopped, once the poor girl ought, according to any biological law, to have slid gratefully into death or unconsciousness, she sat up quite straight in her seat with a sticky, fleshy popping sound, like the noise one hears on pulling the heads off shrimp.

Whatever it was which stared out at them from behind that girl's eyes, it wasn't remotely human. When it spoke, it was no longer in the voice of the girl at all. It would have been impatient, I think, a little peevish and annoyed, as it asked why it had been called to this place before it was time, before the city was ripe.

Then—the springing of the trap. Realising too late what had happened, the thing that wore the girl's skin screeched in rage and fury. It hissed and thrashed and struggled in its chair as, quite impossibly, the cuts on its wrists began to knit themselves together, the skin miraculously reconstituting itself over the slaughterhouse confusion of flesh and blood until, at last, it came to understand the parameters of its entrapment.

The man and the woman watched until the creature in the

chair fell silent and the change began. Unable to bear witness to the alterations wrought upon the body, they left the girl where she sat and retired to the nearest public house, where, on taxpayers' money, they proceeded to fortify themselves with a generous martini apiece.

FORTY YEARS LATER, I moved into that same building. I ate my meals, read the newspaper, kicked off my shoes, leant back on the sofa and watched TV in the room where they cut the wrists of that poor girl. All the time I was oblivious of what had happened there, foolishly (and, as it turned out, tragically) ignorant of the circle of history which was almost complete.

But I'm getting ahead of myself. Until very recently, I knew none of this, and for a long time, I believed that the story of the Domino Men started last year, in slightly more prosaic circumstances, when everything in my life still seemed broadly normal. I thought that it began with my granddad and with what happened to him in the Queen's Head.

CHAPTER 2

T HE FIRST THING YOU SHOULD KNOW IS THAT NO one in my family had ever liked my granddad much. I was always the exception. My mother's opinion was typical and may accurately be gauged by the way in which she broke the news.

"The old bastard's dead," she said, trying to sound sombre but unable or unwilling to remove the last few crumbs of glee from her voice. Then again, more firmly this time, not bothering to suppress the smirk.

"The old bastard's dead."

HE WAS IN A PUB when it happened. Nowhere flashy or picturesque, just another link in a chain, one of those places with the décor of an airport waiting lounge and the ambience of an NHS dentist. It was four weeks from Christmas, the stores were oiling their tills in readiness for the season of consumption and when I picture what happened I always imagine "I Saw Mommy Kissing Santa Claus" or "I Wish It Could Be Christmas Every Day" echoing tinnily in the background.

The old bastard stood at the bar, clasping a pint, flirting with the barmaid, grandstanding for the regulars. Well into his seventies, he looked even older—puce faced and rheumy eyed, his nose stippled with smashed capillaries, those good looks which in his youth had magnetised the attentions of more women than he could count now barely discernible beneath the palimpsests of hard living, old age, regret.

Granddad had a way of drawing people into his orbit, a talent for acquiring an entourage. After he retired to devote the rest of his life to the booze, the quality of his hangers-on underwent a vertiginous decline until by the end it was only the deadbeats who flocked to him, the idlers and the dropouts, the skiving masters and the loafing champs. They were the kind of human jetsam who wash up in the pubs the moment its doors are unbolted and stick at their stools throughout the afternoon, their natural habitat the post-lunch lull, the boozy quiet before the suits trample in. My story started for me at just this time of day, when men like my granddad rule the pub. It began in the hour of the pensioner.

He started to tell a joke, something corny which began, in his favourite formulation, with that whiskery triumvirate of comic stand-bys—an Englishman, an Irishman and a Scotsman. It is a source of endless regret to me that he never got as far as the punchline. I often think that if he had then everything might have been different.

Granddad collected bad jokes, had even written a few of them in his time, and he would have been spinning this one out, hamming up the details and relishing the accents. The courtiers chuckled along with him, sufficiently beered up even at that time of the afternoon to laugh at almost anything, tugged along by the promise of another drink once the joke was done, because Granddad—despite his casual treachery and deceit—could always be relied upon to stand his ground.

This, then, as near as I can reconstruct it, is the joke that he told. As things turned out, it was to be his last.

An Englishman, an Irishman and a Scotsman are summoned before the Queen. They stand there at Buckingham Palace, lined up before her, gawping at the finery of the place like a trio of slack-jawed yokels on a daytrip. The Queen has a commission for them—a kind of favour—and she asks if there's anything they wouldn't do for her. It's the Englishman who steps forward first. "Nothing," he says. "There's nothing I wouldn't do for my Queen."

"Nor I," says the Irishman.

"Nor I," says the Scotsman.

To which the Queen replies: "Would you kill for me? Would you maim and hack and slit for me?"

The witnesses agree that it was at this moment that my granddad's mood changed completely. It was as though all the good humour had been vacuum-pumped from the room.

He winced. A shadow passed across his face. Everyone swears blind that this is what he said next, his voice quaking with emotion: "This is not a joke. This is a secret."

Another wince. Or rather, an expression which began as a wince before growing into a spasm and was well on its way to becoming a convulsion when he pitched forward on his stool and sprawled face-down in the sticky carpet. His companions gaped blearily at him. One or two even wondered whether this might not be part of the fun and were starting to wish that he'd hurry up, get back to his feet and order another brace of drinks, when it became apparent that this was more than play-acting. A murmur of disquiet. A small but noticeable sobering up.

A stranger stepped forward from the back of the pub, where he had been sitting, silent and unobserved, nursing a lemonade with a couple of similarly unobtrusive friends. In a flat, prim voice, he told them that he was a doctor and asked, politely but with the air of someone used to an attentive audience, whether he might be of some assistance.

He wore a dark, old-fashioned suit, a skinny tie and a grubby white shirt with a peculiarly high collar, and he looked completely out of place in that pub, absurdly, embarrassingly incongruous.

No sooner had he appeared than one of his companions, dressed, so far as anyone could tell, in exactly the same quaint way, abandoned his lemonade and trotted up beside him.

Without the slightest trace of emotion, he announced that he too was a doctor and wondered aloud whether he could help to alleviate the situation.

Then, with the woozy logic of a recurring dream, a third stranger, identically attired, strolled up to the bar to casually announce that he'd trained at Barts and that his services were unequivocally at their disposal.

Everyone shuffled back, too befuddled to do much else, as the strangers knelt beside Granddad like the magi turned up by mistake at an old folks' home.

The first of them rolled him onto his back and reached for his wrist, groping for a pulse with forefinger and thumb. After a few seconds, he announced that Granddad still lived. It was only then that any chink of emotion entered his voice. The entourage told me later that it sounded like disappointment.

As the second man speculated about a stroke, a heart attack, an embolism, the last of the strangers took a handkerchief from the top pocket of his jacket, wiped his brow and suggested that someone call a bloody ambulance.

WHEN MUM TOLD ME this story, I stopped her here, my heart cartwheeling in hope. "You told me he was dead."

I could hear the sneer in her voice. "Well," she said. "As good as."

THERE'S SOMETHING MORE YOU ought to know. Each of those men, each of those so-called doctors, spoke with a different regional accent, each so pronounced and distinct as to be immediately recognisable.

Those men were walking stereotypes. They were a bad joke.

They were an Englishman, an Irishman and a Scotsman.

CHAPTER 3

NOTHING OUT OF THE ORDINARY EVER HAPPENS TO me on a Tuesday. It's reliably the dullest day of the week. Even the Tuesday on which my life began its skydive into horror seemed, at first, to be no exception.

I opened my eyes a few seconds before the alarm intended to jangle me awake, rolled across the bed and smacked the machine into silence. With only a little groan at the prospect of another day, I got up, visited the bathroom, washed my hands, trudged into the kitchen for coffee, rummaged around the fridge to see if there was anything salvageable for breakfast and settled eventually for a bruised and doughy banana. But I was disappointed to see no obvious sign of my landlady, no evidence that she was even awake.

We lived, my landlady and I, in a rickety two-bedroom flat in Tooting Bec, SW17. It formed the ground floor of a careworn Victorian house, a short walk from a main street which had about it that distinctively London bouquet, that eau de Tooting—beer, dope and drains; old fish, exhaust fumes, stale urine. The second floor was empty and, so far as we knew, had been for years—something to do, we thought, with some structural infelicity or other. My landlady had been there several years whilst I was still the new boy—freshly ensconced only a month earlier but already resident for long enough to know exactly how I felt about her.

After I had showered and changed into my suit (fraying at the hem, balding at the knees from its overfamiliarity with the dry cleaner), I confess to dallying as I made my sandwiches in the hope of seeing my landlady emerge, gummy eyed and yawning, on a hunt for cornflakes. But her bedroom door remained resolutely closed.

I grabbed my lunch and cycling helmet and exited the flat, careful to double-lock the front door on my way out. It was a cold, clear morning in December and my breath steamed in the air like smoke. It had rained hard in the night and the world had a smeary, dripping quality to it like I was looking at life through a pane of glass damp with condensation. I stooped to unlock the dilapidated bike which I habitually kept chained to a lamppost despite the fact that it had failed to attract so much as a single, half-hearted robbery attempt and that even dogs declined to relieve themselves against its rusty wheels and flaking frame.

Clambering on, I set off, wobbly at first, then gaining in confidence. Down the street, past the corner shop, the video rental store, the King's Arms and the halal pizza parlour, before, sailing by the tube station, I got giddy, felt a head-rush of excitement, swerved into the torrent of traffic and sprinted out onto the main road. From there, it took me somewhere in the region of three quarters of an hour to get to work, pedalling through Clapham, Brixton, Stockwell and Lambeth, the smoke and grit and filth of London billowing in my face the whole way. Even as I cycled, I became aware that I was part of something bigger than myself, a constituent of the great charge into work, the mindless drone-stream to the centre of the city. Underground and overground, in trains, by car, on foot, everybody was elbowing their way in, their eyes on the prize, sparing not a glance for anyone who shared the same quest as them, all of us hurtling forwards in the merciless stampede of the morning commute.

It was perilously close to nine o'clock when I finally squealed to a halt outside 125 Fitzgibbon Street—a squat grey building just down from Waterloo station and a few minutes' walk from the tourist traps on the south bank of the river Thames. The building did nothing to draw attention to itself, although a grimy plastic sign drilled into the wall gave further details for the curious.

CIVIL SERVICE ARCHIVE UNIT
STORAGE AND RECORD RETRIEVAL

Time was when this stretch of the city would have been thriving with rude life but now it seemed either neutered into the sterility of officialdom or else stuffed and mounted for the edification and amusement of visitors like some dead thing in a museum. Wheezy and panting for breath, I shackled my bike in the parking lot beside a bottle bank and a bin for recycling newspapers. In the distance, still garlanded by morning mist, I could make out the turrets of Westminster, the decorous spike of Big Ben, the shining spokes of the London Eye, but I turned my back on the sights of the city and trudged into the building. I waved my pass at Derek in reception, stepped into the lift, took a deep breath and emerged soon after at the sixth floor.

Here was all the comfortable monotony of a day at the office. Grey floors, grey walls, grey desks, grey life. The room was large and open plan and seemed crowded with the usual sounds—the faint hum of computers, the chuntering whine of the photo-copier, the persistent insectoid buzz of ringing phones. I walked to my desk, piled high with stacks of dun-coloured folders, nod-ding at a few of my colleagues as I went, exchanging the usual good mornings and all rights and how was your weekends.

There was a strange girl sitting in my chair.

"You're sitting in my chair," I said, feeling like one of the three bears.

"Hi." She sounded friendly enough. "Are you Henry Lamb?"

I nodded.

"Hi," she said again. "I'm Barbara."

She was in her late twenties, plump, bespectacled and dumpy. She gave me a gauche smile and fumbled nervously with the frames of her glasses.

I still had no idea what she was doing in my chair.

"I'm from the agency," she prompted.

Then I remembered. "You've come to help with the filing."

"I think so."

"Well then. I'll show you the ropes."

BARBARA NODDED POLITELY AS I pointed out the lavatories, the water cooler, the notice board, the fire escapes and the coffee machine. I introduced her to a few colleagues, all of whom looked faintly irritated at the interruption, before, finally, I knocked on the door of my manager. A voice from within: "Come!"

Peter Hickey-Brown slouched at his desk, arms folded behind his head in a clumsy attempt at nonchalance. He had a shock of grey hair which he had grown out too long. He didn't wear a tie. His shirt was sufficiently unbuttoned to reveal tufts of salt-and-pepper chest hair and, more ill-advisedly still, the glint of cheap jewellery. Poor Peter. He'd worn an earring to work for a week last year until senior management had been forced to have a quiet but firm word.

"Peter? This is Barbara. She's come to help us with the filing."

"Barbara! Hi! Welcome aboard."

They shook hands.

"So you're working under Henry?" he asked.

"Looks like it."

Peter winked. "Better watch this one. He knows where all our bodies are buried."

The three of us managed some feeble laughter.

"So what do you prefer? Barbara? Barb?" He broke off, as though struck by a brilliant idea. "How do you like Babs?" He sounded hopeful. "Less of a mouthful."

The girl had a trapped look. "Well, some people call me Babs."

This I doubted. She didn't look like a Babs to me.

Peter strutted back to his desk. "You like music, Babs?"

"I suppose."

Now I just felt sorry for her. Peter behaved like this around any woman younger than himself—a demographic which, perhaps not wholly coincidentally, encompassed most of the female percentage of our office.

"I've just been on the Web booking tickets for a few gigs. You ever heard of a band called Peachy Cheeks?"

"I don't think so, no."

"Boner?"

A shy little shake of her head.

"Arse Bandits?"

Barbara thought for a moment. "Doesn't ring a bell."

Peter shrugged. "I'm not surprised. This stuff's a little out there. It's . . ." He broke off for a stagey chuckle. "It's not exactly what you'd call mainstream." A hideous pause, then: "Allrighty! Great to meet you, Babs. Any questions, my door's always open." And he winked.

Good grief, the man actually winked.

"Sorry about him," I said once the door had clicked shut and we were safely out of earshot.

"Don't be. He seems nice."

"You'll learn. Come on, let's grab a coffee. I'll get us a meeting room."

I found us a room, where we sat for a while, each staring awkwardly into our cup. "I'd better say something about what we do here," I said at last. "What did they tell you at the agency?"

The girl looked apologetic. "Not much."

"We're filing people," I said, starting the usual speech. "Our job is to catalogue every document the civil service produces."

"Sounds riveting."

"It has its moments. Record retrieval can be surprisingly interesting."

"And how long have you been here?"

"Me?" I said, stalling for time—as though she could possibly have been referring to anyone else. "Oh, about three years."

"You've been a filing clerk for three years?"

"It's a living," I protested. "Anyway. On your feet. You ought to see where the magic happens."

The largest of our filing rooms was the size of several tennis courts but still felt cramped and claustrophobic thanks to the enormous metal cabinets which took up every available inch, crammed next to one another like stainless steel commuters. Filled with mouldering paper, packed end to end with dead statistics, old reports, putrefying memos and long-forgotten minutes, the place had the air of a second-hand bookshop which never makes a sale.

"It'll be nice to have some company in here," I said before going on to explain the filing system (a needlessly complicated business of acronyms, mnemonics and numeric codes) whilst Barbara did her best to stifle a yawn.

"This stuff's just the tip of the iceberg," I said. "This is just a fraction of it. Of course, a lot of the older stuff's in an annexe in Norbiton but even there we're running out of space. It's getting to be a real problem."

"You've really been doing this for three years?"

I tried a grin. "For my sins."

"Don't you get bored?"

"Sometimes." Sighing, I admitted the truth of it. "Every day."

FOR THE REST OF the morning, Barbara stood by my side as I filed a batch of records, ostensibly watching me work ("shadowing me," as Peter had put it), though, as I kept catching her sneaking glances in my direction, I wondered if she wasn't spending more time looking at me than at the work. I wasn't at all sure how to take this, although I had my suspicions and it's almost certainly not what you're thinking.

At ten to one, we were back at my desk and I was tussling with a more than usually insubordinate spreadsheet when the telephone rang.

"Henry? It's Peter. Could you step into my lair?"

My desk was seconds from his office but he seemed to derive pleasure from making me come running.

When I went in, he barely looked up from his screen. "New girl settling in OK?"

"She seems fine. Very competent."

"Good, good. I've just had a call from Phil Statham. He's got to do some induction thing with her this afternoon. Safety training. Two o'clock in the conference room?"

"I'll let her know."

"I'd like you to sit in as well."

I cleared my throat. "I've already done the safety course, Peter."

"Sure, sure. But after last month's little blunder . . ."

I blushed.

"You see what I'm getting at?"

"Of course."

"Allrighty. You kids enjoy yourselves, OK?" And he waved a cheaply bejewelled hand to indicate that my audience was at an end.

I PREFER TO EAT LUNCH alone. I like to find a bench, unparcel my sandwiches and lose myself in the flow of the Thames. I can spend an entire hour gazing at the river as it gropes and claws at the banks, watching the scummy hitchhikers who float on its surface—the plastic bottles and the crisp packets, the used condoms, the sodden paper and all the random metropolitan junk which bobs on the black water to be tossed ashore or sucked under. Often I've made myself late watching that liquid history, wondering who has come before me and who shall come after, who has watched that same stretch of river, that same water ebb and flow in its endless mysterious cycle.

On that particular Tuesday, however, I had Barbara with me. She hadn't brought any lunch so we had to go to a sandwich shop, where she blew an hour's pay on a cheese baguette.

The riverbank bustled with London life. We passed flocks of suits and clusters of tourists—the first group strutting with jaded impatience, the last ambling, filled with curiosity and exaggerated wonder. We passed a homeless man juggling for pennies, a crocodile of schoolchildren on a daytrip and a shaven-headed young woman who hassled us for donations to charity. There was a power walker who scurried feyly past, his head set at a comically quizzical tilt, a blind woman and her dog and a fat man in a bobble hat selling early editions of the *Evening Standard* and bellowing out his headline. This was something about the Queen, I think, although I wasn't moved to buy a copy. At that time (my apologies) the royal family had never interested me all that much.

Barbara picked a bench close to the gigantic Ferris wheel of the Eye, and after some desultory attempts at small talk, we settled down in silence to watch its stately revolutions.

As she chomped through her baguette, I couldn't help but notice that she persisted in sneaking little looks at me, shy, curious, sideways glances.

At last she came out with it. "Do I recognise you?"

So that's what it was.

I was spooning out the last of my yogurt. "I'm not sure. Do you?"

I let her flail about for an explanation. "Did we go to school together?"

We did not.

"Do you know my father?"

How would I possibly know her dad?

"Did you used to go out with my friend Shareen?"

Actually, I've never been out with anybody, but I wasn't about to tell her that.

She chewed her lower lip. "I'm stumped."

I sighed. "Don't blame me. Blame Grandpa."

"Do you know," she said, "I thought it was you?"

THIS HAPPENS FROM TIME to time. I can usually tell when someone's about to recognise me. They tend to be the type who watched a lot of telly as kids, who were regularly dumped in front of it by their overworked parents before dinner. I sometimes wonder if there might not be an entire generation who, in some weird Pavlovian way, are actually able to smell fish fingers and chips at the sight of me.

"What was it like?" Barbara asked.

"Oh, great fun," I said. "Mostly." I swallowed. "By and large."

"God, you must have had a riot. Did you even go to school?"

"Course. Mostly we filmed during the holidays."

"Will you do the catchphrase for us again?"

"Do I have to?"

"Oh, go on."

"Don't blame me," I said, and then, again, eager not to disappoint: "Blame Grandpa."

FOR TWO YEARS BETWEEN 1986, when I was eight, and 1988, when I was ten, I played the part of "Little" Jim Cleaver, the wisecracking son in the BBC's family sitcom *Worse Things Happen at Sea*. That said, I'm a terrible actor and I freely admit that my casting was entirely down to nepotism.

It was Granddad's show, you see. He wrote all the scripts, his only major credit after twenty-odd years toiling in the Light Entertainment department of the BBC, something tossed to him as a favour by mates who wanted to give the old guy a break. My catchphrase (actually, often my only line in an episode when they worked out that I couldn't enunciate for toffee and was pathologically unable to emote) was: "Don't blame me. Blame Grandpa"—this invariably delivered on my entrance, as I trotted through the door to the family home and onto the main set. Although gales of prerecorded laughter followed on its heels, I never actually got the joke nor met anyone who did.

After two years of contrived coincidences, pratfalls, one-liners and painfully convoluted cases of mistaken identity, the show was mercifully cancelled and that was that. Just as well, as it turned out. There was no way I could have carried on.

I got ill, you see. I needed to have some operations.

MOST DAYS, IT ALL seems like a dream, like something which happened to someone else and not to me, but even now there are times, when I'm channel-hopping at two o'clock in the morning trying to find something worth watching, that I'll catch a clip of it or an old episode running on some misbegotten cable channel. And there's a Lilliputian version of myself, wisecracking in a falsetto. "Don't blame me," he crows. "Blame Grandpa!"

"YOU MUST GET RECOGNISED LOADS."

"Not loads, no."

"Still acting?"

"I'm a civil servant now," I said firmly. "I'm a filing clerk." I made a big show of checking my watch. "And it's time to get back."

AT TWO O'CLOCK WE WERE sitting in another meeting room watching a man with a whiteboard talk absolute nonsense.

"Hello," he said. "I'm Philip Statham and I'm the safety officer for this department." There were only two of us in the room but he still spoke as though he was delivering his address to a packed-out lecture hall.

Barbara was making dutiful notes.

Philip Statham, she wrote. Safety Officer.

Statham sounded like a stand-up comic of the old school about to launch into the best-loved part of his act, some creaky routine his audience could recite by heart. "You might think," he began, "that an office is a safe place to work. You might think that just because you're not dealing with anything more lethal than a stapler, a fax machine or a ring binder that nothing can happen. You might even believe that accidents don't happen here. That somehow they don't apply to you." He paused, for what I can only imagine he believed to be dramatic effect. "You know what?" He sucked in a breath. "It ain't necessarily so." He tapped the whiteboard with his marker pen for emphasis. "Accidents can happen. Accidents do happen. Every office is a potential death trap. And over the course of the next two hours and a bit I'm going to be giving you just a couple of pointers on how to stay safe." He arched an eyebrow, flared his nostrils. "On how to stay *alive*."

WE HAD SAT THROUGH two videos and a PowerPoint presentation and were about to embark on something Statham ominously referred to as "a little bit of role play" when my mobile phone gave an epileptic shudder in my pocket.

"Sorry, Philip," I said, thankful for the distraction. "Got to take this."

Statham glared as I scuttled gratefully into the corridor but when I saw the caller ID which flashed up on the screen, anything that was left of my good humour ebbed away.

"Mum?" I said. "You mustn't call me at work."

"The old bastard's dead."

My heart clenched tight. "What did you say?"

And she said it again, more firmly this time, not bothering to suppress the smirk.

"The old bastard's dead."

CHAPTER 4

THE FIRST TIME I SAW GRANDDAD AGAIN I DIDN'T recognise him. He had been with me for the whole of my life and I couldn't pick him out in a room full of strangers.

Too cut-up and jittery to risk using my bicycle, I caught the 176 bus opposite the station and sat, anxious and impatient, as it edged its grudging way through the grimy streets of Waterloo, the tarmacked monotony of Elephant and Castle and the minatory neglect of Walworth and Camberwell Green. Down by the river, surrounded by sightseers, gift shops and the eager bustle of commerce, it is easy to forget that the city has teeth, that it has a certain hunger. Out here, it is scarcely possible to forget it.

At last we creaked to a stop, the brakes of the bus whinnying and wheezing like an old nag days from the glue factory, outside the sprawling, red-brick mass of St. Chad's. The entirety of my journey had been spent crammed next to a fat man in a Garfield T-shirt, who ate chicken from a cardboard box and listened to pop music unsociably loud.

I skittered through the big sliding doors at the front of the hospital before spending the next ten minutes wandering about looking lost. Eventually a nurse took pity on me and directed me to the Machen Ward, a soporific antechamber at the rear of the fifth floor sealed off from the rest of the hospital by a thick glass door. Inside, half a dozen elderly men lay stretched out on narrow beds, motionless, silent and still. The room was filled with old-fashioned smells—bleach, soap, floor polish and, everywhere, the insidious odour of decay.

A few beds down, a nurse was wrangling a patient's pillow into place and muttering something she presumably intended to sound soothing.

"Excuse me?" I said.

The woman turned her head to look at me but carried on with whatever it was that she was doing. "What?"

"I'm looking for someone."

"Name?" Her speech was clotted with an accent which sounded like it might be from Eastern Europe.

"His name's Lamb."

She glared scornfully at me, as though I'd just asked if the hospital had a bar.

"He's my granddad," I added, rather feebly.

"Behind you." She shot me another contemptuous look and bustled back to work.

SUPINE AND OBLIVIOUS TO the world, the old bastard had aged about a hundred years since I'd seen him last. Now he was all the things he'd never seemed before—frail and fragile, feeble and faded. White hairs curled unchecked from his ears and nostrils and his skin was drawn tight around the bones of his face. Tubes, wires and metallic lines snaked from his body, linked in some mysterious way to plastic pouches of liquid and a monitor which beeped officiously at intervals.

There was a large window behind his bed decorated, in a

puny stab at festivity, with a single, balding strand of tinsel. Thin winter sunlight played across his chest and lit up the dust which fell about him until it looked like confetti.

I found a chair, pulled it over to the bed, sat myself down and immediately started to wonder whether I should have brought grapes. Flowers? Chocolates? Hard to see how he could appreciate any of them.

I tried talking. Isn't that supposed to help? I'm sure I'd read somewhere that chatting as though everything is perfectly normal is supposed to be good for people in his condition.

"Granddad? It's Henry. I'm sorry I haven't seen you for a while. Work's been hectic. You know how it is before Christmas . . ." But my voice sounded hollow and insincere so I stopped and sat awhile, not speaking, listening to the cold metronome of the machine.

Eventually, I heard someone walk up behind me. From the clack of her high heels and the smell of the only perfume she ever wore, I knew who it was before she even opened her mouth.

"Poor old bastard," she said. "Even I feel sorry for him now."

YOU'RE PROBABLY SURPRISED THAT she even bothered to turn up at all. To be honest, I don't fully understand it myself. But then things always seemed so complicated between them.

MUM CIRCLED HER BIG, meaty arms around my waist and pulled me close. Caught unawares, squeezed anaconda-tight as a tsunami of scent broke over me, I was eight years old again and, for a second, felt almost happy.

We sat beside him in silence. I held the old man's hand whilst Mum produced a book of puzzles and set about working through a page of sudoku with the single-minded pertinacity of Alan Turing squaring up to a fresh cipher from Berlin. The quiet was broken only fitfully, by the beeps of Granddad's machine, the rap-tap of my mother's pen on paper, the occasional passing of a nurse and the distant echo of a telephone. We saw no doctors, no-one came to ask who we were or what we were doing and the other patients who shared his ward made no noise at all, not the slightest squeak or whimper. I'm not sure exactly what I'd expected—death rattles, I suppose, ragged breathing and delirium—but the business of mortality is quieter than you'd think.

We'd sat in the same miserable tableau for at least half an hour when something appeared in the window behind my granddad. First a frond of red hair swaying in the breeze, then a squitty, pinched face, then a yellow safety jacket, a squirt of foam, the underside of a sponge puckering against the pane.

It looked miraculous, as though the man was levitating. The illusion was shattered when the window cleaner peered through the glass, looked directly at my mother and winked. Mum giggled, the sound of it grotesquely out of place here, like laughter in a morgue or a smirk at a cremation.

I gave the man my frostiest look but I'm afraid I saw Mum grin back.

As if in response to this pantomimed flirtation, the life support machine made a chirrup out of sequence, a squeak of distress, an electronic hiccup. I was on my feet at once, the window cleaner forgotten, casting around for someone to help. But almost immediately the machine returned to the same rhythm as before and Mum told me to stop flapping and sit back down again, all the while admiring the window cleaner from the corner of her eye.

She left a short while later, muttering something about meeting a friend for a drink. Evidently I was not invited so I stayed and sat with Granddad, gripping his hand in mine until, eventually, the nurse returned, growled that visiting hours were over and motioned me towards the door. I laid Granddad's hand beside him on the bed and, feeling guilty but grateful, walked back into the light, the beeps of the machine still echoing in my ears.

IT WAS COLD OUTSIDE, already growing dark as the day surrendered to the eager dusk of winter. My breath steamed in the air and I was looking forward to getting home when something immensely improbable happened.

First, there was a noise—a sort of faint yelp, a stifled cry, a distant yell of shock.

Then the air seemed to shudder before me and I glimpsed a blur, a kinetic smudge of red, yellow and black. Finally, there was a dull, decisive *thwump* as something big, fleshy and in pain sprawled by my feet.

I stood very still. I looked away. Then I looked back again just to check that I hadn't imagined it. But there he was, still there.

A man had fallen from the sky, missing me by inches.

Too numb to move, I stared at him and he, barely breathing, stared back. Distantly, I recognised his squitty face, his mop of ginger hair. The earth around the fallen man glittered with broken glass lit up by the artificial illumination of the hospital—a miniature constellation in the earth.

"Henry . . . ?"

How did he know my name? How on earth did a hospital window cleaner know my name?

"Henry?"

"Hello?" Even to my own ears, I sounded stupid. In the distance—shouted orders, the roar of engines, people sprinting towards us.

"The answer is yes," he said. It was a struggle for him to speak and the words forced themselves out in a brittle rasp.

I knelt down beside him and, panicking over what to do next, grabbed for the nearest cliché. "Don't speak," I said. "Don't try to move."

But the window cleaner seemed determined to talk. "The answer . . . ," he said again, his eyes alight with fervour, like this was the most important thing he'd ever say. "Henry . . ." He wheezed again, a terrible percussive rattle. "The answer is *yes*."

Then I was pushed aside as people rushed to help, professional life-savers with their flapping coats and sharply worded questions, a babble of don't touch him and how did he fall and we need to get him inside. Actually, I think the word *miracle* was tossed around more than once.

Even as they took the man away, levering him gently onto a stretcher, trying to calm him down, giving him something to ease the pain, he was still staring at me, mouthing the same words over and over again.

"The answer is yes."

I stared back, frozen to the spot.

"The answer is yes."

He struggled up in his stretcher and tried to shout.

"The answer is yes!"

I SUPPOSE IT'S UNUSUAL to get within spitting distance of thirty without ever having been in love. All I can say is that it's been worth the wait.

I'd met Abbey six months earlier when, having noticed her advert in the "To Let" section of the city newspaper, I had called round to see her about the spare room. I saw from the instant that she opened the door that I'd never want to share my life with anyone else. Dispiritingly, I saw also that she was radiantly beautiful, a shimmering vision in skinny jeans and canary-yellow heels and therefore stratospherically out of my league.

WHEN I GOT BACK from telling about a dozen different people the story of how the window cleaner had fallen at my feet with that unforgettable *thwump*, she was sitting in the lounge, slouched in front of our TV—an ancient old box which she said had been sitting in the place when she'd bought it.

Abbey seemed tired and dishevelled and was doggedly picking her way through a plate of oven chips, but still she managed to look heart-piercingly gorgeous.

I said hello and at the sound of my voice, my landlady struggled to sit upright.

"Sit down," she said, still chewing, reaching for the controller to switch off the TV. "I haven't seen you for days." She thrust her plate in front of me. "Have one of these."

"No, I couldn't."

"Please. I can't finish them."

"Really, I'm fine."

"Have you eaten?"

"Well, no, but—"

"Have one, then."

"Are you sure?"

"Positive."

"P'raps I will. Thanks very much."

"My pleasure."

I took a chip.

"How was your day?" Abbey asked, upon which, for the first time in almost a decade, I burst into tears.

AFTER THAT, WE TALKED. Dabbing surreptitiously at my nose with a Kleenex, I told her about my granddad, the phone call from my mother and the man who'd fallen from the sky. She seemed to sympathise and at one point even made an awkward move towards me as though to offer a hug, although I flinched away and she shifted back.

"Henry?" she said, once the story was told, sounding eager to cheer me up.

"Yes?"

"When's your birthday? You said it was soon."

"Oh." I'd almost forgotten. "Monday. Why?"

"Just wondering." She raised an eyebrow and seemed to be about to say something else when the telephone rang.

Abbey answered. "I'll get it," she said, and looked over at me. "It's for you."

Frowning, I took the receiver. "Hello?"

I didn't recognise the voice. It sounded like it belonged to an elderly woman—crisp and determined, though underscored by a hint of frailty. "Mr. Lamb? Mr. Henry Lamb?"

"Yes."

"Good evening to you, Mr. Lamb. I'm calling on behalf of a firm called Gadarene Glass. I was wondering if I might interest you in having a new set of windows installed."

"Actually I don't own the house," I said. "I only rent a room here. But, in any case, I'm sure the answer's no. And we'd prefer it if you didn't call so late in future. Come to think of it, we'd prefer it if you didn't call at all." The woman tutted at my impertinence and the line went dead.

"Salesman?" Abbey asked.

"Double glazing, I think. Nothing important."

"Oh." She gave me a tentatively hopeful smile. I smiled back and for a moment we stood there just smiling at one another like a couple of idiots, still a little giddy from all this unexpected intimacy, still innocent of the horror which even now was pawing at our door.

CHAPTER 5

A T FIRST, THE NEXT DAY DIDN'T SEEM ANY DIFFERENT. As usual, I woke a few seconds before my alarm whooped its good morning. As usual, I levered myself out of bed, rooted through the fridge for breakfast and hung around hoping for a glimpse of Abbey. As usual, I left the flat disappointed.

I had abandoned my bike in the parking lot at work so I had to trudge down to the underground and strap-hang for eight stops on the Northern line, sucking in stale sweat and halitosis. Consequently, I got into work late and, still half-asleep, retired immediately to the bathroom. I was busy splashing cold water on my face when Peter Hickey-Brown emerged from the stalls, produced one of those combs which look like a flick knife and began to fastidiously scrape back his greying hair. He didn't turn to look at me but just gazed adoringly ahead, a paunchy Narcissus in an office lavatory.

"How's Babs getting on?" he asked, once the posturing was done.

"Fine, I think."

"You show her round yesterday?"

I said that yes, naturally I had.

"Did you take her down to the mail room?"

The mail room? "No. Why?"

"I think she should see it."

"I don't like it down there."

"So? Don't get your knickers in a twist, Henry. Just take her." He flipped on the cold tap, wetted his fingers and teased the hair at his temples back behind his ears. "Phil tells me you had to dash off early yesterday."

"Family emergency."

Hickey-Brown frowned, not from any anxiety for me but purely out of concern that the work of his department might be disrupted, that I might get behind with his precious filing— petrified that if I didn't do my job we'd all be engulfed by an avalanche of ancient appraisal sheets and leprous-coloured meeting forms. "Everything OK?" he asked.

"Don't know," I said. "Honestly, I don't know."

"You're in for a treat," I said to Barbara once I'd tracked her down at the photocopier. "Peter wants you to see the mail room."

The mail room squatted in the lowest floor in the building, stinking, forsaken and unloved. Something was always up with the heating, which meant that down there it was perpetually clammy and warm. A few weeks to go before Christmas and still everyone had a fan on their desk, all of them whirring away bad temperedly, grumbling about being used out of season. The room smelt stale, a pungent blend of perspiration and old socks.

"This is where it starts," I said. I'd given this tour before, to a group of kids in last year's Bring Your Child to Work Day. "This is where the files are sorted."

The room was taken up by four large trestle tables, each stacked high with dun-coloured folders, each populated by three or four workers—the only exception being the last table, whose occupant worked alone. A few of these unfortunates, pimple faced and greasy with perspiration, glanced incuriously over at us as we came in. They were sorting through the files, pulling out minutes, memos, action plans, graphs and annual reports, putting every one in alphabetical order and placing them in a trolley. Later that day, someone would wheel them to the lift and distribute them amongst the floors above. This was the engine room of our department, the business end of the place.

"Big turnover of staff down here," I said. "People don't tend to last long." I pointed across the room to the woman who sat alone and who was busy opening parcel after parcel, filleting the contents with automotive efficiency. "Except for her."

Sausage-fingered, gelatinous and blubbery, she had greasy, lank hair and her face, swollen and pink, had the consistency of Play-Doh. Beside her was a gargantuan bottle of cola from which she took frequent, compulsive swigs, as a baby might reach with blind dependency for the nipple. As usual she was pouring with sweat and her clothes were stained with inky spots of perspiration.

"Hello," I said, realising that I couldn't remember her name. Pam? Pat? Paula? No matter how many times I'd been told it just didn't seem to stick. The fat woman made a slurred noise in reply.

"This is Barbara," I said, perhaps pronouncing my words a little too emphatically. "She's just started upstairs."

The woman made another incoherent noise ("hrellow") and groped again for her bottle of Coke.

As we headed towards the exit, Barbara whispered: "What's wrong with her?"

"No one likes to ask," I said. "It's very sad, really. The poor thing's been here longer than anyone can remember. She's become a bit of an institution."

"Looks like she belongs in an institution," Barbara muttered, rather cruelly.

Governed by a strange impulse, I turned back. Coke bottle midway to her lips, the woman was staring at us, fury blazing from her blancmange face. Feeling suddenly guilty and ashamed, blushing scarlet, I hurried Barbara from the room, away from the grouchy hum of the fans, the omnipresent smell of sweat and the woman's silently accusing eyes. We were both of us relieved to head back upstairs.

AT LUNCHTIME, I MET Mum for a sandwich in Café Nero.

"How long did you stay last night?" she asked, slurping at her latte.

I thought about telling her what had happened with the window cleaner but then, guessing how she might react, decided against it. "Not long. There's nothing I could do."

"He'd always had it coming," she said. "We all know he used to like a drink."

"Will he be OK?" I asked in a small voice.

Mum just shrugged. "Who knows?" She yawned. "Keep an eye on him, won't you? Your Dad would have wanted you to."

"I'm going again tonight," I said.

She seemed surprised. "Really?"

"I want to be with him. It's not like he's got anyone else."

"But who does he have to blame for that? Actually, darling, I was hoping to ask you a favour."

Her motive for lunch had suddenly become clear. "And what's that?"

"The old bastard's house. Lord knows why but I've got a

spare set of keys. Be a dear and pop round in the next couple of days, will you? Just make sure no-one's trashed the place or turned it over." She deposited a bunch of keys on the table with a resolute *clunk*, as though this settled the matter, like there was no need for further discussion.

"We could go together," I suggested hopefully.

"Sweet thing, I'm going away."

"Away?"

"To Gibraltar. With Gordy."

I set my coffee down on the table, frightened of spilling it. "Who's Gordy?"

"He's a mate. Don't fret, darling. He's in the biz."

"Not another actor?"

"Producer, actually. He's booked us into the most marvellous hotel."

"Great."

"Don't look so down. I'm happy. Just keep an eye on the old bastard for us, will you? Give us a tinkle if anything happens."

I stared down at the remnants of my sandwich and nodded.

Mum's handbag began to trill. She pulled out her mobile and clasped it to her ear. "Gordy! No, I'm still with him." Tittering, she turned to look at me. "Gordy says hi."

"Hello, Gordy," I said.

"No, no," she said, suddenly putting on a baby voice. "I think he's Mr. Grumpy 'cause of his granddad." She kissed me on the forehead, waved goodbye, walked out of the café and into the street, still bellowing her endearments, broadcasting her sweet nothings for all the world to hear.

I looked at what remained of my sandwich and pushed the plate aside, my appetite suddenly curdled.

I HAD JUST GOT BACK to my desk when Peter Hickey-Brown summoned me into his office.

A stranger sat beside him. Baby-faced, clear-skinned and enviably exfoliated, he radiated good health. He was a walking advert for diligent grooming. When I came in, he looked at me but offered no smile and simply stared, unspeaking, in my direction.

"You wanted to see me?" I said.

Hickey-Brown, uncharacteristically grave, told me to sit. I was surprised to see that he had put on a tie since the morning and that he'd removed almost all of his jewellery.

"This is Mr. Jasper."

I stretched my hand across the desk. "Hello."

The man just stared. I noticed that he had a flesh-coloured piece of plastic buried in one of his ears and I remember wondering (how naïve it seems now) whether he was hard of hearing.

"I'm Henry Lamb."

Still nothing. Embarrassed, I withdrew my hand.

Peter cleared his throat. "Mr. Jasper's from another department."

"Which one?"

Hickey-Brown looked as though he didn't really know the answer. "A special department. I'm told it keeps an eye on the personal well-being of our staff."

At last, the stranger spoke. "We like to think of ourselves," he deadpanned, "as the department which cares."

Hickey-Brown clasped his fingers together as though in prayer. "Listen. We know that something happened yesterday. Something to do with your grandfather."

The man who had been introduced as Jasper looked at me icily. "What is the matter with the poor old fellow?"

"They think it might be a stroke," I said, just about resisting the temptation to ask why it was any of his bloody business.

"Is he likely to recover?"

"The doctors aren't sure. Though I suspect it's unlikely."

Mr. Jasper turned his eyes upon me but said no more.

I looked over to my boss. "Peter?"

He managed an insincere smile. "We're worried about you. We need to know you're OK."

"I'm fine."

"Sure. But listen. You need any time off—just say the word. Just give the nod."

"Of course."

Jasper was still staring, coolly, unblinkingly.

"Is that all?" I asked.

Hickey-Brown glanced towards Jasper and the stranger gave the tiniest inclination of his head, a motion which might, in the right light, if you squinted a bit, have been a nod.

"Alrighty," said Peter Hickey-Brown. "You can go."

As I walked out, I felt the stranger's unsympathetic eyes boring into my back like lasers.

AFTER WORK, I RETRIEVED my bike and cycled over to the hospital. Although there was no change in my granddad, he was, at least, no worse, and it didn't seem to me as though he was in any pain. I held his hand and told him something about my day, about the fat woman in the basement, my lunch with Mum and the visit of Mr. Jasper.

Someone shuffled behind me. The nurse.

"You recognise your grandpa now?"

I blushed in shame.

"He seems sad," she said.

"Sad?"

"He was in a war."

"Actually," I corrected her, "Granddad didn't fight. He wanted to but they wouldn't let him go. Some kind of heart defect, I think."

The nurse just smiled. "Oh no. He was definitely in a war." She turned and hurried away, the heels of her shoes squeaking on the linoleum floor.

I looked back at my granddad. "You weren't in the war, were you?" I asked, although of course I knew there'd be no reply. "What war?"

HALF AN HOUR LATER, with visiting hours at an end, I was on the ground floor and almost in sight of the exit when I saw a patient I recognised. He seemed quite cheerful, sitting up in bed, propped against a pillow and engrossed in a tabloid, his left leg hanging suspended in plaster. He looked like an extra from a *Carry On* film, the kind of potato-featured background artist who would have ogled Barbara Windsor's wiggle and guffawed at Sid James's dirty jokes.

I stopped in front of his bed. "I know you."

The man looked up from his newspaper. It was definitely him. The squitty face, the shock of ginger hair, the air of insouciant lechery—all were unmistakeable.

"Don't think we've met," said the window cleaner.

"You fell," I said. "You fell at my feet."

"Sorry, pal. Don't remember nothing about it."

I nodded towards the cast and pulley. "You broke your leg?"

"Nah, I'm doing this for shits and giggles. What do you think?"

"Sorry. It's just that you seem . . . I don't mean to be rude but you seem absolutely fine."

"Why shouldn't I be?"

"You fell five storeys."

"Then I'm made of tough stuff, aren't I?" Evidently irritated, he made a big deal about returning to his tabloid.

"Yesterday," I said, "just after you'd . . . landed."

"What?"

"There was something you were trying to tell me. You kept saying that the answer is yes."

He snorted. "Did I? Well, you do funny things when you've had a knock, don't you? Can't have been thinking straight."

"You've got no idea why you said that to me?"

"Mate, I can't even remember." His next look began as truculence but shifted halfway through into one of recognition. "Don't I know you?"

"Ah," I said. "So it's coming back?"

"You're off the telly," he said. "You're a little boy."

My heart sunk. "I was," I snapped. "I was a little boy. Not any more."

"I remember your show. What was it you used to say?"

Now I just wanted to leave. "Don't blame me. Blame Grandpa."

The window cleaner started to chuckle, then abruptly broke off. "Wasn't very funny, was it?"

"Thanks," I said.

"Come to think of it, that show was a real shitcom."

"It's always nice to meet a fan."

"You'd better hop it. Visiting hours are over."

"Well, I'm sorry for bothering you."

"Your mate's waiting." He nodded behind me.

"What?"

"Over there. By the door."

He was right. Standing on the other side of the ward, just by the exit, someone was watching us. He vanished through the door as soon as he clocked me but I'd already seen enough to be able to recognise him as the man from Peter's office. Mr. Jasper.

The window cleaner turned to the soccer results with the air of a reader who does not wish to be disturbed. I left and went outside into the cold but, if he'd ever been there at all, Jasper was nowhere to be seen.

I cycled home, my mind clamorous with unanswered questions.

ABBEY WAS UP, FLICKING through an encyclopaedia of divorce law. My landlady worked in some mysterious capacity for a city legal firm, although the precise details of what she did there always eluded me. I'd asked her about it several times, desperate for any excuse for a conversation, but she was always evasive on the subject, saying that it was too depressingly humdrum to talk about. Whatever it was, I was in no doubt that she was bored of it, as she had complained to me on more than one occasion about wanting to do something better with her life—something more noble, she said, something worthwhile.

"Henry! I was getting worried."

"I was at the hospital."

"No change?"

"No change."

"Sit down. I'll get you a coffee." Abbey was up on her feet and into the kitchen before I had a chance to protest. "Two sugars, right?"

I said a grateful yes and sank into the sofa, relieved that the day was drawing to a close.

Abbey pressed a hot mug into my hands and I thanked her. She was wearing a baggy T-shirt several sizes too big for her and I'm a little ashamed to admit that I wondered whether she was wearing anything beneath it.

She sat cross-legged on the floor. "Henry? Do you . . ." She trailed off, embarrassed. "Do you notice something different about me?"

"Not sure what you mean."

"I mean is there anything different about me?"

Grateful for the opportunity to admire the contours of Abbey's face without her thinking I was gawping, I gazed for a minute or two, uninterrupted.

"No," I said at last. "Not that I can see."

She tapped the side of her nose and at last I saw what she meant—a flash of gold, a small, discreet stud like an expensive outbreak of acne. My first thought was that she'd had it done to impress someone—some square-jawed hunk at work, some broad-shouldered pin-up of the assizes.

"You like it?"

Too tired and guileless to lie, I said: "I prefer you without."

"Oh." She sounded disappointed. "I thought you might like it."

"It's just that you've got such a lovely nose it seems a shame to spoil it." Even as I said it, I could feel myself turning pink.

"Have I really?" she asked. "Have I really got a lovely nose?"

I was just about to stutter out some reply when rescue arrived in the insistent peal of the telephone. As I picked up the receiver I looked back at Abbey and saw that she seemed almost as grateful for the reprieve as I.

"Hello?"

The voice, cracked with age, seemed faintly familiar. "Am I speaking to Mr. Henry Lamb?"

"You are."

"I represent Gadarene Glass. Would you be interested at all in purchasing a new window?"

"Haven't you called before?"

"I have, yes."

"The answer's still no," I snapped, "and I thought I asked you last time not to bother."

Click. The hornet buzz of the dial tone.

Abbey rolled her eyes as I replaced the receiver. "I don't know how they get this number."

I yawned. "Think I'll go to bed."

"Sleep well. But Henry?"

"Yes?"

"If you need to talk . . ."

"Of course."

Abbey smiled. As I turned to go, I saw that she was touching the side of her left nostril, running her fingers over the stud, suddenly, sweetly, adorably self-conscious. I stole another look and felt something unfamiliar, something strange but wonderful, begin to flutter in my chest.

If I'd known at that moment all that was to come, I would have stamped out those feelings right then. I'd have strangled those flutterings at birth.

CHAPTER 6

THE NEXT DAY I MADE UP MY MIND TO GO TO GRAND-dad's house. Not one other member of the family (nor a single constituent of his fair-weather entourage) had emerged to offer their assistance, and as the only relative who had ever admitted to actually liking the man, I felt the persistent tug of responsibility.

The day passed in a blur of routine—Hickey-Brown's jokes, lunch with Barbara, an errand in the mail room, a dirty look from Philip Statham, an eternity spent idling on the computer, staring at my screen and waiting for five o'clock. Once it was over I cycled up to London Bridge, forced my bike onto the train and headed for Dulwich—specifically for 17 Temple Drive, where my grandfather had lived since long before I was born.

Pushing my bike up the hill, I turned into his still, suburban street, past the ranks of plane trees and those signs which hysterically insisted that this was an area under the jurisdiction of the neighbourhood watch. This was time-travel for me. It was a wormhole into my childhood.

Granddad lived in a small terraced house running to seed—books pressed up against the windows, dying weeds curled around the grate, a handwritten sign at the door which read in emphatic Biro: NO HAWKERS.

I let myself in, kicked aside the hillock of mail which had accumulated on the mat and was immediately overwhelmed by an acute ache of sadness. The same smell was everywhere. Fried sausage—fat, greasy and black—the only thing the old man had ever been able to cook. It was what he had invariably fed me when I went to stay at half-term, what was on the table when I got back from those operations at the hospital as a boy, what he'd made for me on the night my father died.

The smell of the past was in my nostrils and I collapsed as though winded into the big armchair in the lounge. At that moment I would have given anything to be eight years old again, for Granddad to be OK, for my father to be alive, for everything to seem sweeter and more innocent.

Something small and soft brushed past my legs and I looked down to see a plump grey cat gazing up at me with optimistic eyes. Tentatively, I reached out a hand. The animal didn't shy away so I stroked it again, at which it started up a contented purr.

"You must be hungry," I said.

There were a couple of tins of cat food in the kitchen cupboard. I opened one and spooned out its contents, which the creature attacked with relish. As soon as it was done, he started to pester me for more.

The cat was not the only thing that seemed unfamiliar. As usual the lounge was filled with books—but they had changed. I remembered dog-eared scripts (Galton and Simpson, *The Goon Show*, *ITMA*, *The Navy Lark*), yards of comedy stacked halfway to the ceiling, but now it seemed quite different. There were volumes here on the most recondite and esoteric subjects—bulky, valuable-looking hardbacks on divination, telepathy, palmistry, the tarot, Freemasonry, Rasputin, metempsychosis, Madame Blavatsky, astral projection, Nostradamus, Eliphas Levi, the preparation of human sacrifice and the end of the world. Books with terrible, wonderful titles. Strange-smelling books, tingly to the touch.

All gone now, of course.

In the past few years I'd not seen Granddad as often as I ought and had barely visited him at home at all. Only twice really—once when I was looking for a job and we'd spent the afternoon trawling the employment sections of the broadsheets, and once again, a few months ago, when we'd done much the same thing searching for flats and he'd pointed out the place in Tooting Bec. After that, once I'd met Abbey, my visits dwindled to nothing.

Guiltily, I told myself the usual homiletic lies—that I'd been busy at work and settling into a new flat, that it wasn't the frequency of my visits but their quality—though none of this made me feel any better about my neglect.

But I still wondered why I hadn't seen any of those books before. I suppose he could have bought them recently but, with their cracked spines, makeshift bookmarks and frequent marginalia scribbled in a hand that I recognised at once as his, they had the look about them of a cherished library.

I was distracted by an optimistic yowl and a renewed, determined pressure on my leg. The cat gave me a disapproving look and padded away to the kitchen. I followed, intending to open another can of food, only for the animal to turn, trot upstairs and vanish into the bedroom. Expecting to find a dead mouse or a week's worth of mess, I followed it inside to discover that here, too, things had changed.

There was a small bed (unmade, strewn with blankets), a table with a coffee-stained copy of the *Mirror* and a wind-up alarm clock which had stopped at 12:14. What was new was the large framed photograph which hung on the furthest wall. It was me as a child—an old publicity shot from *Worse Things Happen at Sea*—buck-toothed and freckly, captured in the midst of summoning on demand another fake grin for the cameras. For a moment, I stood and stared. Seeing stuff from that time is like witnessing the life of a stranger, as though I'm observing events which overtook someone I've never met but only read about in magazines.

I noticed that the picture had been hung slightly askew. The cat craned its sleek head upwards as though he too were staring at it and disapproving of its wonkiness. He began to yowl.

"All right," I said. "I'll get your food in a minute."

I walked over to the picture and tried to readjust it, although it seemed oddly weighted and refused to settle. Irritated, I moved it aside.

It was then that I first started to feel that something was seriously out of kilter here, sensed the first stirrings of the worm at the centre of the apple.

Behind the photograph was a sheet of smooth grey metal. It had no hinges or openings apart from what looked like a small keyhole, its innards filled with pincers of serrated metal. It resembled a piece of installation art or something from a locksmith's nightmare. The thing was an aberration—another mystery in my grandfather's house.

The doorbell rang.

The cat gave a startled meow, ran between my legs and stayed there, quaking. Irrationally, I felt a tremor of fear. There was a second's peace before the bell rang again. I let the photograph swing back into position, padded downstairs and opened the door.

Standing outside was the baby-faced man, Mr. Jasper.

"Hello, Henry."

The sight of him there of all places was so incongruous that, for a moment, I couldn't speak.

"We need your help," he said. "Invite me in."

The cat had followed me downstairs and now crouched between my legs, shaking in fear. "What are you doing here?" I asked at last.

"Aren't you going to ask me in?" Jasper sounded as though he was making the most reasonable request, as though this wasn't strange in the slightest, this unwarranted intrusion into an old man's home. "Your grandfather has put certain safeguards in place. Here and at the hospital. We're going to need your help."

"My help? What on earth do you want?"

"Just let me in, Mr. Lamb."

"No," I said, suddenly afraid. "I think you should leave right now. You're trespassing."

Jasper bared his teeth in a humourless approximation of a smile. As if at the sight of the grimace, the cat wriggled free of my legs and bounded away.

"Have you been following me?"

"You'll regret it if you don't let me in. We'll huff and we'll puff and we'll blow your house down."

"Go away." My voice shook only a little. "I'll call the police."

"Oh, Mr. Lamb. We're above the police."

Then he did something very odd indeed. His head snapped upwards and he stared fiercely towards the ceiling. "I agree, sir," he said, and there was nothing in his manner to suggest he was addressing me. "I thought he'd be better looking too." His eyes flicked over my body. "Slimmer, frankly. And *cleaner*."

"Who are you talking to?" I asked.

Jasper smiled. "I'll go," he said. "But remember that whatever happens next, you have brought it entirely upon yourself."

He turned and walked away. I listened to the click of his expensive shoes upon the pavement but soon even this was swallowed by the sounds of London (the growl of traffic, the howl of sirens, the hectic tattoo of a car stereo) and there was nothing left to prove that Jasper had ever been there at all, nothing to say that he wasn't merely a figment of the city's imagination.

WHEN I WOKE THE next morning, it took me a while to recollect all that had happened since Tuesday. For a few merciful seconds, it seemed as substanceless and evanescent as a dream. Of course, by the time I'd levered myself out of bed, reached for my dressing gown and meandered, bleary eyed and tousle haired, towards the kitchen, everything had come scrambling back and I groaned aloud at the memory.

To my delight, Abbey was already up and sitting on the sofa in her pyjamas. My landlady was the kind of woman who looked sexiest when at her least groomed and at her most irresistible freshly out of bed, unkempt, dishevelled and smelling faintly of sleep.

"Morning," she said.

"Good morning." Although I pined for our meetings, when it came to them, I always found myself a little embarrassed, stutteringly short of words.

"Are you OK?"

"I'm fine," I lied. "Been a weird few days."

"I know."

I swallowed hard. "I could tell you about it tonight, if you want."

"Yeah, I'd like that."

I noticed something different about her. "Where's your nose stud?"

"Oh, I got rid of it. Never really me, was it?"

It was probably my imagination but I was sure I saw her blush.

WHEN I GOT INTO WORK, Barbara was standing over my desk, diligently placing all of my possessions into a cardboard box. Stapler, potted plant, box of tissues, an ancient photo of my dad.

"Morning," I said. "What are you doing?"

"Henry." The girl's face turned white. "Haven't you heard?"

Before I could ask what she meant, the phone on my desk clamoured for my attention.

I picked it up. "Henry Lamb speaking."

"It's Peter. I want a word. Pronto."

I put down the phone and turned curiously to Barbara, who gave me a sympathetic shrug in reply.

"I'd better go," I said, and walked into Hickey-Brown's office without bothering to knock.

A familiar figure stood next to my manager.

"You remember Mr. Jasper?" Peter asked.

"Good morning, Henry," said the well-exfoliated man.

"Morning," I said.

Mr. Jasper smiled. "I'll see you outside."

He left, taking care to close the door behind him.

Hickey-Brown sighed, settled himself down behind his desk and waved a hand to indicate that I should sit opposite.

"Sorry if this seems a bit overwhelming," he said. "I realise you've had a hell of a week."

"What on earth's going on?"

Peter looked at me blankly, whether from discretion or ignorance I couldn't quite be sure. "Mr. Jasper will answer all your questions."

"Oh really? Who is this Jasper anyway?"

"I told you. He's from a special department. Don't look so worried. It's part of the Service."

"He came to my grandfather's house. He said he was above the police."

Hickey-Brown couldn't even meet my eye. "He must have been joking."

"Joking? Why's Barbara packing up my stuff? Are you getting rid of me?"

"You're being transferred."

"I'm sorry?"

"You've made it, Henry. Your filing days are over."

"What?"

"Promotion time, Henry."

"I don't—"

"Better run along now. He's waiting for you."

Hickey-Brown got to his feet and strode past me to open the door, making it palpably clear that our conversation was at an end.

I walked outside, where Jasper was leaning against what had been my desk, talking animatedly to Barbara. She was giggling in reply, stroking her hair, placing a fingertip in the side of her mouth and generally playing the coquette.

Jasper grinned at the sight of me. "There you are!"

Barbara, curiously emboldened, kissed me on the cheek. "Good luck, Henry."

I stood mute and motionless as a shop-window dummy as Jasper thrust the box into my hands. "There you go. We'd better get a move on."

"Now?" I asked.

Jasper nodded.

Barbara squeezed my arm. "Well done," she hissed. "Good luck."

Nervously, I cleared my throat. "Well, goodbye everyone," I announced to the office at large. "It's been great working with you all. I've enjoyed myself. But it looks like I'm moving on." My colleagues ignored me, my only answer the tap of keyboards, the drone of telephones, the lazy burr of the photocopier. Somewhere, inevitably, someone was crunching their way laboriously through a packet of crisps. Cheese and onion, I think. I could smell it.

As soon as we were outside, Jasper grabbed my cardboard box and heaved it into the nearest bin.

"What did you do that for?" I asked, trying not to sound too wheedlingly plaintive.

"Where we're going . . ." The man was striding off ahead. "Take it from me, you're not going to need a potted plant."

I trotted next to him, struggling to keep up. We walked along the South Bank beside the river, past the National Theatre, the restaurants, bookstalls and pavement caricaturists, past the *Big Issue* sellers and skateboarders and the men in furry coats roasting chestnuts, heading towards the great, gleaming edifice of the Eye.

"Where's your department?" I asked.

"You'll know it when you see it."

"I don't understand."

"By the way," Jasper snapped, "I think you should get a new suit. You can't wear that old thing any more. Wouldn't be re-spectful."

"Oh."

"That girl in your office . . . Barbara, isn't it? I don't suppose you happen to know if she's attached?" Jasper's tone had switched from understated menace to something approaching chumminess.

"What?" I asked.

"I mean does she have a boyfriend? Someone special in her life?"

Nonplussed: "I've no idea."

"Hmm. I wonder." He appeared to savour some sort of

mental image before exclaiming: "Perfect, Mr. Lamb. That girl was perfect!"

"What are you talking about?" I wondered if this wasn't some kind of office prank, if for the purposes of someone else's entertainment I'd been yoked to a lunatic for the day. Surreptitiously, I looked around for hidden cameras.

Jasper stopped short. "We're here."

Baffled, I looked up. "But this is the Eye."

"Come inside."

There were dozens of tourists shuffling patiently in line, tortoising forwards a few inches at a time. Jasper barged past them all to get to the front of the queue, and the curious fact was that none of them seemed to object, almost as though they hadn't noticed we were there at all. I observed, too, that for all his bravado and swagger Jasper seemed to be inspecting each of them carefully, like he was searching for someone he knew. More than once, I noticed him turn and nervously scan the line behind us.

"Looking for someone?" I asked.

"The enemy, Mr. Lamb. The enemy are always watching."

"Enemy?" I said, feeling even now that this was most likely to turn out to be some insanely elaborate practical joke.

We reached the front of the queue, pushed past a ticket inspector who offered not the slightest objection to our presence and stood before an open pod filled with a group of Japanese tourists, all of them bristling with guidebooks and cameras, totally oblivious to the two of us.

Jasper gestured into the pod. "After you."

The tourists were still ignoring us.

"But it's packed."

"Trust me."

I didn't move.

"Mr. Lamb, what you're about to see is above top secret.

Breathe the merest word of what you see here today and the most extreme measures will be set in motion against you. Is that understood?"

I nodded, feeling oddly light-headed—like I was in a dream and knew it, that my actions would have no real effect in the waking world.

"Well then. Walk on."

"I can't. It's full."

Jasper seemed to lose patience. "Just go." He pushed me forwards and I stumbled into the pod.

To my amazement, I seemed to pass through the ranks of tourists as though they were no more substantial than mist—will-o'-the-wisps clutching souvenirs, digital cameras and laminated maps of the city.

Jasper stepped smartly in behind me. "Smoke and mirrors . . . ," he murmured, in the kind of tone you might adopt trying to soothe a child woken in the night by bad dreams.

Inside, it was darker and larger than I had expected. Dimly, I heard the door hiss shut and the pod begin its smooth ascent. There was a smell in there which seemed tuggingly familiar, redolent of floating bandages and verrucas. It took me a moment to pinpoint. It was chlorine—the smell of a public swimming pool.

Our view over London was obscured by what appeared to be a large tank of water which took up almost half the pod, as though we had somehow entered an aquarium by mistake. Through it, I could see the landmarks of the city, distended and made strange by refraction—St. Paul's elongated and obscene, the Houses of Parliament shimmering and fragile, the spires of Canary Wharf stretched out and distorted, its citadels of commerce glimpsed as though through the bottom of a clouded glass.

More disconcerting even than this was what floated in the

tank. It was a man, evidently at the extremity of old age, his skin wrinkled and puckered, wattled, creased and liver-spotted. He was naked save for a pair of faded orange swimming trunks and seemed to be floating underwater, his ancient body, backlit by the sun, bathed in a halo of yellow light.

I wondered how he could possibly breathe inside that tank, before dismissing the notion that he could actually be alive as absurd.

Then, impossible though I knew it had to be, the old man spoke. His lips moved underwater yet I heard him as clearly as if he were standing beside me. His was a deep, old, sad voice, full of strange inflections.

"Welcome, Henry Lamb!" he said—and he said it warmly, as though he knew me, like we went back years together, he and I. "My name is Dedlock. This is the Directorate. And you've just been conscripted."

CHAPTER 7

A T THE DIRECTORATE, WE DON'T DEAL IN VOLUN-teers." The man called Dedlock was grinning at me, bobbing up and down with a grisly vigour which belied his age. "You're one of us now."

I opened my mouth to say something but not a single word would come. Instead, I found myself staring at the old man's torso, fascinated by a progression of creases that seemed to strafe his skin, flaps of flesh which throbbed and pulsated as though with independent life.

Gills?

Surely this man couldn't have gills?

Dedlock was glaring. "You find us in the midst of war. And I'm rather afraid we're losing."

For several minutes my mouth had been too dry to speak. Now, at last, I squeezed out a sentence. "War? Who's at war?"

The old man dealt the side of the tank a ferocious blow. Jasper and I flinched backwards and I wondered what would happen if the glass were to shatter and the water gush out, whether Dedlock would flail and flop on the ground like a beached carp. "Secret civil war has been waged in this country for half a dozen generations. This organisation is all that stands between the British people and their oblivion."

I felt concussed. "I don't understand."

"Comprehension is unnecessary. From now on you simply have to follow orders. Is that understood?"

I vaguely remember nodding.

"Tell no-one what you've seen here. There are less than two dozen men alive who know the true purpose of the Directorate."

I managed an objection. "What happens if I say no?"

"To you? Nothing. Absolutely nothing. To your good mother, on the other hand . . . To your pulchritudinous landlady . . ." He seemed to soften slightly. "You'll find your salary many times in excess of your old employment. And we offer a first-rate pension plan. Every cloud, Henry Lamb, every cloud . . ."

I began to get dizzy, felt the room and its impossible occupant slide away from me and become distant and faint, like the world viewed through the wrong end of a telescope.

"Water . . . ," I stuttered. "You're underwater."

"Amniotic fluid," the old man hissed, grimacing as though at some wretched, long-neglected memory. "Not my design." His eyes flicked dismissively over my body. "Were you close to your grandfather, boy?"

I said that I was.

He nodded. "And does the name Estella mean anything to you?"

I just about managed a "no."

"You must have heard something. Did he never mention her?"

"Never."

The man in the tank made an awful clenching sound which I took to be his closest equivalent to a sigh. "If you truly know nothing then the war may already be lost."

"What war? Who are you people fighting? Who is this enemy?"

"You know their name," Dedlock said, his voice filled with rancour and bile. "You carry their likeness with you everywhere you go." A twitch of his lips, as though he couldn't decide whether to sneer or to smile. "We've been fighting the British royal family since 1857. We're at war with the House of Windsor."

I remember blurting out some objection before my limbs turned to rubber, everything started to fade and darkness closed over me.

Dedlock looked on, disdain and disappointment in his eyes. "Dear, dear. It seems we have ourselves a fainter."

My balance went. I stumbled backwards, fell into the arms of Mr. Jasper and, just before I passed out, I heard the old man's voice again, bitter and sarcastic.

"His grandfather would be so proud."

I WOKE THE NEXT MORNING, hours after the alarm clock usually pesters me into wakefulness, punch-drunk and groggy, with a dank, sickly sensation in the pit of my stomach. Beside my bed was a glass of water, a packet of Alka-Seltzer and a small square of cream-coloured card on which was scrawled the following:

Report Monday morning. We'll send a car at 8.

Then, an unconvincingly hearty postscript:

Enjoy your weekend.

As soon as I had showered and felt at least 70 percent awake, I switched on my computer, logged onto the Internet, clicked into Google and typed the phrase: "the Directorate."

It returned not a single hit. According to the most powerful search engine in the world, the organisation which Dedlock had told me was the last hope for the British people did not even exist.

I HAD SUPPER WITH ABBEY before she went out and, fielding her bemused enquiries by improvising something about having got an unexpected promotion, asked if anyone had come home with me the previous night. She shot me an oddly disappointed look. No, she said. She hadn't seen or heard anyone but me.

We did the washing up together and she left to meet her friends, leaving me lolled in front of the television, flicking aimlessly from game show to sitcom to murder mystery, wondering whether all of it wasn't so much lather and bubbles to mask the real truth of the world, the grime, the scum beneath.

ON SUNDAY, PARTLY BECAUSE I couldn't think of anything better to do, partly because Mr. Jasper had peremptorily suggested it, I went into town, where I bought myself a new grey suit, a couple of shirts and some fresh underwear, and where, for a short while, things felt almost normal again.

In the afternoon, I saw Granddad. The ward was busier and noisier than before, cramped with families trooped dutifully in to visit half-forgotten relatives, packing the place with their guilty faces, their bored offspring and wilting bunches of grapes. There they sat, disguising their yawns, making pointless small talk, checking their watches every other minute, counting down till the end of visiting time.

I took Granddad's paper-skinned hand in mine and broke my silence only once.

"What were you keeping from me?" I asked. "What did you have to hide?"

No answer save for the ceaseless reproach of life support.

SUDDENLY THE LULL WAS OVER. I was out of bed on Monday morning, showered and breakfasted at least an hour before I needed to be ready. I sat watching the morning news with its usual countdowns of crisis and disaster, feeling as fluttery and nervous as I suppose I must have done on my first day at school. Abbey drifted into the room in her pyjamas and dressing gown, peerlessly elegant even as she rubbed sleep from her eyes. "You're up early."

"My new job starts today."

"I know." She grinned. "Wouldn't forget that, would I?"

"You might," I burbled. "No-one expects you to keep track of the lodger."

She reached out and ruffled my hair. "Oh, you're more than a lodger."

I turned a shade of damson.

"New suit?"

I said that it was.

"Thought so. But you're not cycling in that, though, are you?"

"Believe it or not, they're sending a car."

Abbey arched an exquisite eyebrow. "You have gone up in the world." She disappeared into the kitchen and re-emerged a few minutes later with a bowl of chocolate cereal. I rose, checked my appearance in the mirror and turned to say goodbye.

"Have a good day."

"You too. Good luck."

I walked towards the door.

"Henry?"

I turned back.

"I really like the suit."

"Thanks."

"You look good . . ." An implication of naughtiness crossed her face. "I definitely would."

There was another silence, still longer than before, during which I cannot honestly say which of us flushed the pinker.

"Bye," I said, and fumbled with the latch, burning with embarrassment and improbable hope. I was halfway down the stairs and almost onto the street when I was struck by a tiny irony. Today was my birthday.

AN ELDERLY BLACK CAB idled by the kerb, a torn piece of card blue-tacked against its window. It read:

Lamb

The driver (unkempt, straggle haired, a stranger to the razor) was engrossed in a chunky hardback book. I tapped on the glass and he wound the window grudgingly down.

"Good morning," I said, trying my best to sound cheerful. "I'm Henry Lamb."

The driver stared at me.

"I was told you'd be waiting."

Another long, sizing-up look, until: "You can call me Barnaby. You'd better get in."

I hauled open the door and scrambled into the back seat. The interior was covered in the kind of long white hairs which smell of wet dog and cling jealously to your clothing for days.

"So you own a dog?" I asked, trying to make conversation

as I strapped myself in and Barnaby cajoled the engine into life.

"Dog? Why would you think I own a dog? Yappy little gits."

A long and very awkward pause ensued. We were passing through the dregs of Stockwell before either of us spoke again.

"What are you reading?" I asked at last, still attempting to be pleasant.

Alarmingly, Barnaby took his eyes from the road to glance down at the title. *"The Middle Narratives of H. Rider Haggard and the Structuralist Problem of Modernity."*

"Sounds a bit heavy going."

Barnaby reacted to this with barely checked fury, as though I'd just insulted his sister. "You think I'm a driver? Just a bloody cabbie? That what you thought?"

I blurted out a ham-fisted retraction. "I'm not sure what I meant."

"Well, I know what you meant. I know damn well what you meant. Listen, before I was recruited by Dedlock's outfit, I was a whole lot more than just a driver."

"Oh, right. Really? What did you do?"

"I was professor of literature at one of this country's foremost centres of excellence. I was an acknowledged authority on fin de siècle peril fiction. So I like to keep my hand in. Big deal. You got a problem with that?"

"Course not." Although taken aback by his belligerence, I was still determined to be civil, the importance of a sort of relentlessly cheerful politeness having been instilled in me by Granddad since the crib. "So . . ." I floundered about for a question. "What made you give up academia for all this?"

"Wasn't given a choice, was I? Those greedy bastards framed me. Got me thrown out of college on the most disgusting charges. The whole business was completely trumped up. There wasn't an ounce of truth in any of it. It was a wicked, stinking pack of lies. You understand me, Lamb? It was all invention. The whole pernicious lot of it. Do you hear what I'm saying?"

"Absolutely," I said hastily. "Without a doubt."

After that, the rest of the journey went by in sullen silence, as we passed through Clapham, Brixton and on to central London via an unusually circuitous route. Abruptly, we turned a corner and found ourselves in the taxi line at Waterloo station.

Barnaby exhaled noisily. "You can get out and walk from here."

IN THE SHADOW OF THE EYE, Mr. Jasper was waiting. A queue of sightseers snaked around him on the pavement—disgorged passengers from those coaches already wallowing by the side of the street.

Strange that in the twenty-first century, the city's greatest attraction should be a bird's-eye view of itself. For all its cocky futurism, there was something Victorian about the Eye. It had a sense of permanence and antiquity, as though it had been there for decades, looking down upon London as it burgeoned and swelled. It is easy to imagine the Elephant Man being taken aboard for a daytrip, staring awe-struck through the glass and wittering on about how terribly kind everyone had been to him.

"Good morning, Mr. Lamb." Jasper can only have been a year or two my senior, yet he invariably spoke to me like I was a school leaver on work experience. "Nice suit." This was said with heavy sarcasm but I mumbled my thanks all the same.

"How do you like our driver?"

"I'm not sure I made the best first impression."

"Barnaby takes a bit of getting used to."

"I can imagine."

"You'd better come up. Dedlock is expecting you."

The pod door was open and I saw the same gaggle of tourists inside as I'd seen on the previous Friday, but today they seemed weirdly frozen, calcified and motionless, like statues pointing towards sights they couldn't see.

"We don't maintain the illusion twenty-four-seven," Jasper murmured. "These days we just can't get the funding."

Bolder than before, I stepped into the mirage and emerged to face the old man. He had swum close to the glass of his tank and his pale fingers were pressed against the pane.

"Good morning," he said. "I trust you had a restful weekend."

"Yes, thank you." My voice was trembling a little. "But I'd appreciate some answers."

"In good time." He swivelled towards my companion. "Jasper? Why haven't you got your hat on?"

Jasper screwed his face up into a sulk. "I had hoped you were joking."

The old man struck the side of his tank and snarled. "Put it on this instant."

Huffily, Jasper reached into his suit pocket, pulled out a pink, neatly folded paper hat and placed it upon his head.

Dedlock gave him a steely look. "That's better." I got a gummy smile and noticed for the first time that the old man had few teeth left—and of those that remained, all were stumps, yellowing, rotting and askew. "We wanted you to feel at home," he said. "Happy birthday, Henry Lamb!"

I fought back the urge to laugh hysterically.

Dedlock flaunted his dental remnants again. "Enjoy your birthday. Celebrate your survival. But pray you never have to suffer as many of the things as me."

The pod shook as it began its ascent and when the man in the tank looked at me again, he was no longer smiling. "Party's over. To business."

"I'd like to know what you want with me." I spoke as calmly and precisely as I could. "I'm nothing special. I'm just a filing clerk. I've got nothing to do with your civil war."

"You're quite correct."

"Oh." I was faintly hurt by this. "Am I?"

"There is nothing special about you, Henry Lamb. Not remotely. And yet your grandfather—he was remarkable. I knew him very well. For a time, we were even friends."

"You and he? Friends?"

"Certainly. Indeed, it's only because he held such inexplicable affection for you that you are summoned here at all. I'm sure that this is how he wanted it to be. When you work alongside someone for as long as we did, you get to know the way they think. And I've little doubt that this is what he meant to happen."

Certain peculiar suspicions were coalescing in my mind. "Granddad was something to do with all this, wasn't he?"

Dedlock and Jasper exchanged watchful glances.

"Was he . . ." I trailed off, hardly daring to articulate the thought. "Was he one of you?"

The old man gave me a long, sober stare. "There was a time, long ago, when I would have said he was the best of us."

"Tell me more," I said. "Right now."

Dedlock turned away and started to paddle over to the other side of his tank. "We're looking for a woman named Estella. Find her and the war is at an end. Your grandfather was the last man alive who knew where she was and I can only hope that he has done us the courtesy of leaving us a clue. I need you to take Jasper to the hospital."

"Why on earth—"

"This is a direct order. Your generation may be a soft and feckless one but you are at least familiar with the concept of an order, yes?"

I said nothing.

"In good time, Henry Lamb, I'll tell you whatever you want to know. Until then—do your duty." And with this final exhortation, dolefully delivered, the old man turned his back upon us and gazed silently out across the city.

CHAPTER 8

WHEN WE ARRIVED AT THE MACHEN WARD WE were told that the old bastard was being washed—a ghastly, ghoulish sponge bath which I had no desire to witness. Jasper and I retreated to the canteen, where we shared an awkward half hour with two lukewarm coffees and a rubbery BLT.

It was only then that I was finally able to persuade Mr. Jasper to listen. During the journey from the Eye, punctuated by bursts of indiscriminate bitterness from our driver, he had sat in solemn silence, ignoring or rebuffing my every attempt at conversation.

"I need to ask you about the war," I said, for what felt like the fifth or sixth time that day.

"Fire away," Jasper said sardonically.

"The House of Windsor . . . they're the royal family, right?"

A yawn, a nod: "Your point being?"

"It's just that I've never thought of them as particularly malevolent. Slightly embarrassing, yes, a bit kooky, maybe, but—"

"They would see London in ruins. They would see the city laid waste."

"Why? Why on earth would they want that?"

Jasper gave something approaching a sneer. "Let's hope you never have to find out."

"Did you know him?" I asked. "My grandfather."

"Before my time. Way before my time."

"But you've heard of him?"

"He's a legend in the Service."

"Why couldn't you have come to see him on your own? Why do you need me?"

"I tried. But even incapacitated, your grandfather is potentially lethal. He's set up some kind of psychic boundary. No-one comes close unless he wants them to."

"What?"

"The Directorate believes in magic, Henry. It always has." Jasper pushed away his sandwich barely touched, prissy disdain flickering across his face. "This plate's dirty." He glanced about him at the café like he was battling to suppress a shudder. "This whole place is filthy. Crawling with disease."

A nurse approached to tell us that we could see the patient now and we got to our feet, my companion more swiftly than I. Mr. Jasper trotted into the ward and over to the prone figure of my father's father with undisguised curiosity.

The old man's eyes were closed, tubes emanated from pale nose and pale mouth, and he seemed weaker and more frail than ever. I couldn't discern a pulse. I only had the word of his support machine that he was even alive at all. Though we had yet to exchange a word, I had seen more of Granddad in the past week than I had for years.

Jasper pulled out what looked like a complicated tuning fork and pointed it at the old bastard's body. It bleeped once, twice, three times, then made a drawn-out chittering sound.

I glared. "What are you doing?"

Jasper, intent on his obscure task, didn't even meet my gaze. "I'm trying to ascertain if he really is in a coma."

"Course he's in a coma."

"Your grandfather's faked his own death at least twice before.

He's a master of disguise. In 1959 he penetrated Buckingham Palace in the company of an Armenian circus troupe disguised as a clown. From sixty-one to sixty-four he lived undetected as a gillie at Balmoral. In sixty-six he bankrupted the head of the House of Windsor's Special Operations Unit in a high-stakes poker game at Monte Carlo. So I think he's more than capable of feigning a stroke, don't you?"

"Not Granddad," I stuttered. "That doesn't sound anything like my granddad."

"Then you never knew him at all." Jasper slipped the device back into his pocket. "But it's real." He sounded disappointed. "Probably the booze." He gazed into the distance, a look of quiet respect on his face. When he spoke again, the effect was that of a humble supplicant offering prayers to his invisible deity. "I'm with him now, sir . . . I'm afraid it's bad news . . . Please. Let's not give up . . . Very well. Understood . . . I'll tell him." Briskly, he turned back to me. "We'll see you tomorrow, Mr. Lamb." He muttered something about enjoying the rest of my birthday and paced bad temperedly away.

"Is that it?" I shouted after him. "What happens now?"

But Jasper left without looking back, strutting onwards towards whatever fresh drama awaited him, and soon the ward was quiet again.

At a loss about what to do next, I sank back into the chair and sat alone for a while, the old man's hand clasped in mine. "Is it true?" I said. "Is any of it true?"

DESPERATE FOR CONVERSATION, I called up Mum.

"How's Gibraltar?" I asked.

No sooner had I spoken than the nurse appeared and waved me out of the room, like a farmer's wife shooing chickens away from the petunias. "No mobiles! Ruins equipment. No mobiles!"

Actually, Granddad's machine had seemed completely unaffected, but, chastened and embarrassed, I did as I was told and took the conversation out into the corridor.

"It's marvellous," Mum was saying. "Just marvellous. Gordy's been such a naughty boy. We're in this wonderful hotel." She broke off to speak to someone and I heard a mention of my name. I imagined her rolling her eyes, deftly miming exasperation. Then she was back on the line. "How are you?"

"Fine," I said, then (discreetly): "Got a promotion."

"That's wonderful."

"I'm not a filing clerk any more."

"Good for you."

"Never again."

"Really, darling. That's fab."

"Mum?"

"Yes?"

"Granddad was middle-aged before he joined the BBC, wasn't he? It was his second career. What did he do before that?"

"Before the Beeb?" She didn't even try to keep the boredom from her voice. "Some sort of civil servant, I think. Nothing glamorous—though God knows he always acted like his shit smelt sweeter than ours. Why?"

"No reason."

"I've got to go, darling. Gordy's booked us a table somewhere. He's looking frightfully cross and tapping his watch."

"Mum?" I said. "I've been thinking a lot about Dad recently."

An eternity of crackling. The vinyl pops and hisses of long distance.

"I'm sorry, darling, it's a terrible line."

"I said I've been thinking about Dad."

"Got to dash. Gordy says the food'll be fab."

She hadn't even remembered it was my birthday.

"Have a nice meal," I muttered. "Have fun."

"Bye-bye, darling."

And then, a tiny acknowledgement that she had, after all, heard what I'd said. "Don't brood, will you?"

The line went dead before I was able to reply.

I walked back into the ward and summoned up a contrite smile for the nurse. "You were right," I said, once the apologies were done. "I think my granddad was in a war."

"It always shows," she murmured. For a moment, there was a chink of humanity, a dappling of sadness in her face before, chilly and professional again, she walked away.

Heavy with half-formed fears and worries, I kissed the old man on the forehead and took my leave at last of that awful mausoleum.

IN THE LONG GREY CORRIDOR which led to the exit, a red-headed man on crutches was clip-clopping ahead of me. I recognised his swaying frond of ginger hair.

"Hello there!"

He craned around to glare at me, his face puce and sweaty from his exertions. "Oh, it's you."

"Let you out quickly, haven't they?"

"Turns out I'm fine."

"You fell five storeys."

"Then I'm a bleeding miracle." He grimaced down towards his crutches. "A limping one, anyway."

"I'm just glad you're OK."

The ginger-haired man looked belligerently at me. "You still don't get it, do you?"

I stared back, nonplussed. "I'm sorry?"

"The answer is yes."

"What?"

"The answer is yes. For God's sake. Have you got that? *The answer is yes.*" The window cleaner took a deep, rattling breath and pivoted himself away.

"What was that about?" I asked, as much to myself as to him.

Taking no notice of me and mumbling a grab-bag of expletives, he made his way unsteadily over to a beaten-up Rover on the other side of the parking lot in which his unfortunate family was waiting and probably wondering why he couldn't have fallen just that little bit harder.

WHEN I GOT HOME TO Tooting Bec and walked through to the sitting room, Abbey was there, wearing a little black dress, surrounded by balloons and smiling sheepishly. An unsuccessful-looking chocolate cake sat on the table, decorated by a single unlit candle.

"Happy birthday!" she said.

"This is unexpected. I don't know what to say."

"Sit down. I'll get you a drink."

She sashayed through to the kitchen, from where I could hear clinking glasses, the jingle of ice, the glug of juice and liquor. She called through: "How was your day?"

"Slightly strange. You?"

"Mostly dull. Till now."

"Thanks for all this. You really needn't have bothered . . ."

She came back into the lounge, carrying two glasses of something fizzy, ice cubes bobbing on the surface.

"What's this?" I asked as I took mine.

"Cocktail," she beamed. "Home-made. Try it."

I took a tentative sip—tingly, sweet, pleasantly numbing. Emboldened, I took another mouthful. Then another. It was only the presence of my landlady that prevented me from downing the thing in one.

"Wonderful! What's in it?"

Abbey arched an eyebrow. "Trade secret." She produced a box of matches and lit the candle on my cake. "Make a wish."

I closed my eyes, blew out the candle and made a wish which, for a short time, came true.

"There's more." Abbey scampered into her bedroom and returned with a soft parcel which she thrust excitedly into my hands. "Here you are."

"This is too much," I protested, feeling a blush start somewhere at the bottom of my neck and gradually stain my whole face.

"I wasn't sure of your size. I've kept the receipt if it's not right."

I tore open the paper to reveal an irredeemably hideous V-neck sweater, precisely the shade of lemon curd.

"It's fantastic," I lied, then lied again: "I've always wanted one of these." Frankly, at that moment, Abbey looked so rapturously beautiful that she could have wrapped me a dead weasel for my birthday and I'd have thanked her for it.

She beamed, I thanked her for a second and third time and there followed a bungling couple of seconds in which I tried to kiss her on the cheek only to chicken out and offer her my hand instead.

"Aren't you going to try it on?" she asked.

I flinched. A lurch of panic in my stomach. "What?"

A smile, almost sly. "The sweater . . ."

As I struggled into my birthday present, Abbey cut us both a generous slice of cake.

"Made this myself," she said. "Could be interesting."

"What do you think?" I asked once I had squirmed inside the pullover.

"Very nice," Abbey said. "Very tasty."

I think I must have blushed again. Certainly I didn't say anything further, and as we sat in silence on the sofa eating cake, Abbey wriggled a bit closer.

"Thanks for the cake," I said. "Thank you for my present."

She sighed with what sounded like frustration. "Henry?"

"What?"

"You can kiss me now."

Like an idiot, I just stared, crumbs of cake cascading from my mouth.

My mobile began to buzz. Abbey said later that she wished I'd turned it off and just leapt on her but I think some pusillanimous part of me was grateful for the distraction.

"Hello?" I said, a little wearily.

"Darling! Happy birthday!"

"Thanks," I said. "Thanks very much."

"Sorry I've not got you anything this year. I'll give you some money when I get back. I know you used to like something to open but you're a big boy now. You'd prefer the cash, wouldn't you?"

"Of course. Sounds nice."

"Are you having a good evening? Doing anything special?" She stopped, suddenly suspicious. "You're not at the hospital, are you? Not with the old bastard?"

"Actually, I'm in the flat. With a . . . friend." I turned to Abbey to check that this description was OK and she smiled impatiently back.

"I'd better go, Mum."

"Many happy returns, darling." At the other end of the line I heard the bass rumble of male laughter.

"Bye then," I said softly.

"Bye-bye, sweetheart."

I switched off the phone and flung it into the corner of the room. Abbey was watching with an amused look. "Your mum?"

"Yes."

"She OK?"

"Sounded fine."

"Good." Abbey stretched herself out and leaned back into the sofa.

"Listen," I said, as calmly as I could. "Before the phone rang . . . Does that offer still stand? Would it be possible—"

Abbey lunged. In a glorious moment, I felt her mouth pressed hard against mine, the honeyed warmth of her breath, the moist intrusion of her tongue. We came up for air and sat gazing at one another, stupid sloppy grins on both our faces. No-one spoke.

Then the phone rang, the landline this time.

Abbey shook her head in silent, irritated warning.

I'm afraid I'm the kind of person who gets superstitious about ignoring the telephone. I can't walk past a ringing phone booth without feeling an irrational stab of guilt. So of course I got up, walked across the room and tried not to sound too out of breath.

"Hello?"

"Henry Lamb?" The voice sounded aggravatingly familiar.

"Speaking."

"I'm calling on behalf of Gadarene Glass."

I felt myself begin to simmer. "I thought I'd told you to stop bothering me."

"So you did. But I felt I really owed it to you to try one last time. Might I interest you in a new window?"

"No," I said flatly. "You might not."

"And that's your final answer? Your answer is no?"

"Absolutely."

The caller said nothing. There followed a long silence as the truth of it smacked me in the face and slapped me viciously around the chops.

"On second thought . . ."

"What?" She sounded utterly exasperated, like a teacher hand-holding a spectacularly dim-witted child through their ABCs. "What's your answer now?"

"The answer is yes," I said, cautiously at first, then growing in confidence. "The answer is yes!"

The line went dead.

Abbey was looking at me as though I was mad. "Who on earth was that?"

The doorbell began to jangle, hectically, insistently, without pause—the kind of ring you'd expect if someone was being murdered on your doorstep.

"Stay there," I said as, fuelled by cocktail, birthday cake and the best kiss of my life, I strode to the front door and wrenched it open.

A little old lady stood outside. With her prim demeanour, outsized glasses and neatly curled hair, she looked as though she ought to be running the jam stall at the church fête instead of standing on my doorstep in Tooting after dark.

Her right hand was pressed hard against the bell. Mercifully, when she saw me, she let go. "Your grandfather said you were intelligent. Evidently, he was blinded by sentiment."

"Who on earth are you?"

"You're in the most terrible danger, Mr. Lamb."

"Didn't I ask who you were?"

"I'm an ally. That's all you need to know for now. I assume your grandfather never told you about the password?"

"My granddad's in hospital," I said. "He's in a coma."

"But he laid plans, Henry. I'm merely playing my part in the process." She peered past me into the house. "Extraordinary. It hasn't changed one bit."

"What?"

"You know by now, I suppose, who your grandfather was? What he was?"

"What he was?"

"Chief field officer in the Directorate. Mr. Dedlock's number one. The leading light in the secret war against the House of Windsor." She lowered her voice. "More kills to his name than any other soldier."

"It's all true then?" I said softly.

"All true, Mr. Lamb. With a good deal of the really unpleasant detail still to come." She seemed to be surveying the street. A battered car, effluent brown, grumbled past and she stared interrogatively at its driver. "I mustn't stay long tonight. They'll have put watchers on you."

"Watchers?".

"Tell no-one you've seen me. Not even Dedlock."

"You know Dedlock?"

"I know them all. Knew them all, at any rate." She gave me a disgusted look, as though I'd just broken wind and laughed about it. "What a hideous sweater."

"It was a present," I said defensively. Then, remembering the gravity of the situation: "I think you'd better come inside."

"Not tonight. The enemy is very close. We'll meet again soon. Until then—tread carefully."

Before I could stop her, she was gone, trotting spryly into the dark. I peered out at the street and could see no sign of those "watchers" she'd spoken about. But I was careful to double-lock the door all the same before I went back into the sitting room, where Abbey, still aflutter from our kiss, was polishing off another slice of cake.

"I was thinking," she said, "how about we go to the cinema tomorrow? I'm not sure what's on—" She saw my face. "What's happened? Who was that?"

"A ghost from the past," I said, before, in a sudden surge of pessimism, adding: "Or the shape of things to come."

CHAPTER 9

SOMEHOW ANOTHER NIGHT HAD PASSED, ANOTHER cheerless journey had been endured with Barnaby and I had come again to the Directorate, back to that glass bubble and its impossible occupant.

"You look tired, Henry Lamb. I do hope that landlady of yours isn't keeping you up nights."

"I beg your pardon?" I asked, starchily affronted that this half-naked ghoul should even know of Abbey's existence, let alone be talking about her in such a way.

Dedlock laughed and a thin trail of bubbles left his mouth, popping as they reached the surface. "An old man's joke," he said, as a second stream drifted after the first. "God knows we need something to laugh about now." In his arthritic doggy paddle, he swam close to the pane and grimaced. "How's your granddad?"

I felt a trickle of sweat creep down my back. "No change. No change at all."

Jasper spoke up, all business. "There is still a sliver of hope. It is just possible that your grandfather left us a clue. We need to see his home."

"You want to go to Granddad's house?"

"It's what he would have wanted," Dedlock said. "Trust me,

it's really very important that you give us your full coopera-
tion."

I thought for a moment. "There is a condition."

A spasm of irritation disrupted Dedlock's face. "What?"

"I want you to tell me exactly what it was that Granddad did
for you."

"Ignorance is a virtue in our business. Relish it. Believe me,
you would not wish to know the truth."

"You owe me an explanation."

The old man banged on the side of his tank, fury bulging in
his ancient eyes. "Just do your duty! Time is running out."

BARNABY DROVE JASPER AND ME to 17 Temple Drive, where
my grandfather had lived out a life far richer and more strange
than I could ever have guessed.

On the journey, I made myself unpopular by insisting we
pull over at a corner shop to buy a couple of tins of cat food. I'd
been feeling profoundly guilty about the old man's pet, terrified
that we would arrive to find the poor animal with its ribcage
poking through its fur, mewling at me in piteous accusation.

At last, Barnaby pulled up outside the old bastard's house.
"Doesn't look like much," he said. "Not for him."

"You knew him?" I asked.

Barnaby summoned up a look of astonishingly undiluted
bellicosity. "Thought you had a job to do."

We stepped out of the car, slammed the doors, and Barnaby
sped into the distance.

Once he was gone, Jasper looked up at the house and wrinkled his nose. "After you."

I fumbled with the key, opened the door and walked inside.
Jasper, embarrassed, hung back, waiting by the threshold.

"Are you all right?" I asked.

"You need to invite me in."

"What?"

Jasper looked at his feet. "You need to invite me in."

"What are you talking about?"

"Your grandfather was prudent. There are snares here, too. Psychic traps and etheric burglar alarms. He's made sure I can't enter without permission."

I grinned. "Like a vampire?"

"Just ask me in, Henry."

"Very well." I shrugged. "Come in."

Jasper stepped inside, looking agitatedly around him as though he expected at any moment to be perforated by a booby trap or tumble through a trapdoor. "We don't want to linger. They'll be watching."

Leaving him to his melodramatics and struggling against the memories stirred by the smell of burnt sausages, I began searching for the cat, scouring kitchen, bathroom and lounge.

"Is there a safe?" Jasper asked.

"Granddad hasn't got a safe," I said.

"He'd have disguised it. It wouldn't necessarily look like a safe. Probably more like a sheet of metal."

For a second, I wavered. Then I made my decision. "You'd better come upstairs."

The bedroom was just as before, mummified and changeless—the coffee-stained newspaper, the clock stopped at 12:14, the photograph of me as a child. I expected Jasper to make some quip at the sight of it, some nugget of sarcasm about *Worse Things Happen at Sea*, but he was fizzing with nerves, glancing feverishly into shadows, jumping like a startled squirrel at the slightest sound.

I moved the photograph aside to reveal the sheet of metal underneath. "This what we're looking for?"

Jasper leaned close, peering at the keyhole and the metal

pincers which ran around the circumference of the hole. "DNA lock," he murmured. "Give me your hand."

"What?" I said. "What are you going to do with me?"

He rolled his eyes. "You're not here for your good looks and your six-pack, Henry. Just give me your hand." Jasper grabbed my left hand. "I need to borrow your thumb for a minute."

"Oh," I said doubtfully.

"Press it against the hole. Make sure you draw blood."

"What? Why do you want me to do that?"

"Like I said—DNA lock. Knowing him, it's bound to be a family thing."

I protested that I didn't understand what he was talking about.

"Henry, please. Just trust me."

"Are you sure?"

"For God's sake, we're running out of time."

Warily, feeling rather as though I'd been bullied into it, I pressed my thumb hard against the hole. The pincers instantly drew blood and I yelped in shock. When I took my thumb away, the metal was stained with red.

With a soft click, the metal sheet slid open.

"See?" Jasper said.

Just as this happened, something furry brushed against my legs. I looked down. "Hello," I said, and the cat purred happily back. To my relief, he looked every bit as plump as before. "I've got some food for you."

"Forget the cat," Jasper snapped. "What's in the safe?"

There was a small compartment built into the wall, entirely empty except for a hardbacked notebook. I pulled it out and saw that someone had pasted a white sticker to the cover, on which was written:

For Henry

So nakedly covetous was the look in Jasper's eyes that I thought he was about to snatch it away from me, like a jealous schoolgirl grabbing at a classmate's love letter.

"What does it say?" he asked. "Quick—what does it say?"

Flipping it open, I saw that the book was filled with familiar handwriting, the pen pressed down so hard upon the paper that every leaf of it was ridged with the outline of letters.

The first page read:

Dear Henry,

If you are reading this, then I have met with some disaster, either by my own folly or at the hand of the enemy. I imagine that you must by now have been inducted into the Directorate and that you will have guessed that there was considerably more to my life—and to yours—than I ever let you know. For this: my sincere apologies.

Both the Directorate and the House of Windsor will be looking for a woman named Estella. The secret of her location has kept the war in stalemate for years.

This book is a list of instructions for how to survive what follows unscathed. You must be certain to follow them to the letter and, above all else, you must trust the Process. Remember that, Henry. Whatever else happens—trust the Process.

The cat nuzzled against my legs and meowed.

"What does it say?" Jasper asked, excitement and relief intermingled in his voice.

"He says it's a set of instructions. Something about a process."

Jasper sounded close to giggling. "We're saved!"

The cat nudged past my ankles, mewed and stalked imperiously to the door. He stopped, looked back and gave a final impatient yowl.

"Do you know?" I said. "I think that cat wants us to follow him."

"Ridiculous," said Jasper, although I noticed that when I walked across the room he was close behind me. Or perhaps it was simply because I had that book and Jasper was drawn to it as a dog to aniseed.

Whatever his motive, it proved fortuitous, because if Mr. Jasper and I had stayed where we were, the two fizzing balls of flame which smashed through the window a minute or so later would have almost certainly hit us square in the face. Instead, they bounced off the wall, dropped onto the carpet and set themselves to burning.

Jasper swore loudly. I just stared, dumbfounded.

In an instant, the room was filled with light and sound. Until then, I had never realised how much noise fire makes, the apocalyptic roar of it. Choking from the smoke, our eyes streaming with tears, we fled the room, stumbled into the corridor and down the stairs, the cat bounding just ahead. Behind us, we heard the bedroom catch ablaze, the whinny of the floorboards, the crackle of cheap furnishings, the splintering of chipboard and plaster. From outside—shouts and screams of panic and confusion. Acrid black smoke blocked our path as I fumbled to unlock the door until, after a small eternity, I got it open, and we staggered gratefully out onto the street.

Already a crowd had gathered, morbidly gripped by disaster. A burly, thick-necked man ran forwards and tugged us from the smoke.

"You two okay?" he asked once we'd finished spluttering. In the distance, I heard the approach of sirens.

"Thank you," I managed at last, dabbing at my streaming eyes. "I'm fine."

"Damn it." The thick-necked man seemed enraged. I noticed

that he wore the same flesh-coloured piece of plastic in his ear as Mr. Jasper. "How the devil did they know we were here?"

"No idea," said Jasper, peevish, singed and soot stained. "Henry Lamb—meet our head of security. Steerforth—meet Henry Lamb."

Mr. Steerforth was not exactly fat, but he had the kind of meaty, rugby-on-a-Sunday physique which makes you wonder how much of it is muscle and how much simply flab. His blond hair looked dyed and was thinning badly, which he had unsuc-cessfully tried to disguise by combing it forwards into a widow's peak. If he had been an American football player, he'd be a grizzled linebacker given one last chance to prove himself in the final game of his career.

"Henry?" Jasper said quietly. "Where's the book?"

I felt like crying. "Inside. I think I dropped it."

Steerforth needed no further encouragement. Despite the fact that Granddad's house had smoke billowing from its door and windows, despite the six-foot tongues of flame which were clearly visible within, Steerforth bounded into the building with the enthusiasm of a puppy chasing his first stick.

I turned to Jasper. "Will he be OK?"

"Steerforth doesn't know the meaning of fear." I couldn't detect whether it was admiration, envy or sarcasm I heard in Jasper's voice—and I wonder now if it might have been some-thing else entirely.

Five or six intolerably long minutes passed before Steerforth re-emerged, a handkerchief knotted around his face, his fore-head smeared with dust and grime, holding something cradled in his arms. To raucous applause from the assembled bystand-ers, he jogged over to us just as a fire engine and two police cars sped into Temple Drive.

"You've got it?" Jasper hissed.

"The book burned."

"What?" Jasper's eyes seemed to swell with exaggerated despair.

"But I did save this little fella."

Steerforth passed me a small grey bundle of fur. Clumsily, I held it in my arms, and as he looked up at me, I could have sworn that Granddad's cat was smiling.

STEERFORTH SUGGESTED THAT WE go for a pint. Various medics and police-people were fussing over us but Jasper had only to mention one word—"Directorate"—for them to dissolve obediently into the night.

Most upsettingly, the cat had done the same, squirming free of my arms and running into the darkness before I could do a thing to stop him. I searched frantically but Steerforth, apparently dying for a packet of pork scratchings, told me to give it up and manhandled me in the direction of the Rose and Crown.

The others went in, despite the fact that it seemed to be hosting some sort of school disco, whilst I hung back outside to make a phone call.

It took a long time for the connection to go through, then: "Mum?"

"Darling?"

Inside, a whoop of delight as "Come on Eileen" arrived on the sound system and the volume swelled.

"Where on earth are you?"

"It's a long story. Listen, I don't know how to tell you this, but . . . Someone's blown up Granddad's house."

Mum sounded bored. "Really?"

"It's been completely gutted."

"Oh." I could hear someone talking to her. "Henry again," she said.

"I was inside when it happened." I was starting to feel rather put out by her lack of concern.

"Sounds thrilling. You'll have to tell me all about it when I get back." She giggled. "Gordy says big kiss, by the way. Big kiss from Gordy."

"Hello, Gordy," I said flatly.

"Look, I'd better go. This must be costing us a fortune. Bye-bye, darling."

Not bothering to say goodbye, I jabbed angrily at the off button.

As I WALKED INTO the pub, "Livin' la Vida Loca" had started up and Steerforth was drumming his fingers on the table in time with the music. When the chorus lurched into view, he began to make weird, bird-like motions with his head as Mr. Jasper, sipping his Baileys, looked on, appalled.

The pub itself was practically deserted. All the real action seemed to be going on in the function room next door, where dozens of teenagers were busy doing one or more of the following: dancing, drinking, snogging, smoking, passing out. The smell of hormones, the heady scent of adolescence, was almost tangible in the air.

Steerforth shoved a glass in front of me. "Lager OK? Nice pint of wife beater?"

"This is a black day," Jasper muttered Eeyoreishly.

Ignoring the signs, prominently displayed, which exhorted us not to smoke, Steerforth pulled out a packet of cigarettes and offered them in my direction.

I shook my head. Jasper looked repulsed and mumbled something which might have been "dirty."

Steerforth peeled the cellophane from the packet. "The

house was our last roll of the dice. You know what we've got to do now."

"Not that." Jasper's voice was shaky and uncertain. "Not them."

"There's no other choice," Steerforth said as he produced a lighter from his pocket and applied it to the tip of his cigarette. I noticed that he had great difficulty lighting the thing since, despite his tone of brusque insouciance, his hands were shaking almost uncontrollably.

Suddenly, Jasper's head jerked upwards, as though he'd been goosed by a ghost. "Good evening, sir," he said. "We were just discussing—" He paused. "Are you quite sure, sir? Is there no other way?" A wince. "You know my opinion on that, sir." A chewing of the upper lip, then a reluctant nod. "Very well. We'll tell Henry."

"What was that all about?" I asked once Jasper had wrapped up his conversation with the invisible man and returned his attention to us. "What have you got to tell me?"

Mr. Jasper looked like he was about to cry. His glass of Baileys was stuck to the wooden table by the glutinous remnants of spilt beer. "This place is filthy," he said. "*Filthy*." A febrile kind of urgency infected his voice. "You were expected, Henry. Did you know that? They told us you'd be coming."

"Who told you? What are you talking about?"

Jasper grimaced, as though every word was causing him pain, each syllable costing him dear. "Somewhere not very far from here, deep underground in their own private dungeon, sit two prisoners of war. They have the blood of hundreds on their hands. They'll never be released alive."

Behind us, the Day-Glo tom-tom of Europop.

"In the course of their sentence, these prisoners have never spoken to a soul. Not one solitary word. And yet, last week, quite casually, they told their guard two things. They gave him a name. And they gave us a warning . . ."

"What's this got to do with me?" I asked.

"They told us about your grandfather before it happened. Then they told us who you are."

"Who are these people? How do they know anything about me?"

"I can't say. But God forgive me—we have no choice but to introduce you."

Steerforth wiped his lips on the back of his hand, making a slurpy smacking noise. "Tomorrow's truth time, Henry. If I were you, I'd drink up. Enjoy your last night of freedom." He took a drag on his cigarette before exhaling a thin grey stream of smoke. He was the kind of man, I strongly suspected, who smoked not because he particularly liked the taste but because he still thought it was cool. He winked at someone over by the bar—a skinny girl in tight black jeans. "'Scuse me, gents." He got to his feet and swaggered over. "A-level totty."

Jasper muttered something bitter under his breath, although I noticed that he never took his eyes off Steerforth.

Suddenly I remembered and glanced down at my watch. "Damn."

"What's the matter?"

"You mean apart from my grandfather's house burning down?"

Jasper nodded distractedly like this was the kind of thing which happened to him all the time.

I bundled up my coat. "I'm late."

"For what?"

"For a date." It was the first time all day I'd felt like smiling.

Before I could leave, Jasper grabbed my arm and held it tight. "Come to the Eye first thing tomorrow. The war hangs in the balance." He sank back in his seat and took a sip of his Baileys. "You'd better go. You don't want to keep Abbey waiting."

I dashed for the door and ran to the train station, grateful to be free. Only later did it occur to me to wonder precisely how it was that Jasper knew her name.

SHE WAS WAITING FOR me in Clapham, a part of the city whose façade of well-monied gentility only barely papered over its dirt and degradation. When I emerged from the tube, a homeless man blundered past me, smelling strongly of faeces.

Abbey stood outside the Picturehouse, traces of irritation marring her beautiful face. I must have looked a real state, as when she saw me her expression changed immediately to one of sympathy and concern. She fussed over me, smoothing my hair, brushing down my jacket, picking charred flakes from my lapels. "What's happened to you? You stink of smoke."

I wasn't sure how much it was safe to tell her. "I was at Granddad's house. There was an accident . . . a fire."

"Oh, you poor thing." She kissed me chastely on my forehead. "You have been in the wars."

"It's complicated."

"Listen, we've missed the film. You're knackered. Let's go back to the flat."

I nodded my grateful assent. "I'm so sorry about tonight."

"It's OK." She grinned. "You'll have to make it up to me."

THREE STOPS ON THE Northern line and we were home again. Abbey made beans on toast and we sat together quietly, the atmosphere between us thick with the unspoken.

"How was work?" I asked at last.

"Same as usual," she said. "Bit boring. Just a couple more rich people getting divorced. I'm starting to think there's got to be more to life."

"I know what you mean."

"Henry?"

"Hmm?"

"What's happening to you?"

I hesitated. "I can't say. I'd love to tell you but I really can't."

"If you ever need someone . . ."

"Thanks."

She leant towards me and kissed me, long and lingeringly, on the lips. I surprised myself by not being too tired to respond.

"ABBEY?" I SAID AS WE lay stretched out on the sofa, our hands entwined, our arms clasped together in tentative embrace. "What would you say . . . what would your reaction be if I were to tell you that a secret civil war has been waged in this country for years? What if I said that a little department in the civil service has been fighting tooth and nail with the royal family since 1857?"

Abbey laughed. "God, Henry. You're so different from the other blokes I've been out with."

Granite-faced, I gazed back at her.

"Please tell me you're joking."

"Of course," I said, despising myself for my cowardice and fear. "Of course I am. Just joking."

CHAPTER 10

F LOATING IN AMNIOTIC FLUID WITH ONLY HIS TRUNKS to protect his wrinkled modesty, Dedlock glowered at me from within his glass sarcophagus. "You failed to retrieve anything of value from the house of your grandfather. The old man's journal is lost to the flames."

"I'm afraid so, yes."

As Dedlock paddled over to me, I was put in mind of a shark I had once seen at the aquarium on a half-term trip with Granddad. Toothless and grey, it can't have killed its own food for years and must have spent half a lifetime chewing on stale meat tossed into the water by its keepers, yet despite all this, it still had murder blazing in its eyes. Looking at it through the glass, I knew that one chance was all it needed, one momentary slip on the part of its owners—and it would grab the opportunity to kill again, seize it with its withered gums and swallow it whole.

"Unacceptable, Henry. You're not filing paper any more. Every secret in that house is in ashes. The only man who can help us is in a coma. And now the House of Windsor is marshalling its forces against us. It is only a matter of time before they make their move."

I was flanked by Steerforth and Jasper, both of whom had

remained strategically silent in the course of my thorough dressing-down. Steerforth looked as though he hadn't shaved that morning and appeared to be nursing a more than usually persistent hangover. A volcanic pimple protruded from his chin.

"We've no other choice, sir," he said. "We all know it."

When Dedlock turned to me, his eyes were glittering with a horrible facsimile of geniality. "Henry Lamb?"

"Yes?"

"The time has come to tell you precisely why we are prosecuting this war—why the House of Windsor is the sworn enemy of this city. The time has come to tell you the secret."

Jasper touched my shoulder. "Sorry. I always liked your innocence."

"You might want to sit down," Dedlock said. "People often find they lose the use of their legs when they hear the truth. I would ask you also not to scream. This is the city's most profitable attraction and I'm loath to scare our visitors away." He grinned again in that same ghastly parody of good humour. "Now then," he said, with what he probably thought of as an avuncular twinkle. "Are we sitting comfortably?"

STEPPING OUT OF THE POD, I walked swiftly through the mirage, past the queue of sightseers and towards the scrap of grass which backs onto the Eye. There, I found myself an isolated corner and proceeded to be copiously sick. When I was done, I straightened up, dabbed at my mouth with a tissue and began to worry about my breath. A seagull landed at my feet and pecked inquisitively at the vomit.

Trying desperately not to consider the ramifications of what I'd been told, I stumbled to the river and stared dully down into its murky waters.

Someone strolled up beside me. "They've told you, then?"

The speaker was an elderly woman, fragile with age but in possession of a certain geriatric poise which suggested that there was little she would not be willing to face down.

"I suppose you've come to sell me double glazing?" I said.

A hint of a smile. "Could I tempt you to a stroll? We don't have long."

Wearily, I agreed, and together we walked along the riverbank, past tourists, buskers, tramps, office workers on an early lunch and truculent-looking kids on skateboards—all of them oblivious to the secret I had just been told, the truth that made a perverted joke of every one of their lives.

"Hits you rather hard, doesn't it?" the old lady said, as though she was discussing nothing more alarming than a national shortage of buttered scones. "You'll get used to it."

"Are you going to tell me who you are?"

"Unlike the rest of them, Henry, I'm going to do you the courtesy of telling you the name I was born with." She smiled. "I am Miss Jane Morning."

"Are you . . . Did he . . ." I gesticulated inarticulately towards the Eye.

"Before his defection to the BBC, your grandfather and I worked together at the Directorate for many years."

"I never knew any of this."

"There are less than two dozen men in England who know of the Directorate's true purpose. Your grandfather loved you dearly but, come now, he was hardly likely to entrust you with one of the best-kept secrets of British intelligence."

"That's why they need me, isn't it? Because of Granddad."

Miss Morning nodded. "The whereabouts of Estella is keeping the war in stalemate. That was always your grandfather's secret. And with him gone"—she looked as though she wasn't sure whether to laugh or cry—"well, as I believe the saying goes—all bets are off."

"You're not making a great deal of sense. Not that anything seems to lately."

"Concentrate, young man. The hunt is on for Estella now. Your grandfather knew this day would come and he planned for it. But something's gone wrong. Certain forces have taken an interest in us and it is most unlikely that we shall survive their attention." She broke off. "You seem frightened."

"Of course I'm frightened. I'm extremely frightened. Probably close to terrified if I'm being honest."

"That's eminently sane of you. But things are about to get a good deal worse. If I know how Dedlock thinks—and I'm very much afraid that I do—then he'll take you to see the prisoners tonight."

"Who are these prisoners?" I asked. "How do they know who I am?"

"You don't want me to say their names. Not out loud. Not in public."

"Why on earth not?"

"Names have power. Theirs more than most. I warn you, Henry. They'll lie to you. If they ever tell the truth, it will be to twist it to their own purposes. Don't take a single wicked word they say on trust. They are chaos incarnate. They delight in destruction for its own sake. And nothing is sweeter to them than the corruption of an innocent soul."

"I don't know what you're talking about."

"Then I fear you may have to discover it for yourself." Miss Morning snapped open her handbag and passed me a discreet square of card. "Call me when you need me. And you *will* need me."

"Can't you tell me more?"

"Not today."

"Why?"

"Because if you knew everything, I doubt you'd find the strength to carry on."

Although this sentence might look a little theatrical on paper, I should point out that it was delivered in a tone which was remarkably calm and matter-of-fact.

"There is one more thing," she said.

"Yes?"

"I have his cat. It found its way to me." A sad smile. "As, in your own way, have you." Then she gave me a crisp nod good-bye and walked into the crowd.

IF I THOUGHT IT would do any good, I'd tell you the secret now. I'd write it down and damn the consequences. But I can't see what help that would be. I don't see how laying before you those terrible truths about the House of Windsor, their insane treachery and their secret lusts, would serve any useful purpose save to infuse your nightmares with a clammy and crepuscular dread.

I STOOD MOTIONLESS, my mind whirling with impossibilities. Then—bathos.

"Henry? Is that you?"

Someone chunky stood in front of me, a sandwich engorged with cheese and pickle clasped half-eaten in her hands.

"Barbara!" I mustered a wonky kind of smile. "How are you?"

"Mustn't grumble. But how are you? How's life in"—she lowered her voice in serio-comic reverence—"the new department?"

I gulped back a bitter laugh, wondering what kind of cover story she'd been fed. "It's . . . challenging."

Barbara grunted and took a noisy bite of her sandwich but seemed to have nothing further to add to the conversation.

"How's Peter?" I asked.

"He's fine," she said between mouthfuls. "Keeps talking to me about all the gigs he's going to."

I rolled my eyes and we shared a moment of exasperated collusion.

"Actually," Barbara chomped on, "I had a phone call from one of your colleagues. Mr. Jasper. Remember? He introduced himself when he came into the office. Tallish man. Lovely skin."

I don't think she noticed me flinch at the mention of the name. What the hell was Jasper doing calling Barbara?

"He's taking me out to dinner," she said in answer to my unspoken question. Then, with a small crescendo of pride: "We're getting pizza."

I couldn't think of anything to say.

"He seems really nice." For an instant, she sounded like a very small girl. "He is nice, isn't he?"

"He's interesting," I said. "Oh, he's full of surprises."

Barbara looked at her watch. "Better go. Nice seeing you again."

"And you," I said politely, meaninglessly, as Barbara lumbered away, leaving me to watch the surge of strangers, wondering if any of them had the dimmest notion of how brittle the world really was.

MY LANDLADY AND I SAT in front of the television in an exploratory embrace, Abbey trying her best to get comfortable with my arm around her, me struggling against that nausea which had settled in my stomach ever since I'd been told the truth about the war.

Abbey had remarked on my pallor but I had admitted only to being worn and exhausted from my new job. I'd not forgotten Mr. Dedlock's threats.

So as not to hurt her feelings, I was wearing the lemon-coloured sweater which she'd given me for my birthday.

She was channel hopping. "Poor bastard," she said as she came to rest on BBC1.

I forced myself to focus on the screen. "Who?"

"Prince Arthur," she said, as the crinkled Prince of Wales moped dolefully across the screen. "Sixty today and still no closer to being king. No wonder he looks so flipping miserable."

"Hmm."

"I mean, look at him. Always so sour."

"Hmm."

"Wife's quite pretty, though. Never understood what she saw in him."

"Uh-huh."

"Are you OK, Henry? You seem miles away."

"Difficult day," I murmured.

"You can talk to me, you know."

I laughed, and judging from Abbey's expression, I imagine the sound cannot have been a pretty one.

Consequently, when the doorbell rang, I was grateful for the excuse to get to my feet.

THE SKY WAS STORMY and black, and Mr. Steerforth was standing on our doorstep. He seemed bulkier than ever, dressed in some kind of flak jacket and the sort of khaki trousers which boast a preposterous amount of pockets. "You all right? 'Cause you look bloody rough."

"I'm fine."

Steerforth snorted. "The secret will do that to you. Better get used to it."

"What do you want?"

"Get your coat. You're going to see them tonight."

"See who?"

"I can't say their names. Not their real names. But I call them . . ." He swallowed hard. "I call them the Domino Men."

"What?"

"Just get your coat," he barked, then, unable to resist a grin: "Nice sweater."

"Who was that?" Abbey asked, her attention half on me, half on the TV, which had now begun to show a montage of the heir to the throne's baby photos.

"It's work. I've got to go out."

"This late?"

"Sorry. Can't be helped."

The look that she gave me was split between sympathy and suspicion. "I wish you could tell me what's really going on."

"Believe me," I said grimly. "So do I."

IT HAD BEGUN TO RAIN, a mean, thin drizzle, and Barnaby was waiting in the car, slouched in his seat, engrossed in *The Dissemination of Irony: The Challenger Narratives Through the Prism of Postmodernism.*

"What a bloody awful sweater," he said, then blew his nose defiantly on the sleeve of his jacket.

Steerforth was already inside.

"Isn't Jasper coming with us?" I asked.

The driver spat out of the window. "Too chicken. Strap yourselves in." I did as I was told and Barnaby started the engine with the dutiful air of a man doing the school run for someone else's kids.

"Where are we going?" I asked.

"You'll know when you see it," Barnaby said.

Steerforth nudged me in the ribs. "Dedlock wants to talk."

"Fine." I looked around for a phone. "How's he going to manage that?"

"Give me a minute." Steerforth screwed up his face as though grappling with the most gruesome kind of constipation. "He's coming through."

Then the big man's face began to twist, flex and gurn; it was possessed by rubbery quivers, spasms and twitches, contorting itself into strange and horrible shapes. He was evidently in considerable pain and it only seemed to end when the man who sat opposite me was utterly transformed. He may still have had Steerforth's body, but through some impossible realignment of his features, he'd become a parody of the old man in the tank. Even his voice was altered, moving into a higher pitch, suddenly wavery with unnatural age.

"Good evening, Henry Lamb," he said.

I stared, astonished. "Dedlock?"

"Do not be alarmed. Steerforth is the pit bull of the Directorate. Some time ago, he submitted to a small procedure which allows me, on occasion, to borrow his physical form."

"Unbelievable."

"Indeed. And speaking of unbelievable . . . What a splendid pullover." The body of Steerforth emitted a series of gurgles which I presumed, after a while, to be laughter. "We've been left with no choice," he said. "Tonight, you meet the prisoners. You need to prise just one single piece of information from them. The whereabouts of the woman called Estella. Have you got that, Henry Lamb? Am I making myself unequivocally clear?"

"Who are these prisoners? How do they know so much?"

"I don't wish to say their names. Not now."

"Dedlock? I need to know who these people are."

It was raining harder now, each drop a hammer-blow against the pane. "My, my." The thing in Steerforth gave a liquid giggle. "Who said anything about them being people?"

There was a final burble, then Steerforth's face, running with rivulets of sweat, went slack and sagged back into its old, familiar lineaments.

"What the hell was that?"

Steerforth yanked a handkerchief from his pocket and mopped his face. "Now you see the price of the war," he murmured. "And we can't afford it. Not by a long shot."

THE CAR SPED ON through the night, passing out of south London, over the river, towards the centre of the city. It was a silent journey except for the deluge which beat ferociously against the windows, the windscreen, the roof.

At last, we headed past Trafalgar Square and turned into Whitehall, stopping outside a metal barricade guarded by a man with a machine gun slung around his neck. Hair plastered to forehead, his uniform sodden with rain, the sentry motioned for Barnaby to wind down the window. "State your business," he said, with all the thoroughgoing charm of a German border official.

"My name is Barnaby. This is Steerforth. We work for Mr. Dedlock."

The soldier peered into the back of the car, then took a stumbling step backwards. "Sorry, gents," he said. Then again, cravenly: "Really sorry."

Barnaby muttered something resentful, wound up his window and drove on towards the most famous address in England.

I think I might actually have shaken my head. "You can't be serious."

Steerforth was unable to keep a hint of pride from his voice. "Welcome to Downing Street," he said.

NUMBER TEN DOWNING STREET is full of false doors. Built, re-built, altered, extended, improved and reconceived over generations by a plethora of architects eager to impress, almost everything done by one designer has later been summarily reversed by another. The result is that the building has acquired the air of a folly, filled with corridors which lead nowhere, staircases that curve gracefully into thin air, doors which open onto brickwork. It is a place of doubles and traps where little is what it seems and nothing can be trusted.

Steerforth led me inside (the door to Number Ten, being perpetually open, has no handle), down a long, tapering corridor which, rather dispiritingly, seemed every bit as grey and nondescript as those in my old office. Eventually, we reached a spiral staircase, the walls of which were decorated with portraits of past prime ministers, beginning with the most recent incumbent before stretching chronologically backwards in time.

Then Steerforth led me down into the past. At first I recognised many of the politicians depicted on the walls—men and women who had held high office in my lifetime—but as we descended, the pictures grew older and increasingly unrecognisable, their costumes changing with the unfurling of the years, from starched collars and cravats to powder wigs and frock coats to lace and frills until, as we reached the lower levels, they scarcely seemed like statesmen at all. The people in those paintings were men of shadows, their faces half-masked and their bodies shrouded in darkness. At the end of the sequence, there were men in animal pelts and furs, hailing from an era of history I wasn't even sure I recognised at all.

At the bottom of the staircase was a lavish library, its walls filled with shelves, packed tight with books—but not the kind of books that one would expect to see here, not parliamentary records, treaties, contracts and points of order, but other, more troubling titles, akin to those I had found in Granddad's house, though stranger still. The tang of the forbidden was in that room. Often I think back to some of those half-glimpsed titles and I shudder.

The only space not taken up with books was filled by a life-sized portrait of a Victorian gentleman, his face still young but starting to show the corruption of age, his dark hair worn daringly collar length, a flutter of grim amusement on his face. I thought I recognised that smile. I have my suspicions as to why, but even now, I shouldn't like to say for certain.

Steerforth walked over to the portrait, pulled out a two-pronged metal tube identical to the device I'd seen Jasper wave at Granddad and pointed it at the picture. There was an electronic whine, a subtle click, and the painting swung backwards. No, not a painting, I saw now. A door.

A halogen light flickered on to reveal the smooth steel walls of an elevator.

Steerforth stepped inside and asked me to follow.

Numbly, wondering why the madness of this life no longer seemed to affect me, I did as I was told.

Steerforth pressed a button, the door hissed shut and I heard the painting snap back into place. Smoothly, the lift began to descend.

"Is there any point in asking where you're taking me?"

The man said nothing.

"Steerforth?"

The lift came to a halt, the doors swept backwards and Steerforth led me into another long corridor. Two guards, both armed, greeted us with grim nods.

On either side of us were glass windows fronting small rooms or cells, as if we were passing through the reptile house at the zoo. It was completely silent save for our footsteps and the shuffles of the guards. As I followed, I saw that there were people in each cell and that every one of them was naked. All seemed ill but their actions careered between the extremes of human behaviour. One raged and gibbered at the sight of us. Another placed his hands imploringly upon the glass, tears curving down his plump cheeks. Another still seemed quite oblivious to us, curled up in a foetal ball, his flabby body quivering in despair. There was even a man who seemed faintly familiar. He let fly a thick stream of urine as we passed before crouching down and enthusiastically licking it up.

"Don't I recognise him?"

Steerforth grunted. "Health secretary. Last but one, I think."

"You're not serious?"

We reached the end of the corridor, the final room, which, in contrast to the rest, lay in total darkness. Another guard stood outside, another machine gun slung around his neck. He sported the eye-popping look of the kind of state-sponsored sociopath who'd not only kill without a minute's hesitation but would probably be looking forward to it.

"We never meant you to see this," Steerforth said softly. "But your grandfather's left us no choice. You've got to go inside."

"You're not coming with me?"

A hesitation. "Please," he said, and his voice seemed to tremble.

"Steerforth? What's the matter?"

The big man sounded as though he were about to cry.

"People think I don't get frightened. But what's in there . . ." His voice grew husky and he began to shake, like an alcoholic about to admit in front of his support group that he has a problem. "They scare me."

"Oh, but you don't mind sending me in?"

"You'll be perfectly safe," he said, although it was obvious he didn't believe it. "They can't leave the circle. Stay outside the circle and I promise you'll be fine."

The glass door glided noiselessly open and Steerforth looked away. "They're waiting for you," he said, and it was impossible not to notice the dark stain that had begun to spread across his combat trousers, snailing down his left leg and towards his shoes. "Go inside," he said miserably.

"Please. At least tell me what to expect."

But the pit bull of the Directorate couldn't even meet my eye.

"Fine," I said. As I walked into the dark, the door slid sleekly shut behind me.

I addressed the blackness, my voice trembling with fear. "My name is Henry Lamb. I'm from the Directorate."

For a terrible moment, there was nothing. Then—light. Blazing, piercing light, almost intolerably bright, making spots of colour jig before my eyes, forcing me to blink fiercely before I became accustomed to the glare. A spotlight picked out a large circular space in the middle of the room, its parameters marked out with white chalk. At the centre of the circle, perched on garishly coloured deckchairs as though they were settling down for an afternoon nap on Brighton beach, were two of the oddest people I have ever had the misfortune to encounter.

Two grown men, well into middle age—one thick necked and ginger, the other slight and thin faced with a cowlick of dark hair. Both (and this was most bizarre of all) were dressed as old-fashioned schoolboys, kitted out in matching blue blazers and itchy grey shorts. The smaller one wore a little striped cap.

They beamed at the sight of me.

"Hullo!" said the larger man. "I'm Hawker, sir. He's Boon."

His companion winked in my direction and that alone was enough to set every nerve in my body jangling. "You can call us the Prefects."

Henry Lamb is a liar. Take nothing he says on trust. He is spinning you lines, sugaring the truth, telling you what he thinks you want to hear. Henry is no innocent. The lily-white Lamb has blood on his hands.

Mercifully for him, we have little interest in simply blackening his name. He has only a short time left before his consciousness is irrevocably snuffed out, an eventuality which renders catcalls and finger-pointing superfluously petty. Instead, we intend to while away these last few days by telling you a story of our own, and you have our unimpeachable word for it that, in shaming contrast to Henry's own self-serving memoir, every syllable shall be the truth.

Brace yourself for a move away from Lamb's quotidian universe of office girls and landladies and the morning commute. Prepare for an Olympian leap from dewy-eyed sentiment about the aged and pubescent longing for the girl next door. This is the story that matters. This, the story of the war, of the last prince, of the fall of the House of Windsor.

I expect you shall find it a good deal more to your taste.

At around the time that Henry the liar was making the acquaintance of Hawker and Boon, the future king of England was listening to a roomful of people who were paid to adore him sing a rousing "Happy Birthday" in his honour.

His Royal Highness Prince Arthur Aelfric Vortigern Windsor was the kind of man whose appearance might generously be described as unusual—not for him the privileged complexions and arrogant cheekbones of most of his ancestors and a good many of that swarming mass of male relations to which he referred, in that long-suffering tone which the nation had come to find faintly irritating, as "the brood." Lugubriously proportioned, thin lipped and pharaoh nosed, Windsor was a man profoundly ill at ease with the twenty-first century. He despised the vulgarities of its culture, the vapid light shows of its television, the unmelodic jabberings of its music, but above all else he hated the manner in which his family, once the most influential bloodline in Europe, had degenerated into a national laughing stock.

This particular day was special, not only because Arthur was celebrating his sixtieth birthday, a milestone in a life which seemed to him increasingly without compass, but also because it was the day on which he had finally accepted a miserable truth. His wife—beloved by her subjects as a radiant philanthropist, sylphlike humanitarian and dispenser of hugs on an industrial scale—no longer fancied him. Naturally, he hoped that she still cared for him, that she at least felt some residual dregs of affection, but it was painfully clear that she no longer incubated the slightest scintilla of physical desire, meeting every one of his advances with barely concealed distaste. Arthur had realised it that morning when, upon his suggestion of a birthday roll around the marital bed, Laetitia had sighed and looked away, a small, darting, sideways glance which confirmed his every fear. In the end she had acquiesced, though wearily, and as she lay dutifully beneath him Arthur noticed her stifled yawns, surreptitious inspections of her nails and regular stolen glances towards the clock.

His mood was not significantly improved by the feudal cheers of his household staff which greeted him on his descent for supper by way of a "surprise" (scarcely that, since something similar had occurred annually since his birth). Arthur gazed at their ham-fisted attempts at decoration and found it difficult to suppress a sigh. He thought the pomp and strut of his official birthday (tra-ditionally held much earlier in the year to avoid a clash with the Christmas season) taxing enough but often wondered whether this ghastly pageant of vulgar good intentions might actually be worse.

There was no sign of Laetitia. Over breakfast, she had com-plained of the first stirrings of a migraine, no doubt laying the groundwork for a plausible absence from the festivities. Arthur would have to face it alone, all the smiling and the shaking of hands and the pleasant inconsequentialities. This was the worst of it, he thought, the awful knowledge that one belongs, almost in one's totality, to other people.

As the assembled domestics launched, wincingly off-key, into "For He's a Jolly Good Fellow" and a troupe of small boys en-thusiastically tossed rose petals in his general direction, the prince noticed a muscular, bulky man, a year or two his junior, shoul-der his way towards him. Here, at least, was an ally.

"Good evening, sir," said the man when he had at last drawn close enough to be heard above the caterwauling. "Happy birth-day."

"Thank you, Silverman."

"Are you quite well, sir?"

"Oh, I'm dandy." The prince tried his best at a smile but, as usual, entirely failed in the attempt. He knew that his smile did not convince. He had seen himself many times on the television, and various acquaintances in what he supposed he was obliged to refer to as "the media" told him that it was regularly used by certain sectors of the press as a stick with which to beat him. It had a rictus quality, an overstretched look quite at odds with the boyish grins and flirty smirks of the new prime minister—a youth with whom the country still seemed inexplicably besotted.

"I have a message from your mother, sir," said Silverman.

"Oh?"

"She sends her apologies for not being able to attend in person."

The prince thrust his considerable chin into the middle distance and mumbled an acceptance. His mother had not appeared in public for years, having long ago removed herself to a modestly proportioned wing of the palace in order to live out an informal and thoroughly deserved retirement. Arthur had not seen his mother for almost twenty months and relied upon Silverman as a go-between. Tired of life in the public eye, the woman was close to becoming a complete recluse, although naturally no-one in the palace seemed at all prepared to admit to this. It suited them all—the fawners, the toadies and the yes-men—to pretend that she would go on forever, monarch in perpetuity.

"I appreciate that this is rather an irregular request, sir. But I understand that your mother would like you to meet someone."

"Who is it?"

"I regret I do not know his name, sir. But the gentleman is waiting outside."

"Now?"

"Your mother believes time to be of the essence, sir."

"But this is my party."

A deferential tilt of the head. "Indeed, sir."

The prince looked about him at the merrymaking, brushed away the rose petals that had accumulated like expensive dandruff on the shoulders of his dress uniform and came to the conclusion that everyone present would have infinitely more fun were he simply to disappear.

Silverman walked towards the big oak doors which constituted the exit and prompted: "This way, Your Highness."

Windsor looked back, hoping for some evidence of his wife. There was nothing. Feeling a pang of sadness rise up in him again, he followed Silverman from the room. Nobody noticed him leave—and, if they did, they scarcely cared.

Silverman led him to a large, circular chamber around the size of an Olympic swimming pool which Arthur was almost certain he had never seen before.

"Silverman? Where is this place?"

"The old ballroom, sir. I believe you danced here as a child."

A vague memory, lambent in his mind. "It is as though I recollect it from a dream."

"That may be so, sir."

A stranger stood in the centre of the room—a slim, blond, narrow-faced man, sharp suited though stripped of a necktie, his hair cajoled into slick, brash spikes. He was the kind of man who seemed to swagger even when he was standing still; the kind of man, the prince reflected, whom women, in their wisdom, find irresistible.

The stranger looked at the prince, conspicuously unimpressed. Not that Arthur was sufficiently naïve to expect awe or admiration—not in these, the dog days of empire—but a little respect would not have been amiss. A bow. The tiny courtesy of a handshake.

"I'm Mr. Streater." The voice of the stranger echoed around the room. "Your mum sent me. I'm sorta her birthday present to you."

"I've never heard of you."

Mr. Streater winked. "Yeah? Well, I've been told plenty about you." The blond man glanced dismissively towards Silverman, who, hovering three paces behind the prince, looked constipated in his concern. "Oi, Jeeves! Sling yer hook."

Silverman rallied with his frostiest smile. "So sorry," he said. "I'm afraid I didn't quite catch that."

"You heard me," Streater snapped. "Arthur and me have got private business here. Man to man."

As Silverman looked towards the prince for guidance, Arthur beckoned the equerry to come closer, lowering his voice so that they might not be overheard. "Could you do something for me, Silverman?"

"Anything, sir. Always. You know that."

"Get word to my mother. Find out why she's sent this fellow. There's something wrong here. Something most improper."

Silverman gazed at the prince, unwilling to abandon him. "I could hardly agree more, sir."

"Good luck, Silverman. Godspeed."

"Yes, sir," the equerry said reluctantly. "Thank you, sir."

Arthur gave a brisk nod, meant dually as goodbye and reassurance. Silverman walked across the ballroom, hesitated for a moment by the door and left. The prince returned his attention to Mr. Streater, who had watched the departure of the other man with a smirk so appallingly insouciant that several of Arthur's ancestors would have had him hanged for treason.

"So then." Arthur glared at the intruder. "What does my mother wish you to do?"

"I've come to prepare you."

"Prepare me? For what?"

"Something's coming, Arthur. A new world."

"If this is a prank or a practical joke, Mr. Streater, I can assure you that I shall not permit it to continue for a moment longer."

Streater did not seem in the least alarmed by the threat. "Easy, mate."

Arthur was astonished at the effrontery of the man. "Mate? I'm not your mate. I've never been 'easy' in my life. And I am hardly accustomed to being spoken to in this manner."

"Yeah?" Streater shrugged. "Bet you're not used to this either."

What happened next seemed almost like a dream. In a few deft motions, Streater rolled up the left sleeve of his jacket exposing his bone-white skin, produced a rubber glove, knotted it into a tourniquet, patted his arm and found a vein. Arthur guessed what was coming and, despite the bile steaming through his chest, he could not bring himself to turn away. With the air of an old-time confectioner dispensing half a pound of sherbet lemons, Streater took out a hypodermic loaded with pale pink liquid, thrust it into his arm, depressed the plunger and sighed with obscene pleasure. Then and only then did Arthur Windsor look away.

When he could bring himself to look back, the syringe and the tourniquet had vanished and the blond man was rolling down his sleeve, grinning wildly, like someone had slashed a smile in his face from left ear to right. "I don't care what anyone says. Drugs are cool."

The Prince of Wales flinched.

From somewhere, Streater had conjured up a cup of tea, which he proffered to the prince. "Oi. Get this down your neck."

Arthur took the cup and drank. The blend was unfamiliar to him but he liked it at once—soothing, rich and aromatically sweet.

"I'm not sure what this is all about," he said. "But I want no part of it. I am a decent human being."

Streater gave him a pitying look. "Grow up, chief. The world's not interested in decency any more."

Arthur turned his back on the man and tried the door, only to find it locked and bolted. "Let me out this instant." Somehow, he succeeded in keeping his temper. "You're already in very serious trouble. Don't make it any worse for yourself."

Mr. Streater shook his head in mock pity. "Stay where you are, chief." He peeled back his lips and grinned. "I'm gonna tell you a secret."

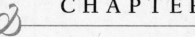

CHAPTER 11

I FEAR THE WORST.

I've just sat down to write, intending to continue the account of my first meeting with the Prefects, only to find several previously blank pages crammed with the opening of someone else's story, a different set of events entirely, some weird interpolation about the House of Windsor.

This has got nothing to do with me. That handwriting is not my own. Whatever you've just read, you can be absolutely certain that it wasn't me who wrote it.

But of course, I know what's happening here. I know what this means.

It means that I am losing.

CHAPTER 12

THE CREATURES WHICH STEERFORTH HAD CALLED, with a shudder in his voice, "the Domino Men" sat on their deckchairs, swinging their short-trousered legs and laughing.

"I say, Hawker," said the smaller man.

"Yes, Boon?" replied his beefier companion.

"Corks! He's not the least bit how I expected."

"Abso-bally-lutely, old top. He's a queer-looking bird and no mistake!"

Boon nodded in enthusiastic agreement. "He's got gangly limbs."

"Fishy eyes."

"A rum sort of gait."

One of them pointed at me. "Everything went wrong with you, didn't it, sir?"

"You're a reject, sir! A misshape!"

"If I was your pa, Mr. L, I'd take you back to the shop and demand a refund."

Peals of laughter, curiously high pitched.

"Sorry, sir." Boon wiped his eyes with the scuffed blue sleeve of his blazer. "Don't mind us."

"We're just a-joking."

"Just joshing."

"Only a bit of banter, sir. Only horseplay. We're really fright-fully bucked to meet you."

As they chattered on, I felt a strange inertia creep over me, the kind of numb fascination you're supposed to experience coming face to face with a predator in the wild, the terrible hypnotism of the carnivore. I stepped a fraction closer—though I wasn't so bewitched that I didn't remember to keep a careful distance from the chalk circle.

"You're the prisoners," I said softly.

"You might say that, sir."

"Indeed you jolly well might."

I stared at them in their absurd little outfits, listened to their ludicrous manner of speaking, and for a moment I wasn't sure that I shouldn't laugh. Such naïveté, in retrospect, given all that I know now.

Hawker beamed. "Frightfully sorry to hear about your grand-papa's fall."

"Terrible pity, sir."

"He was wizard, your granddad!"

"What a brick, sir!"

Hawker's eyes were brimming with dewy wistfulness. "And—oh—he had a lovely sense of humour."

The Prefects exploded into mocking laughter.

I stood silently, determined that these creatures should not get the better of me, that I wouldn't be reduced to cowering at their cell door like the pit bull Steerforth.

As the Prefects finished cackling, Boon leant forward and looked me in the eye. "I take it old fish-face has sent you?"

"He has," I said quietly.

Hawker chortled. "He must be sweating conkers now your

grandpa's popped off. S'pose he's told you to nose out where Estella is?"

"Sad, isn't it?" said Boon before I could reply, although I expect my expression told him all he needed to know. "Predictable."

"Dashed predictable."

"Beastly little prig."

"Greasy ape."

"He needs a vigorous slippering and I don't mind admitting it."

I tried my level best to stay calm. "So do you know," I asked, "where this woman is?"

Hawker waggled his eyebrows. "Rather, my old shoehorn! Your grandpa told us!"

Boon gave a triumphant grin. "If you're nice to us, one day we might even pass it on."

I glared back. "I think Mr. Dedlock will want more of a guarantee than that."

"'Fraid he'll be disappointed then."

"Not today, sir!"

"Nothing doing!"

"No room at the inn, sir!"

"Dedlock told me you knew my name," I said. "How?"

"Oh, but we've always known about you, Mr. L."

"We wanted to see your face, sir."

"We wanted to look you in the eye."

A chill slithered down my spine. "Why?"

Boon flashed another sharky smile. "So that we'll know you when we meet again, sir. Out there in the real world. Just before the end."

They exchanged glances, sly and conspiratorial.

"I think you're lying," I said.

"Oh!" Boon gave a gleeful yelp. "He thinks we're lying. He's only just made our acquaintance, Hawker, and already he's calling us fibbers."

"Getting rather frilly, ain't he, Boon?"

"Fearfully bold."

"The cheek of it. The sheer brazen cheek of it."

"Says what he thinks, doesn't he, our young Mr. Lamb?"

"Oh, he calls a spade a spade."

"Do you know, I rather like that?"

"I respect it."

"Sound fellow!"

"Good egg!"

"Ripping sport!"

"Come and see us again, won't you, sir?"

"How we'd adore another visit."

They laughed uproariously.

"But before you skedaddle, sir."

"Just one more thing, before you cut."

"A quick word about your father, sir."

"Your late, lamented pa."

"My father?" I asked, feeling the stirrings of panic. "What do you know about my dad?"

Boon gave me a subtle look and I felt a heave of nausea.

"Do you want to know how long it took him to die, sir? Trapped in the tangled wreckage of his automobile as the medical chaps tried and failed to cut him free?"

The sound of blood thundered through my head. "How do you know this?"

Hawker smirked. "Four hours, sir. Four unbearable hours before he finally popped off. Wasn't a nice death, was it, Boon?"

"Bally awful if you ask me."

"Protracted, I'd call it. Horribly protracted."

"Golly, Boon, you know some long words."

"So I should, Hawker. You are talking, after all, to the winner of the Cuthbert Cup for Prolixity for five consecutive terms."

"Congratulations, dear thing."

"Thank you, my old hat stand."

Hawker grinned at me. "He bled to death, Mr. L. Nasty gash in the tummy, I think. Absolutely the worst place for it to happen."

"He called for you at the end. He shouted your name as delirium took hold and his bowels let him down."

I turned and banged on the glass window. "Let me out!"

Hawker winced. "Something we said, sir?"

Tears streaming down my face, I slammed my palm into the pane. "Steerforth! Open the bloody door!"

Boon winced. "Hit a nerve, did we, Mr. L?"

I struck the glass as hard as I could. At that moment, I doubt I'd have cared if it had shattered in my hand. "Steerforth!"

Hawker was still smirking. "No need to cut up rough, old thing."

At last, the door slid open.

Boon gave me a wave. "Bye-bye, Mr. L."

"Toodle-oo, sir!"

"Tinkety-tonk!"

They were still laughing when I staggered out into the corridor where Steerforth was waiting, into whose arms I practically collapsed as the door hissed shut.

"I'm sorry," he said, an uncharacteristic tenderness in his voice. "I'm so sorry."

THE RAIN THRASHED AGAINST the car as we were driven from Downing Street, the force of the downpour making it spray back into the air like steam. I sank down into my seat, finding, for once, the omnipresent smell of soggy dog almost welcoming.

Barnaby was hunched forwards, peering past the wipers into the storm, trying to see his way as the rain became torrential. Steerforth was slumped sideways, eyes half closed, hands clasped together. I wondered if he was praying.

In the end, to my surprise, it was me who broke the silence.

"They knew about my dad," I said, feeling my fear begin to ebb away to be replaced with anger, with raw, burning rage at those Whitehall obscenities, those knuckle-kneed monsters who find nothing so unremittingly hilarious as human misery. "How did they know about Dad?"

The pit bull did not reply but gazed solemnly at the floor as though in hope of absolution.

The rain smashed down on the roof; there was a flash of lightning and the timpani growl of thunder, and as the storm illuminated Steerforth's face I saw his features begin to convulse, saw them squeezed, tugged and contorted in something utterly impossible.

For a second, I think I forgot to breathe.

When Steerforth spoke I heard that his voice had once again become a parody of his master's. "Good evening, Mr. Lamb."

"Dedlock?" I said softly.

"Did you get it?" he asked. "Do we know the whereabouts of Estella?"

"I couldn't get them to talk. I'm sorry."

"You're sorry? You've let me down, Henry Lamb. You've let me down and as a result of that failure this city stands on the brink of catastrophe."

"They knew about my father," I said. "They know everything. The smell in there . . . The way you feel when they look at you . . . like needles in your head."

"You have to see them again."

My stomach contracted at the thought of it. "I'm just a filing clerk."

"No objections. You see them again tomorrow." I tried to protest but it was already too late.

As Dedlock departed from his body, Steerforth fell back into his chair, frantically sucking in lungfuls of air. Struggling to breathe, he loosened his tie and flicked down the first few buttons at the top of his shirt.

I caught a glimpse of the big man's chest, and even now, I dearly wish I hadn't. Poor Steerforth—zigzagged in maggot-white scars, scored with old stitches, furrows, grooves and crenellations, the skin repeatedly punctured with pinkish indentations.

Steerforth must have realised what I'd seen, as he swiftly covered himself up, his face aflame with humiliation. "You don't deserve this," he murmured. "None of us deserve this."

BARNABY DROPPED ME A STREET away from the flat and I had little choice but to make a dash for it through the rain. By the time I got home, my clothes were clinging to my body, my shoes felt squelchy and waterlogged and my hair was a bedraggled mop. The first thing I did was knock on Abbey's bedroom door. There was no response, but rather than doing the sensible thing—take a hot shower and retire discreetly to bed—I knocked even harder. At last, I heard the click of her bedside lamp, the rustle of a duvet, somnolent steps towards the door.

"Henry?"

"It's me."

The door opened a crack and my landlady peered out in her pyjamas, yawning, blinking voleishly into the light. My spirits lifted, just a little, to be breathing the same air as her.

"You're drenched. Where the hell have you been?"

"Never mind about that. I want to tell you how I feel."

The hint of a smile. "And how do you feel, Henry?"

"I want to say that you're really special."

"I think you're special, too. But it's late."

"Lunch tomorrow? My treat."

She sounded bemused. "Fine. Sounds nice."

"Fantastic," I said as, pushing my luck just that crucial bit too far, I moved an inch closer to her. "I'd like to kiss you. But I'm rather damp."

"Good night, Henry," she said (not unkindly) before—and there's really no getting around this—slamming the door in my face.

I stood there for a bit in the hope that she'd come back and offer to towel me down or something. But there was no such luck, and, getting tired of loitering and dripping all over the carpet, I had that hot shower and flopped into bed. It was past midnight and I was drifting into sleep when I sat up with a start and began to wonder exactly when it was that the madness of my life had ceased to seem wondrous and bizarre and started instead to become a reality which I simply accepted with the same flint-faced fatalism as Jasper, Steerforth and all those other freaks and victims who had given themselves over, body and soul, to the Directorate.

After the latest bout of mawkish reminiscence from Mr. Lamb, clotted with glutinous sentiment and rendered practically unreadable by the torpidity of his prose, you are doubtless aching to return to the more palatable meat of our narrative. We can scarcely blame you for good judgement. Welcome back, and count yourself lucky that once again you find yourself in the hands of those who understand how to tell a story with verisimilitude and conviction.

As the storm screamed down the Mall and hurled itself against the walls of Clarence House, Arthur Windsor was receiving an unexpected education at the hands of Mr. Streater.

"Get your laughing gear round this," the blond man said, brandishing his teapot. "Wouldn't want you getting thirsty, chief."

"Please don't call me that."

Streater poured the prince more tea. "When I meet a bloke I like I call him 'chief.' And I like you. So tough titty."

Arthur's brow wrinkled in distaste. "Tough what?"

"Arthur," Streater said, allowing his impatience to show. "We haven't got long. Your mother's sent me to tell you a secret."

"Secret? What secret?"

"It's the secret, Arthur. The big one. You've been lied to your whole life. You haven't been ready until tonight. But now a whole lot of shit's about to make a whole lot more sense."

Arthur took a jittery sip at his tea. He kept reminding himself that this was what his mother wanted (wasn't that what Silverman had said?) and he had not disobeyed his mother since he was five or six years old and one of his nannies had found him in the great hall inking beards and moustaches onto portraits of his ancestors.

"Arthur?" Suddenly, Streater was close to him—uncomfortably close—near enough for the prince to smell whatever hung on the man's breath, something cloying, sickly and too sweet.

"I'm sorry?"

"Thought we'd lost you there for a minute, chief."

"My apologies. I have a regrettable habit of wandering alone in the foothills of my thoughts."

"Whatever." The blond man clapped his hands and the old ballroom sank into darkness.

"Streater? What's happening?"

The blond man stayed silent and invisible in the dark.

Gradually, Arthur realised that the darkness was not total. At the far end of the room there was a tiny flicker of light.

The prince moved towards it. To his surprise, as he drew closer, he realised that the light emanated from an old-fashioned oil lamp. Then—an even greater shock. There was someone else in the room. A middle-aged woman running to fat, folds of flesh coiled around her neck, her grey hair curled close to her scalp, a look of disapproval etched indelibly upon her face.

"Hello?" said the prince, determined to act (at least for the time being) as though her sudden materialisation might possess some rational explanation. The woman gazed distantly ahead, and now that he was closer, Arthur saw that she seemed to ripple *and shimmer, like film projected onto heat haze.* "Madam?" he said. "What are you doing here?"

Outside, the storm was getting worse—rain beating at the windows, wind screeching past the stone walls, trying to find egress—but the woman appeared oblivious to it all.

"Don't you see the resemblance?" It was the blond man's voice, maddeningly close.

"Streater?" said the prince. "Switch on the lights."

"No can do." He sounded insufferably smug.

"You caused this."

A giggle in the dark.

"Streater? Who is this individual?"

"Oh, chief, don't tell me you can't recognise your own great-great-great-grandmother? Queen of England. Empress of India. Defender of the faith . . . Albert's missus. Ring any bells?"

Arthur swallowed hard. His instinct for rationalism was shrinking to a pinprick, but still he struggled to accept the truth of what he saw before him. "How is this possible?"

"She's an echo from the past, mate. Just a memory. Chillax. She can't see us. And we can't talk to her."

"What is this?" Arthur said, his voice laced with fear and panic. "What's happening?"

"This," Streater hissed, "is 1857. The year the Indian Mutiny kicked off. Small wonder the old girl's feeling a bit tender. Small wonder this was the year it made its move."

"What made its move?"

There were three distinct knocks at the door.

Streater shushed him. "Watch and learn."

The doors were flung open and a man—another stranger—strode into the room. Dressed every bit as anachronistically as the woman, he was not yet thirty, pleasant faced and athletic, his collar-length hair still boyishly tufty despite his efforts at lacquering it down. He shared the same quality of mirage and translucence as the woman, and Arthur could see that the stranger seemed half-asleep, aggravating his eyes by rubbing them, fiddling distractedly with his collar.

"This is the man who founded the Directorate," Streater explained. "This is Mr. Dedlock."

"Directorate?" Arthur said softly. "I've heard Mother speak of them. Once, when she was in her cups—"

Streater cut him short. "Chief? Just go with the flow."

The lady in the chair favoured the new arrival with a frosty smile. "Mr. Dedlock. Thank you for coming so swiftly and at so unsociable an hour."

"No more than my duty, ma'am."

"What I have to tell you must go no further. Do you understand me? This is to remain a private matter, purely between the two of us. You are here in your capacity as my etheric adviser and I trust that you will honour the sanctity of that position."

Dedlock murmured something trucklingly deferential and the lady went on.

"Last night I had a dream. What is it the poet says? 'I could count myself a king of infinite space and be bounded in a nutshell were it not that I have bad dreams . . .'"

"I believe that is so, ma'am."

"You're looking at me as though I am mad, Mr. Dedlock."

The man from the Directorate, his face a masterclass in discretion, showed not the slightest flicker of emotion. "Nothing could be further from the truth, ma'am."

"I do not think my dream was quite as other dreams. That is to say, I do not believe it to have been a product of too much cream at table or an undigested piece of beef. I believe it to have been absolutely real—as real and as solid as this conversation. You understand me? This was more than mere fancy."

Dedlock, smoothly: "Of course, ma'am."

"Something spoke to me last night while I slept. Something

completely outside the field of human experience. And I am bound to say that it was the most beautiful, the most astounding thing I have ever seen. Mr. Dedlock, I think that I have looked upon the face of a god."

A delicate cough which, to more cynical ears, might have sounded as though it was intended to mask a laugh.

"I had been asleep for barely an hour when it happened. So as not to scare me by appearing in its true form, the god showed itself to me as a great, shining circle of colour."

"A circle, ma'am?"

"Dazzling, impossible shades wholly unlike those that I or any other human being have ever seen before. Colours that surely cannot exist upon the earthly plane. And then, Mr. Dedlock . . ."

"Yes, ma'am? What happened then?"

"Then it opened its eyes." Her own eyes grew watery at the memory. "Hundreds of them, shimmering things as though on a peacock's tail. I heard its voice in my head, deep and ancient, infinitely wise. It told me its name. It is called Leviathan."

"Leviathan, ma'am?"

"That is the closest approximation in our tongue. Its true name, it told me, would resemble a mathematical formula of such length and complexity that it lies generations beyond even our most gifted logicians. To him, our little lives must seem as the scurryings of ants. But he told me that I had distinguished myself." Two spots of colour appeared on the Queen's cheeks. "Leviathan has chosen my family for special attention. To him, affecting human life on earth is as simple as moving toy soldiers upon a board. He will guide us, keep us, protect us. Our empire will flourish. He will keep our borders safe and render us inviolate against invasion."

"It does sound a remarkable experience, ma'am. Has the prince consort—"

"He is with me in this completely. As he is in all things."

"Naturally, ma'am. Quite so."

The Queen looked annoyed at the interruption, at this presumptuous truncation of her zealotry. "From this day forth, my house has a new god and a new religion. Leviathan is the way, the truth and the life." She broke off. "You look suspicious. Do you doubt my revelation?"

Arthur was watching Dedlock as his ancestor was speaking and he thought he saw the young man bristle slightly at this. "Of course not, ma'am. But I would urge caution."

"Caution?"

"The Directorate has dealt with such entities before, ma'am, and they are seldom entirely what they appear to be. Tell me, has this creature asked for anything?"

The Queen wrinkled her nose. "Asked for anything?"

"Such beings usually have some greater motive, ma'am. I doubt he proffers aid simply from the goodness of what passes as his heart."

"Leviathan is not some street waif accosting us for spare change. He is owed homage and sacrifice by right."

"Sacrifice, ma'am?"

"Dedlock, we have seen the way in which you have sneered and sighed. You may be certain that your grimaces of scepticism have gone far from unobserved. Do you not believe me?"

"On the contrary, ma'am. I believe you absolutely. Now I strongly advise you to tell me what it is this creature has asked of you."

The Queen seemed faraway. "There is to be a contract," she said. "An agreement."

"A contract? What kind of a god deals in contracts? Your Majesty, it is absolutely vital that you tell me what you've promised this creature."

The Queen smiled. "Do you really want to know? Leviathan is a god, after all, and must not be denied. What I have done is for the greater good, for the future glory of the house."

"Ma'am . . ." Dedlock was barely containing his rage. "What have you promised this monster?"

"I have promised it London," she said. "And all who dwell in her."

The lights came on; Arthur blinked in shock and when he looked again, the two strangers had vanished. Without them, the room seemed as bare and stark as a squash court.

"What was that?" he gasped.

"That?" Streater said. "That was the first part of your history lesson."

"Was it true? Was any of it true?"

A grin. "Better run along now, chief. Is your birthday, after all."

Dizzy and disorientated, his imagination grown mutinous, the prince stumbled dumbly for the exit.

"Many happy returns, chief." Streater executed a sardonic salute. "And, Your Highness?"

Arthur turned back.

A final smirk, on the razor's edge of cruelty and charm. "Be sure to have another cup of tea before you go."

CHAPTER 13

S O IT'S HAPPENED AGAIN AND ONCE MORE I FIND myself the victim of a crime which surely has to be unique—narrative hijacking, story gazumping, a plot stick-up.

I've no doubt this phenomenon will recur but I'm trying to pretend it isn't happening. I'm doing the grown-up thing here and trying to rise above it. Although there's nothing to stop me ripping out those offending pages, I think I'll let them stand for now. If I allow this thing to run its course, it might buy me time, stave off the inevitable long enough for me to finish what I've started.

So try to ignore it. Gloss over it. Carry on regardless. From now on, I certainly intend to do the same.

I leave these interpolations in place only so that you may have a complete and accurate record of my final days.

WHEN I MET ABBEY for lunch the day after my first encounter with the Prefects, she suggested eating somewhere close to her office, at a place called Mister Meng's Peking Restaurant. I fully intend never to return.

Having unwisely spurned the waitress's slightly condescending offer of an English knife and fork, I was still struggling twenty minutes later with a bowl which brimmed almost full. Needless to say, Abbey not only wielded her chopsticks with embarrassing ease but also, in some strange miracle, made the business of eating egg fried rice and a side order of prawn crackers seem close to sensual. She watched my gastronomic pratfalls with amusement as what little food I managed to pick up spattered down my shirt in Rorschach blots of greasy orange.

Once we had finished chatting of trivial things, she said, apropos of nothing in particular: "I'm really worried about you."

All I could manage in reply was a single "Oh?" distractedly delivered as I was grappling at the time with an especially elusive strip of duck.

"This new job of yours. Yesterday, when you woke me, you were gabbling, you weren't making sense. Like you were high or something."

"Oh," I said again. "Sorry."

"You've changed. Tell me the truth, Henry. Have you got yourself into something dangerous?"

"I've been given a promotion."

"There's more to it than that."

Suddenly lacking the heart to go on, I balanced the chopsticks on my bowl and pushed it towards the centre of the table. "Yes, there's more. But I can't tell you."

"Why on earth not?"

"Because I don't want to put you in danger."

Abbey rolled her eyes and signalled to the waitress. "Fine. Let's just get the bill."

I've never considered myself especially perceptive about women but even I could see that she was upset.

"I'm not sure where you and me are heading," Abbey said. "But I'm telling you now that nothing's ever going to happen unless we're absolutely honest with one another."

"I wish I could tell you," I said. "I really do."

She looked at me sceptically.

"I'm serious," I protested. "It'd be suicide."

"Suicide?"

"Professional suicide," I said quickly.

The waitress drifted up to the table. "Everything OK?"

"Great," Abbey said vaguely. "Thanks."

"What about you?" The waitress sneered down at my half-finished bowl. "Something wrong?"

I mustered a weedy smile. "Not at all. It was lovely. I'm just full, that's all."

The waitress shrugged and turned back to Abbey. "Haven't seen you for a while."

My landlady looked embarrassed. "I've been busy."

"Yeah. I can see that." This must have been meant as a reference to me, as when she said it, the girl glanced dismissively over in my direction. "I'll tell you something for nothing." She leant conspiratorially close. "I prefer the other one."

"Just get the bill," Abbey snapped, and the waitress, chafing at the sudden gear-crunch in tone, scurried away in the direction of the till.

"You've been here before?" I asked.

Abbey couldn't quite meet my eye. "Loads. It's just round the corner from work."

"What did that waitress mean? That she preferred the other one?"

"Haven't the foggiest." Embarrassed, Abbey began to gabble: "Anyway, I'm sorry about earlier. Didn't want to come on too strong."

"You didn't."

"It's just that I'm excited about what's happening between us and I don't want to jeopardise it. I'll have to learn to trust you. Just promise me one thing."

"I'll try."

"What you do . . . It's legal?"

"Completely," I said, although in point of fact the legal status of the Directorate had never occurred to me. That place and its people seemed to exist in some insulating bubble of their own, a carapace of the fantastic which kept them utterly divorced from the real world.

The bill arrived and I was adamant that it should be my treat, claiming that I'd just had a pay raise. This was perfectly true. My first, very generous wage from the Directorate had appeared unheralded on my bank statement the previous day. Abbey was initially determined that we should share the expense but she quickly caved in.

We sat waiting for the waitress to return.

"If you won't talk to me about it," she said, "if you won't let me help you, at least find someone who can."

I laughed. To my ears it sounded alien, bitter and harsh. How long, I wondered, had my laughter sounded like that? "The only man who can help me is in a coma," I said.

Her patience was starting to fray. "There must be someone."

The waitress came back and I was distracted by settling up. "P'raps there is someone," I said once we were on our feet and heading for the door. "Someone who can help."

"Well, then. Make the call." Abbey's mobile trilled to announce the arrival of a text message. She glanced at it. "I have to go. We've got a big meeting this afternoon. Bound to be boring but I'd better be there. Take care of yourself, Henry." She kissed me passionlessly on the cheek, turned and left the restaurant.

I idled on my own for a moment, picked up a mint on my way out and mooched onto the street just in time to see her vanish around the corner. For a second, I felt a compulsion to run after her, throw myself upon her mercy and tell her everything. Instead, I just stood there like an idiot and watched her disappear.

Once she was out of sight, I reached for my wallet and prised free a small square of card. There was a number printed on it and as I typed the digits into my mobile I felt what little lunch I'd managed to consume lurch back up.

When I spoke I had to raise my voice to be heard above the clamour of the city.

"Miss Morning?" I said. "It's Henry Lamb. The answer is yes."

In Ruskin Park, not five minutes' walk from where my granddad lay in hopeless oblivion, the ducks were famished. In the short time that we were there, they managed to devour an entire loaf of wholemeal between them.

Miss Morning looked as prim and fastidious as ever in a pair of tiny black gloves and a powder-blue hat, impeccably poised even as she stooped to scatter gobbets of bread. A couple of adventurous pigeons flew down to pilfer what they could but the old lady shooed them fiercely away.

"Here," she said, passing me a slice. "Make sure he gets some."

I did as I was told and tossed the bread into the path of a particularly sluggish goose who was dawdling dozily by the banks of the pond.

"Why did you call me?" she asked, once the last of the crumbs had been shaken from the bag and the waterfowl, sensing that we had nothing left for them, had waddled away in search of more promising giants.

"The Prefects . . . ," I said heavily.

"So you've met them?" she asked, her expression of wrinkled benignity shifting into something calculating and shrewd. "We should walk. Since we're almost certainly being tracked the least we can do is make our conversation difficult for the bastards to hear."

I gazed around at the grey, deserted park, with its stark trees, its balding grass and unpromising patches of scabby earth. "How could anyone be listening to us here?"

"Eyes in the sky. Don't make the mistake of thinking that the Directorate is just three men and a filing cabinet. You've only seen the tip of their operation." She paused for breath. "But what was it you want to know?"

"Hawker and Boon . . . What are they? I mean, what the hell are they?"

Miss Morning flinched and for an instant I glimpsed the old steel in her, the skein of ruthlessness which must have made her fit for service in the Directorate. "They are the Domino Men, Mr. Lamb."

"The Domino Men? Steerforth used that phrase."

"All history is a game to them and all human lives their pieces. Their weapons are our selfishness, our greed and our cupidity. With infinite patience, over days and weeks and years, they set us up into long unknowing rows until at last, with the merest flick of their wrists, they send us toppling down, one after the other, and clap their hands at the fun of it. They were there at Maiwand, Sebastopol and Balaclava, at Kabul, Rourke's Drift and Waterloo. And all the time—and this I can promise you, Mr. Lamb—as men died around them in the thousands, those creatures were laughing. They were doubled up at the sheer hilarity of it all."

"That doesn't really answer my question," I said, unable, perhaps, to hide my frustration. "Who exactly are these people? What do they want?"

Miss Morning fixed her eyes on mine. "They're mercenaries. Their services are for hire to anyone who cares to pay. At this particular moment in time they also happen to be the key to ending the war. With your grandfather gone, they're the only ones who know the whereabouts of Estella."

"And that's another thing," I said, on a roll now. "Who on earth is this woman? Why's she so important? Dedlock won't tell me."

A grim smile on the old lady's lips. "Mr. Dedlock has always relished his secrets. He hoards them as a miser keeps banknotes under his mattress."

"Please . . ."

"Very well." The old woman cleared her throat. "Estella was one of us."

"You mean she worked for the Directorate?"

"She was the best agent we'd ever had. Passionate, elegant, deadly. Beautiful death in a trench coat. But she's been lost to us for many years."

"Granddad knew where she was. That's what everyone keeps telling me."

Miss Morning nodded. "It was he who hid her from us."

"What? Why?"

"Because he wanted to keep her safe. Because some things were more important to him even than the war."

I sensed that Miss Morning was growing impatient and perhaps I shouldn't have pushed her any further, but I had to know. "There's something you're not telling me."

The old woman spoke softly so as not to be heard by those satellites which she imagined to have turned their lidless gaze upon us, but I could tell that, if she felt that she was able, she would have screamed her answer at me. "I think he loved her," she said. "Loved her with a burning devotion that most of the time you only ever read about in poetry."

I thought of my grandma, whose sullen face I knew only from old photographs and a few half-remembered family stories, and wondered, not for the first time, if I'd actually known Granddad at all. Another betrayal, I suppose. A defection of the heart.

"The hospital is nearby," said Miss Morning. "I think I should like to see him now."

IT TOOK US A QUARTER of an hour to get there. Miss Morning, fatigued from our walk in the park, suddenly seemed much older than before and I wondered how much of her usual appearance was simply a façade shored up by will power and tenacity. I led her to the Machen Ward, and when she saw the old bastard laid out like he was waiting for the undertaker, she staggered into my arms as though she was winded. I found us some chairs, we sat beside him and she took his hand in hers.

The scene reminded me of another time when I'd been in hospital. Years ago, as a child, when I'd been ill and had those operations, I'd been in Granddad's place and he'd been in mine, watching fondly from a distance as Mum grabbed my hand and squeezed it tight.

Miss Morning gazed at my grandfather, her face blank and unreadable. "You foolish old man," she murmured. She inclined her head towards me but did not lift her eyes from the bed. "Will you see the Prefects again?"

"Tonight. I don't seem to have been given a choice."

"Watch your step, Henry. The Domino Men are without morality or compunction. Stop your ears against their lies and their wicked distortions of the truth. Give away nothing of yourself. But keep asking your questions. Be relentless. They will almost certainly offer you a deal but the price they ask is never one you can afford." She put my granddad's arm, followed by its forlornly trailing plastic tube, back on his chest. "As I think he discovered in the end."

I realised she was crying.

At my most haplessly maladroit, faced with raw emotion, I placed a hand on her shoulder and cast around for the platitudes which people usually say at times like these. "Please," I murmured. "He wouldn't want you to cry."

"I'm not crying for him," she said as the tears poured unchecked down her cheeks. "I'm crying for you." She sniffled, dabbed at the corners of her eyes. "I'm crying because of what's going to happen to you."

Enough feckless rambling from Henry Lamb. By the by, we should point out that most of the material in the Chinese restaurant is a fiction—the wretched girl simply wished to rid herself of an undesirable suitor and was trying to find a means of letting the sap down gently. Trust poor Henry to be so hopelessly enraptured by the yielding outline of her figure that he failed to see until it was far too late that the young lady never cared a damn for him at all.

Exhausted from the alarums and excursions of the previous night, the Prince of Wales had retired early to bed. Like the idiot Lamb after his first encounter with Dedlock, he had tried his best to dismiss the episode as a lucid dream or a particularly unfunny practical joke, only for an incident at luncheon to smack the reality of the situation back to the forefront of his attention with distressing force. His mother had replied to his request for information in the shape of a small white square of card, a quarter of which was taken up with a gilt stamp of the royal crest and a listing of her every rank and title. Underneath, written in wavery, doddering capitals, were the following four words.

STREATER IS THE FUTURE

It was a perplexed and weary Arthur Windsor, then, who, shortly after nine o'clock, swaddled in Silverman-ironed pyjamas and clutching his anthology of Rider Haggard, said good night to the muscle-bound servant who stood guard outside his room, folded himself into bed and snuggled up to a pillow.

He fully expected to be sleeping alone. Laetitia had let it be known via Silverman that she wished to spend the night in her private quarters—an increasingly regular occurrence which seemed to Arthur symptomatic of the ebbing away of her desire.

A chapter and a half from the end of She, the prince folded down the corner of the page, placed the book on the cabinet by his bed, switched off the light and, minutes later, fell asleep.

When he opened his eyes again, he was aware that there was someone in the room with him and that it had been her entrance which had woken him. It was not quite pitch black and there was light enough to glimpse a familiar silhouette.

"Laetitia?" he said, suddenly hopeful and aroused. "Did you change your mind?"

As the figure moved closer, he heard the silken music of her most flagrantly erotic nightgown, smelt the barest hint of that perfume which she had worn in the earliest days of their courtship, and closed his eyes in delicious anticipation of what was to follow, praying for her smooth tongue on his face, for her soft hands to rove southwards down his body.

Nothing. Absolutely nothing.

"Darling?" he whispered. "It's been too long. Don't tease me."

Still nothing. Even the scent of her had vanished.

Arthur sat upright, clicked on the lamp by his bed, threw off the bedsheets, got to his feet, wrapped himself in his capacious dressing gown and opened the door.

The guard was waiting. "Evening, sir."

The prince blinked, frantically fishing for a name. "Tom, isn't it?"

"That's correct, sir, yes."

"Have you let anyone into my room tonight, Tom?"

The man seemed affronted by the suggestion. "Course not, sir."

"You haven't let my wife in, by any chance?"

"It was my understanding that the Princess of Wales was spending the night . . . elsewhere, sir."

Was that a smirk? Was this man laughing at him? Good God, how widely was it known that his wife no longer wanted him?

"That's true," the prince said stiffly. "But you'll let me know, won't you, Tom? If anyone calls for me."

"Naturally, sir."

Arthur was on the verge of beating a retreat back inside and was giving serious thought to polishing off the last chapter and a half of She *when he heard Laetitia's laugh.*

"Did you hear that, Tom?"

"Hear what, sir?"

The prince did not reply but walked dazedly away, down the corridor, towards the source of the noise. Hearing it again, the pure, uncomplicated sound of Laetitia's laughter, he found himself fighting back tears, for he had not heard his wife laugh so naturally as this since long before they were married. He reached the end of the corridor but still there was no sign of her.

For an awful moment, he wondered if he might have imagined it, but—no—there it was again, and he began to follow, down another passageway, up a staircase, through a dining room, a drawing room, through corridor after endless corridor, past numerous members of his personal staff who stopped short at the sight of him, pressed themselves into walls and cast their eyes towards the carpet, centuries of tradition having inoculated them against the asking of uncomfortable questions. Arthur moved past them all, too proud to ask for help, stumbling onwards in his dressing gown and slippers, further and further into the labyrinth.

By the standards of the family of Windsor, Clarence House is not especially large nor particularly ancient—certainly, it was nothing like so vast and distinguished as the properties he would eventually inherit upon his ascension to the throne, but as he wandered abroad that night it seemed to him that the house grew bigger than before, that it swelled and budded into marvellous new shapes. Spurred on by the laughter of his wife, he wandered through rooms which he had no recollection of ever having seen before—a hothouse filled with plants of astonishing hues, an immense library stocked with books written in impossible languages, a place which appeared as a strange museum, stuffed with trophy heads of terrible beasts and ancient armour designed for creatures less than human.

At last, he passed into a hall of mirrors, each of which twisted his dressing-gowned form into something gangling and bizarre. Then he saw her, at the end of the hall, waiting on the threshold by the doorway, her favourite nightgown pulled down to reveal a generous swathe of cleavage, slick with sweat. She was smiling, panting, waiting for him to come to her.

"Laetitia!"

When the prince looked again she was gone and the door stood slightly ajar. Shaky and aching with excitement, Arthur dashed on in pursuit.

Inside, Mr. Streater was waiting. Barefoot, crouched on the floor, he was caught in the act of pressing a syringe filled with pinkish liquid into a vein somewhere near the region of his big toe.

"Chief!" Streater's face was suffused with jollity, as though he had just bumped into an old acquaintance at the bar. "You're a bit early." He depressed the plunger.

Wearily, Arthur turned and peered through the door. No hall of mirrors on the other side—just an unassuming stub of corridor that he must have walked down countless times before.

"Streater?" The prince spoke carefully, delicately, swilling each syllable around his mouth as though to test that they were real.

The blond man was pulling on socks and shoes again, stowing away the hypodermic. "What's the matter, mate? You look shocking."

"I think . . . ," Arthur said slowly.

"Yeah?" Mr. Streater sounded impatient, like a home-care worker chivvying along a befuddled charge.

"I think I must have had a nightmare," Arthur said at last. "Just a nightmare."

The prince noticed that Streater had a teapot and a couple of cups. One was filled for each of them.

"I've had word from my mother. She tells me you're the future."

Streater laughed. "We're the future, chief. You and me together." He passed the prince his tea. "Drink up. Time we got started."

Arthur took the proffered cup and had only just had time to raise it to his lips when Streater clapped his hands together, the lights in the old ballroom went out and the pageant began again.

His ancestor, the Empress of India, sat shimmering before him, every bit as cold and monolithic as before, although this time Arthur thought he could detect a certain satisfaction, something almost post-coital in her bearing. She was flanked by three strangers, a trio of men, all in their Sunday best, their hair shiny and slicked flat.

"Streater—" the prince began, but his mother's creature merely waved for him to be silent, with no more respect than a parent might show a persistent child on a long car journey.

"Don't be so impatient, chief. Just sit back and enjoy it." He smirked in the gloom. "I gather there was a time your missus used to give you similar advice."

Arthur was about to protest at this distressingly accurate slur when the door swung open and the translucent figure of Mr.

Dedlock strode in, coat-tails flapping, his face set in an expression of reckless determination.

The old Queen, one hundred and six years dead, turned up her lips in a gruesome approximation of a smile. "To what do we owe this most irregular pleasure?"

The man from the Directorate seemed flustered and ill at ease. "Forgive me, your majesty. Forgive me my haste and my discourteous intrusion. I had no choice but to see you."

The Queen gazed upon her subject, impassive and unspeaking.

"Your Majesty. I do not believe that Leviathan is what he claims. Surely you know that name is written in the Bible? It is the sea beast, the great serpent, the tyrant of the seven heads."

"Really, Dedlock." The Queen was tutting like a ticket collector faced with a recidivist fare dodger offering up some deliriously complicated excuse. "There is no need for such theatrics. Leviathan said you might react like this. He told me last night that there will be doubters."

"Last night, ma'am?"

"He came to me again in a dream and told me what I must do. I am to construct a chapel beneath Balmoral in his honour. He will keep our borders safe. He will maintain our empire and ensure that this country remains in the hands of my house for all time."

"Have you never considered, ma'am, that we may achieve all of that without the help of this Leviathan?"

The Queen did not seem to have even heard the question. "I don't believe you've been introduced to my solicitors," she said. "They have been hard at work upon the contract." Like clockwork mannequins, the men behind the Queen stepped forward. "I'd like you to meet the firm of Wholeworm, Quillinane and Killbreath."

The first of the men thrust out his hand. When he spoke, it was in the rich, plummy tones of the cream of England's boarding schools. "It's a pleasure to meet you, Mr. Dedlock. I'm Giles Wholeworm."

The next lawyer stepped forward, his hand also extended. "Jim Quillinane," he said, in the musical lilt of the Emerald Island. "Ah, it's a rayle pleasure to make yer acquaintance."

"Robbie Killbreath," said the third of the lawyers in a thick Scots brogue. "Good tae ken you."

"Gentlemen," said the Queen. "You have your orders. You know where to find the boy? Has Leviathan given you directions?"

Wholeworm bowed his head. "Yes, your highness."

"I know I can rely upon your discretion. We will meet again tomorrow."

The advocates nodded their understanding and, careful never to turn their backs upon the monarch, edged slowly, and with painful respect, from the room.

"Amusing, aren't they?" said the Queen after they had left.

"Ma'am?"

"What is it, Mr. Dedlock? What do you want now?"

"I want you to think, ma'am. Please. Consider carefully before taking any action you might regret."

"Come back tomorrow. Then you shall see. By the time we are finished, you will fall to your knees and worship with me."

"Tomorrow, ma'am? What's happening tomorrow?"

The Queen leant towards Dedlock, and even from his distant vantage point, Arthur Windsor thought he could see the lights of madness dancing in her eyes. "Something wonderful, Mr. Dedlock. Something glorious. Tomorrow, Leviathan is coming to earth."

CHAPTER 14

H EADING BACK TO THE FLAT, HALF AN HOUR OR SO
after saying goodbye to the old lady, I noticed that a
dead ringer for my old bike, which I'd abandoned at work on
the day of my initiation into the Directorate, had been roped
around the exact same lamppost to which I used to lasso my
own. That's curious, I thought. What a coincidence.

Inside, I found Abbey sitting at the kitchen table and shar-
ing a bottle of wine with the very last person I would have
expected.

"Barbara?"

Unflatteringly dressed in chunky knitwear, her hair in some
abortive attempt at a bob, the dumpy girl giggled in greeting.
"Henry! Hello!"

"What on earth are you doing here?"

"I brought your bike back. You left it at work." A hint of
a blush suggested itself at the peripheries of her cheeks. "I've
chained it up outside."

I was quite touched by this. "That's very kind of you. I'd
completely forgotten about it."

"You don't need it for your new job?"

"Not really. They usually send a car."

Barbara beamed in admiration.

Abbey broke in. "We've just been getting to know one another," she said. "I did say that Barbara could leave the bike with me but she seemed to have set her heart on seeing you."

Barbara flushed pink.

Abbey gave me a meaningful look. "We thought you'd be home sooner."

"I've been at the hospital."

Barbara looked sympathetically deflated at this and Abbey shot her a look of profound irritation.

"Oh, I'm so sorry," said Barbara. "Is there any change?"

"I'm not sure there'll ever be."

"Have a drink," Abbey said quickly. "Join us."

I sat down, poured myself a glass of wine and asked Barbara how she was getting on at the office.

"You know how it is. More files than we know what to do with. Even the Norbiton annexe is running out of space now. And Peter's been acting funny."

"No change there, then," I said, and Barbara laughed dutifully.

"They keep sending me down to the mail room." The pudgy girl leant over to me. "That lady down there, the fat, sweaty one. She gives me the creeps."

"Oh, I know," I said. "I remember. But how are you?"

As Barbara chattered on, Abbey curled back into her seat and gulped sulkily at her wine.

"I had the most wonderful evening the other night with your Mr. Jasper," Barbara said.

A shiver of suspicion ran through me. "You did?"

"Lovely man. So attentive."

I felt troubled by this, though I was uncertain why. "Are you seeing him again?"

"Definitely," she said, with just a touch too much certainty. "Hopefully . . . ," she added.

Abbey yawned, then gaped in fake astonishment at her watch. "God. Is that the time?"

"What a tedious woman," she said, the moment poor Barbara had gone.

I was in the kitchen, putting the kettle on. "Wouldn't call her tedious."

"Clearly she finds you fascinating."

"Sorry?"

"Coming all the way round here just to drop off your scrapheap of a bike. It's embarrassing."

"I thought it was a nice gesture."

"Nice gesture?" Evidently, this suggestion was absurd. "I think she's after you."

I could hear the kettle boiling. "What do you mean 'after' me?"

Abbey folded her arms. "I can see it in her eyes."

"That's ridiculous. Why would Barbara be interested in me? Anyway, do you want a coffee or not?"

Abbey stalked from the room. "Good grief," I muttered. "Surely you can't be jealous?"

My only answer was the slam of her bedroom door.

I WAS GIVING SERIOUS THOUGHT to knocking on that door, to taking Abbey in my arms and confessing that I was falling for her in the most hopeless, overwhelming kind of way (and that I wasn't in the slightest bit interested in Barbara), when the doorbell began to clamour for my attention.

The driver from the Directorate slouched on the threshold. "Fetch your coat," he grunted. "The Prefects want a word."

I made as much noise as I humanly could in retrieving my coat and preparing to leave the flat, but Abbey didn't emerge from her bedroom and I was too proud to tell her that I was going.

BARNABY HAD RADIO FOUR playing in the car, some piece of late-night esoterica with a couple of professors sparring crustily over the early works of H. G. Wells.

"Academics," Barnaby spat as we drove past Tooting Bec station and began the usual protracted escape from south London.

"But weren't you one of those once?" I asked mildly.

"Yeah," Barnaby said, his voice bristling with an even greater than usual distillation of belligerence. "Difference is—I knew what I was talking about. Still would, as a matter of fact, if those bastards hadn't set me up. If they hadn't concocted that farrago of—"

"Where's Jasper tonight?" I asked, eager to avoid another venting of the Barnaby spleen. "Where's Steerforth?"

The driver grimaced. "Too chicken. Couple of nancy boys, the pair of them."

"I don't believe they're cowards," I said quietly. "It's just Hawker and Boon. They've got a way of making you feel afraid."

A grunt from the front seat.

"Have you ever met them?"

"No," he said, although I could tell by the way he said it that he was lying.

I was about to ask more but Barnaby turned up the volume on the radio as high as it could go and refused to answer any further questions for the duration of the journey.

THE PHALANX OF REPORTERS and photographers who often loiter and preen outside Number Ten in daylight hours had long since retired to bed, and those who were left—the soldiers, the guards, the plainclothes policemen—all parted before me without the slightest murmur of a challenge and I marvelled again at the skeleton key effect of the words "the Directorate."

This time I had walked into Downing Street alone. Barnaby still sat in the car outside, gloomily turning the pages of *Erskine Childers and the Drama of Utopianism: (Re)Configuring Bolshevism in "The Riddle of the Sands."*

If anything, the sense of oppression, of walking blithely into the gingerbread house, felt even stronger this time. I moved through the library, stepped behind the painting and descended into the depths, past the silent gallery of freaks and ghouls, and tiptoed along the twilight corridor until I reached the final cell, the dreadful resting place of the Prefects.

The guard, his hands white knuckled around his gun, nodded brusquely and I think I was able to detect, buried somewhere deep in his mask of military indifference, a flicker of concern, the merest suggestion of compassion.

Inside, the Domino Men were waiting, their gnarled, hairy legs swinging to and fro in their deckchairs. Everything seemed identical to my last visit, the room as pitilessly stark as before— except for one peculiar addition.

There was an ancient television set in the centre of the circle, cranked up far too loud. I heard the blare of canned laughter, the squeak of poorly delivered wisecracks, the silken voice of one of our most prolific character comedians, but it was only when I recognised the tremulous soprano of my nine-year-old self that I realised with a jolt exactly what it was that those creatures were watching.

On-screen, my younger self walked onto a set which always wobbled and delivered my catchphrase to cyclones of tape-recorded mirth.

Hawker and Boon were staring sullenly at the television, like it was a lecture on photosynthesis which they were being forced to sit through in double-period science.

The smaller man groaned. "Dearie me."

Hawker shook his head sorrowfully. "I've got to be honest with you, old top."

"Got to be frank."

"It ain't the funniest thing I've ever seen."

"Let's be candid here, Mr. L. It's about as funny as cholera."

"It's about as funny as . . ." Hawker thought for a moment, then sniggered, "A nun with leprosy."

A dirty smirk twisted Boon's features into something rubbery and grotesque. "And we should jolly well know."

I moved before them, careful to keep outside the circle.

"Why are you watching that?" I asked, as I caught the familiar plonk and grind of the theme tune.

"It really is a clanger, isn't it, sir?"

Hawker switched off the television, his lips pursed in a moue of distaste. "What a turkey, sir! What a tip-top stinker!"

Boon passed his hand to and fro in front of his nose, as though waving away an imaginary pong. "Phew!"

"Coo-ee!"

I let them finish. "I want you to tell me where Estella is," I said as calmly as I could.

Hawker looked at me blankly, then cupped a hand to his ear. "Who?"

"Estella," I said flatly, knowing that he'd heard me perfectly well the first time.

"Oh right! You should have said, sir! We were going to tell you the other day but you dashed out 'fore we got to it. Rather rude, I thought. Bit cheeky."

"Dashed ungrateful," said Boon. "'Specially since we'd bent over backwards to make you feel welcome."

"Where's Estella?" I said again, trying my best to remain toneless.

Boon got to his feet and surveyed the little limits of his cell. "Do you miss it, sir? The old show?"

"The old routine?"

"The roar of the greasepaint?"

"The smell of the crowds?"

Though the Prefects squealed with laughter, I was careful not to let my expression alter. "Where's Estella?"

"Pity you're such a terrible actor, isn't it, Mr. L?"

"S'pose you might have made a career of it if you'd been any good. But you're nothing now are you, sir? Is he, Boon?"

"Certainly not, my old satsuma. He's a real nobody."

"Where," I said, my voice at last betraying my impatience, "is Estella?"

"What a grump."

"Someone's in an awful dudgeon."

"Young Mr. Lamb's got up on the wrong side of the bed today."

I glared. "I need to know where she is."

"Yaroo!"

"You've got a rotten temper, Mr. L."

I tried my best not to listen. "I want to know where Estella is."

"And you think that'll be it, do you, sir? You think, once you find the lady, they'll let you trot back to your old life? Bad luck, old chum. No-one ever leaves the Directorate. You'll croak in the harness."

"Where's Estella?" I said.

Boon smirked. "Even chaps who don't sign up for Dedlock's mob end up dying for it," he said. "Even your daddy, for instance."

I felt tendrils of panic begin to stir inside me. "Don't talk about my father."

Hawker clapped his hands in joy. "Splendid, sir! You were starting to sound like a stuck record."

"Your pa," said Boon, "he never signed up for the Directorate. Your granddad didn't tell him a thing about it."

"He wanted him to have a normal, dull sort of life."

"And he did, didn't he, Mr. L? Your pa—he was the dullest man you ever knew."

I protested. "That's not true!"

"Goodness me, but that fellow was a dullard!"

"And yet . . ." Boon smirked.

Hawker rubbed his hands together. "We did your granddad a favour once. We told him about the Process."

"The Process?" I felt myself on the edge of the precipice. "What are you talking about?"

"And we didn't ask for much in exchange, did we, Hawker?"

"Certainly not, Boon. We're not greedy boys."

"It was the smallest of favours. The tiniest trinket."

"What," I gasped, "did he promise you?"

"He promised us his flesh and blood," said Hawker.

"And we were ready and waiting on the day of your father's accident."

"*Accident!*" Hawker crowed. "Oh, my little lambkin, now you know the truth of it."

"We peered into the tangled wreck of his car as he lay dying and we jeered and laughed and poked him with a very big stick."

The monsters were doubled up with laughter now, jackknifed in hilarity.

"The look on his face," said Boon, "as he lay there sobbing! He thought we'd come to save him!"

"Do you remember," Hawker gasped, forcing the words out amidst eruptions of laughter, "how we poured petrol on his legs?"

I did my best this time. I didn't holler or scream or beat my fists fruitlessly against the glass walls of the cell. Nor was I tempted to blunder into the circle. Instead, I simply walked calmly over to the door and knocked for the guard to let me out.

"Ta-ta!" one of the Prefects shouted. "Come and see us again soon, won't you, sir?"

"Better luck next time, Mr. L!"

More laughter. I heard the television blunder back into life, heard those brash inaugural chords, the old soundtrack to my life, before anything evil had entered in.

As I stumbled back out into the corridor, my only hope was that the bastards hadn't seen that I was crying.

WHEN I GOT HOME, Abbey was waiting for me, sitting at the table in the front room, dressed in a man-sized T-shirt and nursing a mug of hot blackcurrant squash.

"Hi," she said.

"Hello," I said carefully and, after a few seconds of trying to guess what sort of mood she was in, decided to chance a smile.

To my relief, she smiled tentatively back. "I'm sorry about earlier."

"No. I'm sorry."

"I saw you with that girl . . . I suppose I just overreacted."

"Honestly," I said, taking off my jacket and throwing myself onto the sofa. "I'm not interested in Barbara."

As Abbey grinned, I noticed how thin her T-shirt was, how it seemed to accentuate and draw the eye to the curves of her chest.

"How was your work thing?" she asked. I wondered if she'd noticed the way I'd been looking at her.

"Oh, you know," I said. "Bit knackering."

"Let me get you a drink, then."

"A glass of water would be lovely," I said, and I heard her pad away into the kitchen.

When she came back, she passed me a glass, but no sooner had I raised it to my lips than I felt her hands in my hair, her breath on my skin.

"Abbey?"

The water was forgotten, hastily abandoned on the table, and all at once she was kissing my neck, my cheeks, my temples. For an instant, her tongue flicked inside my left ear and I shuddered in pleasure.

"I'm sorry," she breathed. "Poor Henry."

She manoeuvred herself in front of me, then sat down on my lap.

"Abbey?"

"Shh." She kissed me hard on the lips and I responded in kind (as best I knew how).

"I didn't expect to feel this way," she said, once we'd come up for air. "Not so soon. But there's something about you . . ."

Giddy with the moment, I risked a joke. "I'm irresistible."

"Don't spoil it," she chided, placing her hand on mine, guiding it beneath her shirt as somewhere deep in my stomach I felt the same lurch of panic I'd felt the first time we'd kissed, the awful anxiety of performance, the insidious terror that one might not measure up.

"Are you sure?" I asked.

She kissed me again, I kissed her back and I was just beginning to relax and enjoy myself when my mind was wrenched back to that terrible cell, to the gargoyles in the chalk circle and the relentless cackle of the Prefects.

The next thing I knew, Abbey was no longer sitting on my lap but standing over me, concerned, disappointed, smoothing down her T-shirt.

"What's the matter?" she asked.

"I'm sorry," I said. "I really wanted to—"

"It's fine."

"I hate to let you down."

"You're not," she said, although I would have been deluding myself not to recognise the frustration which tinged her voice.

"It's just that I've had a long day. A lot's happened."

"Of course."

"And . . . Oh God—" Something halfway between a sob and an irresistible urge to vomit began to force its way up my body—the great, indigestible tumour of the truth.

Abbey stroked back my hair, held me close, whispered in my ear: "What is it? What's the matter?"

"I'm sorry." I was gulping back tears. "But there's something I can't stop thinking about. Something in my past."

Abbey kissed me on the forehead. "Let it out."

"I need to tell you . . ." My nose had started to run and I could feel grief and rage take hold. "I need to tell you how my father died."

The heir to the throne woke the next morning to find Silverman standing over him holding a breakfast tray, a large pot of tea, a sheath of correspondence and a fresh edition of the Times, all of it balanced with the kind of dexterous skill one can acquire only through decades of experience.

"Your Royal Highness. Good morning, sir."

Arthur wriggled up in bed. "Plump the pillow for me, would you, Silverman?"

Obediently, the equerry patted the pillow into place.

"I have sleep in my peepers," said the prince.

With great tenderness, Silverman teased out the granules of dust which had accumulated overnight at the edges of the prince's eyes. He walked over to the wardrobe and laid out his master's outfit for the morning—crisp grey suit, starched white shirt, underpants emblazoned with the prince's crest and a choice of half a dozen ties, all of them in varyingly sombre shades of mahogany.

Once the equerry was done, the prince asked: "What do the papers say? Be a good chap, would you, and summarise the headlines."

Silverman scanned the front page. "The prime minister is flying home from Africa," he said, and at the mere mention of the man, the prince rolled his eyes in exasperation. "A new *health secretary has been appointed. And a rock musician has been arrested for punching a traffic policeman."*

"What else, Silverman? What aren't you telling me?"

"I'm not sure I know what you mean, sir."

"Nonsense. You're utterly transparent, man."

The equerry cleared his throat discreetly. "There is a small article about your mother, sir."

"My mother?"

"Some wholly unfounded piece of speculation about the state of her health."

"What are they saying, Silverman?"

A moment's hesitation, then: "It would appear, sir, that the headline is: 'At Death's Door?'"

"How do they know? It's not like anyone's even seen her for months."

"It's only a newspaper, sir. They are peddlers of exaggeration and hyperbole."

"I do wonder when she'll show her face again. You know, of course, that she never liked me all that much?"

"I'm sure you must be mistaken, sir."

"Never liked Laetitia either, come to think of it. Of course, that's why Mother won't see me any more. She thinks I'm weak. She thinks I'm squeamish. And I suspect the public tend to concur. It's really most unfair."

Silverman cleared his throat. "Will that be all, sir?"

Arthur took a sip of his tea and eyed his breakfast. "Thank you, Silverman. You may go."

The equerry backed towards the door.

"There's just one more thing."

"Sir?"

"What do you make of this Streater fellow? Seems a rum sort."

"He does not appear to be a man in whom I would be altogether happy to place my faith, sir."

"Oh?" Strangely, the prince seemed almost affronted by this. "Well, I'll say this for him. He makes an uncommonly good cup of tea."

"Is that so, sir?"

"I'm seeing him later, as it happens. He's in the midst of telling me the most extraordinary story. Something about my great-great-great-grandmother. Something about a contract."

"Good Lord, sir."

"Good Lord, indeed, Silverman. It's all madness, of course."

"Indeed, sir."

"I don't suppose you've ever heard of something like that? Any rumours of that nature?"

"There are always rumours, sir." Silverman bowed his head. "If there's nothing else . . . ?"

Arthur Windsor waved the fellow away and sat in silence for a while, alone with his boiled egg, his suspicion, his storm-cloud thoughts.

An hour or so later, he left his room and, brushing aside offers of assistance from various members of his household staff, walked swiftly to the old ballroom, not stopping to question his haste or wonder why he was hurrying with such rapidity to meet a man whose company, in the normal course of life, he would have found distasteful in the extreme.

Arthur arrived at the appointed time to discover his host already waiting for him, drinking tea and smirking.

Streater didn't bother to get up when the prince walked into the room, just grunted once and slurped noisily at his cup.

"Mr. Streater?"

There was another lip-smacking sound before the sharp-featured man looked up. "Be with you in a minute, chief. Just having my brew."

"I'm thirsty."

"Thirsty?"

Arthur Windsor became uncharacteristically meek. He seemed to shrink back, withdraw into himself, a royal snail edging into his majestic shell. "What I mean to say is that I'd really like some tea."

Streater drained his cup and set it on the table beside him. "What was that, mate?"

"I said I'd really like some tea."

"Bad luck, chief." Streater sounded not in the least apologetic. "Think I've just had the last of it." He belched expansively.

The prince looked stricken.

"Sorry about that."

"Are you quite sure?" Arthur said, his voice wavering under the weight of disappointment. "Might there not be a little left behind?"

Streater shrugged. "Doubt it. But I'll check anyway." He popped the lid off the teapot, peered inside, paused, wrinkled his nose and said: "You're in luck, chief. There's a few dregs after all."

Arthur's voice was glutted with relief. "Dregs will be fine."

Streater poured out about half a cup and passed it to him. "Happy now?"

Arthur gulped it down in one. "Much better. Thank you, Mr. Streater."

The blond man flashed his sharky smile. "We ought to crack on with your education. Your mum doesn't want us to drag our heels." Like a ringmaster about to introduce the prize of his menagerie, he clapped his hands and the room instantly grew dark. "Tea down, chief. It's look-and-learn time."

By now it had started to become almost predictable—the past shimmering into existence, coalescing and becoming real before the prince's eyes. There was his great-great-great-grandmother, sat behind her desk. There was Mr. Dedlock, founder of what (according to Streater) was to become the implacable enemy of his family. And there, marching through the doors like the spearhead of some bureaucratic army, were the Englishman, the Irishman and the Scotsman, the triumvirate who constituted the firm of Wholeworm, Quillinane and Killbreath. By their side was someone the prince had not seen before, an adolescent boy—squat featured, his face pocked with acne, his hair in hopeless clumps, his mouth twisted into a vacant leer.

The long-dead Queen bared her teeth in welcome. "Is this the child?"

The Englishman, Mr. Wholeworm, spoke first. "It is, ma'am."

Next, the Irishman stepped forward. "And he was exactly where Leviathan said he'd be."

Strangely, the boy seemed unafraid, allowing himself to be herded into the presence of the monarch, his expression fixed and incurious.

Dedlock, who had until now been standing at the Queen's right hand, moved into the light. "Why is the boy so quiet? Why does he not scream and mewl?"

The Englishman spoke up. "He has been bred from birth to act as a vessel for Leviathan."

Impatiently, the Queen waved away the explanation. "Bring him to me."

The boy was ushered forward.

"Gentlemen," purred Arthur's great-great-great-grandmother, "I think this child should kneel before his Queen."

The Irishman placed a hand on the boy's head and guided him down onto the floor.

"You've done well," said the Queen. "Now give me his wrists."

Quillinane nodded. Almost tenderly, he took the child's hands and turned them palms-outwards towards the monarch.

"Gentlemen, what I am about to do may cause you some distress, but I wish you to know that however my actions appear to you, they are executed for the greater glory of our empire and for the continued inviolacy of these shores. Stiffen your sinews, gather up your resolve, harden your hearts. Leviathan has warned me that there may be those amongst you who suffer from nerves or who lack the stomach for necessities. I only hope that we are man enough to stand the sight of blood." Whilst she had been speaking, the Queen had teased out a slender knife from a hiding place in her left sleeve—a sleight of hand which had gone entirely unnoticed by all who were present, meaning that what happened next took everyone by surprise.

In two swift surgical motions, the head of the British Empire slashed into each of the child's wrists. Blood bubbled up.

"Come here, boy," she said, dropping the knife, seizing the boy's wrists and pressing down hard. "Now, bleed," she hissed. "Bleed!"

Later, bringing to bear all the logic and common sense which had fled in the face of the horror in the ballroom, Arthur realised that pressing down so vigorously upon the boy's wrists ought rightfully to have staunched the bleeding. It should have stopped the flow of blood, not the opposite. Certainly, it shouldn't have sprayed out in the way that it did, not in those nightmarish geysers of iridescent crimson.

Dedlock ran towards the Queen. "This is monstrous, Your Majesty!" He tried to wrest the boy free, but against all logic, the woman's grip proved too strong.

Wholeworm, Quillinane and Killbreath merely looked on, swapping the occasional anxious glance between them, content on this occasion simply to observe.

"Silence!" barked the Queen. "You are all of you accompliced to this day."

Dedlock's face was purpling in rage. "I will not condone such butchery!"

The boy crumpled to the floor, scarlet pooling fast around him.

"What have you done?" Dedlock said. "What have you become?"

The Queen seemed unmoved by his appeal, fired up as she was, supercharged by passion. "Hush," she said, her voice trembling with fervour. "Leviathan is here."

The boy sat up straight, a human jack-in-the-box in a spreading lake of blood. He made a noise when he moved. They all heard it—a sticky, fleshy popping sound, like the noise one hears on pulling the heads off shrimp.

He smiled.

"Good morning," he said, although the voice did not sound altogether like that of a child. "Greetings to you all."

The Queen's left hand hovered near her mouth in a posture of girlish excitement. "Leviathan?"

The boy's lips twitched upwards. "I am here, Your Majesty."

"Then everything was true?"

"All true. All quite true."

Dedlock approached the child. "Leviathan?"

"You must be Mr. Dedlock," said the boy. "The doubter. The cynic. Not that Dedlock is your real name. Why not tell us the name you were born with, sir? Surely that is not a thing of which to be ashamed?"

"What are you?" Dedlock asked.

"A higher being, sir. One who moves amongst the angels. One who hears the music of the spheres."

"You're not human?"

"I am a creature of air and starlight, Dedlock. A thing of clouds and moonbeam."

"*What is it you want? What do you want with London?*"

The boy turned towards the Queen. "Shall we tell him, Your Majesty?"

She giggled. "The excellent firm of Wholeworm, Quillinane and Killbreath has drawn up our contract."

The Scotsman stepped forwards. "All above board," he purred, his voice full of Caledonian pride for a really well-crafted legal document.

"Ma'am?" Dedlock's voice bristled with barely suppressed fury. "Surely you cannot be ready to sign away the city to this monstrosity?"

Behind them, the boy was laughing, blood and mucus in his throat conspiring to lend the sound the quality of a struggling cistern. Raising himself to his feet, the child clip-clopped over to the monarch.

Dedlock looked as though he was going to throw up. "Majesty!"

The boy reached the desk and placed a hand on top of it. Blood oozed around the inkwell, spread fast across the blotter, seeping scarlet into the walnut wood below. "Dear lady. Please sign. Feel at liberty to use my blood."

The Queen took out a pen and dipped it in front of him. "So kind."

"No!" Dedlock was so close to the monarch that, for a moment, it seemed almost as though he might strike her.

"Leviathan wishes only to guide us," said the Queen. "This is simply his due."

The boy squirmed over the desk. "Sign, Your Majesty!"

"Ma'am," said Dedlock. "I implore you not to sign that paper. And I tell you again that this being is not what he claims. What god has need of signatures and contracts?"

"Time grows short," wheedled the boy. "Sign the paper."

"Ma'am!"

The child smiled. "Without my help, by the end of the century, this country will be overrun. Foreigners everywhere! Savages at the gates! The streets crimson with the blood of innocents! Sign, Your Majesty! Sign!"

Dedlock was near to begging. "Majesty, please. What does the creature want with London? What will it do with the city?"

"My mind is made up, Mr. Dedlock," she said—and the Queen of all that is pink on the map scrawled her sanguinary signature.

"Ma'am!" Dedlock was distraught. "I cannot—I will not—tolerate this."

A royal glare. "You have little choice, sir."

"On the contrary, I will devote every fibre of my being to stopping you. I will dedicate the whole of my life to bringing this Leviathan to justice. I shall pit every resource of my organisation against your house of malice."

"You would declare civil war? War between crown and state?"

"It grieves me to say so, ma'am, but you have left me with little choice."

Just as Mr. Dedlock strode from the room, self-righteous wrath in every strutting step, the boy toppled forwards, face-down, onto a floor sticky with blood, the last flicker of life in him extinguished.

It was over. Streater struck his hands together, the room blazed with light and the outlines of the spirits faded into dust and sunshine once again.

Arthur, his eyes stinging from the glare, craned his head to look at his mother's messenger with piteous confusion in his face. "Is this the truth?" he asked.

Streater grinned. "All true, chief. All true. But the really juicy question is—what happens next?"

CHAPTER 15

W HEN I WAS SUMMONED THE FOLLOWING MORNING into the presence of Mr. Dedlock, I found him to be quite unlike his usual self—pensive, melancholy, consumed by a bleak nostalgia.

"I chose to be stationed here," he began, apropos of nothing in particular. "Did you know that?"

The day was bright with the cruel sunshine of winter and as our pod neared the apex of its revolution we were granted a view of the Houses of Parliament at their most ingratiatingly picturesque.

"The Directorate could have been headquartered anywhere. But I chose the Eye. Why? Because I wanted to see what we're fighting for. You understand? I love democracy."

I wondered where this was heading.

"Sleep does not come easily to me. Not any more. But here, a stone's throw from the cradle of democracy, here at least my dreams are not so black." He gargled meditatively. "Can you guess what I'm going to ask you to do for me?"

"I expect you'll want me to see the Prefects again."

Dedlock observed me gravely through the glass.

I chose my words as tactfully as I could. "I'm not sure they're going to help us. And when I see them . . ."

"Yes?"

"I feel like weeping."

"I understand how you feel, Mr. Lamb. I've met them once myself, a long time ago and a world away." He sighed. "They are the ones who did this to me. Did you know that? They gave me these." Tenderly, his fingers brushed the sides of his torso, sliding over those strange flaps of skin which I had taken to be gills. "You're surprised? Of course I wasn't born this way. They made me like this. They turned me into their idea of a joke."

"I hadn't realised . . ."

"I know better than anyone what they're capable of. But we need to find Estella and it seems that you are still the only man they'll talk to.

"They told me terrible things . . ."

Dedlock swam to the edge of the tank. "I'll explain everything, I promise. But for now—go back to the Prefects. Find Estella."

"I'll do my best," I said, although even the thought of returning to the hideous subterranea of Downing Street sent a liquid tremor through my bowels.

"You'll do better than that, Henry Lamb. You'll have to. The war's in your hands now."

IN THE DAYTIME, Downing Street seemed a different place— almost friendly, peopled with flocks of policy makers and power brokers, think-tankers, politicos and wonks, but the illusion vanished as I descended underground, past the bottled ranks of madmen, who simpered, scowled and wept at the sight of me.

The guard outside the Prefects' cell let me pass with a nod of recognition. Inside, the television was gone but the circle was filled with a vast amount of food—trifle, liquorice, sausages on sticks, éclairs, green jelly, slabs of Neapolitan, currant buns, biscuits in the shapes of jungle animals, cans of Tizer and sherbet dip.

My tormentors waved.

"What ho, Mr. L!"

"Hello, sir!"

"Hawker," I muttered stoically. "Boon."

The ginger-haired man thrust a teetering spoonful of trifle into his mouth. Some of the cream and at least one of the cherries splattered down his shirt and tie.

"Super tuck we've got here, sir!"

"Jolly good feed!"

"T'riffic nosh!"

"What's the occasion?" I asked warily.

"Can't you guess?" Hawker chortled.

There was something I had to ask them. Something I hadn't even mentioned to Dedlock. "Last time I was here you spoke about my dad again. You said you were there the day he died."

Boon had produced a box of macaroons and was stuffing them mechanically into his mouth in a joyless production line with the weird tenacity of some oriental eating champ. He swallowed and reached out again for the contents of the box.

"How can you have been there?" I asked. "How is it possible that you were by the side of that motorway when you've been trapped here for decades?"

Boon seemed startled by my question. He spluttered, a stream of half-chewed macaroon spraying into the air like green mist. "You really think we're here against our will?" He wiped the crumbs from the corner of his mouth. "You think a little line of chalk can stop chaps like us from mooching out whenever the fancy takes us?"

Hawker downed a dainty ham sandwich with its crusts cut off. "We're only here because we want to be," he said, and hiccoughed.

"Why are you eating all this stuff anyway?" I asked in exasperation.

"It's our last night here, sir!" said Boon, swigging from a bottle of ginger beer. "Thought we'd jolly well celebrate."

"You know what they say, sir, about the condemned man's last meal."

"What's going on?" I asked.

"Golly," said Boon, mock sympathetic. "Haven't you worked it out yet?"

Hawker waggled his eyebrows at me. "Bit slow, are we, Mr. L? Bit of a turtle brain today, my old lamb chop?"

Boon turned to his accomplice. "Lamb chop! I say, that's rather good." He sniggered as Hawker ladled jelly into his mouth. "Can't believe we didn't think of it sooner."

I raised my voice, just a little, just enough to get their attention. "It's your last night here?"

"Course it is, sir!"

"Abso-bally-lutely!"

I glared at them. "Why's that?"

"Because today's your lucky day, Mr. L."

"I haven't come to listen to your lies," I said. "Just give me the location of Estella."

"Oh, but we can't tell you that, sir."

"No, no. You're perfectly hopeless with directions."

"We'll take you there ourselves, sir. Introduce you face to face."

"What do you bastards want?" I asked.

Hawker looked scandalised. "Cheek!"

Boon tutted noisily. "Naughty old lamb chop. Wherever did you pick up language like that?"

"What do you want?" I asked again, trying to stay calm.

"Just a small thing."

"Nothing too big," said Boon. He had helped himself to

more jelly and it was dribbling glutinously down his chin. "But we would like to ask a little favour . . ."

As soon as I was clear of Downing Street, I took out my mobile and phoned Mr. Dedlock. Exactly how this worked, since I had never seen the least evidence of any communication device in the pod (let alone a sub-aquatic one), I really couldn't say.

"Henry?" the old man rasped. "Have you seen them?"

"They've agreed to take us to Estella. God knows what's changed their mind."

"This is excellent news."

"But there's a condition."

"Tell me, boy."

"They want you dead." I swallowed hard. "And they want to choose the manner of your passing. Apparently they . . . Well, they've got something specific in mind."

There was an achingly long pause and when Dedlock spoke again, I could detect a change in his voice, a note of sadness, even of relief.

"You'll have my answer," he said, "in one hour."

As soon as he had gone, I dialled another number.

My heart lifted when she spoke. I hadn't realised how swiftly I'd come to find her voice so comforting.

"Hello?" she said. "Who is this?"

"It's Henry, Miss Morning. I need to see you again." I tried to suppress the quivering vibrato in my voice. "It's time I knew the truth."

Trying to forget the sticky, fleshy popping sound which the boy had made when Leviathan had sat up inside him, Prince Arthur Windsor left Mr. Streater's presence and headed not, as one might have supposed, back to his own quarters, to seek out Silverman or his wife, but rather towards the official front door, the gateway, of Clarence House. Half a dozen servants, thrown by this unscheduled, impromptu abandonment of the day's agenda, were around him within minutes, enquiring as to his plans, making polite offers of assistance and discreetly attempting to slow his progress. As the heir to the throne edged increasingly close to the open air, they frantically signalled for the prince's regular security detail to be torn from their recreations and summoned to his side.

Arthur was polite to them all, his lifelong unease with the family's mastery of the servant class manifesting itself in a flurry of apologies and regrets, but he was nonetheless adamant that he wished to change his plans for the day in order to pay a visit to the palace. There was no longer any need (as there might have been ten or even five years earlier) to enquire as to whether or not his mother was currently in residence. The palace had become her hermitage, far from the public gaze despite its location at the heart of the city, though it had always struck the prince that the place seemed less of a spiritual retreat than a paranoiac's bunker, as though she was expecting some imminent catastrophe and had elected to bury herself deep, hoping to wait out disaster.

A Jaguar was ready for him at once and, several imploring calls having been made to the Metropolitan Police, when the prince sank back into the downy seats the roads had been cleared for him to proceed from Clarence House towards Buckingham Palace. No traffic light was ever red for Prince Arthur Windsor and no zebra crossing, lollipop lady or rogue pedestrian ever provided the slightest impediment to his regal procession through the city.

When he arrived at the palace, a platoon of secretaries, equerries and ladies-in-waiting were gathered in anticipation of his arrival. Although he waved them aside, they buzzed and clustered around him, like beggar children accosting a man of evident wealth and munificence strayed too far from his usual habitat. As he walked, the throng of domestic staff seemed to grow in number, dozens of them trailing behind him like the anxious tail of a meteor. They were running some sort of interference—the prince could tell that much—trying to slow him down, offering an abundance of plausible-sounding reasons for him to turn back.

Arthur ignored them all and walked on through the mazy corridors of the palace that glimmered with a casual wealth to which he was long inured. He knew where he was heading. He was absolutely certain where his mother would be—squirreled away in the north wing of the palace, hiding from the world in her private suite.

When he arrived with the mass of attendants still behind him, Arthur discovered the great wooden doors to be closed and fastened and two palace servants—burly, pugilistic types squeezed uncomfortably into dark suits—standing in front of them, arms folded, unfaltering stares in place, like bouncers at the most exclusive club in the world.

"Her Majesty is not at home to visitors," one of them said in a dull, perfunctory voice which tacked heedlessly close to discourtesy.

"I think she will be at home to me," said the prince.

"No, sir," said the other man. "Not even to you."

"She sent me a letter," Arthur said.

"A letter, perhaps, sir. But not an invitation."

"Listen here. I have a perfect right to see my mother. God alone knows why she has decided upon this perverse seclusion of hers but something is going on in my house and I think she may be able to tell me why."

Like a guardsman in a busby ignoring the antics of a tourist angling for a photo opportunity, the men seemed entirely unimpressed by what, according to the standards of the prince, amounted almost to a tirade.

"Her Majesty's instructions were most specific, sir. We are to admit nobody."

Blood was rushing to Arthur's head, dyeing his cheeks red with frustration. In desperation, he leant towards the doors and shouted. "Mother? Are you in there?"

Everyone stared at him, a little embarrassed.

"Mother!"

The men at the door had started to move towards him as though intending, gently but firmly, to eject him from the premises when a frail, cracked voice issued from just behind the door. Several of those present—a brace of private secretaries, two telephonists and a maid—found themselves picturing the Monarch with her ear pressed up to a glass held against the door.

The voice was unquestionably hers—probably the most famous in the British Isles—reedily nasal, impeccably enunciated, a relic from an earlier and more decorous age.

"Arthur? Go away! Shoo! Skedaddle!" She seemed to relish that last word in particular, audibly enjoying the unfamiliar taste of the vernacular.

"Mother!" the prince wailed back, and for a moment, it was as though the servants, the advisers, the ceremonial train of lackeys and right-hand men had melted away and there was nobody else in that place but them, mother and son, still struggling to communicate after all these years. "Who is Mr. Streater? Is it true what he told me, about Leviathan? Why won't you see me?"

There was a hissing sound from next door, then: "Have you still not disposed of that bitch of a wife?"

Several of the servants who had followed the prince from the moment he entered the palace at least had the good grace to look awkward at this, to turn to one side and choose not to gawp quite so openly as the rest. None of them, it must be noted, actually walked away.

"Mother . . ." There was a conciliatory cadence to the prince's voice now, like that of a diplomat, faced with some intransigent warlord, trying his utmost to be reasonable. "I know we've never exactly seen eye to eye, but really—"

"Eliminate the girl, Arthur. Then we may talk." There was a sliding, shuffling noise from the other side of the door which seemed to indicate that the speaker was retreating.

The prince stepped back. "Honestly, Mother. You can be most unreasonable at times."

No answer came save for that same sliding, shuffling motion, growing ever fainter, as though something of immense bulk was dragging itself into the distance.

When the prince turned to face the assembled onlookers, there was an expression on his face which, to those who did not know him better, might almost have looked dangerous. "Take me home," he said, and silently, respectfully, they did just as he had commanded.

By lunchtime, the prince was surprised to find that he could barely wait to get back to Mr. Streater.

Usually, luncheon with Silverman was a joyous affair, brimming with talk of their schooldays, or of their time together at an expensively dour university, or of the prince's short-lived military career (an almost wholly wretched experience save for the one spot of light that was Mr. Silverman—as faithfully attentive a batman as he had subsequently proved a valet, equerry and aide-de-camp). On that day, however, the prince could muster little enthusiasm for any of it. Silverman's well-oiled anecdotes seemed so much conversational sludge, the food felt rubbery and tasteless and the wine turned to vinegar in his mouth. His one thought was to get back to Streater, to hear the story of his ancestor and, above all else, to drink another cup of tea.

The prince prodded his dessert away after less than a spoonful. "I should go. There are things which require my attention."

"Is everything quite all right, sir? You seem rather distracted."

"I'm fine," Arthur snapped, and immediately felt guilty for it. "Really, I'm fine. Now I'm so sorry. I must go, I've a very important meeting this afternoon."

"I've seen your diary, sir." Silverman gazed unflinchingly at his master. "And I saw nothing in there for today. Nothing at all."

The prince drew breath, opened his mouth and, guppy-like, closed it again.

He was saved by an embarrassed tap at the door. A young servant shuffled into the room, his head bowed low towards the carpet.

"Sorry to trouble you, sir." Well into his twenties, he still looked like a teenager, his voice squeakily uncertain with protracted adolescence. "There's a phone call for you, sir."

"Well, tell them to call back."

"It does sound important, sir."

Suddenly, the prince was interested. "Is it Mr. Streater?"

The servant sounded bewildered. "No, sir. It's your wife."

He took the call in his study. "Laetitia?"

"Arthur, what on earth is going on?"

"What do you mean?"

"Don't try to hide it from me. You went to see your mother today. Something is definitely up."

"Well, perhaps we could discuss this at a more convenient time? Perhaps tonight . . . after lights-out?"

"I've no stomach for that at the moment. I thought you understood that. I need you to tell me what's going on right now."

"I haven't got time to talk. I have a meeting."

"A meeting with that Streater creature?"

"How do you know about Streater?"

"Silverman told me."

"Did he really?"

"Ring me when you're ready to tell the truth, Arthur. I can't go on like this."

She slammed down the phone.

Arthur sometimes wondered whether anyone was listening in on these calls of theirs, an enterprising underling, a junior butler with an eye on the chequebooks of the national press. Sometimes he even wondered whether he and Laetitia ought not to at least try to keep pace with modernity and invest in a pair of portable telephones. He strongly suspected that such an act would play well with the public, that it might finally and unequivocally prove him to be a man of the people, a modern prince almost psychically attuned to the lifestyles and concerns of twenty-first-century youth. Arthur scrawled a note to Silverman on the subject and, still muttering to himself like an unusually well-dressed wino, began the long walk to the old ballroom.

Mr. Streater's trousers were concertinaed round his ankles and he was enthusiastically engaged in shoving a hypodermic needle deep into a vein somewhere in the region of his left thigh.

Arthur double-taked into the corridor, making certain that no-one had seen. "What are you doing?"

"Gets tricky after a while," Streater drawled, "finding a new vein."

"I can imagine."

"Just a little pick-me-up after lunch." The blond man stowed the hypodermic in one of his pockets and Arthur felt a pulsation of disgust.

"I've just bolted down my food," the prince said softly. "I've been rude to my best friend and I've refused to speak to my wife. Why the devil can't I stay away from you?"

"Gotta be my magnetic personality." Like a used car salesman drawing a customer's attention to the pride and joy of the forecourt, Streater gestured towards a china teapot on the table. "Up for a cup of tea?"

At the mention of tea, the prince seemed enthused. "Do you know, I think I am."

"What were you saying about your wife?" the blond man asked as he poured the heir his first cup of the day.

Arthur seized it hungrily. "She says she needs to talk to me."

"That right?" Streater laughed. "She wants you to jump and you ask how high? Is that how it goes with you?"

"No," Arthur protested. "That is, I—"

Streater put his hand on Arthur's shoulder. "Word to the wise, mate. Don't put up with any backchat. Give birds an inch, they grab a bloody mile."

Arthur seemed barely to have registered what Streater had

said. He held out his cup, already drained. "Listen here. Is there any chance of a drop more?"

Streater smiled and filled the cup again. "We should press on. Your old mum's keen to finish your education."

"Why?"

Streater gave a savage smile and clapped his hands together, at which the thin, wintry sunlight faded away as though a cloudbank had rolled in front of the sun. As the prince sat riveted, clasping his cup of tea, a figure began to materialise at the corner of the room, the strange shade of Windsor's great-great-great-grandmother. Beside her—the silhouettes of Wholeworm, Quillinane and Killbreath.

"Thank you for coming, gentlemen," said the Queen.

The lawyers nodded as one.

"We regret the unpleasantness with Mr. Dedlock on the last occasion we met."

"Not at all, ma'am," said the Englishman. "I'm sure that Mr. Dedlock will one day come to see the light."

"Oh, I doubt that very much, Mr. Wholeworm. I think we're in for a long and bloody struggle. Whether Mr. Dedlock approves of it or not, Leviathan is here to stay. But the truth can be entrusted only to a few. Only the most worthy of my successors will be told—and only then when the time is right."

"Amen," chorused the lawyers.

"We are the inner circle. We know the truth. Leviathan will take the city only when it is ripe."

"How will we know, ma'am?" the Irishman asked. "How will we know when London is ripe?"

"I am not certain, Mr. Quillinane. As I understand it, there are certain atmospheric conditions which must be met before the city is acceptable. Certain questions, too, of population. But I know that I shall not be here to see it."

Various obsequious protestations at this.

"No need for flattery, gentlemen. I shall be long dead when Leviathan comes again. But the firm of Wholeworm, Quillinane and Killbreath . . . now they shall not."

"Ma'am?" the Scotsman asked. "What dae ye mean?"

"Leviathan has blessed you all. Your service to the crown will continue for far longer than you could ever have dreamed. You are to be his eyes and ears on earth. You will not taste death, gentlemen, until the very end."

Wholeworm's face had turned white. "Ma'am? What are you suggesting?"

"You shall be eternal lawyers, in the service of Leviathan far beyond the natural span of your lives."

They stared at her, struck dumb with horror.

"Now, now, gentlemen. Please, do not thank me. You know how easily I blush."

"Your Majesty—" Quillinane stepped forward, hoarse voiced and shaking. "Please—"

"No, Mr. Quillinane. That's quite enough. I envy you. You shall be here to see Leviathan in his full glory. You will be here to bear witness as he blesses the people of this city."

Streater clapped his hands and there was light again.

Arthur realised that his body was damp with sweat. "It's coming, isn't it? That's why you're showing me this. The city is ripe. Leviathan is coming soon."

Streater cocked his head in a sort of nod. "Leviathan's already here, chief. It came to the city in 1967."

"What? How is it possible?"

"It was summoned here but some clever bastard trapped it."

"Trapped it? What do you mean—trapped it?"

"It was chained by the Directorate. By one of Dedlock's men."

"Good God. Is the man dead now?"

"As good as." Streater smirked. "Leviathan's here, chief. Close by. In the city somewhere, imprisoned. But don't stress. It's all in hand. We're pretty confident that his rescue's only a matter of days away."

"This can't be right. This feels so wrong. Good God, Streater—my own family—"

"Relax," Streater purred. "Chill out."

"Why did Mother want you to tell me all this?"

"She wants you to be ready, chief. For Leviathan. For your ascension to the throne. And before that, for something she wants you to do. A necessary chore."

The prince was still sweating and had begun to shiver and tremble like a street-corner alcoholic. "I'm gasping for a drink. Is there any more tea? Might I have some more tea before we finish?"

The prince didn't spot it but a tiny smile of triumph flickered on Streater's lips. "Why not?" he cooed. "A little drop can't hurt."

CHAPTER 16

MISS MORNING LIVED WITH A MONSTER.

Even so, it was immediately clear that she was also lonely. Her house, a large four-bedroomed place in the snooty precincts of South Kensington, whilst grimily bohemian, lacked the imprint of any life but hers. Her fridge, when I caught a glimpse of its contents, was stockpiled with ready meals, instant snacks and suppers for one.

More than this, I scarcely recognised her when she came to the door, dressed in a flowing grey smock, her hair worn long and pre-Raphaelite around her shoulders, her hands covered in what looked like clay.

Once I had stepped inside and we were walking through to the heart of her home, I blurted out: "You seem different."

Her only answer was a smile, like a mother to a son who's just worked out the truth about Father Christmas. We walked down a chilly hallway, through her sparse kitchen and into a large light-filled extension which jutted from the rear of the building. Formed entirely of glass, it felt pleasantly warm, like a giant greenhouse or the tropical rooms at Kew—comforting and almost homely, or at least it seemed so until I saw the beast.

The room was filled with clay sculptures, each depicting the individual body parts of some bizarre, impossible monster. Here were tendrils and tentacles and black-skinned teeth, there were talons and claws and, over by the window, a gigantic eye, milk-white and scored as though by chisel marks.

I murmured: "I never knew you were an artist."

"I dabble. It's a hobby I discovered after I left the service." She asked the minefield question: "What do you think?"

"It's weird," I said, trying to be tactful. "There's a lot of black. A lot of tentacles."

She nodded. "I only seem able to approach my subject in parts."

"Is it some sort of allegory? Something modern and difficult?"

"On the contrary, Henry. This is life drawing."

Before I could ask any more, something small, grey and very familiar padded into the studio, looked over at me and mewed.

"Hello there," I said, feeling absurdly disappointed not to get a reply. I made that strange high-pitched kissing sound that everyone seems to make around cats, at which the animal trotted meekly over and allowed me to stroke the underside of his chin.

"He recognises you," Miss Morning said.

I agreed, and I have to admit that my spirits lifted, just a tiny bit, at the knowledge of it. "It's astonishing he found you," I said.

"You know what he is, don't you?"

I was tickling the animal's belly by now, making it squirm and purr with pleasure.

"The cat is your grandfather's agent in the waking world. He is the old man's familiar."

Gingerly, I removed my hand from the cat's tummy. "What do you mean?"

"It's the old man's servant, an avatar, an extension of his self. A distillation of sheer willpower cloaked in flesh, fur and whiskers. He sees through its eyes and it has all his guile, all his wisdom. Your grandfather chose its form but it may also be able to change its shape."

I looked down doubtfully at the animal. "Alternatively, it might just be my granddad's cat."

"Is there something you wanted to tell me?" Miss Morning asked pleasantly. "You sounded agitated on the phone."

Looking warily back at the feline, I dropped my voice almost to a whisper. "Are you sure it's safe to talk?"

"I sweep this place twice a day for bugs. We're as secure here as Dedlock in the Eye. Probably safer."

I took a breath, before the truth came out in a torrent. "The Directorate is going to let the Prefects lead us to Estella. And it's going to happen soon."

The old lady gazed at me gravely and murmured: "There's no fool like an old fool. By which yardstick, that old man's a moron. But why have you come to me with this?"

"I need to know what happened with Estella."

Miss Morning tottered towards a colossal fang and rested on it for support as she released a long, rattling sigh. "You'd better sit down," she said at last.

I lowered myself onto a tiny wooden chair which looked as though it had been stolen from a classroom.

"Your grandfather loved Estella," Miss Morning began. "Adored her. He was the only one who loved her for who she was and not simply for the contours of her figure. But he let it happen to her just the same."

I shuffled uncomfortably in my chair.

"At the end of the sixties, we were losing the war badly. An entire division had just been wiped out on field exercises in the Malvern Hills. Leviathan was coming and we had no means of stopping it. Your grandfather grew desperate. He started to consider the most extreme solutions. Even this . . . Against all advice and his own better judgement, on April fourth, 1967, he summoned the Prefects. He told them everything. Begged for their help. They thought for a while—Hawker scratching his head, Boon sucking on a sherbet lemon—before they told him how to stop the beast. All they wanted in return, the only thing they asked for ... Well, I'm sure they haven't lost any time in telling you that."

My stomach turned over and I thought of my father's last, frantic moments of life, gasping for breath on the hard shoulder of a motorway.

"In exchange, the Prefects told your grandfather about the Process."

"The Process?"

"You've heard the phrase before?"

"From the Prefects, yes. And it was in Granddad's journal. Why? What is it?"

"The Process is high science and low magic. It bends time and compresses matter."

"I'm afraid I haven't got the faintest idea what you're talking about. Your mouth is open and there are words coming out but I don't know what any of them mean."

Miss Morning sighed. "The Process transforms a person into a vessel. It turns them into a living prison, a jail to hold the monster. We needed a volunteer. Someone strong. Someone psychically tough. They would require certain preparations ... incisions to the brain ... Then we were to take them to a place of power."

"What do you mean? A place of power?"

"An old site. Somewhere charged up with psychic energy. Marked out with certain signs and sigils."

"And then what?"

"We had to make them bleed, Henry. We had to slash their wrists and let the life dribble out of them. Until they were empty. Until they were hollowed out."

"That's murder."

"No. Not quite murder. That was the art of it."

"And you went along with this?"

"We had no choice. Believe me. Can you guess who they chose as the vessel?"

The answer was grotesquely obvious. "Estella."

Miss Morning gave a bleak twitch of her shoulders. "Dedlock insisted on her. So we went through with it. The whole thing."

"Where did it happen?" I asked.

"You don't need to know about that. I doubt you'd like the answer." She looked at me as though I was expected to figure something out, to make some leap of logic here. I probably just looked blank.

Miss Morning went on. "It was a night of dark miracles. When we cut that woman's wrists they healed right back up again."

"Impossible, naturally."

"Naturally. But we saw it happen. Your grandfather and I were both there. Poor Estella—not quite human any more. A medieval mind would say that what we did was to cut out that woman's soul. Leviathan came to earth and we bound it in a jail of flesh and bone. Like a genie in a bottle. Like a spider in a jar." She seemed to shrink back at the memory. "We made a prison cell from a human being. I don't expect that was right of us. But there it is. Estella was an empty shell of a woman once we were done. The strain of keeping Leviathan inside her had shut down most of her motor functions. She became sluggish, glazed, absent. Two days later, I was babysitting our safe house at Mornington Crescent when the Prefects strolled through the door and announced that they wanted to turn themselves in."

"Why?"

"They said their conscience had too much to bear. They told me that they were ready to give themselves up."

"You didn't believe them?"

"Of course not. They're playing some larger game. That chalk circle no more holds them than a shopping bag would restrain an ocelot."

I frowned slightly at the metaphor.

"Your granddad quit the service and took Estella with him. He went home to your grandmother and a couple of days later, Estella disappeared. He would never tell us where he hid her, even under the severest provocation. The Directorate has men who specialise in persuasion but your grandfather never spoke about it. Not once. So you see why they need to find Estella so badly. She's not the key to the war. She *is* the war."

Miss Morning and I stared uneasily at one another across the curve of a clay tumour.

My phone shivered in my pocket. "Excuse me," I said as I retrieved it, terrified at what news it might bring.

It was Mr. Dedlock. Our conversation was brief and almost entirely one-sided.

"What did he say?" the old lady asked as soon as I was done. "Spit it out."

"Dedlock has agreed to their terms." My voice was trembling despite my attempts at moderation. "The Prefects will be moved tomorrow."

Miss Morning looked at me sadly and turned away. "Then I think it's time you went home and enjoyed what little time you have left, because, believe me, everything's about to go to hell." I got the impression that, in Miss Morning's world, this constituted fruity language indeed, reserved for use only in the very teeth of catastrophe.

I WAS RUMMAGING THROUGH my jacket pockets, trying to locate my key, when the door to our little flat in Tooting Bec was shoved open and Abbey stood before me in her dressing gown, her hair still damp from the shower, her pinkish face scrubbed clean of cosmetics, smelling all over of caramel-scented moisturiser.

"I was worried."

"I'm fine." I walked inside, shut the door, locked it, drew across the chain. "Had to work late, that's all." I shrugged off my coat and hung it on the hook.

"Are you cross with me?"

"Why would I be cross with you?" I glimpsed bare flesh beneath the dressing gown. She seemed fragile, doll-like, and I had never before felt a more irresistible compulsion to embrace her.

"I just thought that after what happened last night . . ." She was chewing on her lower lip. "After what *didn't* happen . . ."

I took her in my arms, clasped her close and kissed her on the lips, not caring about the consequences, not worrying for once if I might make a prat of myself.

"Henry?" she asked tremblingly once our lips had finally parted and my hand had begun to slip unthinkingly downwards.

Silently, I led her to my bedroom, where, as gently as I could, I slipped away that gown, brushed my fingers across her breasts, dropped to my knees and began to kiss every part of her.

LYING IN WARM-SKINNED INTIMACY, we had just begun to drift into a doze when the grouchy buzz of the bell wrenched us back into the real world. Abbey snuffled her disapproval but I disentangled myself, pulled on T-shirt and boxers, and plodded to the door, acutely aware that the evening's pleasures were already evaporating into history. The bell jangled again and as

I reached for the handle, I wondered whether an unexpected ring at the door after midnight had ever, in the whole history of the world, been a herald of good news.

It was Jasper, giddily energetic, like a child high on tartrazine.

"I think it's a mistake," he said, stepping into my home uninvited.

I rubbed at my eyes. "Don't know what you're talking about."

"You haven't heard?"

"Heard what?"

"The Prefects are being moved tonight."

"That can't be right. Mr. Dedlock was quite specific."

"Misdirection. Either that or he's changed his mind. You'd better get your clothes on." Jasper was ignoring me. Abbey had emerged from the bedroom and stood blinking in the corridor's electric light, her modesty shielded only by a set of artfully positioned towels.

Jasper smirked. "You must be Henry's landlady."

Abbey shot me a look made up in equal parts of bewilderment, irritation and accusation.

"So sorry to barge in like this," Mr. Jasper went on. "Though I've actually been interrupted myself. Just in the middle of squiring young Barbara around town. Wonderful girl. So clean . . ." He smiled dreamily. "I'll give you two a moment, shall I?"

I steered Abbey back into the bedroom, where I apologised profusely, dressed, thrust a comb through my hair and tried to prepare for a night out with Dedlock, with Hawker and with Boon.

"Could you distract him for a minute?" I asked once I was fully clothed. "Just get him talking. I need to make a private call."

"Why?" Abbey asked. "Who the hell are you phoning?"

"Please. No questions."

"One day, Henry, you're going to have to tell me everything."

"I promise. But for now . . . ?"

Abbey plastered on a hostess smile and we went back together into the sitting room, where Jasper was flicking through a magazine and swigging briskly from a bottle of water. He tapped his watch.

"Two minutes," I said. "Just got to go to the bathroom."

As I left, I heard Abbey talking, trying her best to distract him. "Lovely to meet a colleague of Henry's. Now tell me, 'cause I've always wondered . . . What is it you do exactly?"

I FLUSHED THE TOILET and crouched beside the bowl, partly to disguise the sound of my voice, partly to fox any listening devices which might have been hidden nearby. It didn't occur to me at the time to question how naturally I'd taken to such precautions.

I took out my mobile phone and dialled a number which must have rung a dozen times before it was answered.

"It's Henry," I hissed. "Sorry to wake you."

Miss Morning sounded older now, as though she'd aged ten years since I'd left her. "I was not sleeping, Mr. Lamb. Just too afraid to answer."

"They're moving the Prefects tonight."

No reply.

"Miss Morning? I said, they're moving them tonight."

A heavy sigh. "Then I assume you've made a will. I trust you've set your affairs in order. I hope you've prepared yourself for the worst."

He never slept with her, of course. As guarantors for the truth, we think it our duty to make that absolutely clear. Naturally, he would have liked to have done so, but we can assure you that he never laid so much as a finger on any part of her. In fact, unless something remarkable happens in the next few days, the miserable man will die a virgin.

At around the time that Mr. Jasper was standing on Henry's doorstep, the heir to the throne of England awoke with a wretched headache, an urgent need to urinate and a terrible hunger gnawing at his soul.

He had no idea how he had ended up in bed, no recollection of staggering along the corridor, of peeling off his clothes and falling onto the mattress, no memory at all, in fact, since he was last in the ballroom, taking tea with Mr. Streater.

Streater. If the prince was certain of just one thing then it was this: he needed to see that man again. Only Streater would understand. Only Streater could make the world tolerable again. Only Streater could ease the craving, the black desire, the burning need.

The extremities of his body tingling with pins and needles, the prince swung himself out of bed and wrapped himself in his dressing gown. Every noise seemed too loud, every light intolerably bright. He used the telephone by his bed to make two calls—the first to Mr. Silverman, the second to his wife. Both, he was told, were unavailable.

In the end the prince had to wake an underbutler named Peter Thorogood to ask the only question which seemed to matter to him any more.

"Where is Mr. Streater?"

Although Peter Thorogood thought that the prince appeared out of sorts, he politely pretended not to notice and simply directed him to the room which Streater had commandeered upon his arrival at Clarence House.

However, once the prince had left (Arthur was adamant that he did not wish to be escorted), Peter Thorogood telephoned his superior, a butler called Gilbert Copplestone, to inform him that the master was acting erratically, that his speech was garbled and his gait had become eccentric. Copplestone conveyed these fears to the head of the household, Mr. Hamish Turberville, who then telephoned the prince's permanent secretary, Galloway Pratt, who called Kingsley Stratton, his contact at the palace, who spoke to his lover, a lady-in-waiting named Eloise Clow. Four hours later, the Queen herself had heard the news about the behaviour of her only son. The message which she sent back was alarmingly simple.

Everything is proceeding according to plan.

As Arthur weaved his way down the corridors of Clarence House, he saw what had descended outside—a thick fog, a pea-souper—and it is a measure of his increasing instability that he pondered at length whether the weather was real or a trick of his mind.

It turned out that Mr. Streater was staying in an unusually unassuming wing of the house, halfway down a corridor of single rooms traditionally designated as quarters for chauffeurs and scullery staff. Exhaling asthmatically with relief, Arthur knocked at the door and waited.

When the sharp-faced man opened up, he was fully dressed and beaming. "All right, chief?"

"Let me in."

Streater stepped back and watched the heir to the throne totter inside. The room was almost monastic—bare white walls, cheap furniture, a single bed with its duvet rumpled and distressed. There were no books, keepsakes or mementoes, nothing to suggest any life beyond the palace, with just one exception—a framed photograph of a young woman, a pretty brunette in skinny jeans.

Arthur all but tumbled onto the bed. "You know what I want."

Legs splayed, immobile but somehow still swaggering, Streater sat opposite on the only chair in the room. "Do I though, chief? Do I really?"

"Is it true what you told me? About the deal? About my family?"

"Come on, you gotta know the answer to that."

"So Leviathan is real? The war . . . I'm a part of it?"

"Chief, chief, chief. I think we both know that's not why you're really here."

Windsor blinked vaguely, as though he'd forgotten what he was about to say.

"Spit it out," Streater said. "Tell us what you've come for."

"You know what I want."

"Maybe I do, chief. Maybe I do. But perhaps I'd just like to hear you say it."

The prince's Adam's apple yo-yoed in desperation. He felt salt in his mouth, the panicky taste of sweat. "I was wondering . . ."

"Yeah?"

Arthur's eyes were pleading. "I was wondering if you happened to have any more tea."

Streater laughed. "Tea?"

The prince ventured one of his unconvincing smiles. "Yes, please."

Mr. Streater shook his head in mock sorrow. "Oh, Arthur. You've got it bad, haven't you, old son? But since you asked so nicely . . ." He reached into the holdall by his feet and pulled out a hypodermic loaded with pink fluid.

"For God's sake," the prince muttered, "now's not the time to be fooling around with that stuff. I need tea."

Streater cocked an eyebrow.

"What is that muck you put in your veins anyway?"

Mr. Streater did not smile. He seemed more serious than Arthur had ever seen him before. "The name of the drug is ampersand."

"Ampersand? I've never heard of it."

"Ampersand is my mother." Streater spoke slowly, intoning every word, as though this was something sacred to him. "Ampersand is my father. Ampersand is my lover, my life. Ampersand, Your very Royal Highness, is the future."

Arthur moaned. "Please . . ."

Streater sat down on the bed and began to roll up the prince's sleeve.

"What are you doing?" Windsor was too enfeebled to move, too broken and pathetic to offer the least resistance.

"I'm giving you what you want, chief. Giving you what you need."

"Explain yourself."

"Surely you've worked it out by now? It's in the tea. It's always been in the tea."

"Streater?"

"You've been taking ampersand from the day we met." The blond man was slapping the inside of the prince's arm, searching for a vein, brandishing his needle. "You're one of us now."

After that, His Royal Highness Prince Arthur Aelfric Vortigern Windsor did not speak again but lay back, gave in and let the sharp-featured man do it to him.

When the thing was over, he wept with gratitude, joy and a terrible sense of submission. He kissed the hands of Mr. Streater, he licked his palms and sucked his fingers. He made awful promises and horrid vows. He bartered his soul for another cup of tea.

CHAPTER 17

I STEPPED OUT OF THE CAR AT THE FURTHEST END OF Downing Street to find a world fallen into darkness. In open defiance of the TV's predictions of clear skies and moonlight, an impenetrably dense, freakishly pervasive fog had descended upon the whole of London.

Fog was everywhere. The city was steeped in it—thicker than smoke, saturating clothes, sinking insidiously into lungs. It was as though we had been dragged back half a dozen generations to the era of the gas lamp and the hansom cab, the ancient queen and the advent of the war.

I was struck by the thought that perhaps such an age was not so far away as it seemed, that it was only the short lives of human beings which gave the illusion of distance. Perhaps, from some greater vantage point, the span between the age of Victoria and our own would appear no more than a handful of seconds, a few spasms of the little hand around the clock.

The whole of Whitehall had been sealed off and the most famous street in England was crowded with the sounds and sights of war. Arc lights blazed impotently against fog banks. Men in uniform swarmed around an armour-plated vehicle which had been backed close to the door of Number Ten and there was everywhere the glint of gunmetal, the growl of orders, the dull jangle of weaponry. These were preparations for disaster, it seemed to me. This was insurance against catastrophe.

As I emerged from the car, Mr. Steerforth materialised by my side, flint faced and grave, in his element surrounded by military strut and bustle.

"You're with me," he snapped, and strode away. As I followed him towards Downing Street, the fog closed in around us.

We were close to the door of Number Ten and Mr. Jasper was in sight when Steerforth passed me a pink, flesh-coloured piece of plastic, shaped something like a tadpole. "Dedlock wants to speak to you. You know how to use these?"

I started to complain, asking whether this was really necessary, when Steerforth thrust the thing hard into my left ear. A tendril groped its way into my earhole. I felt a savage poking through to the doughy wetness beyond and cried out in pain and shock. Although the pain ended almost at once, I was left with an unshakeable unease, a permanent, shivery sense of intrusion. I heard a familiar voice, too loud, in my head. "Good evening, gentlemen."

I imagined him grinning gummily, staring down across the river from his eyrie.

"This is the form tonight will take. The Prefects have already been released from their cell. They are to be taken from Number Ten under guard and placed in the armoured vehicle which I imagine you see before you now. From here, they will direct us to Estella. The end of the war is in sight. I would suggest that this is cause for jubilation."

Steerforth spoke up. "With respect, sir, I strongly recommend that we stand down tonight. There are too many variables in this fog. We should wait until we're in control of the situation."

"We have total control, Mr. Steerforth."

"We can't see more than half a yard in front of our faces, sir. I don't think you understand the risks—"

"It is you who does not understand, Mr. Steerforth. We cannot afford to wait. Do you think the House of Windsor is sitting idle? Do you think that they would surrender in the face of a touch of fog? They will be preparing themselves for the endgame. We cannot sit idly by and watch this city slide into chaos."

"I'm aware of the stakes, sir."

"No!" Dedlock shouted. "You are not! You have no idea what I've given up to make this happen!" I felt a twinge of pain in my head and pictured the old man splashing in his tank, impotent and enraged. I tugged at Jasper's sleeve and asked if there was any way to turn down the volume.

Jasper tried to shush me, but it was too late, and Dedlock was growling in my ear again.

"Are you trying to shut me up, Mr. Lamb?"

"No, no. Of course not."

"I think you'll find me a difficult man to silence."

"Sorry," I said, and mercifully, the conversation rolled on.

I felt my mobile phone shiver in my pocket and pulled it out as discreetly as I could. There was a text message from Abbey.

Thinking of you x

That little X made my heart soar. It made me want to sing.

Steerforth was still protesting. "Please, sir. Please reconsider."

"You've been working for the Directorate for thirteen years, Mr. Steerforth, is that correct?"

"Almost fifteen, sir."

"You've served in Algeria, Khartoum and the Sudan. And you're frightened of a bit of London fog?"

"It's not the fog which scares me, sir. I'm frightened of what it might be hiding."

"This discussion is at an end. Do not question my authority again."

ALL AT ONCE, a hush fell upon Downing Street, an atavistic silence.

Two figures strolled through the black door of Number Ten—creatures dressed as schoolboys, forced to walk unnaturally slowly, shuffling in tiny steps like old men. A metal chain ran between their ankles and their hands were shackled and cuffed in front of them. They were as criss-crossed and tightly bound with manacles and locks as was the ghost of Jacob Marley.

Hawker and Boon were flanked by men with guns, killers who eyed their captives with the keen suspicion of keepers at the most dangerous wing of the zoo. Weapons were trained upon every part of the Prefects' bodies by Directorate officers with paranoiac minds and itchy fingers, who were trained to murder in an instant and to relish it.

Yet Hawker and Boon were laughing. They were positively full of mirth, beaming and winking at one another as though they were on a school trip on the last day of term.

"Corks!" said Boon. "Fresh air! Have you missed it, old thing?"

"Rather," said Hawker. "It's absolutely topping!"

"Course we're used to having the run of the playground. Such a shame the beaks kept us in detention so long."

"Asses."

"Swine."

"Rotten brace of polecats."

"I say," said Boon, and I had a terrible feeling that he was looking at me. "Isn't that Henry Lamb?"

"Beards! It's old lamb chop."

"Lamb chop! Over here!"

Had they been able to raise their arms, no doubt they would have waved.

For six long minutes they stood there, keeping up their ceaselessly see-sawing conversation, their endless, babbling cross-talk, until they were marched at gunpoint into the back of the armoured van.

As the door clunked shut, a man in uniform jogged up to Steerforth. "Sir?"

Steerforth looked irritated at the interruption. "What is it, Captain?"

"We've got a civilian, sir. She's asking to see Lamb."

"I thought we'd sealed the whole street off."

Spots of colour appeared on the man's cheeks. "We've no idea how she got in. It seems she . . ."

"Yes?"

"It seems she slipped through . . ."

"Keep her detained until after this thing's over. Least she deserves for poking her nose in."

"She knows more than she should, sir. She's naming a lot of names . . ."

Before Steerforth could reply, an elderly woman trotted impatiently out of the fog. "Henry? There you are, dear. I've been looking all over for you."

Miss Morning was wearing her public face again and she seemed correspondingly older, more frail than before.

She advanced upon Steerforth. "You must be the new boy."

Steerforth looked affronted. "I've served the Directorate for fifteen years."

"Like I said. The new boy."

"Everyone," I said, trying to ease the tension. "This is Miss Morning."

"Thank you, dear," the old lady said. "They know who I am."

Dedlock was shouting. "Who's there? Steerforth, let me see."

Mr. Steerforth looked as though he were going to be sick. "Now, sir? Does it really have to be now?"

The growl of the head of the Directorate: "Let me in."

Poor Steerforth. He convulsed once, twice, three times, his face squeezing and contorting in agony.

"Miss Morning?" he said. The body was Steerforth's but the voice, cracked and bitter, belonged unmistakeably to Dedlock. "Time, it seems, has not been kind to you. Or even mildly understanding."

Miss Morning thrust out her chin pugnaciously. "And how is life underwater, Mr. Dedlock?"

"What are you doing here?"

"You're about to do something very stupid indeed."

"I'm doing what is necessary to win this war."

"The Prefects don't care a jot about your war. They're playing a larger game."

Steerforth's face was turning a terrible scarlet colour. "I've outmanoeuvred them."

"Come now. You've done no such thing. This situation is entirely of their own devising."

"I am the one in control here."

The old lady sounded tired. "Oh, but they'll escape."

"Escape?"

"Of course, they'll escape. They're the Prefects."

Steerforth turned towards the soldier. "Captain, make sure this presumptuous secretary is put in a holding cell." The captain placed a hand, slightly squeamishly, on Miss Morning's shoulder but she scarcely seemed to notice.

"Why can't you see?" she said. "This is their fog."

"Move them out," Dedlock snarled before, all at once, Steerforth's face sagged back into its familiar lines.

We stood and watched, transfixed in solemnly respectful silence, as the armoured vehicle reversed out of Downing Street, turned laboriously and began to progress down Whitehall, creeping through the fog.

"You mustn't let this happen!" Miss Morning said, jerking at my sleeve.

"What can I do?"

Perhaps I am retrospectively crediting myself with too much perspicacity but I was unable to shake the feeling that what we were watching was somehow less than real, that we were just spectators and that all of this was merely an illusion.

"Dedlock!" Miss Morning was almost shouting now. "Unless you finish this right now, people are going to start dying."

In monumental indifference to the old woman's warnings, the vehicle continued its stately progress down Whitehall. Bikes rode close by on either side. Dozens of guns were trained at it, ready to fire at the slightest sign of trouble.

It was then that we noticed something was wrong.

It began as a trickle, a thin line of red smoke, curling out from under the doors. I watched it grow larger, as though a fire had been lit within. Then great clouds of red smoke were pouring out, streaming into the fog, staining the night scarlet.

Dedlock bellowed in our ears: "What's happening?"

"I see it!" Steerforth ran towards the van as it skidded to a halt, and the rest of us followed.

Dedlock: "What the hell's going on?"

Miss Morning appeared by my side. "It's happened already. They just couldn't help themselves."

The old man was screaming out his fury. "Mr. Lamb?"

"I don't know," I snapped. "I can't make anything out in this fog."

As we drew closer to the vehicle, Steerforth opened the door and clambered inside. The fog made it impossible to be certain what had happened, although, of course, I think I already suspected. All of us did, I suppose.

At last we were close enough to see.

Jasper was talking to his master. "It's bad, sir. It's really bad."

I stared into the van and saw the truth of it. The vehicle was empty. The prisoners were gone. The Prefects had vanished in a puff of smoke.

Miss Morning turned away. "It's finally happened," she murmured, her voice shot through with bitterness. "The Domino Men are loose."

CHAPTER 18

WHAT HAPPENED NEXT WAS CHAOS IN ITS PUREST form.

Cries of panic and disbelief, Dedlock screaming in our ears, the rattle of weapons, the jabber of gunfire, the bellow of Steerforth's commands as he screamed phrases so dismayingly hackneyed I thought I would only ever hear them on television. "Secure the perimeter!" "Go, go, go!" "Damn it, I want them alive!" And all around us, the ceaseless swirl of fog.

Mr. Jasper had turned the colour of chalk. "How did they do it?" he asked. "How was it so easy?"

"It's a game," Miss Morning murmured, a grim kind of satisfaction in her voice, a melancholy I-told-you-so crouched behind each syllable. "It's always been a game to them."

Steerforth turned to the soldier who still stood, stricken with shock, by his side.

"Captain? Give me a status report."

In the palm of his right hand, the soldier clutched a PDA which displayed an electronic street map of Whitehall.

"They're on the move, sir." He stabbed a finger towards two smudges of black that were barrelling across the screen. "They're heading towards the roadblock."

"Then we can still catch them." We all heard it then in

Steerforth's voice—that awful Ahab mania. "I need twenty volunteers."

THE PIT BULL OF THE Directorate got his volunteers that night—more than he had asked for. All the killers who were there lined up before him—brawny men in khaki, the kind who'd been good at games at school, now trained to murder on the say-so of the state. The captain was amongst them and as he strode across to join the others he thrust his screen into my hands. I began to protest but he pressed it towards me with such insistent vigour that I felt I had no choice but to accept. It made me uneasy, this piece of high technology which turned men's lives to pixels and reduced mortality to a mouse click.

As Steerforth was yelping more orders, exhorting them to bring the Prefects back alive, Miss Morning was shaking her head. "What a waste," she murmured. "And they all seemed like such nice young men."

Steerforth must have heard because he spun around to face her. "They're the best. They'll run those bastards down. You have my word."

"Those creatures are death incarnate, Mr. Steerforth. Take it from me—your men won't stand a chance."

The soldiers sprinted into the fog, and as I scrutinised the screen, I saw twenty spots of white hare after the Prefects' trails of black.

"Oh dear, oh dear," Miss Morning said pityingly. "When will you people learn?"

The next few minutes were a study in impotence. Powerlessly, we watched as the white chased the black. We watched as the two colours met somewhere at the very tip of Whitehall and we watched as, one by one, the splashes of white were extinguished.

"No . . . ," Steerforth whispered.

"Boys will be boys," Miss Morning murmured with what, under the circumstances, I suppose should count as gallows humour.

Dedlock was shouting in our ears again. "Are they dead? Are they all dead?"

Jasper tried his best to calm the situation. "It would seem so, sir, yes."

"Where are they now?"

I consulted the PDA. "Moving out of Whitehall. Heading towards Trafalgar Square."

"Then find them!" Dedlock screamed.

A vein twitched on Steerforth's temple. "Please, sir . . ."

"What is it, Mr. Steerforth?"

Despite the arctic tinge of the night, the man was sweating prodigiously. "I'm afraid, sir."

"Steerforth! We do not have time for your soul-searching!"

Jasper moved to the burly man's side and placed a hand discreetly on his arm. "You're Mr. Steerforth." His voice was gentle but underscored by steel. "You're the hero of the Directorate. There's nothing you're afraid of."

At the time, I assumed that Jasper was doing his best to support a friend and colleague, trying to cajole him into action. Now I'm not convinced that there wasn't some other, darker agenda at work.

The voice of the old man crackled in our ears. "Stop bleating! Do your job!"

Steerforth seemed to come to a decision. He straightened himself up, pushed back his shoulders and snapped a reply. "Yes, sir!" Turning to the few of us who were left, he said: "I'm going after them. Who's with me? Who's bloody with me?"

"Steerforth?" Dedlock snarled. "Bring me their heads!"

"Yes, sir!" And again, filled with the unfettered joy of hara-kiri: "Yes! Sir!"

As Steerforth pelted into the fog, Jasper and I started, reluctantly, to follow.

I have never claimed to be a hero and I'm happy to admit that I was absolutely terrified. It wasn't long before we came across the first of the corpses, the body of the young captain, contorted in death, splayed out on the Whitehall street like a doll abandoned by children who play too rough. I almost tripped over him and, at the sight, swallowed back a sick-bag surge of nausea and despair.

"What is it?" Dedlock bellowed in my earpiece. "What can you see?"

"Casualties, sir," said Jasper.

"Bad?"

"Couldn't be much worse."

We walked on in silence, respectful though full of fear, treading through the fog past the ranks of the fallen.

Somewhere out of the billowing banks of mist came the voice of Mr. Steerforth: "I'm at the roadblock, sir. Everyone's dead." There was a swell of hysteria in his voice. "Did you hear me? Everybody's dead!"

"Mr. Steerforth!" Dedlock barked in everybody's ears. "Moderate your tone!"

"Don't you understand? Those things are loose in London. Nothing's safe now. They'll turn this city into a charnel house."

"Clearly you're not robust enough to cope. I'm taking charge of this operation personally."

"With respect, sir—"

"I don't give a tinker's cuss for your respect," Dedlock snapped. "Just give me what I want."

"Please—"

It was too late. There was a grinding, crunching sound, the noise of clanking cogs and arthritic gears—and when Steerforth spoke again it was in the voice of Mr. Dedlock. There could be no question what had happened.

"Slaughter!" His voice was filled with fury. "Slaughter on the streets of London."

The rest of us hurried towards him, terrified of what we might find.

In our earpieces, Dedlock spoke again through Steerforth. "They're heading towards Trafalgar Square. I'm going after them." Then—"I can see them! I'm in pursuit."

Somewhere ahead of us, he was dashing after the Prefects. It may have been my imagination but through my earpiece I was sure I could hear the malevolent lullaby of their laughter.

I CAN IMAGINE HOW it would have gone, how they would have taunted and teased him, showing just enough of themselves—a flash of blazer, a glimpse of gnarled knee, a distant glint of penknife—just enough to keep him going, to feed him hope and lead him on.

WE EMERGED AT THE MOUTH of Whitehall to find the roadblock in ruins and yet more tragedy, stumbled over in the fog.

Dedlock was screaming. "I can see them! I've got them in my sights."

Jasper and I moved towards Trafalgar Square, where only the base of Nelson's Column was visible, the great man's view being mercifully obscured.

Steerforth was still shouting that he could see them, that he was going to bring them back and make them pay—although we could make out nothing ahead but endless fog.

Through our earpieces, we caught a fragment of conversation.

"Hello, sir!"

"You're looking a bit peaky!"

"Not feeling yourself, sir?"

Much laughter at this, then a scuffling sound, then a thud, then a sickening crack.

Dedlock's voice: "Forgive me. I have to leave you."

Then, strangely, Steerforth's again: "Please, sir. Don't leave me like—"

He was interrupted by what sounded like a scream. There was an animal whine, cut abruptly short, the abattoir shriek of metal on bone. Then another sound, a bouncing, rolling noise like a bowling ball as it speeds towards the skittles.

Sometimes I dream about what we saw come wobbling out of the fog towards us, sliding over the tarmac of Trafalgar Square. I felt a powerful urge to vomit and even Mr. Jasper seemed to have tears (or something like them) swelling in his eyes.

It rolled to a stop a few centimetres before it reached me, saving me the embarrassment of having to halt its progress with my foot as though it were a child's football kicked into the street.

Dedlock spoke again into my earpiece. "I think . . . I think Mr. Steerforth may have passed away."

None of us replied. Jasper sank onto his haunches and, almost tenderly, picked up the disembodied thing. Still, there was silence.

"Apply yourselves!" Dedlock was shouting again. "Get me a status report."

"The Prefects have disappeared," I said flatly. "They've gone."

"Gone?"

"They must have known we'd put tracers on them," Jasper

muttered wearily. "There's only two of us left here, sir. What do you want us to do?"

Dedlock hissed. "I want you to find them!"

"With respect, sir. You've seen the casualties we've taken. You'd be sending us to our deaths."

Then—a bitter order. No apology. No trace of sympathy. "Go back to Downing Street."

WE TRUDGED FORLORNLY TO Number Ten, where Miss Morning was waiting. At the sight of what Jasper was carrying, she seemed to tremble on the edge of tears.

"Now you understand," she said quietly.

Dedlock spoke again. "I'm sending in a whitewash team to deal with this mess. Our first priority must be to find the Prefects. They're still our only link to Estella."

"More than that," Miss Morning said. "They would tear this city apart simply because they're bored."

"There are other resources available to the Directorate," Dedlock said. "I'll see all of you again at nine A.M. at the Eye for a council of war. Until then—get some rest. Guards will be posted at your homes. You're dismissed."

Miss Morning, who, lacking an earpiece, had not quite been following all of this, turned to me and said: "Tell him I'll be seeing him tomorrow."

"Sir?" I said. "Did you hear that?"

"Why would I want her?" he asked. "What do I need with a bloody secretary?"

"Tell him I understand these monsters. Tell him I know what makes them happy."

There was a long pause. "Very well. Bring her. I'll see you in five hours."

SOON AFTERWARDS, BARNABY ARRIVED to take us home. Miss Morning and I clambered wearily into the cab but Jasper elected to stay behind, clinging to what was left of Steerforth with a disturbing tenacity.

As we drove, I saw that Dedlock's whitewash team had already moved in—a phalanx of people in what looked like full-body anoraks, the personification of unsqueamish efficiency with their scrubbing agents and wire brushes, their sponges, sprays and tweezers. The street was lined with polyester bags the size of coffins, zipped up snugly to hold the dead.

We were negotiating the circle of Trafalgar Square when a van screeched past us, speeding towards the seat of power. I caught a glimpse of its passengers—more killers, tooled up and bristling with eager death.

"Jackboots," Miss Morning murmured. "Dedlock's reserves. The chase goes on." She yawned and settled back into her seat, bleakly deferential to defeat.

We were too exhausted and distraught for much conversation, but as Barnaby drove us through the glum streets of Elephant and Castle, Miss Morning muttered: "I've seen them."

"What?" I'd been staring out of the window, doing my best to forget.

"Whilst the rest of you were gone. I saw them. They were watching it all."

"Who was watching?"

"The three," she whispered. "The three are moving again."

"What are you talking about?"

"You know them, Henry. The Englishman. The Irishman. The Scotsman." Even after all the lurid horrors of the night, at this I felt a peculiar frisson of disgust.

I turned my face away from the old woman and stared through the window. All I could see was my own reflection in the glass—a haggard, weary man with pity and accusation in his eyes.

DAWN WAS SKULKING OVER the horizon and the fog was just beginning to lift when Barnaby dropped me back outside the flat in Tooting Bec.

I let myself in, set the alarm to give me four hours' sleep, unpeeled my clothes and sank gratefully into bed, wriggling under the cocoon of the duvet, hugging it close for comfort.

When I woke again it seemed like mere minutes had passed, although the officious chirrup of my alarm insisted that it was past eight o'clock and that I had less than an hour to present myself at the Eye.

To my surprise and delight, Abbey was in my bed. She gave a little groan at the alarm.

"Thanks," she said when I switched it off. She moved close to me and wrapped her arms around my chest.

"You've come back."

"Of course I've come back."

I kissed her on the forehead and I think my hand may have inadvertently brushed against her breasts. She gave a husky sigh of pleasure.

"Oh, Joe," she murmured.

For a moment, I wondered if I had imagined it, but then she said it again, quite clearly, as though to leave me absolutely no room for doubt, no merciful space for self-delusion. "I can't believe you've come back, Joe."

"Joe?" I wondered aloud. "Who's Joe?"

When I looked again, Abbey's eyes were fluttering shut, her lips slightly parted as though in provocation for a kiss, and the last good thing in my life had just begun to dribble away.

For the first time in his long and privileged existence (with the regrettable exception of an indiscretion during his university freshers' week, kept from the media only by the application of an improbably large donation from the royal purse) the Prince of Wales woke up the following morning without the faintest idea of where he was or why.

As soon as he came to after a peculiarly troubling dream (something about a little boy and a small grey cat) he felt the first flailings of panic. Struggling into an upright position, he surveyed the room in which he had woken—small, functional, yet dimly familiar. Beside him, on the floor by the sofa on which he had presumably passed the night, was a little heap of items which had nothing whatsoever to do with his life, stock props from the horror reel of someone else's existence—tourniquet, syringe, a vial of bubblegum-pink liquid. It was around this time that the prince realised that he was wearing nothing more than his boxer shorts (florid, festooned with hearts and pineapples, purchased by Silverman at Laetitia's request). Arthur had no memory of having stripped off his clothes and realised that someone must have done it for him. It was only when he noticed Mr. Streater, face-down on the bed and dressed in a silver thong which flossed insouciantly between his buttocks, *that Arthur Windsor remembered the sight of the needle, the fizz of the liquid in his veins.*

His emotions upon this realisation were complex. Naturally, there was shame, a certain amount of humiliation and a large portion of self-chastisement, but there was also—and this was something that the prince was able to admit to himself only much later, when events had sucked him in, seemingly beyond the point of no return—a sneaking, secret pleasure, the shuddering joy of the forbidden.

Arthur retrieved his clothes from where Streater had abandoned them on the floor and began to dress himself. As he struggled on with his shirt, he noticed the neat, professional puncture mark on his left arm—the first, we are grieved to have to tell you, of the many which were to come—and felt a spasm of disgrace and self-pity. More than once his eyes drifted across the room and alighted upon Mr. Streater's bottom, the smoothly pert contours of which he compared to his own sagging, haemorrhoid-ridden posterior and felt a deep swell of sadness.

Taking care to close the door as softly as possible, the prince tiptoed from the room and headed back towards his own. Aware of his wretchedly dishevelled appearance, he moved as fast as he could, keeping his head down low, praying that he would attract no attention. Relieved to find that there was no-one on guard outside his quarters, the prince locked himself inside, took a shower and tried to make himself presentable, whilst all the while a hideous lust was dragging at his soul, hectoring, pleading, begging to get it what it needed.

The prince felt a flare of concern. Where was Silverman? Why had he not come to find him last night? And, worst of all, why was he not here now, to dress him? Arthur Windsor could count the number of times in his adult life when he had been forced to clothe himself on the fingers of a single hand.

He sat on his bed, reached for the telephone and dialled

Silverman's private number. It rang incessantly without reply. Confused, the prince rang through to the Clarence House switchboard.

"Hello?" The voice was young, female and, like the majority of her generation, tinged with the taint of estuary.

"This is the Prince of Wales."

"Good morning, sir."

"To whom am I speaking?"

"This is Beth, sir."

"Ah yes." The prince had a vague memory of false nails and hoop earrings. "Good morning to you, Beth. I'm trying to get through to Mr. Silverman. But he doesn't seem to be picking up his telephone."

"One moment, sir."

There was a click and a pause before Beth spoke again. "His private line's working fine, sir. I'll look into it and get back to you."

"Many thanks to you, Beth. I'm most grateful."

"Thank you, sir."

The prince set down the receiver, paced, vacillated, chewed his fingernails, watched the little hand on his watch go 360 degrees, then picked up the telephone again. He tapped in a number which rang interminably before it was answered.

His wife sounded out of breath. "Who is this?"

"Laetitia?"

"Arthur? Is that you? Where have you been?"

Strangely, Arthur thought he heard a male voice on the other end of the line. His wife's breathing seemed to grow heavier. "Darling? What are you doing?"

"Nothing. I've just woken up."

"Nothing? Is that the truth? Is there something going on I don't know about?"

"Of course not. I told you. Anyway, shouldn't I be the one asking you that question?"

Arthur heard what sounded like a grunting sound on the other end of the line. "I rang to ask for your help," he said, disgust pushing its way into his voice.

"I'm so sorry, Arthur. This isn't really a good time. I don't feel at all well. I've got to go."

Without warning, the line went dead.

Forced, without Silverman, to make his own decisions, the prince had picked out a charcoal-coloured suit and was dallying by the mirror, trying everything he could to make himself appear less pop-eyed and exhausted, when the telephone rang again.

"Laetitia?"

"It's Beth here actually, sir."

"Beth?"

"We spoke a moment ago, sir. I'm calling from the switchboard."

"Beth! Of course."

"I've located the whereabouts of Mr. Silverman, sir."

The prince brightened. "Splendid. Where is he?"

There was a moment's hesitation. "He's in the Princess of Wales's quarters, sir. He's with your wife."

Arthur crept along the corridor which led to the large suite of rooms occupied by his wife, unsure of what he would say to her, struggling, like some Canute of infidelity, to hold back the tides of suspicion. The prince was not a man who sought or thrived on confrontation. If things had turned out differently, we suspect that he would have said nothing at all and done his best to ignore the telltale signs, perhaps retreating to his apartment to wallow in melancholia. But, as you shall see, that is not how events unfurled.

When the door to his wife's suite was unlocked from the inside, Arthur scurried back along the corridor, pressed himself flat against the wall and peered around the corner.

The door opened and Silverman strolled out, chased by the laughter of the prince's wife. He tried to remember the last time he had made Laetitia laugh like that and came to the knife-twist conclusion that he never had. Not once.

Silverman was saying something impossible. It was hard to tell at such a distance and the prince was no lip-reader, but it looked like an invitation. An invitation and a promise. The equerry winked in a manner which we can only think to describe as salacious.

"It's got to be our secret." This was Laetitia, calling from inside.

The equerry snorted, winked again, closed the door and swaggered away down the corridor, upon which the prince had no choice but to emerge from his hiding place.

The man did not even have the decency to seem embarrassed. "Good morning, sir."

"What were you doing in my wife's quarters, Silverman?"

"She required my advice, sir."

"Your advice?"

"That's correct, sir."

The prince looked at his old friend and now saw no treachery in his face, no skulduggery or lecherous deceit. "I needed someone to dress me and you weren't there."

"I'm so sorry, sir. I was on my way. You are not usually awake so early."

"What time is it, Silverman?"

"Barely seven, sir."

"Barely seven? Good God."

"Is everything all right, sir? Is there anything I can attend to?"

"Of course not," Arthur snapped. "How can everything be all

right? I needed you to dress me and, as you can see, I've had to do that myself." Without giving the equerry a chance to reply, the prince turned on his heel and stalked back to his rooms.

Inside, for a heartbeat, the mask slipped. He collapsed on his bed and let out a moan, the doomed cry of an animal dying in a trap. Then he collected himself, took a deep breath, reached for the phone and waited for his last true friend to speak.

"Yeah?"

"Mr. Streater. So glad you're awake."

"Just got up. What can I do you for?"

"Please. Come to my rooms. I need you."

"Sure. I'll get dressed. Be right over."

"And Mr. Streater?"

"Yep?"

"Bring me some ampersand."

Down the telephone line, the prince could almost hear Mr. Streater's smile.

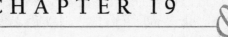

CHAPTER 19

AT NINE A.M., THE LAST OF THE DIRECTORATE GATH-
ered in the Eye for a council of war.

When the pod doors opened and Miss Morning and I
walked inside, Jasper was already waiting. He was wearing the
smug, self-satisfied expression of a man who's just had a long-
cherished dream rubber-stamped by someone who can actually
make it happen. I didn't like that look, as you can imagine. I
didn't like it at all.

Dedlock swivelled in his tank and splashed noisily through
the fluid. "Henry Lamb! Miss Morning!"

"You seem cheerful," the old lady said, understandably suspicious.

"Mr. Jasper has good news."

"You've found the Prefects?" I asked.

"My jackboots have yet to track them down. But Jasper . . .
Jasper may have given us the means."

Miss Morning stepped up to Mr. Jasper, a wrinkled Holliday
at the OK Corral. "What exactly," she said, "are you propos-
ing?"

"The Blueprint Programme," said the smooth-skinned man,
a gleam of triumph in his voice.

As usual, it was left to me to ask the necessary question. "And what's the Blueprint Programme exactly?"

"To track the Prefects," Jasper explained, "we need a hunter. Someone ruthless. Someone tenacious. Someone with a talent for getting their hands dirty."

Dedlock chipped in. "The Directorate may have lost Estella in 1967. But we did not let her make her sacrifice without persuading her to leave us with a memento."

"A memento?" Miss Morning's wizened frame seemed suddenly animated by rage. "What did you do?"

Dedlock spoke lightly, conversationally, like he was discussing the weather or the football or giving directions to tourists. "We made a copy of her etheric signature."

"Her what?" I asked.

"Her essence, Mr. Lamb. Her animus."

Miss Morning was furious. "Why?"

"So we could copy her abilities. So we could replicate the highlights of her mind in someone new. And we've finally found a way to do it."

"But we're looking for Estella," I said. "Aren't we? I mean, isn't that what all this has been about?"

"We need her physical form, yes," said Dedlock. "We need the real Estella. But this is something quite different. I take it you've heard the phrase 'Set a thief to catch a thief'?"

Jasper delved into his jacket pocket. He pulled out a silver pill and, like a soothsayer picking through the skeleton of some sacred animal, held it aloft for our scrutiny. "In this pill," he said, "is the essence of the best field agent in the history of the Directorate. It only needs to be ingested for the subject to begin the transmogrification into a second Estella."

"How remarkable," Dedlock murmured.

"How wicked," Miss Morning snapped.

"What exactly are your objections?" Dedlock asked Miss Morning.

"That boy's grandfather would be appalled by this blasphemy," she said. "It's illegal and immoral. It disgraces the memory of a woman who gave up everything she had in the hope of keeping this city safe."

I noticed that the old man couldn't bring himself to look her in the eye. "The Blueprint Programme is already sanctioned. But I've made it very clear that our subject must be a volunteer." He splashed towards Mr. Jasper. "You understand that? A volunteer. We're not barbarians."

Jasper rolled out his answer, smoothly prepared. "Naturally, sir. But bear in mind that we'll need a woman in excellent physical condition, someone with a lively, eager mind, someone . . . clean."

"Clean? What are you talking about—clean?"

"Trust me, sir. Estella was a formidable woman. Anyone we choose will be grateful for the improvement."

Miss Morning was practically spinning in fury. "Disgusting. These methods are beneath you."

Dedlock sighed. "We do whatever it takes. You understand me? Things have changed since you were last in the game. The world is much less genteel now." He swivelled in my direction. "Mr. Lamb?"

I was starting to hope he'd forgotten me.

"I want you to go to the hospital. Hawker and Boon have unfinished business with your grandfather and it's just possible they might try to see him. Don't look so worried. I'll put a security detail on you. Morning? Have you anything useful to contribute?"

The old lady looked defiant. "I've a lead of my own I'd like to follow."

Dedlock glared suspiciously at her. "Very well. I'll see you all back here at six o'clock. Jasper, I expect to see your hunter. Now—get to work!"

THERE THEN FOLLOWED AN embarrassing ten minutes of small talk and chit-chat as the pod took a little age to complete its revolution and reach the ground again.

WHEN WE STEPPED OUT of the Eye, Jasper was still wearing that same look of smug vindication. I think I knew even then, although I lacked the slightest sliver of evidence to prove it, that he had been waiting a long time for the programme to go ahead and that all this suffering and death had ever meant to him was a chance to test his wretched theories. For this, I never forgave him. The rest of his betrayals I can live with, but for that, for his part in the inception of Blueprint, I can't imagine I'll ever find a shred of clemency.

Miss Morning, still denouncing the rank immorality of the man in the tank, walked away down the South Bank, off to pursue her nebulous lead. I can't say I was unhappy to see her go. She was starting to unravel, sinking into confused, directionless rage, and I found the spectacle of it upsetting. It would have been better for her if she'd never got involved with the Directorate again. Better, perhaps, for us all.

"Jasper?" I said.

The baby-faced man, urgently tapping into his mobile phone, didn't look up. "Shouldn't you be with your grandfather?"

"I wanted to ask . . ."

"Yes?"

"This Blueprint Programme. This pill of yours. Who are you going to feed it to?"

"Don't get yourself all riled up, Henry."

A horrible suspicion had begun to claw towards the forefront of my brain. "You are going to find a volunteer, aren't you? Dedlock—he said it's got to be a volunteer."

"Leave it to me, Henry. I've given Blueprint a lot of thought."

"I'll just bet you have," I said. "Christ, you've been grooming someone, haven't you?"

"Look." Mr. Jasper was gazing over my shoulder. "Isn't that your landlady?"

He was right. Abbey was strolling over the grass towards the Eye. She smiled, waved, and I waved back, but when I turned around to confront Mr. Jasper he had already disappeared.

Abbey drew close enough to kiss me—a brief meeting of lips and, to my surprise, a swift intrusion of tongue.

"Hello," I said once she had stepped away.

"What's that?" she asked, staring suspiciously at my earpiece.

I shrugged, sidestepped the question. "It's for work. But what are you doing here?"

"I'm up in town for a meeting. Wondered if you were around for a quick coffee. I was going to ring but, well, here you are."

"Love to," I said. "But I've got to go to the hospital. See my granddad."

"I thought you were working."

"I am. It's . . . It's kind of connected."

"Then I'll come with you."

"Really?"

"Yeah. I'd love to meet him."

"If you're sure . . ."

"Course I'm sure."

"He's not at his best at the moment. Not very chatty."

Abbey laughed. "Come on. We'll get the bus."

⚭

THE 176 BELCHED TOWARDS DULWICH, hissing and snarling through the sullen traffic. The bus was almost empty, and despite my situation, there was something rather pleasant in sitting on the top deck with Abbey whilst everyone else was hard at work. The world of the Prefects, the Directorate and the Blueprint Programme suddenly seemed a world away, something pulpy and ridiculous which had happened to somebody else. The grotesque reality of it all was brought back only when I turned in my seat and noticed the black car that was following us—Mr. Dedlock's promised watchman.

"Hope I didn't wake you this morning," I said.

"Course not. But I was impressed you were up so early after last night."

"I had to go to work."

"God. This promotion . . . They're pushing you hard, aren't they?"

I shrugged. "Making me work for my money, I suppose."

"Money?" she said. "Is that why you're doing it?"

"No, not just money," I admitted.

She nodded sagely. "Job satisfaction. That's what I'd like, too. It'd be wonderful to do something important. Something really worthwhile."

"What, like charity work?"

"Maybe. I'm not sure, to be honest with you. Perhaps I'll know it when I see it. I'd just like to make a contribution."

"I think I understand."

"I've missed having you around the flat," Abbey said softly. "I've missed you."

"Me too," I replied, and we sat in contented silence, enjoying whatever mysterious connection it was that we had begun to share. Naturally, I had to go and ruin it.

"Abbey?"

A soft smile. "Yes?"

"Who's Joe?"

The smile fled from her lips to be replaced with a trembling impostor. "Where did you hear that name?"

"You whispered it this morning. You called me Joe."

Abbey didn't reply but only stared out of the window, her pretty face filled with sadness and regret.

"Abbey?" I said. "Abbey?"

"Joe's no-one." She mustered a feeble, unconvincing smile. "He's a ghost, that's all. Just a ghost."

Strutting into the Prince of Wales's private bedroom without even bothering to knock, Mr. Streater shouted: "Chief! Get your glad rags on! We're going out!"

Arthur wandered in from the bathroom, his scanty hair still heavy and dripping with Brylcreem following his tragically inexpert attempts at styling it.

"Out?" said the prince, searching around for a towel. "What do you mean 'out'?"

"Don't stress. Nothing heavy. I've got a coupla buddies I'd like you to meet, that's all." Streater picked up a towel abandoned on the floor and tossed it over to him. "You looking for this?"

"I can't go out," said the prince. "I'm meant to plant a tree at a primary school this morning."

Streater made calming motions with his hands. "Mate . . . Mate . . ." He slid something out of his pocket—another syringe loaded, inevitably, with the candy sizzle of ampersand. "You want some of this?"

Desire twisted inside him and the prince, submitting again to the demands of his new, remorseless mistress, could only nod dumbly.

Streater's answer was a wolfish smile. "Then you're coming with me."

". . . I need some now."

"You can't even wait till we're in the car?"

"Streater, please."

The blond man cupped his hand over his left ear. "Can't hear you, chief."

"For God's sake, man. Please."

"OK then."

With the terrible proficiency of the expert, Streater rolled up the prince's sleeve, tapped a vein and plunged in his syringe. A tiny pressure on the plunger, a murmur of ecstasy from Windsor and the thing was done, already easier than before, a little more seductively natural every time.

"Come on then," Streater said as the prince, now dazed and wide eyed, rebuttoned his shirt sleeve.

"Streater? I had a dream last night . . ."

"Yeah?"

"About a little boy and a grey cat."

The blond man shrugged. "With this shit inside you," he said, "with this gunk gumming up your veins—take it from me, that's only the beginning."

No-one tried to stop them as they walked out of Clarence House, strolled into the staff parking lot and climbed inside Mr. Streater's effluent-brown Vauxhall Nova. Dimly, the prince wondered why not a single person had lifted a finger to challenge them, why they had done nothing to save him from himself.

In fact, the incident of his departure had not gone unnoticed. There was gossip promiscuously exchanged amongst the household servants, there was tittle-tattle in the scullery, idle talk amongst the grooms and scandal whispered in the ears of ladies' maids—but remarkably not a single one of them ever went to the press about it. Although if you knew of the reprisals conducted in

*secret by the House of Windsor against those it considers disloyal
this might not seem so surprising.*

"Do you like it?" the blond man asked once Arthur was inside
and staring vacantly through the windscreen, past the grime and
squashed flies which the wipers had formed into protractor-neat
curves and whorls.

"It's a nice car, Mr. Streater."

"Now, that's where you're wrong." Streater turned the key in
the ignition and started, quite unnecessarily, to rev the engine.
"This isn't a car. It's a pussy wagon." He smirked. "I've lost count
of the quim I've had in that seat you're sitting in right now."

Arthur flinched.

With ridiculous rapidity, they drove out of the parking lot,
squealed down the length of the Mall and braked extravagantly
before the gates, whose guardians, long inured to the whims and
eccentricities of their employers, allowed them to pass without
comment.

Streater wrestled the steering wheel towards the City. "Something the matter, chief? Something on your mind?"

The prince turned his heavy-lidded eyes towards his companion. "My wife, Mr. Streater. I think she . . ."

Streater had to coax him. "Yeah?"

"She and Mr. Silverman. I think they may be . . ."

"Yeah? What are they doing?"

Arthur screwed up his face. "I think they may be having"—his
voice diminuendoed to a whisper—". . . relations."

"So they're shagging?"

The prince gazed mournfully at him. "I think it's just possible
that may be the case, yes."

"Unlucky, mate. Having your missus get schtupped by another
bloke. It's humiliating. But you've only got yourself to blame."

"What do you mean?"

"What I mean, Your Royal Highness, is that you let her get away with too much shit. You gave her everything she wanted from the get-go so there was nothing left for you to bargain with. She got bored. Birds are like that." Streater broke off to honk at a schoolgirl. His tongue darted out of his mouth to wet his lower lip. "Wouldn't throw her out of bed for eating prawn crackers." He wound down the window and bellowed a suggestion of staggering vulgarity.

The prince hardly seemed to notice. "Tell me, Mr. Streater," he murmured. "And in this matter I should appreciate your candour. What would you suggest?"

"Treat 'em mean, mate. I'm not saying that's an original thought, but that doesn't make it any less true. Women like to know who's boss. There's a reason why blokes like me get more pussy than we know what to do with, while blokes like you end up with your wife tupping around behind your back. You know what that is?"

Slowly, solemnly, the prince moved his head from side to side.

"It's because you're afraid of women and I'm not. I know how to play them and I know how to give them what they want. It's a game, Arthur, and the sad thing—the bloody tragedy of it—is that blokes like you just never learnt the rules."

"So am I to take it, Mr. Streater, that you've never been in love?"

In the kind of voice which made it very clear that he would answer no more questions on the subject: "Just once."

On Shaftesbury Avenue, Streater swerved blithely into a bus lane and the prince enquired where they were going.

"Not far. I promise."

"But I am to plant a tree today. The children are expecting me."

"Sod the children!"

The prince just blinked. "What was that?"

"Sorry," Mr. Streater muttered. "Sorry, mate. Didn't mean to blurt that out."

Streater brought the car to a halt just outside the bleak terminus of King's Cross station in a space reserved for emergency vehicles, switched off the engine, yanked open the glove compartment, pulled out a ragged, faded baseball cap and passed it to the prince.

"What's this?"

"It's your disguise, chief."

The prince was just becoming used to this unfamiliar thing perched on his head when the doors at the back of the car were flung open and a couple of fat men squeezed themselves inside, along with the smells of grease and roadkill.

One of them shuffled his bulk forward to stare at Arthur. "This him, then?" he said in a mockney growl. "Bugger me, he's uglier than I expected."

The other one thrust a cardboard container running with oil and slime under the nose of the heir to the throne.

"Golden arches?" he asked, bafflingly.

Arthur never learnt to tell these two apart. They seemed almost identical—both thick necked, both jowly and unshaven, dressed in grubby shirts, frayed jackets and stained raincoats. They both smelt the same, too—of the street, of bad money and of corruption.

"I'm Detective Chief Inspector George Virtue," one of them said. "This fat wanker's Detective Sergeant Vince Mercy."

"What is the meaning of this?" asked the prince, only just keeping the incredulity from his voice.

"Little field trip," one of them said. Virtue? Mercy? It was so difficult to tell. "Little bit of R 'n' R."

"Just sit still," Streater snapped, "we're going inside in a bit."

"You're catching a train?" Arthur asked hopefully.

Streater looked as though he was about to remark that the prince should just wait and see when someone tapped on the windscreen, scurried round to the back of the car and, miraculously, crammed himself in beside the fat policemen.

The newcomer was sweaty and nervous, had greying hair (too long) and wore an embarrassing amount of gold jewellery. "Streater?" he said, and nodded towards the prince. "Who's this? What's he doing here?"

This question elicited a more than usually large grin from Streater. "This is Arthur Windsor. Arthur, this is—"

"Mr. X," the man interrupted, suddenly frantic.

"For Christ's sake. This is the next king of England. If you can't be upfront with the Prince of Wales, who the hell can you be straight with?"

The man seemed embarrassed. "Of course. Sorry. I'm Peter." He stuck out his hand, and instinctively the prince shook it.

On the back seat, one of the policemen belched, and for a vile moment the smell of half-digested Big Mac lingered in the atmosphere.

"Time to move," Streater said, and opened the door, admitting a merciful blast of cold air.

Together, the five of them walked into the station.

"You've probably been wondering exactly what ampersand is . . . ," Streater said.

One of the fat men laughed. "Tasty!"

Streater went on as though the interruption had never happened. "Fact is, it's a natural substance. Grows by itself under certain conditions. Peter here . . . what's the word you'd use, Pete? He gathers it, he . . . harvests it for us."

The grey-haired man flushed pink.

"But demand's seriously outstripping supply. The kids are lapping it up so we've had to find a way to replicate. A mate of mine has a mate who knows a man who did time with a guy who's shagging the sister of a bloke in France who's tight with a sympathetic chemist. Result—ampersand manufactured by the ton. We're off to meet our courier off the train."

Detective Sergeant Vince Mercy slapped his hands together in glee. "New delivery! Fresh meat!"

Streater grinned. "Welcome to the real world."

The blond man led them into the station and down the escalator to the Eurostar terminus, where they took up positions by the coffee shop. Arthur kept the baseball cap pulled down over his face but was strangely disappointed to find that not one member of the public so much as glanced at him.

Streater bought Peter and the prince a latte (oddly, not offering to do the same for the two policemen) and they all stood suckling at the plastic teats on their cups, trying not to look suspicious. One of the fat men jabbed Arthur in the ribs. "Has he told you how it's done, guv?"

"I'm sorry?"

"This bird we're meeting. She'll be carrying the stuff inside her."

"What do you mean?"

The other detective leered and Arthur was assaulted by a venting of his rancid breath. "Obliging little cow swallowed ampersand in a prophylactic. We'll strain it out of her later."

"That's horrible."

"That's life, mate. We weren't all born with a silver spoon up our jacksie."

Streater looked up from his conversation with Peter. "Everything OK, chief? You seem worried."

Arthur was stuttering his way into a reply when a train's worth of people emerged from the exit gates, last amongst them a dark-haired woman just on the cusp of middle age.

"Here we go," grunted one of the policemen. "I'd recognise that wiggle anywhere."

Peter seemed even sweatier and more nervous than before. "No," he muttered. "Something's wrong."

Streater shot the man a sharp look. "What?"

"Look at her. Something's up."

They all stared as the woman moved across the floor. It was as though she was drunk but trying her best to walk in a straight line, staggering under some appalling strain. As she drew closer, they saw that her skin had turned a violent shade of pink.

"Oh God." Peter was whimpering. "Oh God."

"What is it?" Streater snapped. "What's happening?"

All the blood had drained from his face. "I think it's split inside her. If she's ingested that amount of raw ampersand . . . Christ knows what'll happen to her."

None of the men, not even the policemen, had any answer to this. They all just stood in silence and watched the inevitable unfold.

The woman staggered again, stumbled forwards and lurched onto the ground. Arthur made a move to help but Streater grabbed his arm to hold him back.

A couple of customs staff had seen the woman fall and hurried over but it was already too late. Her face grew more florid, seeming to bloat and swell far beyond its natural size. Shiny, bulbous boils rose upon her face, and even from a few metres away, Arthur could see that they were filled with lurid pus, moving and squirming with some life of their own. Her body seemed wracked with a tremendous pressure from within, shuddering like a blocked water pipe after the taps have been left running. Once or twice, Arthur tried to turn away but failed to do so, morbidly riveted by the spectacle of it.

The woman was still shaking. A keening, piteous moan escaped her as a crowd began to gather, impotent yet transfixed.

At the end, Arthur's view was mercifully obscured, but he heard the sound she made when she died. One could hardly miss it—it was the hearty impact of a water balloon on a summer's day—and he saw the aftermath, too, the spreading pool of bubblegum pink which crept along the station floor, staining the stone with ampersand.

Peter was retching into his handkerchief. Virtue and Mercy were shaking their heads in grim disbelief. But Mr. Streater only smirked. "Just goes to show," he said. "Turns out you really can have too much of a good thing."

And he smiled his secret smile.

CHAPTER 20

OFTEN, LATE AT NIGHT, WHEN I CAN'T GET TO SLEEP, I wonder how Jasper did it.

I don't suppose he even found it difficult. Something like that . . . it would get to me. It would prey on my mind. But Jasper? It never seemed to bother him in the slightest.

You've probably already guessed who he phoned the moment he left me at the Eye. And you can imagine how he sweet-talked her into coming out for lunch. Somewhere posh, he would have said, somewhere swanky. My treat. And the girl, already flattered by his attentions, by the gentlemanly way in which he had conducted himself and the evident sincerity of his intentions, would have been helpless at the invitation.

Later, after it was done, Jasper told me that he never laid a finger on her. But we know the truth. We know what kind of man he was. We know he wouldn't have been able to stop himself.

You'll have to forgive me if I sound bitter. Given my condition, I actually harbour surprisingly little resentment, but there's something about this part of my story which never fails to enrage me. Something also in the fact that if I'd just been that little bit sharper, that tiny bit more alert, I might have been able to stop it completely.

So Jasper called her up, asked her out for an early lunch and she agreed. She would have scavenged some makeup from her colleagues and spent an eternity in the ladies' before coming to meet him, her heart pitter-pattering at the prospect of another date with this dapper, uncomplicated man apparently unburdened by baggage, kinks or hang-ups. Jasper would have been waiting punctually outside the office and taken her to a restaurant which he knew should impress her but which he would never dream of visiting in the normal way. It had to be somewhere no-one knew him. It had to be somewhere he wouldn't be recognised.

He would have listened to her chatter as the wine arrived, asked about the office gossip, nodded politely on hearing that her boss had called in sick that morning and pantomimed interest when she told him about the fat woman in the basement. He would even have put up with her gauche flirtations during the starter, and it would only have been when she left the table to powder her nose that he would finally have made his move.

To a man like him, it probably didn't even feel like a moral decision. A circular silver pill dropped discreetly into her drink. It would have effervesced briefly, then dissolved, and by the time Barbara came back to the table she would never have guessed that anything had transpired at all.

But it's the thought of what must have happened next, once the meal was over and the pill had set itself to work—it's that and the terrible betrayal it represents which, as I write, makes me sick to my stomach.

AT THE TIME ALL this was happening, I was ushering Abbey into the Machen Ward and presenting her to the pitiful shadow of my grandfather. The place seemed quieter than ever. The bed opposite Granddad, occupied the last time I'd visited by a portly bald man whose face had been covered almost entirely with burst blood vessels, lay conspicuously empty.

We found a couple of chairs and lowered ourselves down beside him.

"Granddad," I said. "I'd like you to meet Abbey. My girl-friend."

I turned to check that this description of her was OK to find my landlady staring at the old bastard in disbelief. "I know him," she said.

"What?"

"I know him," she said again.

"You can't. That's impossible."

"Henry, I've met him before."

"When?"

"Through the real estate agent. He was the man who sold me the flat."

SHE TOLD ME TOO MUCH about him and in too much detail for me ever to believe that she had imagined it or that she was making the whole thing up. She told me how they'd met when she'd looked around the property for the first time, how they'd hit it off straightaway, even if (and there are no surprises here) she was unable to shake the suspicion that the old man was flirting with her. She'd told him a bit about her life, how she was looking to buy her first home and that she might take in a lodger to make the mortgage. Apparently, Granddad had said that he'd taken a liking to her, and in the end he accepted her offer even though it was considerably less than others he received.

It was like he had chosen her. That was how Abbey put it. It was as though he had singled her out.

"What's going on?" Abbey asked once she had finished.

I didn't have an answer for her but in the end I managed

a shrug and a lopsided smile all the same. "Listen," I said, "I know an absolutely dreadful café just down the corridor. Can I buy you lunch?"

As I watched Abbey take delicate, surgical stabs at a puny bowl of salad, I decided that I had to ask her again.

You'll probably think this bizarre, given the mystery of my grandfather, given that people had started dying, that society was tumbling down around us and that there were a couple of mass-murderers on the loose who actually had a nickname for me. You'll probably argue that I should have been concentrating more on the war and less on some imbroglio in my love life. But, then, what do you know? You weren't there.

"Abbey?" I asked as she speared an anaemic tomato. "I want you to tell me who Joe is."

The tomato bounded away from her fork. Abbey looked angry enough to snap the cutlery in two.

I persisted. "I need to know. You said his name twice this morning. Say I misheard. Say it's the name of your cat. Just tell me something."

Abbey pushed away her salad. "Joe was someone I used to go out with. Just an ex."

"I see."

There was a man on the other side of the canteen, dark suited and crop haired, a copy of *Martin Chuzzlewit* held conspicuously out in front of him, the outline of a weapon clearly visible in his jacket pocket. He looked over at me and nodded. One of Dedlock's jackboots, of course. He didn't look like the sharpest tool in the box. It wouldn't have surprised me if he was holding that book upside down.

Abbey hadn't noticed him. "I was with Joe for a while," she said. "Quite a while." She seemed to be choosing her words very carefully, deliberating over each one. "But not any more. We haven't spoken in months."

"You still have feelings for him?"

"God, no."

"But you whispered his name this morning in your sleep."

"Habit, Henry. Don't read anything into it."

"How did you meet him?" I asked. "How did you meet *Joe*?" I couldn't help but infect that last word with a bitter spasm of contempt and immediately I disliked myself intensely for it.

Abbey didn't meet my eye or challenge my tone, but just gazed ahead of her at the salt and pepper on the table. "He lived in the flat," she said.

Something wobbled in my stomach. "In the flat? In my room?"

Abbey nodded. "It had to finish." My beautiful girlfriend chewed her lower lip at the memory of a time about which I knew nothing, and I felt the steel-capped kick of jealousy. "He'd lost his way. He was getting into something dangerous."

"Tell me more." I knew that I was interrogating her now but somehow I couldn't bring myself to stop. Some grubby curiosity in me wanted to know it all.

"He was unpredictable," she said. "Crazy, sometimes. Dangerous. Not like you. Not like you at all. You're not dangerous. You're . . ." She searched for an adjective. "You're sweet." At last she looked up at me, tried a smile, thrust her hands across the table to clasp mine.

"Sweet," I said softly, and never had the word sounded so damningly joyless. I swallowed hard and asked the biggest question of all. "Do you miss him?"

With the screech of metal on linoleum, Abbey pushed back her chair, suddenly bustling and irritable. "I have to get back to the office. Don't bother to see me out. I'll get a cab."

After that, all that was left for us to do was to swap frosty goodbyes and vague promises to meet up in the flat.

I trudged back to sit with my grandfather. I sighed. "You've got all the answers, haven't you?" I said, but all I got was the usual dead-eyed stare at the ceiling, the irritating bleeps of life support. I lost my temper. My voice cracked. "You old bastard!"

BY THE TIME BARBARA returned to the office, she was feeling queasy. By 2:30 P.M., she was feeling physically sick. Down in the basement, when it got really bad, she had to steady herself against the fat woman's chair until the nausea subsided.

By three P.M., the poor girl thought she might throw up at any moment. Peter Hickey-Brown had slunk in whilst she was at lunch, muttering some sheepish excuse about a dentist's appointment. She had no choice but to knock on his door and ask him to let her go early. Too distracted by something on his computer to offer much resistance, he just nodded, not even looking up from his spreadsheet, meaning that Barbara was free of the office and heading towards the station not more than ten minutes later.

The tube journey must have been difficult. In addition to the violent ructions of her stomach, she would have had a piercing headache, her vision would have been blurred and uncertain, and she would have found herself perilously unsteady on her feet. Once she had got off the tube, it was only a short walk home. She lived with her father and two cats.

Or, at least, that's how I've always imagined it.

The old man—and he would have been old, I think, an elderly father some years into a mostly miserable retirement— would have emerged from his study to find out what his daughter was doing back from work so early. Not wanting to bother him, she would have said that she was feeling a little poorly but that it was nothing to worry about, nothing for him to fuss over. Always uneasy around female illness (all that oozing, all that bleeding and perspiration), her dad would have ducked gratefully back into his den. Perhaps I'm being unjust to the man but I've always imagined him turning his music up loud to cover the sounds from upstairs as his daughter cowered in the bathroom, first the sounds of vomiting, the tears, the stifled moans, the swallowed cries—then much, much worse. I imagine him with a large collection of LPs, and for some reason, when I torture myself by picturing what happened, it's always an old Elton John song I hear: "The Bitch Is Back."

Poor Barbara, trying to be quiet in the bathroom. Poor Barbara, who'd do anything not to be a burden to her dad. Poor Barbara, trying to be quiet as she threw up what felt like half her stomach lining, as something impossible took hold of her body and poked and pulled and twisted. Poor Barbara, who didn't even scream when her bones started to stretch and elongate of their own accord, as her flesh alternately boiled away and swelled up, as her eyebrows shortened, her lips grew bulbous and her cheeks shrank away to almost nothing. Fully expecting to discover now that this was death, she somehow managed to crawl into her room and lie down, whimpering, on the bed. Eventually, when the pain had just begun to recede, she got up the courage to look in the mirror. Only then, only when she saw what they'd done to her, did she finally scream.

And then, at 5:30 P.M., Mr. Jasper came to call.

Silverman came running as soon as he heard, dashing along the corridor, skittering down hallways, practically bouncing off the walls, panting, perspiring, raggedy breathed. He knocked on the door to the prince's private suite and walked in without waiting for an invitation. They had been friends for too long to worry about protocol, been through too much together to let etiquette stand in their way.

Even so, the prince looked annoyed at the interruption. He sat on the edge of his bed, breathing deeply, his face the colour of semolina and wearing the look of a bunny on the motorway who knows that he will never make it to the verge in time.

The ghoul Streater stood over him, one hand placed, with casual proprietarialism, upon the royal shoulder. Silverman thought he even noticed a gentle squeeze.

"What is it, Silverman?" It was barely lunchtime, yet the prince sounded exhausted.

"We were all so worried about you, sir. You were out on your own without any kind of security detail—"

"Why does anyone give a fig how I choose to spend my time?"

"The tree-planting ceremony at the school, sir? The children were most disappointed." At this, Silverman gave the prince a mildly reproving look—an expression which had often done the trick in the past, tweaking the royal conscience when they were both serving in the regiment and Private Wales had contemplated feigning sickness to wriggle out of training. Today, however, the prince scarcely seemed to notice that Silverman was in the room at all.

Mr. Streater looked the equerry up and down. "We went out, OK? I wanted Arthur to meet a couple of mates of mine."

"Mates?" In other circumstances, Silverman might have found a certain humour in this, but today, one look at the pained and perplexed face of the prince was enough to quell the slightest hint of humour. "Why on earth would he be interested in your mates?"

Streater strutted over to the equerry and glared unflinchingly into his face. "What's wrong with my mates? You think they're not good enough for him?"

Silverman did what the middle classes usually do when confronted by blatant aggression. He backed down and started to apologise. "I didn't mean any offence. I'm sure we're both just as concerned about the prince's welfare—"

Streater cut him dead. "Piss off."

"Pardon?"

"You heard me. Sling your hook."

Arthur pulled at the man's sleeve, more like a little boy than ever. "That's enough. Silverman. I think it's probably best you leave. I'm in excellent hands here."

Silverman knew that something was disastrously wrong but decades of deference and duty ordered him to simply bow his head and shuffle towards the door. "If you're sure, sir."

"Quite sure," said the prince. "In fact, I've never been more sure of anything in my life."

Silverman left the room feeling a horrible certainty that the situation had just passed the point when it could be safely contained. Unsure to whom he should turn but desperate to do something to help, he walked swiftly to his study, where he poured himself a generous gin and tonic and began to set arrangements in motion for an emergency meeting with the Princess of Wales.

As soon as the equerry had gone, the prince gave a dolorous sigh.

Streater patted him on the back. "Nice one, chief. You didn't lose your rag. Thousands would've. Personally, I'd have lamped him. Wiped that greasy little smirk off his face. He's laughing at you, chief. All the time. That man and your missus, they're pissing themselves behind your back."

"I can't take it . . . ," Arthur murmured. "Silverman and Laetitia . . ."

Streater shrugged. "You saw the bloke. All panting and out of breath. Looked like he'd dressed in a hurry. Reckon he was still balls-deep in her when we got back."

Arthur stared bleakly down at the elaborate weft of his carpet, a gift from some sheikh or other whose multi-syllabic name temporarily eluded him. "I can't get the image of that poor woman out of my head."

"What woman?"

The prince made a pathetic little moaning sound. "At the station."

"Oh, her. Well, that's life, isn't it? Her choice."

"Surely she didn't choose to die like that."

"Them's the breaks, Arthur. Them's the breaks."

"Can ampersand do that to anyone?"

"Only if you take way too much. Listen, mate, ampersand's special stuff. It's priming the population. It's making them ready."

"Ready for what?"

"For Leviathan. Keep up, chief. It's more than a drug. First time I bought it off Pete at a gig, it changed my bloody life. I'd tried all kinds of shit before but this was something new. Lights. Colours. All kinds of trippy shit. I heard a voice."

"I've heard no voice."

"Give it time. With me—you couldn't shut it up. Told me I'd been chosen . . ."

"I can't stand this," said the prince. "I believe I have begun to see what it is we are travelling towards and I cannot endure the thought of it."

"I know what'll cheer you up," Mr. Streater said. "This'll put a bit of lead in your pencil." His hands retreated into his jacket pockets to re-emerge, predictably, with the sickening accoutrements of addiction—the tourniquet, the vial, the syringe.

"No," Arthur muttered. "Put that stuff away. There's been too much today."

Streater's voice took on a wheedling tone. "Come on, Arthur. Just a little hit. You must've missed it."

The prince managed a final, token piece of objection: "Under the circumstances, I'm not sure it's appropriate—"

"Shh." Streater put his fingers to his lips. "Not another word, chief. Not another peep. Just gimme your arm."

Arthur began to fiddle with the cuffs on his left sleeve.

"The other one. Wanna fresh vein."

He did as he was told.

"There you go! Now, lie back . . ."

The prince stretched out upon the bed and let Streater do it to him again, savouring the tingly sense of anticipation, the needle's teasing bite, the soothing warmth as the ampersand flowed into his system. He closed his eyes and slipped away—and as he slept he had the dream again, about the little boy and the small grey cat.

He woke to find sweat cooling unpleasantly on his body, Streater gone and the telephone by his bed ringing loudly.

The prince rubbed his eyes and struggled towards the receiver.

"Who the bloody hell is this?"

The voice was deep, gruff and filled with oddly mirthless laughter. "Hello, guv."

"To whom am I speaking?"

"The name's Detective Chief Inspector Virtue, guv. You're on speakerphone with DS Mercy. We met earlier today."

Arthur wondered how on earth they had got hold of his private number.

"You all right?" one of them asked.

"Thank you, Detective. I am perfectly well."

"It's just that I've been thinking. Well, we've been thinking. About your missus. Course we've seen her on the telly. Succulent piece. Nice tush."

Another voice chipped in now and Arthur could picture all too easily his bloated jowls and sunken chin, his fat lips smeared with animal grease.

"We've been thinking about all the things she lets him do to her. About his hairy arse in her face."

The other one again: "We've been picturing their screws, guv. Their quickies. Their tumbles. Their knee tremblers.

"We've been imagining the mucky bits on your behalf, guv. Been wondering who likes it dirty. Who likes it rough. Who puts what in where."

"I hope you appreciate this, guv. We're looking out for you here. We're watching yer back."

The conversation which followed was a long one, endlessly, inventively upsetting, and by the time detectives Virtue and Mercy had finished speaking, the prince's eyes were red and raw from weeping.

CHAPTER 21

WE WERE WAITING AT THE DIRECTORATE IN EX-
pectation of a miracle. That was what the odious
Mr. Jasper had called her—"a genuine, irrefutable, copper-
bottomed miracle."

Dedlock's squad of killers had found nothing, Hawker and
Boon were still at large and the air seemed to crackle with a
perplexing combination of urgency and exhaustion.

I stood apart from the others, staring out of the pod, past
the illusory tourists and towards the real world, where, beyond
the mirage of camera wielders and guidebook flourishers, I
could see the snake of real punters waiting patiently in line.
Past them—the lights of the South Bank, the neon and halogen of real life.

A hand on my shoulder. "You look tired, Henry."

It was Miss Morning, more battle weary than ever.

"I am," I said. "And I'm starting to wonder whether this miracle of Jasper's is ever going to turn up."

Mr. Jasper strolled over to us, a look of smug self-satisfaction
uncurling itself across his face. "Trust me," he said, "she'll be
worth the wait."

In this, if in nothing else, Jasper was right. As we watched, the queue of tourists began to part in wonder and envy as a woman, a stranger, strode through the crowd and stepped smartly into the pod like she belonged there. The door hissed shut and we began to move, but with a judder, as though even the Eye itself had been thrown off kilter by the newcomer.

Straightaway we knew that she was what we'd been waiting for, that she was Jasper's miracle.

She was tapered, statuesque, with a mane of jet-black hair, and the curves of her exquisite figure were encased in a tightly belted trench coat which flapped about her like a cape. She was flawlessly complexioned and what light make-up she had applied served only to accentuate the splendour of her cheek-bones, the imperious curve of her nose, the glacial sensuality of her lips. Most striking of all were her eyes. Once they had been turned upon you, it was impossible to imagine denying her anything she might desire.

There was something terrible about this woman. Hers was the bleak beauty of nature, the desolate grandeur of an ice field, the awful grace of a tiger stalking its prey.

But the most surprising thing of all was that I thought I recognised her from somewhere.

"Barbara?" I asked.

I looked closer and I was certain. It was her. A stretched, plucked, distended parody of her, perhaps, but unquestionably the girl from the office all the same. She favoured me briefly with a condescending glance but did not offer a reply.

"Gentlemen." Jasper was wearing the look of the cardsharp who knows he can never lose a game. "This is our hunter."

The woman did not smile or bow or in any way acknowledge the introduction but gazed at us in much the same way that the first Cro-Magnon may have surveyed a gathering of Neander-thals.

"Remarkable," Miss Morning murmured. "Repugnantly immoral, of course, but still—remarkable."

"Barbara?" I asked again. "It is you, isn't it?"

She turned her head in my direction with a motion that was strangely mechanical. I noticed that she already wore the same earpiece as the rest of us and I wondered if I might not be able to hear the whir of motors, the clank of gears.

"Hello, Henry," she said, and I could tell from her voice that it was still her. Changed, alchemised, transformed, but somehow still Barbara. Her perfect lips formed words as though they were still learning how. "Barbara's in here somewhere. Buried very deep. She says hello." The word "hello" was spoken as though it was barely familiar to her, alien and slightly dirty, like a judge struggling with the patois of some young offender brought before him in the dock.

I turned to Jasper. "What the hell have you done to her?"

He giggled. "I've made her better. This is Estella come back to us. This is victory."

"Enough," Dedlock snapped. "I want proof."

Barbara sashayed past and walked as close to the tank as she could. "The first Estella is inside me. And she knows you, Mr. Dedlock." Why, at this, I was put in mind of Marilyn singing "Happy Birthday" to the president, I really couldn't fathom.

"Estella . . . ," the old man stuttered. "You've come back to me."

"It's good to be back, sir," she said, although her voice was wholly without conviction.

The man in the tank squirmed. If it had been possible for us to see, I have no doubt that Dedlock's upper lip would have been coated in sweat, in the shifty rime of mendacity and betrayal. "How much do you remember?"

"I remember almost everything."

"*Almost* everything?"

"I can recollect some of the smallest details of Estella's life. I can remember a great deal of the existence of poor Barbara. But I am more than either of them."

The head of the Directorate looked afraid.

"Gentlemen, we're wasting time." Barbara paced briskly back to the centre of the pod. "The Directorate has frittered away the last twenty-four hours. We should have the Prefects in custody by now."

"Tell me," Dedlock said in a little boy's voice. "How do we find them?"

"The answer's been staring you in the face. Any one of you could have worked it out for yourself."

Most of us could no longer stand to look at her so we gazed dolefully at the floor or stared shamefacedly out of the window, like a line-up of new arrivals at the kind of penitentiary where they favour throwing away the key.

"Dedlock," snapped Barbara. "Bring up a heat map of the city."

"I don't know what you mean."

"We don't have time for your game playing. Just do it. Say a ten-mile circumference from Whitehall."

Dedlock's fingers twitched in the water and behind him, miraculously, we saw the lines of London shimmer into existence, the streets and roads form themselves out of the fluid in some impossible liquid cartography. Overlaid upon the familiar landmarks were splashes of yellow and orange.

"A heat map's no good," Dedlock protested. "Everything has a signature."

Barbara raised a hand to silence him. "The Prefects are creatures of fire and sulphur. Watch the screen. They will reveal themselves."

Amidst the blurs of oranges and yellows, there appeared two jets of red.

Others in her position might have found it hard not to sound triumphant, but Barbara's voice held no trace of vanity or conceit. "There. We have our men."

"Somewhere in Islington," Dedlock muttered. "I'll get an exact grid reference."

Barbara turned away from the tank and started dispensing orders. "Jasper—get Barnaby to meet us. I want to drive directly to the site. Henry and I are going in together."

"Me?" I said, my guts clenching like a fist at the prospect of another confrontation with the Domino Men. "What on earth do you want me for? You look pretty capable yourself."

"Oh, I'm immensely capable, Mr. Lamb, but for some reason these creatures seem to have taken a shine to you."

For a moment, Jasper looked at his creation almost doubtfully. "I'll organise the jackboots. Get the place surrounded. We'll take them by force."

"Hawker and Boon cannot be stopped by conventional weaponry," Barbara said. "How much more blood do you want on your hands before you learn that simple lesson?"

"Then what can stop them?"

The ghost of a smile appeared on Barbara's impossibly perfect lips. "Miss Morning. How pleasant it is to be working alongside you again."

The old lady squinted at Barbara. "I'm not sure precisely what you are, young lady. But you're not Estella. You're something new."

"You know what I need. Get me the weapon."

"I thought it was lost."

"Then you were misinformed. The old man hid it in the safe house."

Miss Morning smiled faintly. "Such a clever fellow in his own way."

"Find it and bring it to me."

Miss Morning nodded.

Starved of attention, the man in the tank beckoned Barbara back across the room. "I have the address. It's somewhere on Upper Street. But where on earth could a couple of grown men dressed as schoolboys hide in Islington?"

"There's a little place I know."

"Is that so?"

"Yes, sir."

"It's good to have you back, Estella."

"It's good to be back, sir."

"And so wonderful to see that everything's been forgiven and forgotten."

Barbara peered into the tank and the head of the Directorate shrank from her gaze. "That's all in the past, sir." She bared an unnaturally bright white set of teeth. "That's water under the bridge."

Mercifully, at that moment, the pod's revolution was complete, and we were pushed back out into the freezing night air.

BARNABY WAS WAITING. Barbara had climbed into the passenger seat and Jasper was clambering into the back when Miss Morning tapped me lightly on the shoulder.

"You need to call home. Tell Abbey I'm coming round."

Exhausted from the battering of the past few days, my brain couldn't really compute this information. "What?"

"Just tell her I'm on my way."

"OK . . . Why are you going to my flat?"

"That flat isn't your flat. It's a Directorate safe house."

"What?"

"Henry, it's where we carried out the Process. It's where we cut poor Estella. Don't act so surprised. Why else do you think your granddad was so keen for you to live there?"

The window at the front of the car whirred down. "Henry," Barbara said quietly—although this new softness in her tone made me feel more afraid of her than any shout or scream would have done. "Get in the car."

"You have to go," Miss Morning said. "I'll explain later."

For a second, I hesitated. Then I heard Barbara's cool, clear voice ("Time is of the essence, Henry") and I climbed in beside Jasper. Miss Morning slammed shut the door and as the car drove away, she mouthed something at me. A single word. I couldn't quite make it out, but now, looking back on it as the days of my life almost certainly dwindle into single digits, I'm certain I know what it was.

"Sorry."

JASPER WAS FIDGETING, interlocking his fingers, touching the end of his nose, fiddling with his chair, periodically clearing his throat and then, growing bored with the rest, poking me in the ribs.

"Isn't she wonderful?" He nodded towards the front, where Barbara was giving our driver directions in the dispassionate tones of a satellite navigation system.

"Why did it have to be Barbara?" I hissed. "Why did you have to choose her?"

"She was perfect, Mr. Lamb. Just perfect."

Swallowing my disgust, I took out my mobile and stabbed in Abbey's number.

Barbara swivelled round, suddenly suspicious. "Who are you calling?"

"My landlady."

"Make it quick, then."

As it happened, I only got her voicemail. "Hi, Abbey," I said, almost in a whisper, acutely aware that the others were listening. "Listen, I know this might sound a bit odd but I've got a friend coming round to the flat. Is there any chance you could be there for her? Help her out with anything she needs. I can't explain. But it's really important. Anyway, I'll call you later. And . . ." I couldn't begin to articulate what I wanted to say. "I'm thinking about you a lot." I broke the connection.

Jasper, still buoyant from his triumph, started smirking knowingly at me, but I ignored him and took to staring moodily out of the window.

We moved into the city and were passing a department store, open late for Christmas shopping, festooned with fluorescent Santas, blinking baubles and Day-Glo snowmen, when Barbara suddenly said: "Pull over here."

"Why?" Barnaby asked.

A hint of a smile. Or perhaps just a trick of the light. "We're going to need costumes."

AT THE FAR END OF Upper Street, sandwiched between the kind of newsagent that makes most of its money from the magazines on its top shelf and a place which will sell you fried chicken at four o'clock in the morning, there was a nightclub called Diabolism.

Its name was a vestigial piece of pretension from an old proprietor who had nurtured plans to take the place upmarket. Unlike him, his successors knew their market.

Once a week, every week, the club hosted an event called Skool Daze, which, with its melange of cheap alcohol, hoped-for promiscuity and chemically induced good humour, seemed no different from any other evening at Diabolism—except for a single innovation. In an attempt to recapture the carefree sybaritism of their adolescence, everyone who came through the door had to be dressed in an approximation of a school uniform.

So you see now why Barbara insisted that we stop to pick up costumes.

It should go without saying that she looked extraordinary. She had picked out a skirt which displayed an impressive amount of leg and a blouse which, generously unbuttoned, revealed the aerodynamics of her cleavage. She was gorgeous—ravishingly, ridiculously so—yet I felt not a flicker of desire for her. The more time I spent in her company, the less real she seemed, as though she wasn't quite there, more like a fantasy come to strange half-life instead of a real woman. It was only when I caught occasional glimpses of the Barbara I knew, in the way that she moved or a sudden dimpling of her cheeks, that I remembered the essential tragedy of the woman.

I'm rambling, of course, doing my best to avoid having to describe how Jasper and I climbed reluctantly into our little outfits, our shirts and striped ties. I couldn't find shorts to fit me so I had to make do with rolling my trousers up above my knees. Actually, it was a look that Jasper almost pulled off, even if he did resemble the kind of kid who always came top of the class in mental arithmetic. I just looked ridiculous.

We left Barnaby in the car, engrossed in *Peril Fiction and the Yellow Movement: The Fallible Narrator in the Lives of Sexton Blake*. The photograph on the back cover was a younger version of our driver, uncharacteristically clean shaven, quietly pleased with himself, full of expectation for the future.

"I might have a sniff around in a bit," he said, glancing up from his book. "See if there's any sign of the enemy."

I wish now that I'd said something to him. Thanked him, perhaps, for giving us a lift. Shaken his hand or something. Told him to let the bitterness go and enjoy what little was left of his life. But how could I have guessed? How could I have known that I was never going to see him again?

We strode over to the club. There was a ridiculously weedy bouncer at the door, sporting a little spiv's moustache like no one had bothered to tell him that the Blitz was over and we didn't have rationing any more. He smirked at Barbara as she walked past and nodded brusquely at me, but just as Jasper was about to strut through, he held out his arm to stop him.

"Sorry, sir. Couples only."

Jasper looked at him in astonishment. "What did you say?"

"Couples only. That's the rules. Makes it a level playing field, you see."

"Just let me through," Jasper said, and tried to push his way past. All I can say about the struggle that ensued is that the bouncer must have been very much more forceful than he appeared.

"OK." Jasper stood back, put his hand in his pocket and produced a twenty-pound note. "Would this help change your mind?"

"Rules is rules," the bouncer said sententiously.

"Fine." Jasper dragged out another twenty-pound note. "How about this?"

The moustachioed man just shook his head.

"Brilliant," Jasper snapped. "London's only honest bouncer. Listen here," he said, and I could see that he was on the cusp of losing his temper. "Right now, inside your club, there are a couple of creatures who'd think nothing of making every woman in this city a widow just because they're bored. Now, for God's sake, let me pass."

"No offence, sir. And I don't mean to be rude. But would you mind awfully buggering off?"

I'd been watching this performance with no small amount

of amusement, but when I turned to look at Barbara there was nothing but stern professionalism on her face.

"Mr. Jasper," she said. "We can't afford to waste time out here. See if you can gain access with another party. Henry and I must go inside."

Jasper whined, "You could disable this man with a twitch of your wrist."

"I don't want to draw attention to us," she said.

"You can't leave me out here." He contemplated his pale, almost hairless legs and shivered. "Not like this."

Barbara gave him a look of sardonic dismissal, turned her back and vanished into the club. As I followed, she spoke quickly into her earpiece. "We're at the club, sir. Near the targets. We're going dark."

Dedlock's voice in both our ears: "Understood. And good luck."

At the door, we both paid ten pounds to a woman who sat slouched on a stool chewing gum, who then grudgingly invited us inside.

Diabolism turned out to be a large concrete space packed with several hundred people swelling and roiling in an ocean of sweaty desperation. There seemed to be a vaguely festive theme, and I recognised the song which was making the floor thump and quiver as a dance remix of Earth, Wind and Fire's "Boogie Wonderland," which had climbed alarmingly close to the top of the chart that year. There were firemen's poles fixed around the room, about which the uninhibited could cavort. It was the kind of place which served Bacardi Breezer by the pint, and I'm afraid I hated it on sight.

Every single person was dressed the same. They were literally in uniform. Tiny skirts, ties draped suggestively around bare necks, scarves knotted round heads like bandanas. The club insisted that the minimum age of entry was eighteen and I can confirm that everyone present appeared very comfortably over that limit. A good many, in fact, looked as though they had not seen eighteen for several decades, a fact unflatteringly revealed at intervals when the strobe lighting illuminated their faces, accentuating every crease and wrinkle, each pockmark and pimple. The floor sucked at my feet and for the first time in years I felt again the bilious fear of adolescence, the hideous terror of being expected to dance.

As Earth, Wind and Fire segued into Europop, Barbara took me by the hand and hoiked me through the crowd towards the bar, where she fetched me a drink in a plastic cup. When we spoke we had to shout in order to be heard.

"Eee shred shred tout!"

"What?" I yelled.

She leant close to my left ear and shouted: "We should spread out!"

I nodded in response and, clutching my drink, walked away from her, slaloming between gyrating couples.

It turned out to be easier than I could have hoped. A few minutes later, I saw them, recognising them at once from the backs of their heads, two men sipping cocktails at the bar, one burly and ginger-haired, the other slim and dark. I looked around for Barbara but she had already disappeared into the crowd, and I knew that if I were to go for back-up now I could lose the Domino Men all over again and we'd have to start from scratch. So (I think not unheroically) I did the only other thing I could. I walked up behind Boon, intending to administer a brisk tap on his shoulder, but as I was almost upon him a tubby redhead dressed for hockey practice blundered my way and I tripped forwards, slapping the Prefect hard on the back of his head.

When the little man turned to face me I saw immediately

that he was not Boon. Nor was his companion—a tall, pugilistic-looking man with an interesting scar on his left cheek—Hawker. Both appeared incensed.

I tried a weak smile and mouthed a "sorry" but neither of these improbable clubbers seemed swayed by my contrition. The smaller one grabbed my shirt and yanked me close enough to smell the beer on his breath.

"Sorry!" I shouted again. "Thought you were someone else."

The ginger-haired man pinched my nose between his forefinger and thumb and forced me up on tiptoe. I squeezed shut my eyes in expectation of a thorough pummelling when my nose was suddenly released and I was able to place both feet flat on the ground. The men were pointing at me and laughing. I couldn't quite hear what they were saying but I could guess.

Don't blame me . . . Blame Grandpa!

Not for the first time, I felt a warm surge of gratitude for *Worse Things Happen at Sea.*

Somebody seized my hand and I was dragged away from my admirers. Barbara's face was close to mine and she was shouting. "Henry! Stop clowning about!"

She gave me a look which, if not actually outright contemptuous, at least bedded down somewhere in the lower reaches of derision. She strode back into the crowd and I was about to do the same when I felt an angry buzzing in my left pocket. I pulled out my phone and tried to answer, but conversation proved hopeless and I was forced in the end to retreat to a stall in the gents', where the music at least subsided to a tectonic rumble.

"Hello?" I said for what must have been the sixth or seventh time in a row.

"It's Abbey." She sounded infuriated.

"Sorry. Couldn't hear you out there."

"Henry, your friend's turning the flat upside down. She's

been in our bedrooms. She's chucked half the fridge out onto the floor. She's in the corridor right now, tapping the walls to see if they're hollow. What the hell's going on?"

I swallowed hard. "I know it must seem strange. But, please, let Miss Morning do whatever she needs. I'll make it up to you. I promise."

Abbey still sounded profoundly irritated but I thought I could detect at least the beginnings of a thaw. "Listen, about our conversation earlier. About Joe. I want you to know that I don't have any feelings for him any more." It was obvious that this wasn't easy for her to say. "I'm not on the rebound."

"Thanks," I said. "Thank you for saying that." Someone blundered into the toilet, bringing the antic roar of the dance floor with him.

"Where are you anyway? I thought you were working late."

"I'm at a club."

"You're where?" The thaw was retreating now and a new ice age had begun.

"In a club," I repeated. "Diabolism." Adding quickly: "It's for work."

"Well, who are you there with?"

"Just a colleague," I said, trying to sound meek and innocent.

Abbey's voice seethed with barely suppressed fury. "And what's her name?"

"It's complicated . . . But I suppose you could say I'm with Barbara."

"Unbelievable! We have one tiny disagreement and you're out with another woman."

"Abbey, please. It's really not like that."

"You'd better hope you've got a really, really good explanation for this." There was a strange shattering sound from the other end of the line. "Christ."

"What was that? What's happened?"

"Your friend. She's just put her foot through our TV."

"What?"

"Goodbye, Henry."

I suppose she must have put the phone down then.

I left the stall and stepped over to the sink. There was a man there, a Diabolism employee who squirted soap at my palms before guilt-tripping me into paying him a pound for the privilege.

"You chatting to your lady?" he asked, and I realised that he must have overheard the whole of my conversation. "You talking to your woman?"

"Yes," I said stiffly. "I suppose I was."

"Giving you grief, was she?"

"In a manner of speaking."

"You want my advice?"

"Not particularly," I said, but the man didn't seem to hear me.

"Forget her. Have a good time. What your lady don't know won't hurt her. What happens in Diabolism stays in Diabolism."

"Thanks for that," I said, and, just about resisting the urge to snatch back my pound, strode back out into the heart of the club.

THE HOURS WHICH FOLLOWED were amongst the longest of my life. I patrolled every inch of the dance floor. I scrutinised the faces of lip-locked couples. I stepped over a pool of vomit, drank three cocktails, two bottles of beer and a pint of tap water into which I'm certain I saw the barman spit. I tried to blend in by dancing.

It was late, well into the small hours of the morning, when I saw them. After the inaugural chords of Alice Cooper's

"School's Out" were greeted by whoops of delight from the regulars, I'd retreated to the bar, where I stood half-watching a couple of overenthusiastic young men whirl themselves around the firemen's poles. Then, caught in a lightning flash of strobe, I saw their faces and my insides turned to water. I started to move across the floor and searched around desperately for Barbara but she seemed to have disappeared. When I looked again at the pole, the Prefects had vanished, their places taken by a couple of paunchy men who I'd never seen before in my life. I was starting to wonder if I hadn't imagined it when someone slapped me hard on the back.

As I turned to face them the incessant music of the place seemed to recede into the background and I could hear them both perfectly, like voices in my head.

"Crikey! If it isn't old lamb chop," said Hawker.

"Hello, old man," said Boon.

"What are you doing here?" I said. "You promised you'd lead us to Estella."

"And we will, sir."

"Keep following, sir. We'll see you right."

"We're just having a bit of fun first."

"Only larks, sir."

"We're stretching our legs, sir."

"Getting a breath of fresh air."

"Going the scenic route, sir. Taking the dog for a walk and getting a dashed good yomp into the bargain."

"What are you talking about?" I asked.

"I'd get out now, sir, if I was you."

"I'd cut."

"Why? What are you planning?"

"We've just time for one more prank before the end, sir."

"Just time for a damned good bibbling."

"Don't look so worried, old man."

"Trust the Process, Mr. L."

"No!" I shouted. "Please—"

I was interrupted by a drunken quartet of middle-aged wo-men in nylon skirts and sweat-soaked blouses dancing past me in an inebriated attempt at a conga line. By the time they'd staggered past, the Prefects had vanished again.

I struggled through the crowd, looking for Barbara, but it was already too late.

A minute later, all the lights in the building went out.

And a minute after that, the sneezing began.

Blissed out on the contents of another syringe and half-succeeding in holding back the tides of his suspicion, there were times, as he hunkered down in the passenger seat of Mr. Streater's Nova, that the Prince of Wales felt almost content. Then, a moment later, everything would crowd back around him, he would remember the appalling details of the past few days and life became bleak and impossible again. This was the rhythm to which he was already growing accustomed, this awful see-saw of emotions, the heaven and hell of the drug called ampersand.

For a few minutes, he drifted into an uneasy sleep and had the dream again. When he woke, the man behind the wheel was swearing noisily at a passing motorist.

"Mr. Streater?"

"What?"

"Why is his grandfather to blame?"

"What are you on about?"

"I keep having this dream—"

"Christ." Streater tugged an Evening Standard from the car floor and tossed it over to him. "Do the crossword or something."

Arthur shuffled in his seat and stared blankly at the print but the words swam persistently away from him.

"How long will it be?" he asked.

One of Streater's hands was on the steering wheel, the other was engaged in teasing his hair back into its usual spikes. "What's that, chief?"

"How long before Leviathan is let loose?"

"Not long now. It's all going according to plan. The beauty of it is we hardly need to lift a finger. The enemy are doing all the hard stuff for us."

Arthur seemed to be having great difficulty forcing out his words. "And what will happen once it's freed?"

"Things are gonna get a lot more interesting around here. Take it from me, everything's gonna change for the better."

The prince groaned, flailed in his chair and gave in to despair again, sinking gratefully into darkness.

When he opened his eyes there were two men sitting in the back of Streater's car. One of them leant forward.

"Remember us, guv? DCI Virtue? DS Mercy?"

Both were eating kebabs and they held aloft their supper in congealed greeting. They smelt, as before, of grease and animal fat.

When the prince glanced up into the rearview mirror, he was somehow not completely surprised to see that Virtue and Mercy were not reflected there, that the spotty glass showed only empty seats.

"What's happening?" he asked numbly. "Where are we heading?"

"Nearly there," said Mr. Streater.

As Arthur peered out of the window, the lights of a tube station slithered by and the prince reflected sadly that he had ridden only twice on the city's underground system, both occasions engineered by his squad of experts in public relations. This seemed to him to be a pity since those places had always felt so welcoming and full of cheer.

Streater drove away from the main road and down a couple of side streets, eventually emerging in a small patch of concrete dappled with junk and debris, round the back of what appeared to be some kind of pub or nightclub. There were a couple of cars already there, a motorbike, an abandoned shopping trolley and a stack of soggy boxes. There was also the faint, disagreeable rumble of popular music.

"What are we doing?" Arthur asked plaintively. "What is this place?"

Virtue and Mercy rolled out the back of the car, short of breath even at this mild exertion, their exhalations fogging the air, their boulder bellies swaying in sweaty sympathy.

"I'm going into the club for a bit," Streater said. "Gonna do a bit of business. Gotta shift the last of the ampersand."

"The last of it?" Arthur despised himself for not being able to keep the panic from his voice. "Surely it hasn't run out?"

"Don't worry, chief. Not long now and everyone's gonna have more of the stuff than they know what to do with. That sound good to you?"

Poleaxed by another surge of pain and self-pity, the prince was unable even to gasp out a reply before the door was slammed in his face. Mr. Streater took out his key ring and pointed it at the car. All the locks on the doors slammed down. Arthur struggled with the handles to no effect.

His window was open a little and he called out to his tormentor: "Let me out."

Streater strode away but one of the fat men turned back.

"Stay here, son!"

The other one growled. "Keep an eye on the motor."

The next few hours passed like a fever dream, in a whirl of lucid hallucinations, fantasies of sexual envy and sporadic, doomed assaults at the Standard crossword.

The prince was interrupted twice—first by a gaggle of revellers teetering past, all of them dressed, improbably, in some strange parody of school dress. This Arthur shrugged off merely as ampersand phantasmagoria and returned to his descent.

The second time he was disturbed by the car being noisily unlocked. Virtue and Mercy clambered in the back, settled into their seats, greeted Arthur with a belch and began to munch anew on the remnants of their kebabs.

"Where's Streater?" Arthur asked.

The fat men gave their answer through mouths full of pita bread.

"Still inside," one of them said. "You know how he gets when he's shifting that stuff . . ."

The other one sniggered. "Birding it up."

After this, for a long time, there was just the sound of mastication—rhythmic chomping echoing in the prince's ears like the approaching stamp of some still-distant army—until:

"Oi oi!" Vince Mercy wore the look of a gambler whose horse has just romped home to an easy victory.

A young couple, dressed like the others in a lascivious parody of school uniform and in the latter stages of inebriation, had tottered up to the car, leant against the bonnet and proceeded to extravagantly grope one another. The girl's skirt rode up almost to her hips and the policeman was whooping his appreciation when the lady (who seemed to the prince to be placing herself at serious risk of hypothermia) pushed away her beau, stumbled a few steps and let fly a stream of lumpen vomit. Her companion merely laughed and hit her joshingly on the back, and as soon as she was done, the girl joined in the laughter. The pair wandered away into the night, spattered with puke yet still cackling.

In the back of Mr. Streater's Nova, Virtue and Mercy were laughing with them.

One of them jabbed a sausagey finger in Arthur's face. "Reminds me of your missus!"

"Way I hear it, she wouldn't even brush her teeth afterwards. She'd just get straight back down to it."

"Please . . . ," whimpered the prince. "Please don't . . ." But this only made the detectives laugh all the harder, their flabby bodies shaking with hilarity, halted only when someone smacked down hard on the car roof.

A couple of middle-aged men stood outside, both grinning wildly. They too were dressed as schoolboys.

"Good Lord!" one of them was shouting. "I know that face!"

"It's the best boy!" the other man called back. "It's teacher's pet."

Desperately, Arthur turned around to his companions, but, impossibly, both Virtue and Mercy had completely disappeared.

Arthur quivered in his seat, wondering what fresh indignity was about to be visited upon him, when there came a righteous cry from the other side of the parking lot.

"Abominations!" A dishevelled man in a brown raincoat was pointing a gun in the direction of the schoolboys. "Wretched pieces of putrescence!"

"I say, Boon," said one of the men in a tone of mild, pleasurable surprise, like one trainspotter to another on noticing a particularly uncommon diesel chugging towards them up the track. "Do you think that's us he's talking about?"

"I rather think it might be, Hawker. Anyway, isn't that old Barnaby?"

The grizzled man gestured at them with the gun. "Get on your knees!"

The schoolboys laughed. "Do you ever go back, sir?"

"Go back?" said the man they had referred to as Barnaby. "What do you mean?"

"Back to your old college, sir."

"Back to your alma mater."

"Don't suppose they'd let you in now, sir. Not after what happened."

"Cruel, wasn't it, Mr. B? The things they said."

"They must have really hated you, sir, to make up all those stories."

"And they were stories, weren't they, sir?"

"There wasn't any truth in them?"

Barnaby shouted: "Shut up! Just shut up, you lying monstrosities!" But even as Arthur slunk down in his seat, trying his best not to be noticed, he could see that the man was severely rattled, tripping and stammering over his words.

It was no great surprise, then, that as the schoolboys ambled over to the stranger he did nothing to halt their progress. They walked so close to him that they were almost touching, as though, under different circumstances, they might be on the precipice of a kiss, a tender and mutually respectful exchange of saliva.

"Still collecting stamps?" the little man shouted, and stamped brutally down on Barnaby's foot. This shouldn't have hurt all that much but Barnaby winced, gasped and staggered backwards, his arms windmilling uselessly in the air. Boon stamped down again whilst Hawker shouted out encouragement.

"Still collecting stamps, sir?"

"Still collecting stamps?"

The bigger of the two schoolboys grabbed the man by the ears and stretched them out. "Haven't seen you for ears and ears!" He cackled and the ginger-haired one joined in.

"Ears and ears and ears!"

Pinioned to his seat in terrified fascination, the prince none-theless found time to ensure that the doors really were locked.

Outside, as Barnaby fell to his knees, the schoolboys were laughing.

One of them thrust his hand into his blazer pocket, tugged out a fistful of black, faintly volcanic-looking powder and flung the lot of it in Barnaby's face. The man looked up in bafflement. His nose twitched cartoonishly for a second or so before he unleashed a gargantuan sneeze. Then another. Then, inevitably, another.

Barnaby mewled. "What have you done?"

The ginger-haired man released him, gave him a hearty slap on the back and bellowed: "Keep up, sir! It's sneezy powder."

The other one snickered in complicity. "Wizard wheeze!"

Barnaby was still sneezing. One of the schoolboys produced a grimy handkerchief and passed it to him. He clamped it to his face and sneezed and sneezed and sneezed. When the rag was taken from his face it was splattered with red.

"Please . . . ," he stammered. "Stop this . . ."

Blood had started to streak its way like lava from his nose, flowing across his lips, down his chin, dribbling onto the ground.

Hawker sniggered. "Why should we stop, sir, when we're having such fun?"

Barnaby's body had passed the point of total exhaustion and was barrelling towards shutdown. When he sneezed again, a pink strip of gristle was borne out on a sea of snot. "What's your plan?" he gasped, with helpless pleading in his eyes. "What is this leading towards?"

The schoolboys laughed. "Plan, sir?"

"Gosh, whatever makes you think we've got anything so hoity-toity as a plan?"

"This is our glory, sir!"

"Our bally glory!"

Then, with the Prefects cheering him on, Barnaby gave a final nasal eruption and toppled face-first onto the tarmac. He landed with the same crack a hardcover book makes when one bends it back too far and snaps the spine.

"Well, that sneezy powder certainly works, doesn't it, Boon?"

"Jolly well does, old chum. Most efficacious."

Boon turned towards the car. Arthur tried to slide further down into his seat but it was too late. The schoolboy grinned.

"Good evening to you, sir!"

Hawker looked across and raised his hand in salute. "What ho, Arthur!"

"Sorry we can't stay for a powwow but we're already running late."

" 'Fraid we've got to cut, old man."

"See you anon, sir!"

"Tinkety-tonk!"

The schoolboys ran into the building and Arthur was left alone in the car with only a dead body cooling on the tarmac for company.

Seconds later, the door to the warehouse clanked open and Mr. Streater emerged, accompanied by the opening chords of some pop track or other.

"School's out for summer . . ."

He stepped adroitly over the corpse and got into the car. "All right, chief?"

The prince wasn't listening. "They killed him . . . ," he murmured.

Streater shrugged. "Looks like."

"Your friends were useless. They vanished. They disappeared."

"Who are you talking about? What friends?"

"The detectives. Virtue and Mercy."

Streater smirked as he twisted the key in the ignition. "Never heard of them. I expect that'll be the ampersand, squire. Hallucinations come as standard. They're often personifications of whatever parts of yourself you keep repressed. I saw ballerinas, believe it or not. But I wouldn't worry about it if I was you." He reversed the car quickly on the tarmac, turned and headed swiftly out of Islington, towards home. "Whichever way you slice it—it's all going according to plan."

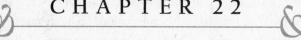

CHAPTER 22

I T WAS THE LAST NIGHT OF THE DIABOLISM CLUB.
After what unravelled there, I don't suppose anyone had
the stomach to carry on. The building was demolished, the
ground concreted over, and I understand that there are currently plans to build some kind of monument, a memorial or a
tombstone, on the spot where Diabolism used to stand.

It happened two minutes after Hawker's salute and sixty seconds after all the lights in the building had flickered off. When
someone eventually managed to get a couple of them going
again, it was already too late. The place had turned insane.
Adults dressed as children were screaming, sobbing, trying to
escape; hundreds of liquored-up revellers frightened for their
lives were charging for the doors in a stampede born of mortal
desperation. Every one of them was sneezing. There was a cacophony of nasal distress. The air was filled with saliva, snot
and tears, with mucus, spit and foam.

I was the lucky one. Immediately after the lights had gone
out and just before that black, volcanic dust had sprayed down
from the sprinkler system, I felt a soft hand clamp itself over my
mouth and another apply itself firmly to my back and steer me
towards the exit, jostling nimbly through the mêlée.

Later, I learnt that fifty-four people were hospitalised just trying to reach the door.

"What happened?" I gasped, once we were outside and Barbara had taken her hand away from my mouth.

The Directorate's hunter raised a hand in her usual semaphore for silence. The weedy bouncer was still standing there, petrified and helpless, as his club vomited up its clientele.

Barbara snapped: "Call the emergency services. Tell them they have a disaster." The man nodded stupidly and obeyed.

Whilst I did my best to calm a young woman whose nose had already started to spurt blood, Barbara, brisk and unflappable, spoke into her earpiece.

"Sir?"

The voice of Mr. Dedlock echoed in my head. "I trust you have good news." He paused. "What is that rumpus?"

Barbara's was a calm, still voice amongst the chaos. "The Prefects appear to have sprayed everyone inside the building with some sort of sneezing powder, sir."

"Why on earth would they want to do that?"

"Why do little boys do anything, sir? For fun. For larks."

"Where are those knobble-kneed bastards now?"

Barbara took out her PDA. "I can see them, sir. We can track them."

"Then get after them!"

"People are dying here," I said.

The old man was incensed. "If you don't do your job, this city as we know it will cease to exist."

"I'll get the car," said Barbara. "We'll bring them in."

"Do it." A final snarl from Dedlock, then merciful silence in my head.

Barbara ran out of sight to get the car before I could think of anything to say.

I did my best to soothe the girl in my arms, tried to staunch the blood, told her to breathe deeply and think about not sneezing. After a while, it seemed to calm her, so I did what I could for some of the other victims until, at last, a fleet of ambulances blared onto the scene. I was easing a man whose body was close to rupturing into the arms of a paramedic when Barbara pulled me roughly to my feet. Her trench coat was back, billowing about her in the breeze.

"We're leaving. Now."

"But these people—"

"There's nothing you can do for them."

"Where's the car? Where's Barnaby? Where's Jasper?"

"The car is burning. Barnaby's dead. And Jasper's gone."

Already, I was growing accustomed to Barbara's delivery of bad news—catastrophe snapped out in telegraphic monosyllables. "Burning? Dead? Gone?" I asked, but she was already running. I left the paramedics to do their job and sprinted after her. "Barbara!"

She pelted on, ignoring me. There was a crackling in my ear and I heard the voice of Dedlock. "What's happening?"

Barbara: "We're tracking them."

"You mean you've let them get away?"

"The club's in chaos. It masked their escape."

Dedlock snapped some final, bitter instruction and broke the connection. The two of us dashed into the darkness of the city. Soon my breathing was ragged and I had an agonising stitch in my side but Barbara, sprinting into the distance, appeared quite unaffected. I was about to lose sight of her completely when she gave a yelp of frustration.

When I caught up, she had stopped short and was staring at her PDA in furious disbelief.

I panted. "What's happened?"

She struck the machine hard. "They've vanished."

"What?"

"Disappeared. Dropped off the map." Her shoulders sagged at the news and for a second or two I thought I caught a glimpse of the real Barbara, trapped behind that immaculate façade. "They're playing with us."

Once I had sufficiently recaptured my breath to form whole sentences again, I said: "You saved me. I ought to thank you."

"No need."

"How come you weren't affected? By the sneezing powder?"

"My respiratory system is vastly superior to yours. I can go three hours without having to draw breath."

"Remarkable," I said, even now incredulous. "And Mr. Jasper did all this just by giving you a pill?"

Barbara nodded. "Despite his considerable personal failings, Jasper is the most brilliant chemist of his generation. The Directorate takes only the best. The prodigies. The wunderkinder." Her eyes passed over me as though she'd suddenly remembered something. "And you, of course, Henry."

She walked on.

"Where are we going?"

"We're tracking the Domino Men. We're following their spoor."

"But we've lost them! This is pointless."

Unspeaking, she strode ahead.

THE LONG NIGHT HAD TURNED into early morning and the first glimmerings of dawn had just begun to dilute the greyness of the sky when we chanced upon a side street filled with parked taxis clustered around an all-night café like piglets at a teat. We had been walking for what felt like hours and I suggested to Barbara that we at least take the opportunity to get a coffee. I had even begun to wonder whether she required sustenance at all in the traditional human sense, so I was surprised

when she quickly concurred with something approaching gratitude in her voice.

I'd rolled down my trousers and ditched the old school tie so
that when we walked inside, I looked normal again—or at least
able to pass for it. The place was filled with cab drivers amongst
whom there appeared to be little or no camaraderie. They sat
in their ones or twos, morosely clasping plastic cups, scanning
the sports pages of yesterday's newspapers or gazing dead eyed
at the smeary bleakness of the Formica table tops. Even the appearance of Barbara in their midst occasioned little more than
a rustling of tabloids, a weary leer and a single, pathetic wolf-
whistle which shrivelled into nothing after my companion's
gaze flicked across the culprit. I got us a couple of coffees and
we sat together at a table by the window.

"Do you remember when I started at the office?" she said,
after we'd both swallowed a mouthful or two of what turned
out to be surprisingly decent coffee.

All of a sudden, her voice sounded different and I experienced a stab of hope. "Barbara?"

A brief flash of smile. "Barbara's always here, Henry. Even
if it doesn't seem that way. But I asked you a question. Do you
remember my first day?"

"Of course."

"You were kind to me. You showed me the file room, that
sweaty woman in the basement. You introduced me to Peter
Hickey-Brown."

I pushed aside my memories of everything which had happened since then—from my grandfather's collapse to the carnage at Diabolism—and I ventured a smile. "God, that man's a
prat. Do you remember—he tried to impress you by naming all
the gigs he goes to?"

Barbara tried to laugh at the memory. It was a painful thing
to hear. A forced rasp, a throaty hiss, a mechanical chatter.

"I'm glad you remember," I said softly.

"It's strange." She sipped her coffee. "There are parts of Barbara's life I can recall so clearly. Her father—my father—taking me to church on Christmas Eve. Midnight mass. The way his hand felt in my mine. But I can't remember if Barbara ever kissed anyone. I can't remember what happened to her after she went to lunch with Mr. Jasper."

"I'm so sorry."

"I don't know how I can explain this to you. Somehow my memories are also infused with those of the woman they call Estella. She had such a life, Henry. She'd avert national disaster and scarcely blink. But I'm not either of them now. Not fully Estella. Nor fully Barbara."

I gazed at her, partly in admiration, partly in fear. "Jasper seems to think you're some kind of superhuman."

She snorted. "You know what I think I am?" she asked. "Honestly?"

"Go on."

"I think I'm a cul-de-sac. I think I'm a dead end." She got to her feet. "And I think I need to try to pee."

As Barbara walked into the back of the café I suddenly remembered something. I fumbled for my phone and punched out a text message to Abbey.

So sorry. Been a horrible night.

Can't wait to see you again.

I pressed send although I didn't expect a reply for several hours.

Barbara returned from the bathroom. I tried to draw her back into a discussion of the transformation which had overtaken her but it seemed that our moment of intimacy had melted away as quickly as it had arrived. She asked if I'd like another coffee. I said yes, and whilst she was ordering at the counter my phone shuddered in my pocket to announce the arrival of a text message.

> So glad you're ok. Can't wait to see you too.
> Sorry I didn't tell you about Joe.
> I missed you holding me tonight.

Then, best of all, the letter X repeated three times.

"Girlfriend?" Barbara asked, setting another coffee in front of me.

"Maybe," I said. "Not sure, to be honest."

"Is it the girl we met? I mean—that Barbara met. Your landlady?"

I nodded.

"Have a little happiness together, Henry. Grab it while you still can. You're lucky." Barbara stretched herself out felinely. "I know that's not for me."

"Surely," I said, "looking like you do . . ."

She just stared ahead. "You know that they fought over me . . ."

"Who fought over you?"

"Dedlock and your grandfather. I can't quite recall the details. Not yet. But I know that there was a struggle. Backstabbing. Treachery. Nothing changes. Jasper wanted me, too. He tried to touch me."

"Jasper?"

"I say only that he tried, Henry. He made the attempt. That's all you need to know."

"And Barnaby? What about him?"

"Barnaby's dead," she said flatly. "They killed him."

"Who?"

Rather disgustingly, she spat into her coffee. "You know their names."

Suddenly, mercifully, Barbara's PDA bleeped for attention. She seized it and grinned. Two small spots of black had reappeared on the screen.

"Gotcha."

I felt a paroxysm of fear. "Where are they?"

"Oh, very good." Barbara laughed, and this time it sounded almost natural. But there was no happiness in her laugh, no genuine mirth. "Very droll."

"Barbara," I said softly. "Where are the Prefects?"

"You know the address. We both do. They're at One Twenty-five Fitzgibbon Street." Now Barbara's laughter sounded a hairs-breadth from tears. "They're at our old office."

By the time we got to the Civil Service Archive Unit, it was almost nine o'clock and a stream of grey-faced men and women was slouching despairingly into work. The safety officer, Philip Statham, walked straight past and didn't even recognise me.

Barbara was outlining the situation to Dedlock. His voice crackled in our ears. "What are they doing in there? What the hell are they doing?"

"I think this is it, sir," Barbara said. "I think they're here to find Estella."

"You know something?"

"Nothing concrete. Just ghosts."

Engrossed in their conversation, I slowly became aware that someone was shouting my name.

"Henry!" Miss Morning was walking along the pavement towards us, clutching a carrier bag. Strangely, she appeared to be smiling.

The croak of Dedlock in my head: "Who is it?"

Barbara told him.

"What does she want?" he spat.

Miss Morning reached us, still brandishing her plastic bag like she'd won it at bingo. "Tell that unhappy old man that I have our salvation in this bag. Are the Domino Men inside?"

"Yes," we said, pretty much simultaneously.

"Thought so."

I asked her why.

"You think your job was an accident, Henry? You think anything in your whole life has been left to chance?" She took the carrier bag out from under her arm. There was something heavy inside which she unwrapped with the reverential care of a priest opening a fresh delivery of wafers. "Your grandfather built this."

What was in the carrier bag was an impossibility. Shaped like a revolver and constructed with perfect intricacy, it was formed entirely of glass, glinting in the early morning sun, the product of a technology so far out of step with contemporary thought that it almost qualified as science fiction.

"He hid it in your flat," Miss Morning said. "I discovered it behind your television."

"So I've heard," I muttered. "What does it do?"

The old lady smiled again. "It's going to stop the Prefects."

"How will it do that?"

"Your grandfather promised it would work. But Henry?"

"Yes?"

"If anything goes wrong in there. If we get separated. Trust the Process, won't you?"

"What?"

"When the time comes, you'll know what I mean. Just promise me—trust the Process."

With impeccable timing, my mobile phone began to trill.

When I saw who it was, I think I might actually have groaned aloud. I turned away from the others, hit the answer key and sighed: "Hello, Mum."

"Gordy's a shit. He's a shit like all the rest."

"Are you still in Gibraltar?" I asked gently.

"God, no," she said. "Back home now, thank Christ. Jesus, what a disaster. The man's an absolute bastard."

"Not a good holiday, then?"

"It was a catastrophe. His only topic of conversation was his exes . . ."

Barbara tapped me on the shoulder. "Time to go in now."

"Mum?" I said. "I'm sorry. But I've got to get to work. I'll call you later, OK? We can catch up then. Have a natter."

Mum gave a protractedly theatrical sniff. "If a day at the office means more to you than a conversation with your mother—"

"Bye, Mum." I finished the call and turned back to Barbara.

Miss Morning, still holding that insanely improbable weapon, had begun to walk towards the office, tottering heroically onwards in little-old-lady steps. We easily caught up.

I spoke quietly so that only Barbara would hear me. "Something I've never understood . . . if Estella's in there—the real Estella—then what do we do when we find her?"

"It's not going to be nice," she said. "Not nice at all." Barbara's face had turned chalk-pale and she seemed to move more mechanically than ever, propelled forward by some irresistible force. "I'm afraid we're going to have to kill her."

Slimy with sweat, oppressed by spasms which shook the whole of his body and struggling to swallow the lake of bile in his throat, the next king of England crouched in the passenger seat of Mr. Streater's Nova and whimpered about the end of the world.

The driver's gaze passed casually over the prince, his voice a twitch of disdain. "What's up with you?"

Outside, a gaggle of girls, belt-skirted, orange-peel-skinned and mountainously stilettoed, lurched and reeled along the pavement. Streater honked the car horn, at which one of the revellers raised her middle finger in contemptuous salute.

The driver sniggered. "Always liked a woman with a bit of attitude. With a wiggle in her walk and steel in her arse. You're the same, aren't you, chief? You like a girl who knows what she wants and how to get it. Your missus is like that. Just a shame these days it's not you she wants."

The prince whimpered again, a pitiful, helpless threnody, like the sound a puppy makes on catching a glimpse of the veterinarian's knife and guesses, too late, what is to come.

"Up for some tunes, chief? Something to blow away the cobwebs? Something to get us in the mood?" Streater's left hand drifted away from the steering wheel towards the glove compartment, clicked it expertly open and unleashed an avalanche of old cassettes. Arthur moaned and Streater noted, with something akin to satisfaction, that his charge had actually begun to drool. He tossed a handful of tapes onto Arthur's lap.

The prince stared dumbly down at them and saw that they were all identical, all labelled with the same short word.

"What is this . . . ," he began, squinting at what was written in front of him as though he was not quite certain of its reality, "What is this . . . Boner?"

Streater grinned. "That's my old band, chief."

"Band? You're a musician?"

"Played bass. Used to do a lot of gigs. How else do you think I met Pete?" Streater plucked out a tape and thrust it into the mouth of the car's cassette player. "Here we go. Let us know what you think."

The prince groaned again, Mr. Streater pressed play and the car was filled with the beehive roar of static. There was a moment's silence, followed not, as Arthur had expected, by the cacophony of modern music but by a clipped, strangulated voice, a masterclass in received pronunciation.

"Good morning, Arthur."

At the sound of it, the prince wriggled up in his seat, wiped his mouth and felt the distant pull of lucidity. "Mother?" he said.

He turned to Mr. Streater, intending to ask the meaning of this strange recording, only to see that the blond man was rhythmically tapping his fingers on the steering wheel and humming, a little discordantly, as he drove, as though he was joining in with some chorus or refrain which the prince was unable to hear.

The tape went on. "Of late, I have been thinking a good deal about the first stalking party your father took you on. You must have been terribly small. Six, perhaps, or seven."

The eyes of the prince moistened at this, for he knew what was coming, knew with what he was about to be confronted.

"You seemed so eager for the adventure. I recall that for once I felt a small measure of pride in you—that warm maternal glow which one is often told that ladies in my position are expected to feel. But then, as usual, you lived down to our expectations. You came home early and in tears. You had walked out with the rest of them but when the moment came for the belly of the kill to be slit open and for you, as the most junior member of the hunt, to receive the honour of having its blood laid across your forehead, you began to cry. You mewed as though you were still a baby. You refused to be blooded then and have spurned it ever since. That awful woman you married has done nothing to encourage you. You have turned out so spineless, Arthur, that I saw no choice but to place you in Mr. Streater's care. I only hope that he has prised some semblance of manhood from you."

Mr. Streater winked.

"It saddens me that you are to be the only heir of the House of Windsor. I suspect that by the time you hear this, Leviathan will be on his way at last. I do hope you are blooded in time. I pray you are man enough to welcome our saviour and do what needs to be done. I only hope that at long last you can make me proud."

The tape spooled to a finish and Arthur slumped miserably in his seat. "I never liked the sight of blood," he said at last. "Why is that so wrong of me?"

Streater laughed. "Tough titty, chief. Gonna be a lot of it about in the next few days."

"What do you mean by that?"

"I mean that Leviathan's gonna make a few changes. A few improvements to the city. I mean that you're expected to help out."

The car slowed down, almost home now, back in the familiar alley of the Mall, the Nova processing with high seriousness along the wide stone channel. At last, the blond man pulled up outside Clarence House.

"Get out, chief. I'm not stopping. There's still some shit I've gotta sort."

Arthur groped for the door handle and, like a one-night stand on the morning after, stepped unsteadily, dazed and humiliated, from the car.

"Oi!" Streater had wound down his window and was leering out of it like a lecherous cabbie hoping for a tip. "I've got a couple of things for you."

"What?"

"Here's a little pick-me-up." He shoved a shrink-wrapped syringe into Arthur's hands. "And here's something else. Just in case." He shoved an object into the prince's hands and, too late, Arthur saw what it was, caught the glint of dawn light on gun barrel, and felt nauseous at the sight of it, green with disgust.

"I don't want a gun."

"Just take it, chief. Remember what your mum said? You've gotta be blooded. And you might need it. What if you see something you don't like? What if you're confronted with the truth?"

The window hiccoughed upwards. Streater revved the engine and, without so much as a wave of goodbye, turned the car and hot-rodded back into the city.

Stowing into his jacket pocket the accessories of a criminality from which, only a few days earlier, he would have believed himself completely removed, Arthur trudged indoors. Servants were already up and about, doing whatever it is that servants do— wiping, scraping and polishing, making ready, making clean. As the prince passed by, they stopped, looked down at the ground and said nothing. They asked no questions. Discretion had been bred into them and even at the sight of their master reduced to the status of a bum, all of them held their tongues.

Overcome with desire, helpless with craving, the prince lurched into an alcove and, with a grim facility which would have horrified anyone who had ever loved him, injected himself with another hit of ampersand. He sighed in dark delight. It was only when he was finished that he noticed that an under-butler was standing opposite, his eyes still cast feudally towards the ground. Making a stab at dignity, flailing towards decorum and falling horribly short, the prince rolled down his sleeve and tottered past.

The under-butler's face burned with shame. Just as the prince was almost out of sight, he said: "Sir?"

Slowly, the prince turned around, dumbstruck by the insolence.

"I'm sorry, sir," said the man. "But I have to say something."

"What?" hissed the prince.

"Fight it, sir! You have to fight it!"

The prince stared at the servant. No doubt he had passed the man a thousand times, but his face was entirely unfamiliar to him. The fellow had a strange, whiskery moustache and an air of almost feline sleekness.

"What . . . ," he began. "What did you say?"

"I said you've got to fight it," said the under-butler again. "For the sake of us all, you have to snap out of this."

The man backed away and disappeared, his courage evidently all used up.

Arthur tried not to think too hard about this strange interlude and lurched on towards his quarters.

He heard the sounds before he even reached his door. Animal noises. Grunts and groans. Yells and screeches. He paused outside. Had he been mistaken? No, there they were, the sounds of passion, almost comical in their volume and excess. There were squealed suggestions of the most indecent nature. There were hoarse commands and whimpered pleasures. The prince heard his oldest friend yelp in delight and his lover moan in delirious abandonment.

As ampersand gurgled through his synapses, slimed down his

nervous system and surged along his bloodstream, the prince felt the weight of the gun in his pocket and knew what he had to do.

He opened the door and walked inside. Who knows what he saw behind that door, what grotesquerie, what lurid pornography, what leering simulacra.

You might reasonably expect at this point, when the drug ampersand had almost completely destroyed his capacity for reason, for us to tell you about a couple of gunshots, to be told about the ferocious whip-crack of that revolver echoing around the corridors of Clarence House.

That wasn't to be. Instead, two minutes later, the prince simply re-emerged, as inside the sounds of romance went on unabated.

Only one thing had changed in this picture. A single, unremarkable detail which none of us could have predicted but which immediately made everything different.

There was a small grey cat strolling by his side.

In the corridor, two old acquaintances stood waiting. Each held a pasty in his hand—half-eaten, their glistening insides dripping onto the floor, where they clung glutinously to the plush strands of carpet.

"Evening, cock!" crowed Detective Chief Inspector George Virtue.

"Wotcha!" bugled Detective Sergeant Vince Mercy.

"Why are you here?" Arthur asked.

One of the fat men wiped his meat chop of a hand across his nose. "Bottled it, didn't you, scout?"

"Couldn't go through with it, could you?"

"Wassock."

"Toss-pot."

"Nonce."

"You gonna stand about and let people laugh at you?"

"You gonna let them take the piss?"

"Be a man, guv."

"Get yourself blooded."

Arthur stared, a little more understanding inching into his consciousness. "What did you say?"

"Blooded, guv."

"That's what he said. Get yourself blooded."

The prince stared at them both, suddenly hopeful, suddenly aware of the possibility for redemption. "Gentlemen?" he said, sounding for the first time in days something like his old self.

"Yeah?" Mercy asked through a mouth of semi-digested mulch.

"I don't believe you're real."

"Oh, that's gutting, mate."

Arthur went on. "I can't believe what I'm hearing from that room. Or what I saw in there either. It's an illusion, isn't it? It's a trick being played on me by ampersand."

"Don't know what you're on about, pal."

The prince glared at them. "Why?" he asked. "Why do you want me to kill my wife?"

"What's the matter with you?" Virtue shouted. "There's a bloke in there porking your missus and you're wasting time yammering with us."

Deliberately, Arthur turned away from them (behind him, their cries went on—"Do it, you arsehole!" "Pull the bleeding trigger!") and, his gun lowered, went back into the bedroom.

As the ampersand-filter descended from his eyes, he saw the truth of it—Laetitia on the bed, alone and fast asleep, curled up under the covers, the picture of innocence and chastity (though perhaps looking a little heavier than Arthur could remember having seen her before).

Back outside, the detectives Virtue and Mercy had disappeared. The prince fell to his knees in relief, wracked with sobs at how close he had come. At first he didn't even notice what had walked in beside him and begun to nuzzle against his legs.

Arthur Windsor wiped his eyes, dabbed the snot from his nose and, miraculously, managed a kind of smile.

The grey cat looked up at him and purred.

"You again," whispered the prince.

The cat purred, seemed to smile and stalked closer to the downed prince, pleased at what had been averted, knowing the dangers which still lay ahead but ready at last for the endgame.

The prince fell back upon the floor as the cat came closer. He was about to say something more, to offer the animal some thanks, some further words of gratitude, when exhaustion washed over him and everything faded away. The last thing he saw was a feline face, small and grey, filled with wisdom and concern, opening its mouth as though it was about to speak and, at long last, explain it all.

CHAPTER 23

A T 9:01 A.M. THAT TUESDAY MORNING, MR. DEREK
Mackett, who had dedicated the great majority of his
working life to safeguarding the Civil Service Archive Unit,
waved two of the most notorious killers in British history past
reception without even asking for their ID. It was the only
blot on a career which (with its 100 percent attendance record
and five-time commendation for loyal service) stood otherwise
unblemished.

Mackett was never able to forgive himself for the over-
sight. How could he have failed to stop two people who
transparently had no business in a civil service building without getting them to sign in for guest passes? How could he
have blithely hurried them through, even going so far as to
speed them on their way with a gruffly avuncular smile and a
friendly nod? Why did he think that there was nothing at all
suspicious in two grown men dressed as schoolboys wandering
into an office block? Why couldn't he have smelt the blood-
lust on them?

The counsellors were good with him, awfully decent and
kind. They told him that the Prefects were able to warp per-
ception, that they were masters of deceit and that Mr. Mackett

was far from the only person responsible for what happened. But Derek took his job very seriously indeed, and as far as he was concerned, the buck stopped with him.

I heard that he died last month, not so much of a broken heart as of fatally punctured professional pride.

AT 9:02 A.M., THE PREFECTS were in the lift, chittering excitedly to one another, ascending towards the uppermost level. Theoretically, there should still exist CCTV footage of their journey, but you might not be altogether surprised to learn that the tapes for that day show only electric snow, that they are filled end to end with the miserable vacuum of static.

AT 9:03 A.M., HAWKER AND BOON arrived at the tenth floor and the carnage began.

Their first victim was Philip Statham, the safety officer. He was leant over his desk, engrossed in a book of sudoku, when Hawker and Boon strolled up to him, sliced away the front of his fan, deftly switched it on and pressed Mr. Latham's face into the spinning blades. Blood on the puzzles. Desktop dappled, in a hideous kind of artistry, with red.

A secretary by the name of Emily Singer saw this happen. I understand that she has never fully recovered from the experience and insists, to the ever-diminishing patience of her husband, that she is unable to sleep with the lights out. On that Tuesday, however, Mrs. Singer showed some presence of mind. She screamed as loudly as she knew how, smashed the fire alarm with its little plastic hammer and dashed pell-mell for the exit. This should have meant that the population of the entire building began an automatic evacuation onto the street, but for some reason the mechanism malfunctioned, failing to make any sound at all. A satisfactory explanation for this has yet to be advanced.

Singer escaped to the exit but many of her colleagues were not so lucky. They were corralled against the photocopier by the relentless storm of Hawker and Boon, who moved amongst them with penknives flashing and teeth shining, their eyes bright with the reaper's joy on the first day of harvest.

"What ho!" said Boon, as he forced the hand of a Timothy Clapshaw (who I vaguely remember and who I think had something to do with accounts) into a paper shredder.

"Top of the morning to you!" said Hawker, energetically staple-gunning the hands of a brusque PA called Sandra Pullman to the surface of her boss's desk. "I don't suppose any of you fine fellows have seen Estella?"

Anyone who could speak protested that they had never heard of the woman, let alone knew where she was.

Hawker shook his head in disappointment. "That's a dashed shame."

Boon heartily concurred. "If you'd only tell us, Hawker and I might think about giving all this up."

"Too true, my old tup-weasel. We'd throw in the towel."

Someone from HR whimpered that no-one knew what they were talking about.

"She's here somewhere," Hawker brayed. "I can jolly well nose her."

"Just so, old top. But at least we can have a bit of fun while we're looking."

At 9:08 a.m., Hawker and Boon moved down to the ninth floor just as Miss Morning, Barbara and myself were attempting to fight our way up towards them. On the stairwell, wading against the fleeing masses, I bumped into Peter Hickey-Brown.

"Christ," he said. "What the hell are you doing here?"

"Hello, Peter," I said.

He sounded close to hyperventilating. At the time I assumed that he was simply overwhelmed by panic.

"Just leave," I snapped. "Run for your life and don't look back."

Hickey-Brown gave a limp, lolling kind of nod, pushed past us and skipped girlishly down the stairs.

"They're on the top floor," Barbara shouted. "The sooner we can intercept them, the fewer people need to die."

I realised that someone was missing. "Where's Miss Morning?"

AND SO IT WAS that at 9:12 A.M., on the eighth floor of the Civil Service Archive Unit, Hawker and Boon ran, almost literally, into an old acquaintance.

Miss Morning stood before them—my grandfather's glass gun held outstretched in both hands, her gnarled little finger curled around its crystalline trigger, her arms shaking only slightly, trembling almost imperceptibly in the face of their blazered malevolence.

OF COURSE, I CAN ONLY take an educated guess at what happened next.

"Hawker," the old lady said softly. "Boon. You haven't aged a day."

The ginger-haired man grinned. "Whereas you, old girl, look absolutely hideous."

"Miss Morning . . . ," Boon said heavily. "Didn't you ever feel rather left out? Everyone else had a made-up name and you had to get by with the one you were born with."

"That was my choice," Miss Morning said, unflinching. "They offered me Havisham but I chose to keep my own."

"Course you did." Boon winked. "Course you did, old thing."

Hawker mimed the stroking of a long imaginary beard. "Itchy beard!" he shouted. "Itchy beard!"

Then Boon was doing it, too, yelping out the same esoteric phrase. "Itchy beard! Itchy beard!"

Miss Morning was fed up. "Behave!" She pointed the gun towards Hawker's head. "You know who built this. You know what it can do." She pulled back the safety and the device made a splintering click.

Suddenly, Boon looked pitiful and afraid, more child-like than ever. "Please don't pull the trigger, Miss Morning."

"Oh, please don't do it, miss."

"It's really going to sting."

"Pretty please!"

Without a second's hesitation, without so much as a shiver of conscience or doubt, the old woman shoved the weapon hard against Hawker's head and pulled the trigger.

The Prefect collapsed wailing to the floor, screeching in melodramatic agony. For almost a minute, Miss Morning was actually fooled. For a while there, she actually believed she might have won.

HAWKER SAT UP WITH a big grin on his face and mimed a little wave. He and Boon fell about laughing.

"That should have stopped you," Miss Morning muttered. "He promised. He promised it would cut you down."

She was still protesting as Hawker and Boon advanced upon her, their bodies visibly quivering at their own incorrigible naughtiness.

"Nothing stops us, old girl," Hawker said, as he hoisted the pensioner into the air by her throat. "You really ought to know that by now."

Boon had his penknife drawn in anticipation of the coup de grâce. "You silly sausage."

AT 9:15 A.M., we found them, crouched above her like starving dogs over a savaged rabbit. I'll always be able to remember the sight of it, the degradations they put that woman through at the end. There are some things it's impossible to ever truly forget—they imprint themselves on your retina and stay there, refusing to budge, like a ghost image on an old computer monitor.

At the sight of me, the Prefects beamed. "Henry!"

"Lamb chop!"

"What have you done?" I shouted.

Boon laughed, his hands extravagantly dripping blood onto the carpet tiles. "Just having a bit of fun, old fruit."

"Just larking about."

"Where's Estella?" Barbara strode towards the Prefects, as coldly implacable as ever and apparently unaffected by the death of Miss Morning. Certainly, she stepped over her corpse as though it was of no more significance to her than a sandbag.

Hawker and Boon seemed not in the least intimidated, although I noticed something unexpected in their reaction, an expression on their faces I'd never seen there before and which I suppose I'd thought I never would. It was curiosity.

"I say," said Hawker, as Boon let out an amused whistle. "What the Dickens are you?"

Barbara glared. "Where's Estella?"

"No idea," said Boon. "The old man only gave us the address. But come here anyway, you wonderful thing. We ought to have a bit of a chinwag."

Warily, Barbara walked over to him. He whispered something in her ear, some poisonous lie or vicious half-truth, some dangerous arrangement of words.

I knelt beside the mutilated body of Miss Morning. Although she was dead, her eyes hadn't stopped staring wildly towards the ceiling and her pupils still seemed engorged with fear. The only thing I could think to do was to close them and, beneath my breath, murmur something halfway between an apology and a benediction.

"Henry?"

Barbara was shouting at me and the Prefects were gone.

"What did they want?" I stumbled to my feet. "What did they whisper to you?"

"Not now, Henry." Remarkably, she smiled. "I've been a fool. I know where Estella is."

Barbara ran from the room and I had no choice but to follow and abandon poor Miss Morning where she lay.

Only then did I realise where we were heading and who would be waiting for us. Certain things were starting to become clear. We were running towards the basement, you see. Running towards the mail room.

I had begun to appreciate the complexity of my grandfather's design. How carefully he had arranged my life! With what diligence had he nudged the playing pieces of my existence into place. Now I understood why, in those long chats in his lounge, as both of us sat rapt over the newspapers, he had been so adamant that I should look at the flat in Tooting Bec, why he had encouraged me with such avidity to apply to the Civil Service Archive Unit.

I finally understood who was waiting for us in the basement and why the old bastard had sent me here to watch over her. I had even begun to chew over the significance of those operations that he had paid for me to undergo as a child.

But I saw also that his plans had not, in his absence, unrolled themselves altogether smoothly. There had been unanticipated flaws, human errors, problems it would have been impossible for him to have foreseen.

Problems like Peter Hickey-Brown.

THE BUILDING WAS COMPLETELY empty now and the terrified employees of the Archive Unit had fled into the streets. There was only one exception, one loyal worker still at her post. The fat woman, the sweaty one. When we reached the mail room, she was exactly where she always was, sorting through files with her usual sluggish roboticism. At the sight of us, she grunted in greeting.

I walked over and looked into her sweaty blancmange of a face, her features swollen and distended by decades of overeating—and at last I saw the truth of it.

"Estella?" I said.

The woman was in pain. Something was inside her, pushing and tugging and clawing to get out. Something trapped—like a genie in a bottle. Like a spider in a jar.

The door opened behind us and there was an unexpected voice at the far end of the room. "Hello, Henry. Hello, Barbara."

It was Peter Hickey-Brown—dazed, hoarse and uncharacteristically emotional. "I knew you'd be coming for me," he breathed.

Barbara seemed curiously unflummoxed even by this latest contortion of events. "Do you know, I thought it might be you?"

Hickey-Brown walked across the room, heading for the woman.

"Stay away," Barbara warned.

"Please," Peter wheedled. "Please. Just let me touch her one more time."

"Did you enjoy touching her?"

"Of course," said my old boss. "Of course, I did."

"I have a . , . sympathy with this woman," Barbara said. "I know you got off on it."

"Hey," said Hickey-Brown. "Am I denying it?" He giggled. "Oh, but she tasted so fine. Finger-licking *good*."

I cleared my throat. "Would there be any chance of an explanation?"

"Leviathan has been engineering its own escape," Barbara said. "The beast has been changing this woman's body, tampering with her DNA. It's done something to her sweat—given it the properties of a hallucinogen. Ever since Hickey-Brown discovered this he's been harvesting it, replicating it, selling it on. He's been dealing in Estella's sweat and calling it ampersand."

My former line manager shrugged. "I go to a lot of gigs."

I stared at him. "How the hell did you manage that? I mean, what on earth were you doing to discover it in the first place?"

"She was so delicious," he said simply. "I couldn't resist."

Unable to restrain himself, like a pastry addict passing a trolley of cream buns, he made a dash across the room, his fingers outstretched, clawing at the air, grasping for the prize. I suppose he wanted to touch Estella again, one last time. The need, the hunger in him, outpaced all rationality, any last remaining strand of common sense.

He was nowhere near the woman when Barbara flung him

aside with as little effort as it takes you or me to bat away a wasp with one of the Sunday supplements. Hickey-Brown crashed to the floor and I heard a loud, final crack as his neck broke, his gig-going days gone for good.

Barbara's attention shifted to the fat woman—the original Estella, the mould from which she was made. She strode over to her, crouched down and, in a weirdly maternal set of gestures, stroked her cheek, smoothed back her hair and cooed.

Estella gazed up at this weird, impossible reflection of herself with utter bewilderment in her sunken eyes.

"What have they done to us?" Barbara asked. "What the hell have they done?"

ESTELLA BEGAN TO COUGH. It started as a simple clearing of her throat and graduated to something hacking and painful before becoming a terrible convulsion as all the phlegm and mucus within her rattled towards an exit.

"Barbara?" We both of us just stood there, watching the beast inside tear that unfortunate woman apart.

Barbara was in shock. "You have to kill her," she said slowly.

"Me?"

"If you don't, then Leviathan will get loose. The city will be overrun. The casualties will be without number."

The woman coughed and wheezed and spluttered. She shuddered and shook and she was rent apart.

"I can't," I said. "I can't do it."

Barbara produced a slender knife, tailor-made for gutting, and thrust its handle into my hand, not saying a word.

Then—something extraordinary. Something impossible and fantastic in a day already characterised by both.

What came first was the smell (so pungent that it drowned even the stale sock odour of the basement), the sudden scent of fireworks coupled with the lingering aftertaste of sherbet dip. It was followed by a violent disturbance in the air, a bewildering rush of colours—blue, pink, brown and black.

Finally, impossibly, the Prefects rippled into existence, materialising on either side of Estella.

Boon pursed his lips and tutted. "Nasty cough."

"Sounds like she's got a frog in her throat," said Hawker.

"Awfully big frog!"

"More like a toad!"

They cackled deliriously.

Hawker slapped Estella on the back. "Come on, old thing, let it out!"

She groaned but he slapped her again anyway and Boon joined in too, until they were both hitting her, smacking her hard and enjoying it, sniggering as they competed for who could strike the woman with the greater ferocity.

I gripped my fingers tight around the handle of the knife and stepped forward, knowing what I had to do. I still have no idea whether I would have been capable of it. I strongly suspect, in the end, that I wouldn't have.

Estella was coughing so hard that she had begun to exhaust herself. She lolled back in her chair, helpless against the sedition of her own body. Her jaw dangled open, her mouth was agape and she was staring fixedly towards the ceiling.

She shuddered again and cried out—not a cough now but a great and terrible wail of agony. I watched, spasming with nausea, as something streamed from her mouth. Liquid and fleshy, it forced its way out of her in something like a beam of pulp and skin—like a laser made of meat.

Given the volume of matter which was expelled from her body it must have been quite impossible for it ever to have been fully contained inside her. But I was growing well used now to impossibilities.

As it left her body, the beam punched a neat, surgical hole through the ceiling, cutting through the masonry of 125 Fitzgibbon Street and rising through the eleven levels of the Archive Unit as easily as a bullet would pass through paper. It blazed out to the sky beyond and disappeared.

"Barbara?" I asked in a very quiet voice. "What do we do now?"

But the woman was gone.

The last of the beam escaped Estella's body and she slid to the floor.

When I looked again, the Prefects had vanished and I was left alone with the fat woman.

Flakes of plaster drifted onto my head, debris from where the roof had been punctured. The building bellowed and groaned, its structure fatally weakened by the hole stamped through its centre, its dignity in tatters thanks to that mutinous jab from its bowels.

"Henry?" The woman was still alive and better able to speak now that the beast was gone.

I wiped away the black sludge which still lingered at the corners of her mouth and asked: "You know who I am?"

"Of course. Of course I do." She reached up and tugged at my sleeve. "Give my regards to your grandfather."

I promised that I would but I'm not sure she even heard me.

"Having Leviathan inside you . . . ," she said. "It brings out your true self. Shows the world what you really are." An ominous splintering sound came from the roof. "I've failed."

I squeezed her hand, trying to reassure her.

"Leviathan is loose," she said. "It's called for reinforcements. They will not make the same mistake a second time."

Another cracking sound from overhead, a second flurry of plaster and dust, another encore of debris.

Estella grimaced. "You'd better get out of here."

I struggled to lift her up, pawed at her shoulders, tried to get purchase on her blubber. I did my best to save her.

"Go," Estella wheezed after a minute or so of this gruesome tango. "Just go."

As the building began to shake in rehearsal for its downfall, I set the woman back onto the floor and tried to make her as comfortable as I could. Her eyelids fluttered shut and her face relaxed. I kissed her twice on the forehead.

But I'm afraid that I left her there all the same and, as the place started to crash down around me, ran for the final time from 125 Fitzgibbon Street and the offices of the Civil Service Archive Unit (Storage and Record Retrieval).

Outside, it had begun to snow. But this was not like snow which anyone had ever seen before. It was beetle black, sticky to the touch and subtly unnatural. As I emerged onto the street, a crowd had gathered, their attention split between the collapse of the building and the arrival of the snowstorm.

They were catching flakes of it in their hands, speculating about what it might mean. A man in a suit, standing apart from the rest at the edge of the pavement, was laughing at the sight of it. Just laughing and laughing and laughing until he exhausted himself with his own hysteria.

Behind us, with a volcanic rumble, the building crumpled, cracked and fell in upon itself, burying the woman who had kept Leviathan beneath eleven stories' worth of paperwork and filing.

IN THE EYE, DEDLOCK watched the snow fall, looking helplessly on as the sky grew black, failing to fend off a gnawing suspicion that what he had been afraid of for most of his long life had finally come to pass.

A woman stepped into his pod. She had vengeance in her

eyes, murder in her heart and something terrible clasped in both hands.

"Who's there?"

Flakes of black snow flung themselves at the pod window and dribbled downwards, smearing the pane with ebony.

"Who's there?" Dedlock asked again. "What do you want?"

Barbara trod forwards into the light, and although she was smiling there was no true amusement on her lips.

"Hello, sweetheart," she said.

TWO AND A HALF MILES away, in the Machen Ward of St. Chad's Hospital, my granddad was busy defying medical science.

At the very instant that the snow began to fall, his life support gave a squeal of cacophonous dismay, he sat upright in his bed and his eyes flicked impatiently open.

Although it was barely ten A.M., the view from his window was darkening and spotted with black.

I wonder what he thought when he saw it. I wonder what went through his mind. And I wonder if he knew, even then, that it was already too late for all of us.

CHAPTER 24

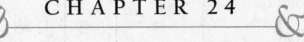

W HAT FOLLOWS IS MY TRANSCRIPT OF A RECORDING which I have been able to retrieve from the remains of the London Eye—a black-box recorder salvaged from the scrap metal of the city's premiere attraction.

When these events took place, my grandfather had just regained consciousness and the snow had been falling for about ten minutes.

As Barbara strolled into the light and Dedlock saw what she had clasped in her hands, he felt fear—real, irrefutable, bowel-quaking fear—for the first time in more than a century.

"Think, my dear," he hissed, his voice already acquiring that wheedling plausibility which had sent generations of Directorate agents to their extinction. "Don't do something you might regret."

Barbara strolled closer, all smiley now, twinkling, light on her feet, like a party hostess greeting the first of her guests. She positioned a forefinger in front of her lips. "Shh," she said, and called him by a name I'd never heard before.

In his tank, the old man hissed in anger. "No-one's called me that for a long time."

"And why is that, I wonder?"

"Nobody's dared."

"You prefer Dedlock?" Barbara said airily, still sounding as though she was merely making polite conversation with acquaintances she barely knew. "I always thought these code names made us seem so silly."

"You think so? Well, if anyone's left alive after today, I'll be sure to look into it."

Barbara merely smiled, slightly blankly, like she was handing out canapés.

The old goat in the tank, that impossibility, that living affront to the laws of science, was playing for time. Even as he spoke, he was wondering if he might be not be able to contact someone on the outside, weighing up the odds of his raising the alarm before it was too late. Desperate for a distraction, he clenched his fists and behind him a map of London shimmered into existence, street after street of it smudged with black, eclipsed with the taint of Leviathan. "What are you doing here? Where are the Prefects? Where's Henry Lamb?"

When she spoke again, Barbara's voice was leeched of all emotion. "You know what's happening. Leviathan is loose. All we ever did was stave off the inevitable for a few years. The blink of an eye for a creature like that."

"Don't say that," Dedlock said. "I never give in. If there's one thing you can say about my long life, it's that I've never given in. Not once."

Barbara yawned. "Your life. Your long, long life. Do you have any idea how tired everyone is of hearing about that? One hundred and seventy-five years of anecdotes and tall tales."

"If it hadn't been for me, this city would be a slave colony by now. You'd have been born into chains."

"You know, a lot of stuff's been coming back to me this morning. There's a lot of Estella in this strange body that Jasper fashioned for me. In the last few hours, her memories have been flooding back. You asked me what I was doing here . . ."

"Yes?"

"I've come to ask you a question."

"Fine time for questions when the world is shattering around us."

"Why me? Why did you choose me to imprison Leviathan? You must have known you were handing me a life sentence."

Dedlock swam close to the glass of his tank. "It wasn't a choice I made lightly. God knows, I've had to live with it."

"You've had to live with it? You?" Barbara blazed in fury, her face lit up with rage, like Moses when he first set eyes upon the golden calf. For an instant, she held what was in her hands high in the air. Then, recovering her equilibrium, she lowered it. "I've seen what you allowed Estella to become. A mute in a basement, pawed at by a greasy little man. Harvested for my sweat."

"Blame loverboy for that. It was he who hid you from us. And anyway we didn't have much choice. You were the only one strong enough to hold the beast in thrall. And things *were* a little pressing at the time. Tell me, my dear, what would you have done?"

"I know the real reason you chose me."

"Do tell."

"You said you loved me once. Do you remember that?"

An uneasy splash. "Perhaps. I might have experienced a momentary spurt of affection. I might once have believed myself to have feelings—"

"You never had feelings for me. You certainly never loved me. You wanted to possess me."

"What's the difference?" Those last words emerged as a snarl. Dedlock paused and tried to compose himself, and when he spoke again it was in more collected tones, intended to mollify, to soothe, placate and appease. "But you were so beautiful, my dear."

Barbara was unmoved. "Beautiful, yes. And young. And trusting."

"But you were attracted to me. That was real. I could taste it."

"What could I possibly have wanted with you? You used me. Worse than that, I let myself be used."

"I'm not proud of what we did. But—oh!—you were magnificent. You were always at your most beguiling with a blade in your hand."

"You're sick. And getting sicker by the hour. Look what you've done. Hijacked the body of this poor girl."

Dedlock rallied to his own defence. "That girl should thank us! We've made her beautiful! She was only a filing clerk before she came under the influence of the Directorate."

"She was happy before!" Barbara shouted, then, checking herself: "I was happy before."

"You can't have been."

"Do you understand what your man's done to me? The alterations he inflicted with his wretched pill?"

"Mr. Jasper didn't wish to trouble me with specifics."

"I'll just bet he didn't. So allow me to enlighten you. I don't sweat any more. I only need to breathe three times an hour. I've tried my best but I no longer eat or drink or shit. And I've been neutered. What was between my legs has been fused shut."

"Like an angel," the old man murmured.

"Like a monster! A parody of a woman!"

"We need you," Dedlock said quietly. "The city needs you."

Barbara shook her head in pity. "Oh, sweetheart. Have you not realised it yet? The city is lost."

She raised the axe which she grasped in her hands high above her head and brought it savagely down against the glass of Dedlock's tank.

First, the old man whimpered.

Next, he leaked fat, tadpole tears which dripped down his cheeks like rain.

Then, at last, he begged.

But he did not apologise, nor did he show the merest shred of remorse for his actions, and so in consequence Barbara merely continued her assault. The part of her which was Estella had dreamt for years of this moment, had spent decades in the basement plotting and scheming towards this man's comeuppance, and so, even in the face of his wailing pleas for pity, she simply struck again, and struck harder, redoubling her efforts as the old man thrashed and squirmed and wailed. Cracks appeared in the glass, turned into fractures and fissures, widened into fault-lines until the contents of the tank began to gush forth, geysering into the room. A final blow shattered the tank entirely, evacuating everything into the pod. London washed out with it, the city sluicing across the floor.

Barbara watched as Dedlock flailed and flopped upon the ground, helpless as a beached carp, gasping and wheezing for air as the gills on his sides trembled in pitiful failure. He looked up at her pleadingly but there was no clemency in her eyes.

"This is what they planned," she said. "This is how the Domino Men wanted you to die."

"Would you . . ." Poor Dedlock, struggling to breathe, drowning on dry land. "Would you believe me if I said I was sorry?"

Barbara bent over his trembling form, and for the first time since her poisoning at the hands of Mr. Jasper, she seemed to show a filament of compassion. She stroked his hair. She kissed him chastely on the cheek.

"Too late," she said as she sat cross-legged beside the body of her tormentor, gazed out of the window at the gathering snowstorm and settled down to watch the end of the world.

✣

WHATEVER IT WAS, it wasn't snow. It looked the same, of course. There were superficial similarities and for a second—if you were indoors, say, and looking out at it—you might even have been fooled. But once you'd touched the snow, once you'd held it in your palm and felt it close to your skin—then you wouldn't be fooled any longer.

It settled thickly, dense and compacted, on the ground, on rooftops and car hoods, like it wasn't planning on budging, as though it was here for the long haul. It didn't seem at all prepared to melt, not even in the centre of the city where real snow rarely lasts beyond the hour.

The only time it did what it was supposed to do was when it landed on human skin. There it melted straightaway, seeping past the epidermis, snuffling down into the pores. Oh yes, it was happy enough then. This stuff—it loved the human body and we were all as sponges to it, as blotters are to ink.

Apart from me, strangely. That stuff slid off my skin in seconds as though it couldn't find a way in.

THE SNOW HAD JUST BEGUN to fall when the hospital phoned to tell me the news.

I hailed a cab and asked to be taken to St. Chad's. On the way, I asked the driver to pull over by an ATM, where I withdrew a couple of hundred pounds. I felt oddly certain I'd be needing it.

As I passed through the streets, I saw that the panic had already started. People left work early, before it was even lunchtime, and headed wordlessly home to their families. The supermarkets were packed with hysterics stocking up on tinned goods, grabbing armfuls of imperishables, cramming their trolleys with beans and cereal and chunks of pineapple. Everywhere else was shutting up. All across the city, windows were being closed, curtains pulled, doors locked and bolted.

I experienced symptoms of my own. The earpiece which had been in place ever since Steerforth had put it there, on the night that the Prefects had escaped, suddenly fell out, dropping to the ground like a dead insect, shrivelled and useless. On the floor of the taxi, I ground it into slime.

I took out my mobile and dialled a number. Abbey picked up straightaway and I pictured her beautiful face darkened by a frown of concern.

"Henry? Darling, are you OK?"

Even though the world was slipping into nightmare, I felt a pang of pride. It was the first time she'd ever called me by that endearment. By any endearment, come to think of it.

"I'm fine," I said. "You?"

"I'm still in the flat. I didn't fancy going into work today."

"Very wise."

"Where are you now?"

"I'm heading for the hospital. Then I'm coming home."

"I've got a terrible feeling about all this. For God's sake, hurry."

In the hospital, there was that same quality of barely suppressed panic—as though an army were approaching and we were all in preparation for a siege. The Machen Ward was empty except for an old man who lay stretched out, his breathing ragged and asthmatic, muttering under his breath. I couldn't understand exactly what he was saying but it sounded filled with regret, with sadness and self-pity at roads not taken, at the shabby predictability of his choices.

The usual nurse was standing by the window, watching the

sky blot with black. If she heard me enter, she evidently didn't think it worth a reaction. She must recently have been outside because her shoulders were dappled with black snow.

"Excuse me?" I said.

Still the woman stared, watching the flakes of black as they curled and pirouetted to earth, shimmying down like goose feathers.

I tried again. "Hello?"

She turned around. Her face, formerly hard-lined and rigorous, had softened, the creases in her skin had smoothed out and, endearingly, dimples had materialised upon her cheeks. She seemed dozy but content, sleepily post-coital.

"I'm looking for my granddad—"

She smiled. "I know who you're looking for. And you're too late. He's gone."

"What do you mean, he's gone? Up until an hour ago, he was in the kind of coma you lot said he'd never come out of."

"He discharged himself," the nurse said blithely, as though comatose septuagenarians had leapt from their beds and bolted for the exit on most days of her working life. "He said he had things to do. But he left you a note. Over there. By the bed."

I strode over to the wretched National Health Service cot in which the old bastard had been so long entombed and saw that the nurse was right. There was a message scrawled for me, written on a page ripped from a notepad.

> Dear Henry,
> Go home.

It was signed in his usual scrawl. Below that, a postscript.

> I am serious. *Go home.*

Nothing else. Just that. And to think I was hoping for answers.

The nurse was speaking again. "You mustn't worry about him. He's with friends. I saw them from this window."

"Friends? What friends?"

"Two men in fancy dress. They were dressed as—"

I cut her short. "I know what they were dressed as."

The woman laughed. There was an undercurrent of naughtiness to it, as though she'd just been unexpectedly tickled somewhere intimate. "You know what's coming, don't you?"

"What?"

Another discomfitingly sensual laugh. "The city is ripe and Leviathan is coming to take it as his own."

"What did you say?"

The door was flung open and someone clattered in behind us. The nurse swivelled away and returned her attention to the gathering dark.

The new arrival shouted my name and I barely had time to hear the strutting clack of her heels and catch the familiar odour of her perfume before she was upon me and I was enfolded in her fleshy arms.

"Oh, Henry . . ."

"Hello, Mum," I said.

She was covered in snow. A thick swathe of the stuff was clinging to her clothes, and although traces of it were still discernible on her hair and eyebrows, the rest must long ago have sunk into her skin.

"He's a shit, Henry. I was the latest in a very long line. I was a notch on his bedpost." She broke off, having finally realised what had happened. "Where is he? Where's the old bastard?"

"He's gone. It would seem he's defied medical science and made a dash for it."

Mum sounded dazed and bewildered. "That can't be right, can it? That's not possible."

By the window, the nurse turned her head towards us, slowly, as though heavily drugged. "Leviathan is coming." A look of zealotry burnished her face. "Such a glorious day."

For an instant, Mum just stared at her, then she gasped as though she were short of breath, lumbered forwards and crashed into a chair, sending it skidding across the floor.

"Mum? Are you OK?"

All at once, she seemed terrifyingly old. "I'm OK," she murmured. "Don't know what came over me. Just a little turn."

"I think we should leave."

"So many of them, Henry. All those women. And not just women, either. It's the only thing he'd talk about. I couldn't stand it. I—"

"Let's go, Mum. I don't think it's safe here any more."

"Not safe?" My mother looked afraid. "Whyever isn't it safe? Is Gordy here? Is that it?"

"Come back to the flat. I don't think you should be on your own."

Then, without warning, my mother was smiling again, a dopey, blissed-out kind of grin. "Have you seen the weather, Henry? Don't you think it's beautiful?"

I grunted in reply, took her by the arm and steered her firmly towards the door.

"Leviathan is coming," Mum said. "Leviathan is coming to earth."

At the sound of these words I felt rancid and sick but I did my best not to show it. "Let's get out of here," I said briskly. "Let's take you home."

As we walked from the room, I heard the nurse begin to laugh. An instant later, the old man in the bed joined in. Mum and I left the Machen Ward backed by the stereo laughter of people whose sanity was steaming into the distance and wasn't even bothering to look back.

We scurried through the hospital as fast as we could. The beds had emptied out and the patients—even the worst of them, even the most long-term and permanently horizontal—were on their feet, milling in flocks, trailing tubes and splints and bandages. I learnt later that a doctor had returned from a lengthy outdoor cigarette break to open every single window in every single ward, encouraging the black snow to enter in and billow hungrily over all those consigned to the care of St. Chad's.

The staff were endeavouring to keep them in line, doing their best to put everything back in its proper place, but the ill, the old and the dying were having none of it and persisted in wriggling free. The scariest thing was that it was becoming hard to tell the professionals from their charges, the keepers from the beasts.

As we pushed our way past, it felt like I was one of the first to have any idea what was happening, the first to understand the gravity of the situation, like the man who runs to the top deck of the *Titanic* the moment the lower levels begin to flood only to find the band bickering amongst themselves about what to play next.

When we reached the exit, Mum didn't want to come. She seemed to want to stay with the patients, and I had to use some considerable force to propel her out of the door, into the dark and the snow. Behind us, the situation grew worse. I didn't turn back but I heard scuffling and brawling and wild laughter—the forest-fire spread of insanity.

THE ROADS WERE PACKED, almost completely gridlocked as the population struggled to escape the city. There were horns, raised voices and shaken fists, quarrels and arguments lip-read from behind glass—anger feigned to hide the fizzing surge of panic. For a while, we walked, me half-dragging my mother, as she seemed to luxuriate in the snowfall and shuffled only very reluctantly onwards until, miraculously, I saw a taxi drive by, its light still switched on. Warily, the driver stopped for us, but it was only when I brandished a wad of notes that he seemed to even entertain the idea of letting us inside. I gave him everything I had and told him to take us to the flat in Tooting Bec. Mum was still bleating and muttering darkly but I strapped her in and told her, politely and with a lot of love, to shut up and behave herself.

We had just escaped from Camberwell Green when my mobile phone shuddered in my pocket, as though in sympathy with the distress which surrounded us.

The line whirred and crackled, like the soundtrack to an old newsreel, and it took me a moment to recognise the voice.

"Henry? It's me."

"Who?"

"Mr. Jasper. Though I think you ought to know now. My name . . . my real name . . . It's Richard Price."

I thought for a moment. "Is that supposed to mean something to me?"

"No. I just thought . . . I thought you ought to know my real name."

"Thanks." I really couldn't think of what else to say. "How are you?"

"Fading fast."

I asked him, not without a certain measure of impatience, what on earth he was talking about.

"I'm in a hotel room," he said. "Somewhere expensive. Somewhere clean. So very important, I think, to die somewhere clean."

"What are you doing there? Can't you lot help? This stuff—this snow—it's doing something to people."

Jasper chuckled indulgently, like a mother to her little boy who won't stop jabbering about his first day at school. "I've swallowed some pills, Henry. Swallowed a lot of pills."

"For God's sake, why?"

"Because I touched her."

"Touched who?"

"Only once. I want to make that absolutely clear. I only touched her once. But I had to. You understand? What man wouldn't?"

"Who? Who did you touch?"

"The goddess, Henry. The new Estella. She was so perfect. She was smooth between the legs." He wheezed in exhalation. "Do you forgive me? Henry? I absolutely need you to forgive me."

"I don't suppose it matters now," I said, watching fistfuls of black flakes throw themselves in kamikaze assault against the windows.

"It's all over. The great serpent is coming." Mr. Jasper ("Richard Price") coughed, a thin rasp which turned, horribly, into something gushing and wet. "You've seen the snow?"

"Of course."

"Do you know what it is?"

"I'm . . . I'm not sure."

"It's ampersand, Henry. Ampersand pouring from the sky."

Another rattling breath, the line went dead and the snow fell more densely and more heavily than before, ceaselessly, without mercy, pouring onto the city like tears.

CHAPTER 25

THREE DAYS WAS ALL IT TOOK FOR LONDON TO RUN into the arms of chaos. The city embraced it willingly, all too eager to swap her staid old suitors of simmering calm and disgruntled order for this fresh admirer, this master swordsman of panic, anarchy and fear.

WE ARRIVED BACK at the flat late that afternoon. Several times during the journey the driver had come close to turfing us out of his cab. He was going to make a break for it, he said, get the hell out of the city before catastrophe struck. It was only by stopping at another ATM and clearing out all that was left in my account that I was able to persuade him to take us home at all.

On the long drive Mum had got much worse, alternately enraged over old mistakes and infidelities, and weeping over what was hiding in the snow. By the time I got her into the flat, she'd grown almost delirious and Abbey, who, I noted with a warm glow of affection, was working hard to batten down her own panic and disquiet, had to help me put her into my bed, swinging Mum's legs indecorously onto the mattress, stripping off most of her clothes, settling her down and doing our best to make her comfortable.

I'm sure it was wrong of me to think about such things at a time like that, but I realised, with a tingly thrill, that this unexpected houseguest would mean I'd have no choice but to share Abbey's bed that night.

I brought Mum a glass of water, persuaded her to drink and, as she seemed finally to swim back to lucidity, introduced her formally to Abbey.

"You two an item?" she asked, as I wiped a strand of spittle from her lips. "I always thought you were gay." She gurgled, spumes of spittle dripping from the corners of her mouth. "Never saw you with a woman. Assumed you were a woofter."

"What's happening?" Abbey asked when I came back into the sitting room and, frightened, we held one another just a little too tightly on the sofa. "Henry, what's happening?"

"The worst thing you can imagine," I said. "That's what happening. The absolute worst thing you can imagine."

"No," she snapped. "I'm fed up with all these secrets. I want to know exactly what's going on. I want you to tell me the truth."

So I took her in my arms and, as gently as I could, I told her everything—from what had happened on the day that Granddad collapsed, to my history with the Prefects, to all that I knew about the snow. When I'd finished, she just nodded, thanked me for my honesty and reached for the TV remote.

On the tiny screen of Abbey's portable television (rescued from the attic after Miss Morning had smashed up its predecessor) we watched the news as the terror began. The hoofbeats of disaster were there in every story—an epidemic of suicide; the churches, synagogues and mosques filled beyond capacity;

neighbour turning upon neighbour; violence on the streets, widespread, indiscriminate and hysterical. Bewilderment led to confusion, confusion to fear, fear to panic—panic, ineluctably, to death.

At six P.M., the prime minister called an emergency session of Parliament. One hour later, the government was advising everyone to stay in their homes, exhorting us not to venture outside. At eight P.M., we heard that the hospitals were overloaded, filled with manically gibbering patients (many of them former members of staff). At nine P.M., perhaps inevitably, martial law was declared—and at 9:25 P.M., the telephone rang in our lounge.

I was checking on Mum when it happened. She seemed to be sinking into a kind of delirium, muttering about something coming out of space to swallow London whole. The strange thing was that when she spoke about it, it was with a pronounced lilt in her voice, an intonation of delight, as though she was actually looking forward to the death of the city.

When I got into the sitting room, Abbey was staring at the phone, gazing at it warily, like it was about to jump up and bite her. I asked her why she hadn't answered.

She bit her lip. "I'm scared."

I seized the receiver. "Hello?"

I didn't recognise the voice. It was a man, about my own age. "Is Abbey there?" he asked.

I said nothing.

"I need to speak to Abbey."

"Who is this?"

Now the voice had an undercurrent of belligerence, barely disguised. "This is Joe. Who're you?"

"I'm Henry Lamb," I said, and slammed the phone down hard.

Abbey looked at me, wide eyed and shaky. "Who was that?"

"Wrong number," I said, and the way she stared at me it was like she knew that I was lying.

I TOOK A GLASS OF WATER in to Mum and got her to struggle up and take a couple of sips before she sank back onto the mattress again.

"It's all happening so fast," she murmured.

"Don't, Mum," I said. "Don't try to speak."

She groaned softly. "Didn't think it would end quite like this . . ."

Her eyelids fluttered shut. I kissed her once on the forehead, made sure the duvet was tight around her and left her alone.

NEXT DOOR, ABBEY WAS already in bed, dressed in a man-sized T-shirt, tense, fidgety and chewing on her fingernails. Self-consciously, I stripped to my boxers and climbed in beside her.

"How's your mum?" she asked.

"Not sure," I said. "A bit shaky."

We both knew that I wasn't ready yet to admit the truth of it. At least not aloud.

"She seems nice," Abbey said. "From what I could tell."

"Well, you're probably not meeting her at her best."

"Probably not."

There was a moment's awkward silence.

"Henry? Do you think we're safe here?"

"Yes. I think we are," I said. "My granddad told me to go home."

"I did a bit of research on this house once," Abbey said, suddenly eager for a chat. "It's been here longer than you'd think."

"Really?" I said, grateful for the shift in conversation, happy for any old nonsense to be spoken as long as it filled the silence.

"Back in the last century, before this place was divided into flats, there was a psychic who lived here."

"A psychic?"

"A spiritualist, yeah." She giggled, and that giggle, it was wonderful to hear. "Crazy, isn't it?"

"I think a lot of dark stuff's happened here in the past," I said softly. "I don't believe anything's been an accident in my life. Not even this place."

The moment of good humour had passed.

Abbey sighed, rolled over and switched off the light.

Later, as we lay together in the dark, she said: "I can't believe I've found you. You're my second chance, Henry. I always wanted to do something worthwhile with my life. Something that makes a difference. With you, p'raps I finally can."

I squeezed her hand and she squeezed mine as outside the snow continued to fall, covering the city in a second skin, in a carapace of jealousy and spite.

IN THE NIGHT, THERE were strange sounds—shouts and moans and smashing glass. Once, just after midnight, we heard a whispered invitation at the letterbox. Certain promises were made, certain boons offered in exchange for services rendered, for a number of small concessions.

But we held one another close and tried to stop our ears against it, knowing that this was our haven and that to leave the flat could mean the end for either one of us.

I SUPPOSE THERE MIGHT be some bitter kind of irony in the fact that the next day was Christmas Eve. In all that had happened, I'd started to forget that there was supposed to be anything festive going on at all.

When I woke, Abbey's side of the bed was empty and cool. I wrapped a dressing gown around myself and walked through to the lounge to find her on the couch watching television, a mug of something hot cupped between her hands, riveted by the cataclysms unfolding on-screen.

She didn't even look up. "The city's in lockdown," she said. "They've set up checkpoints at the edge of London. People've seen soldiers. They're saying they're shooting to kill."

I sat beside her on the sofa and hugged her close.

"Everyone's gone mad," she said. "They've all gone mad."

I kissed her gently on the forehead, smoothed back her hair and whispered something treacly and cloying.

"Thank you," she said, and smiled.

"I need to check on Mum."

She nodded distractedly. "Henry?"

"Yes?"

"What do we do?"

"We stay here," I said firmly. "We stay in this flat and we wait it out. As long as we're together—as long as we're in here—then nothing can touch us."

"But there are people outside I care about. What about them?"

"Everything I care about's right here." I sounded perhaps a little colder than I had intended.

"You think your granddad's dead, don't you?" she said.

I walked away.

Of course, I blame myself.

Mum was fine when I checked on her. Her breathing was shallow and she was still murmuring and moaning to herself, but she didn't have a temperature and seemed, if anything, to be slightly calmer than before. I did what I could, gave her water, mopped her brow and, just before lunch, helped her lurch uncertainly into the bathroom, even cleaning up the subsequent mess.

I'm not a bad son, that's what I'm saying. I did my best.

Abbey and I were having lunch, eking out the last of our bread and fruit, when we heard the scream.

In the bedroom Mum was on her feet and almost fully dressed, lacing up her shoes with jerky, robotic motions, muttering endlessly about the snow.

She'd managed to tear out some of the fitted carpet, peeling it back to reveal old floorboards underneath. Here she'd uncovered something extraordinary—painted markings, sigils, signs and symbols daubed in faded red upon the wood.

"Mum?" I said, moving warily towards her and trying not to think too hard about what I'd seen on the floor. "What's all this, Mum?"

"He sold your father. Did you know that? For the sake of his putrid little war he bargained away your dad. And you know what scares me now? I think he's sold you, too."

"Are you talking about Granddad?" I asked.

"That man," she rasped. "That vicious man. It was always his idea."

"What was?" I said. "What are you talking about?"

"The telly . . . Your father and I never wanted it for you. And then—those operations. He paid for them. Oh, Henry. Incisions to the brain."

I edged closer. "Mum?"

Then I made my mistake. I placed a hand on her shoulder. It was the gentlest restraint, the kindest holding-back, but that was not how my mother saw it. She gave a roar of outrage and pain. Until then, I don't suppose I'd ever thought her capable of making such a sound. If I hadn't snatched my hand away as quickly as I did, I honestly believe that she might have bitten it.

My voice trembled. "Mum, what are you doing? Please. Get back into bed."

She bared her teeth and hissed. "Leviathan is coming. We must all go out to meet him."

Hunched forwards, simian in motion, she pushed past me and sped towards the front door. Abbey appeared and stepped uncertainly into her path but Mum just slapped her out of the way. Abbey squealed in shock and I saw that my mother had drawn blood on her cheek.

Mum reached the door and unlocked it, suddenly, helplessly desperate to be outside.

Stupidly, I touched her arm again and she snarled back something terrible. Even now, I'm unable to bring myself to set down those words.

She wrenched open the door and I saw the scene outside, a window onto what the city had become. Chaos, smoke, endless snowfall. Dozens of men and women in the same condition as my mother, loping through the snow, all of them streaming in the same direction.

They no longer seemed like people at all. Drones. That was how I thought of them now. Just drones.

Mum stepped into the street and sniffed the air.

"Don't go!" I shouted.

But she paid me no attention. Mum gave another cry of fury and triumph, and ran into the street to join the others, into that exodus of the damned.

"Mum!"

She didn't turn back. I stood on the threshold, wondering what to do, uncertain whether to give chase, knowing that she wouldn't thank me for it. A few seconds more and she was lost to the snow and my decision had been made for me.

I stepped back inside and snapped shut the door, just as Abbey emerged from the bathroom, clutching a wad of tissue to the side of her face.

"She's gone," I said.

At FIVE O'CLOCK that afternoon, the television went black. With the exception of half an hour of the test card on BBC1, there was nothing on any channel except static and inter-ference. Snow outside, snow inside, blackness crept all over London. A few hours later, the lights went out as well and we lost power for good.

Abbey and I went to bed, too scared to sit up in the dark, not brave enough to pay any heed to the strange sounds we heard from outside, the rustlings and stampings, the whinnies of terror, the orgiastic cries.

Much later, as we lay close to one another, we heard the same hissing at the letterbox as the night before, the same whispered invitation. But we held each other tight and stopped our ears against it.

As I'M WRITING THIS, I feel a flicker of hope. You know what I'm talking about. You must have noticed it yourself.

The other handwriting, that other story, has gone and there have been no more interpolations, no more intrusions, for days.

Maybe everything's going to be OK. Maybe there'll be no need for that journey I thought I had to make, for that appoint-ment of ours in the wilderness. Perhaps at last I'm really free.

As Abbey and I tried to sleep, outside an old man was running. I didn't know it at the time but he was very near to us, almost in sight of our door.

His flight had not gone unnoticed. He was being tracked, although not with any subtlety or grace as he could hear them blundering behind him, wheezing and squealing in weird pleasure. There was a whole tribe of them, dumb but implacable, tireless, without morality, the new face of mankind.

The old man was growing weary and out of breath, his years of active service in the Directorate long behind him, weakened by his days in a hospital bed and ground down by the spectacle of his darkest fears become reality. No-one would have blamed him for giving up. Thousands would have done just that, long ago. In medical terms, he shouldn't even have been on his feet. But he didn't give up. He kept going, forcing his ancient body onwards through the snow and the dark, pushing himself far beyond endurance just to try to reach me before the end.

He was less than a street away when they found him, the herd driven mad by the snow, inflamed by the ampersand in their systems.

Every breath felt like fire. Each step was an ordeal. He could feel them at his back. Determined not to slow down, at the last instant he tripped, fell forwards, grazing old hands, bruising old skin, until at last he righted himself and turned to face the mob, courageous and unflinching.

He would have fought, I know that. He would have fought tooth and nail to the end.

Sentimental nonsense.

We know the truth. The old man had his wrinkled cock in his hand when they came for him. They cut him down mid-dribble, his body made unrecognisable, battered by a thousand boot-heels, stamped into the snow by an army of our commuters.

Even this, of course, was very much more than he deserved.

ABBEY AND I WOKE WITH the dawn, too distraught and too scared to kid ourselves that we were going to get much sleep.

I managed a wan sort of smile. "Merry Christmas," I said.

"Merry Christmas, Henry."

We hugged, and I was clambering out of bed to get us some tea when Abbey reminded me that the power had gone. No tea, then. No heat, either, and the pair of us lost no time in wrapping ourselves in multiple shirts and jumpers, self-insulating in worn vests, old cardigans and favourite sweatshirts.

WE HAD BEEN UP for a couple of hours, in which time we'd scraped together a meagre breakfast, held one another tightly and swapped tender pledges of devotion, when there came a knock at the door—a sharp, brisk tap, all business.

I ran to open it. "Granddad?"

A stranger stood on the threshold. A man not much older than me, slim, blond and sharp featured, his hair cajoled into slick, brash spikes.

"You must be Henry Lamb," he said.

"Who are you?" I asked, although I think by then I'd already guessed the answer.

"I'm Joe," he said, sardonically extending his hand. "Joe Streater."

You hoped that we had gone?

We were only resting. We were relaxing, taking a little down-time, stepping back to gain a better perspective on all that has been laid before us to date. It is of vital importance (Leviathan has always said so) to maintain an equable balance between leisure and our working lives. But now our lunch hour is over and we have returned to work with a revitalised sense of purpose and a determination to succeed that I think you will find to be steelier and more implacable than ever.

We thought it might be of interest to adumbrate something of what occupied Arthur Windsor whilst the execrable young Henry Lamb was barricaded into his flat in Tooting Bec, crying into his pillow and quivering in the arms of his landlady.

Details follow, and as ever, unflinching accuracy is guaranteed.

As the prince slept upon the floor of his palace, a small, grey cat trod softly through his dreams. He told Arthur the truth about the war, he told him about the innumerable clashes between Dedlock's men and the House of Windsor—a secret history of the British Isles which had run beneath the surface of public life for more than *one hundred and fifty years. He spoke of the Process, of Estella's sacrifice and of the dark miracle of Tooting Bec. He spoke of the one who had been prepared to take Estella's place, a boy groomed almost from birth to contain Leviathan and who now needed only to remember a simple formula, an incantation to activate the Process and close the ancient trap. And the small, grey cat spoke, too, of the prince's part in it all, his responsibility to deliver the boy into the belly of the beast. If the boy is the bullet, said the cat, then you, Your Highness, you are the gun.*

When Arthur opened his eyes again, he was at once aware that something had changed, that something had tipped and shifted in the balance of the world which meant that no day would ever seem quite the same ever again. As he rose, awkwardly and painfully, to his feet, something of what had happened came back to him and, with it, certain details of his peculiarly troubling dream. But the prince tried to shake it off, stretching, yawning, attempting to persuade his eyes to focus, forcing himself back into wakefulness.

He looked around for the cat, but if it had ever been there at all, it had long since vanished. Only then did he notice what was happening outside. Snow. Jet-black, ebony snow, hurtling towards the earth.

He felt a strong compulsion to go outside—to run, not walk— to stand and luxuriate in that snow, to roll in it and, gawping happily into the sky, catch flakes in his mouth. But something else, some quieter impulse, persuaded him to stay indoors. It cannot have been later than lunchtime, yet it already looked dark outside. The prince walked up to the windowpane and it seemed to him that there were figures moving in the unseasonal gloom and that he recognised many of their faces—staff, servants, even one or two that he might have been moved to call friends. They were standing in the snow, allowing it to land upon their clothes and settle onto their skin, and they were laughing, all of them, gazing up towards the heavens, emitting loose peals of demented laughter.

Remembering more now of what had taken place, Arthur's thoughts turned to the well-being of his wife and he hurried into his quarters. There she was, mercifully safe and sleeping as soundly as before, although the prince wondered if her slumber didn't seem alarmingly deep. How can she not have been woken by the ruckus outside?

Gently, he pulled aside the covers. Lovingly, he brushed his fingers against her face. "Laetitia?" he whispered. "Laetitia, it's me."

No reaction. Not a murmur or a flickering of the eyelashes or even (how grateful would the prince have been to hear this) a tiny, indecorous snore.

"Laetitia?" The prince shook her, carefully at first, then with increasing vigour. "Laetitia!"

She was breathing, at least. Leaning closer, he could detect an unfamiliar smell on her breath, and as he arranged his wife upon the bed, tucking her in with almost maternal concern, he concluded with a guilty kind of sadness that she must have been drugged. In this, if in pitifully little else in his almost entirely useless life, Arthur Windsor was correct.

He picked up the telephone and dialled Mr. Silverman's number. It rang for an eternity without reply. He slapped at the cradle then dialled down to the switchboard. Whoever picked it up said nothing.

"Hello?" said the prince.

There was a low burbling sound at the other end of the line which might almost have been a laugh.

"Who's there? Speak up!"

The same sound again—wet and gurgling. "Good afternoon, sir. This is Beth speaking."

"Beth? We've spoken before, haven't we? Good God, that seems a lifetime ago now. Listen, I'm trying to get through to Mr. Silverman."

"I'm afraid that will be quite impossible." Her voice sounded distant, flat and almost robotically toneless.

"Impossible? Why the devil will it be impossible?"

"The playing piece named Silverman has been removed from the board."

"What on earth are you talking about?"

The girl called Beth seemed not to have heard the question. "Have you been outside yet? Into the snow? You really ought to, you know. It's so pretty, sir. Like ashes from the sky."

"Now listen here, young lady—" the prince began, but the woman interrupted him without a thought.

"It's coming, sir," she said. "You know that, don't you? It's almost here. And the time has come for you to pick a side."

"I've chosen my side," the prince said firmly.

Beth just laughed at this, that same moist chuckle, before there was a tutting click and the line went dead.

Suddenly, as though all the fight in him had been used up in his conversation, the prince felt overcome by great waves of nausea and exhaustion. Something inside him spasmed once, twice, three times, each more urgent than the last. It was all he could do to stumble into the corridor, where he was copiously sick. This done, he wiped his mouth, retreated back into the bedroom and closed the door (just managing to lock and bolt it) before he collapsed onto the bed beside his wife and passed out.

It was dark when he awoke. He was flat on his back, a hand was on his shoulder and a familiar face was swimming hazily into view.

"Arthur?"

The prince blinked, tried to sit up, winced. "Darling? Darling, is that you?" The prince attempted a rueful grin but discovered that smiling seemed to hurt him now, that it cost him dearly.

"Arthur? Are you going to tell me what's been going on? I've heard the most fearful noises."

"Leviathan . . ." Arthur tried to push himself up. "I think Leviathan must be here." The prince was in the most relentless, unstinting kind of pain. He wanted to say more, to explain as much as he could, wanted more than anything to beg Laetitia's forgiveness, to throw himself upon her mercy and plead for the balm of her understanding, for her sweet clemency. But he found himself unable to speak a single word—his throat tight and dry, his innards churning and swirling in a tempest of gastric distress, his head pounding with a fusillade of thunderclaps.

Just before he sank back into unconsciousness and the horrified face of his wife vanished first to a distant point of light and then into absolute nothingness, Arthur Windsor was granted clear and unambiguous knowledge of what was happening to him. These are withdrawal symptoms, he thought, having attended several lectures on the subject as part of the work that he did for a spectrum of young people's charities. I am in withdrawal from ampersand.

Shortly before he went under, he managed to croak out a few words. "Stay in here. Promise me that you'll stay in this room."

But by then he was already sliding into unconsciousness and he never heard his wife's reply.

The next twenty-four hours were a study in pain and terror. There were moments of relative lucidity when he saw Laetitia and heard her voice quite clearly, moments when he sensed that she held him in her arms, rocking him gently as a mother would a child, even (although this may have been an auditory *hallucination) that she was singing to him, some old melody part-remembered from his childhood. Once when he awoke, she persuaded him to drink a little water. On another occasion, when he emerged momentarily from the deep mists of his mind, he discovered her seated before him on the bed eating the most peculiar combination of food—peanut butter ladled directly from the jar, gherkins, pork scratchings, sardines. For some time afterwards he believed (quite erroneously) that this had simply been some overheated imagining of his. Certainly, it grew almost impossible for the prince to tell what was real and what were merely tricks, snares and booby-traps laid by that ampersand which still fought for a foothold in his system. There were the sounds that he heard from outdoors, the screeches and whisperings, the savage cries of triumph. More than once, he discovered himself clutching at Laetitia's arm and imploring her not to leave him. The shutters were down, so he could not see outside, but there existed not the slightest doubt in his mind that it was still snowing. He even believed that he could hear it, the ceaseless patter of the snow, the unending fall of ampersand from the sky, and as he lay in this febrile state, he was visited by memories of old sins. He saw the face of Mr. Streater contorted into a malevolent grin. He saw the woman at the station explode all over again, as though in slow motion. He even thought that he heard the laughter of Virtue and Mercy, although he never saw them, their power fading, perhaps, even then. But whilst he longed for it, the small, grey cat never visited him again. Something in the prince told him that the animal's strength was very weak now, if, indeed, it had not been extinguished altogether.*

The future king of England slept and dreamed and sweated. His wife lay beside him, doing everything that she could to ignore the terrible roars and shouts from outside, noises strangely echoed beside her as her husband swam in and out of consciousness, calling out unfamiliar names and screaming for forgiveness, his body a battleground for forces beyond her comprehension.

And so it went for a day and a night until, early in the dawn of the third day, as the prince seemed at last to be coming back to her, Laetitia heard a firm, decisive knock upon the door.

"Who's there?" she cried out, shaking her husband hard to stir him. "Arthur? Someone's at the door."

The prince groaned, stirred and clutched at his forehead in a theatrical gesture which Laetitia had hitherto believed to be confined to stage drunks.

Then it came again—the same solemn tapping.

Laetitia looked around for something with which she might defend herself. Although the room lay in sepulchral gloom (the power having gone out almost forty-eight hours earlier and the emergency generator secreted beneath Clarence House failing only a very few minutes thereafter), it was still possible to see that the place was tastefully studded with objects of breezily incalculable wealth—several immensely rare vases, pottery fragments which were believed to predate Christ, a glass case of butterflies, all extinct—but none of them looked as though they might prove of much use as a weapon.

Arthur was at least sitting up now and had taken to rubbing his eyes, with hands clenched into fists like a child woken in the night. Laetitia was about to urge him into action when, from the other side of the door, she heard just about the most welcome voice in the world.

"Ma'am? Are you all right?"

Relief gushed into her voice: "Silverman?"

Behind her, Arthur, on his feet and searching for something on the floor by the bed, started to mumble a warning, but Laetitia ignored him and opened the door onto an old friend.

It was a friend, however, sadly changed. Mr. Silverman stood upon the threshold, badly bruised, stained in mud, grease and blood, his left hand horribly mangled as though he had dipped it, for some inebriate dare, into the spinning rotors of an uncompromisingly efficient piece of farming equipment.

"Silverman! My God!" The prince, leaning against the end of the bed, seemed to be stowing something into his trouser pocket. "What the devil have they done to you?"

The equerry stepped inside, closed the door and began to speak, briskly, urgently, but without obvious emotion, like a junior officer returned alone to HQ to deliver news of some catastrophic rout. "Mr. Streater took out some of his frustrations upon my person, sir. Shortly before imprisoning me in one of the wine cellars."

"But you escaped?" Laetitia asked.

"Indeed, ma'am."

Arthur gestured towards the gory remnants of Silverman's hand. "But not, it seems, without some cost to yourself."

"This is nothing, sir." The man looked hideously pale, his skin taut and glossy with sweat, but it was still possible to discern a blush. "It's a scratch."

"Can you tell us what's going on out there?"

Silverman appeared to sway slightly on his feet. "I think you might be able to teach us something about that, sir." There was a trace of recrimination in his voice—not obvious and probably invisible to anyone who did not know him but to Arthur and Laetitia strikingly and uncomfortably apparent.

"I've made mistakes, I know—" Arthur began.

Silverman cut him off with a gesture. "No time for that, sir. The city's being eaten alive."

"What?"

"It's the snow, sir. It's driven everybody mad."

"And Streater? What happened to him?"

"He's gone, sir. Took one of the Jaguars. He said that he had to look up an old friend. Although he was good enough to stop by the cellar for a few words. He seems to believe that he'll actually be rewarded for what he's done."

The prince straightened up, mopped his forehead, pushed back his shoulders, cleared his throat, and despite his evident exhaustion, the unkempt brush of his hair and the wildness which capered in his eyes, he looked, just for an instant, unmistakeably a king. Then his shoulders slumped, his posture sagged and he was only Arthur again. "I want you both to listen to me. This is what is going to happen. Silverman. I need you to stay here to look after Laetitia." His wife began to object but Arthur waved away her protestations. "I'm going outside," he said. "There is somebody I need to find."

Silverman sank gratefully onto the bed and nodded in grave approval.

"Good luck, sir."

"But if you're going outside, the snow—"

Arthur shook his head. "Something tells me I've built up a resistance." He bent down and kissed his wife on her forehead.

"Be careful," she said.

The prince reached into his pocket and pulled out the gun that Mr. Streater had given him what felt like a small eternity ago. "I have this," he said.

He nodded once, then, without saying goodbye, opened the door and stepped outside.

The house had been comprehensively ravaged and despoiled, as though an all-night party exclusively attended by vandals, incontinents and graffiti specialists had only recently moved on. Steeling himself against the sight of it, Arthur stepped through rubble and rubbish, over broken glass and furniture reduced to matchsticks, skirted around slicks of blood and trails of indescribable fluids before, at last, he emerged into the open air.

If anything, the devastation was even more advanced out here. Several vehicles were gutted and aflame and there were at least two bodies, which he tried not to examine too closely. As memories of what the cat had told him moved to the forefront of his brain and a more exact notion of what it was that he had to do began to form, he searched around for some means of transport.

When he saw it, he laughed out loud (a bitter, caustic sound). The only remaining car which seemed remotely roadworthy was an old Vauxhall Nova, effluent brown, the stink of Mr. Streater's treachery still boiling off it. Swallowing his laughter, Arthur Windsor strode across to the car of his enemy, wondering if the man had actually been arrogant enough to leave his keys in the ignition.

And there, for the present, we shall leave him. For all that he believed himself capable of some species of Dunkirk courage, the Prince of Wales was undeniably a coward, a milksop and a fool, stepping dumbly into the role suggested by a small grey cat, whose owner, we are very glad to be able to report, was at that time either dying (slowly, with great and exacting pain) or else already dead.

The tragedy of it all—the sheer, mindless folly of these people's actions—is brought home by the knowledge that we were only ever trying to help. However unfairly we may have been represented in these pages, you may be absolutely certain of the fact that Leviathan is here for one purpose only—we are here to tell you the good news.

CHAPTER 26

JOE!" ABBEY STOOD BEHIND ME IN THE CORRIDOR. "What the hell are you doing here?"

The blond man flashed a Hollywood grin. "Come to rescue you."

My landlady blushed. "You'd better get inside. Shut the door. There's things out there that—"

Like some laconic traffic cop, Joe Streater held up his hand to halt her. "They won't bother me."

"Why not?"

Streater shrugged. "Kind of a long story."

Still flushing crimson, Abbey stumbled over her words. "Henry, this is Joe. Joe—meet Henry."

The two of us glared at one another, both measuring and sizing up, the veil of civility already close to rending.

His examination complete, Joe gave me a dismissive smirk, and for this alone I could cheerfully have punched him on the nose.

Abbey touched me lightly on the arm, pivoting me away from the interloper. "This is awkward. I know that. Really, really awkward. But could you just give us a minute on our own? We'll go in the sitting room. There's some stuff we need to get straight."

"Fine," I said. "Dandy."

Frothing with rage and envy, I stalked off into the bedroom, sat on my bed and took deep, calming breaths. What seemed like a thousand different scenarios suggested themselves to me, none of them remotely optimistic.

A few minutes later and feeling no better, I succumbed to the inevitable, got to my feet, tiptoed outside the sitting room door and tried my best to eavesdrop.

Streater sounded calm and laid-back, his voice wheedling and full of flattery. Abbey was less controlled, quickly sliding into tearful hysteria. I realised that I'd never heard her like that before. She'd always struck me as essentially unflappable.

Should we pity Henry Lamb? There's something so pathetic about the man that we can never quite bring ourselves to do it. The idea that someone like his landlady would ever look twice at him were she not recovering from the abrupt cessation of an earlier entanglement is palpably absurd. The idiot Lamb was never much more to her than a man-sized comfort blanket.

EVEN NOW, I'M NOT SURE what passed between the two of them, but the first time I was able to catch exactly what they were saying, it was his voice that I heard.

These are the words of Joe Streater: "A new world is on its way. And if you wanna survive then you've gotta come with me. Stay here, and everything you know and love is gonna burn."

I leaned closer, trying to hear more, but just as Streater finished his speech, the door was flung open and I scurried goonishly backwards, almost tripping up.

Abbey hovered, tear stained, in the doorway. "Were you listening?"

I stuttered out a denial.

Behind her—friend Joe, grinning snarkily.

My landlady stepped out into the corridor and pulled the door shut on Streater.

"I can't believe you were listening," she said.

"Well, wouldn't you?"

"Just give us a couple of minutes, OK? There's lots of stuff we need to talk through."

I spoke as evenly as I could. "I can imagine."

"This is difficult for me. I'm confused."

"Well, how do you think I feel?"

"Sweetheart, please."

I managed a bitter sort of smile. "Do you know, he's not at all how I expected?"

Abbey conjured up a little smile—tentative, hopeful. "Oh? Why's that?"

"I didn't think he'd be so fucking ugly."

A long, brittle silence. "That's disappointing." There was a flinty pragmatism in her eyes which I'd never seen there before. "That's unworthy of you."

She opened the door to the sitting room and for an instant I caught an almost subliminal glimpse of Streater. I can't be sure that this is what I saw or whether it's something I've imagined since, filling in the gaps with all that I've learnt, but I'm almost positive that I saw him brandishing a syringe, filled with pale pink, effervescent liquid.

Then Abbey slammed the door and I saw no more.

You can imagine the true scene here. A pretty girl, resigned to sitting out the apocalypse in the company of a bloodless mummy's boy, is overjoyed at the arrival of an old flame. The contest is over before it has begun, the better man is victorious and all that remains is to find a way to eliminate the lodger.

THE REST WAS SOUND EFFECTS—a muffled declaration of affection, a wet, puckering sound, a moan of pleasure, a round of male laughter. Then swift strides across the room, the snap of the door as it was wrenched open again and Joe Streater was back in my face.

"Henry Lamb!" he said, walking up to me. "Weird coincidence."

"I don't believe in coincidence," I said, trying not to flinch. "No such thing."

The blond man flashed another savage smile. Silently, as though this was just another chore to carry out, quickly and briskly, before getting on with the rest of his life, he punched me hard in the stomach. Unprepared for this eruption of violence, I jackknifed in pain. My mouth bubbled with nausea. Streater pulled me upright and then he did it again—administered another pile-driving punch to my gut. As I stumbled, totally unable to muster the least defence, I saw Abbey watching as her boyfriend expertly beat me up, evidently appalled, her hand hovering towards her face as though to ward off what she was witnessing.

Fancy that.

It is our theory that the girl was laughing and that the hand hovering near her mouth was merely a device to disguise her smile.

※

STREATER DRAGGED ME into the sitting room, grabbed a chair from the table and forced me down into it. I made a grim, scuttling attempt at escape, which was quickly and permanently proved futile. Joe produced a thick roll of duct tape from somewhere (I wouldn't put it past him to have brought it with him) and lashed me to the chair, taping up my hands and ankles with practiced efficiency, winding a strip tight around my mouth. Already there was blood on my teeth, the taste of metal and, with it, the promise of vomit.

When he was finished, Joe Streater winked at me. "All right, chief?"

Abbey put a hand on the blond man's arm. "Is this really necessary?"

Streater answered her with a kiss and I had no choice but to watch as she met his lips with hers and gave every impression of liking it.

Joe came up for air. "Take me next door," he said, his voice filled with casual authority, with the certainty that he would never be disappointed. My Abbey smiled and led him from the room.

The next few minutes were a little difficult, trussed up in that chair, immobile, tasting blood and shame in equal measure as, from next door, I heard it all. Abbey and Joe in their scrabble to undo shoelaces, the clink of belts being unstrapped, the rustle of clothes being torn away and then—the creak of the mattress, the persistent rhythm of the headboard, the moans and squeals and ululations of delight. I wonder if she enjoyed it. I wonder how she possibly can have done.

※

Of course, she enjoyed it. How could she not? The fumbling ministrations of Henry Lamb, gauchely performed and inexpertly delivered, had scarcely raised her heartbeat. Her mind was ever on the lithe form of Joseph Streater. All the time she was with Henry, whenever the lodger kissed, caressed or tentatively nibbled, she was thinking of Joe. And when Streater took her to bed that afternoon, it was like coming home. It was a glorious, orgasmic vindication of her choice.

ONCE IT WAS OVER, Abbey came to say goodbye.

She asked me if I was crying. Grimly, I shook my head.

"I suppose you must be wondering why . . . why I've chosen him and not you. It has to sting, all this. It's got to rankle."

Through the duct tape, I groaned in affirmation.

"I hate to say it, Henry, but in the end it wasn't difficult."

I groaned again.

"You're too nice," she said. "You've got to have a bit of steel in you and Joe . . . Well, Joe's iron straight through."

This isn't you, I wanted to say. God, Abbey, this isn't you at all.

"Joe knows what I want," she said. "And the thing is—you never got to know me at all." She smiled sadly. "But we're still friends, aren't we? We'll be better as friends, I think. Better as mates."

I shook my head.

"Listen, Joe and I have to go now. There's a lot for us to do. I'm sorry. Truly." She kissed me on the forehead and walked away.

I heard the smack of the front door, the snap of the key in the lock, and for a short while, all was silence.

I THINK I MUST HAVE passed out. When I opened my eyes, it had grown dark, the blood on my wrists had dried to crusts and I felt a burning desire to urinate. But I wasn't alone. I could hear people moving about outside.

Someone come to find me? Abbey returned, stricken with conscience? Granddad?

I heard the rattle of the door, footsteps coming towards me, whispers which spoke my name. A faint hope ignited itself within me.

There was light in my eyes. A torch in my face. Hands reaching towards me.

I moaned a frantic greeting.

My rescuers grinned. "Hello, sir!"

"What ho, old top!"

The ginger-haired man yanked the tape from my mouth and I yelped in pain.

"You look a bit peaky, sir!"

Oh God.

"Please," I muttered. "Please . . . Please help me . . . I know we've had our differences. But for God's sake, let me go."

One of them giggled. "Sorry, lamb chop. That's not really on the cards."

Boon looked around him and smacked his hands together cheerfully. "Where's the little lady, then, sir?"

"Where's the missus?"

"Popped out, has she, sir?"

"Gone to borrow a cup of sugar?"

"Please . . . ," I said. "You can see what's happened here. Please untie me. That's all I ask."

"Oh no, sir."

"Couldn't do that, sir."

"Point of fact, this is how we expected to find you, sir. This is where your grandpapa told us you would be."

"What are you talking about?" I said, wriggling my arms beneath the rope.

"He liked your ladyfriend when he sold her the flat, sir."

"Thought she was quite the dish, sir."

"Thought she'd be perfect."

"Perfect?" I said. "Perfect for what?"

A wide grin stretched itself across Boon's face. "Perfect bait, sir," he said. "With which to set the trap."

Hawker pulled at each of my hands, wriggling them free from the tape and exposing my wrists.

"Now then, Mr. L," said Boon, "have we ever told you about our penknife?"

"It'd be queer if we hadn't, sir," Hawker chortled. "We tell most of the chaps. It's got a bottle opener and a corkscrew and a how-de-ye-do for getting stones from horses' hooves."

The pressure on my bladder had grown intolerable until, miserably, I felt warm piss spurt into my pants and start to soak my trousers.

Hawker dug into his blazer pocket. With evident pride, he produced a long knife and brought it close to my left wrist.

I screamed. "Please! What are you doing?"

Boon sniggered. "We're good boys."

"We're the sturdiest chaps in school."

"We're only doing what your grandpa wanted."

Cold steel on my skin.

"I shouldn't fret, sir."

"Buck up, Mr. L!"

"It's all part of the plan."

"All part of the Process."

Hawker cut into my wrist, slashing downwards in swift, vertical motions, following the path of the vein. Blood bubbled up. With hideous expertise, he did exactly the same to my other wrist.

As I screamed, Boon touched the brim of his cap. "'Fraid we've got to dash, sir."

"But we want you to know it's been a real pleasure."

"We've had ripping fun!"

"Such larks!"

"Such japes!"

"Ta-ta, sir!"

"Tinkety-tonk!"

With the smell of fireworks and sherbet dip, they shimmered and disappeared, and I was left alone in that wretched room, already too weak to cry out, watching my life pool away from me onto the floor. I stared down until I couldn't bear it any longer. I closed my eyes, lost myself in the pain and sucked in a few last breaths.

A short while later, my heart stopped beating altogether and I burrowed down into the darkness.

CHAPTER 27

I'VE JUST SEEN WHAT I WROTE YESTERDAY. OBVIously, you realise what's happened. The other storyteller (the interloper, the spite merchant) has returned and I no longer have complete control of my pen.

So this is it, then.

A race to the finish.

CHAPTER 28

U NEXPECTEDLY, I OPENED MY EYES.

It was as if I was waking up from an unusually vivid and visceral dream. I felt groggy and dazed and there was a sour taste in my mouth but the symptoms were no worse than those you might expect from a medium-strength hangover.

I was still bound to the chair but there were no cuts to my wrists. They chafed against the duct tape but they weren't bleeding now, nor did they even appear to be grazed. Of the Prefects, there was no sign.

The pieces of tape which tied me to the chair seemed suddenly easy to remove. They slipped away like shrouds.

I stood up, shaky, slightly nauseous, quivering with pins and needles, but otherwise conspicuously unharmed.

I thought of what Miss Morning had told me about Estella—of how her skin had healed right back up again after the Directorate had bled her to the point of death. I remembered, too, what she'd hinted about the history of this place. I wondered about what my mother had uncovered in the bedroom, the significance of those sigils, signs and symbols, wondered about exactly what had been done to me in those operations I'd undergone as a child.

A couple of minutes ensued during which I tried to dismiss

everything that had happened since Joe and Abbey had left as a hallucination or nightmare, but deep down I knew that something had been done to me, something set in motion. I even knew its name. Like everything else, Granddad had made sure of that.

The Process.

We count ourselves as no friends of his but in the final analysis it must be said that Henry Lamb was poorly used. The things that he allowed to be done to him were immoderate and inhumane. But the real tragedy lies in how bovinely he accepted it all.

Even now, his humiliations are far from at an end.

I TOOK MY LEAVE OF the flat and strode outside. The snow had finally stopped but its fall had rendered London strange and unfamiliar. The drones were everywhere. I couldn't see them but I could sense them, moving past me, bustling onwards, hastening into the centre of the city. They seemed to be saying something and gradually I made it out—the same chant, heard on every street corner, in every home, the same word, repeated over and over in a mantra of fierce joy.

"Leviathan! Leviathan! Leviathan!"

But for the first time in weeks, I no longer felt afraid. For so long, fear had been a part of my daily life, a car alarm whine which had swayed my every decision, stifled my imagination, stunted my morality.

I had only stepped a few metres from my front door when I saw it. Almost completely hooded in black snow, it was still immediately recognisable from the corkscrews of white hair which emerged like unusually hardy plant life through the darkness and the nose which jutted out like that of some ancient statue discovered in the dust.

The body of my grandfather.

As understanding began to percolate through my system, I fell to my knees with the same force as if I'd just been struck hard on the back of my legs. Tears crept from my eyes. I made no sound but began, reverentially, to scrape away the snow from his face, a patient archaeologist revealing, inch by inch, his cracked and weary features.

Then I heard the cry, much closer than before.

"Leviathan! Leviathan!"

With it, I could hear their raggedy breath and smell the weird electric tang of their sweat. Slowly—very slowly—I looked up.

There must have been twenty of them at least, arrived like hooligans at a wake, all with flushed pink faces, all shambling towards me in the kind of frantic clump you get emerging from a tube station at rush hour. "Leviathan . . . Leviathan . . ."

I struggled up. "Can't you fight it?" I asked a big bearded bloke in a postman's uniform who appeared to be leading the charge. "At least try."

He growled and lunged. "Leviathan . . . Leviathan . . ."

I was just beginning to wonder if it might not be about to end here, after all, at Granddad's side, when the postman's head erupted, unexpectedly prettily, in a fountain of pink and red. He didn't have time to cry out before he toppled to the ground, everything from the neck up a leaky scrag of gristle and bone.

I turned around. An old brown Vauxhall Nova had pulled up outside my flat and there was a man who I thought I recognised hanging out of the driver's window and holding a smoking gun.

"Get in!" he yelled. "Get in the car!"

The drones had cowered back at the gunshot but already

they had begun to regroup and were starting to move towards me, their new leader a fat man dressed from head to toe in pinstripe.

For the last time, I reached down and took the old bastard's hand. "This is my granddad," I called back. "I can't leave him."

The man in the car looked at me as though I was an idiot. "There's nothing you can do for him now."

"You don't understand. He's . . . he's the most important person."

"Leviathan!" Stomach bulging through striped shirt, fat hanging heavily over belt, the new leader of the drones was clumping purposefully in my direction, the rest of them following cloddishly in his wake.

"For God's sake! Get in the bloody car!"

I looked at what was coming towards me, squeezed Grand-dad's hand and made my decision. "Sorry," I said, "I'm so sorry," and I turned on my heel.

I ran over to the car and scrambled inside. My rescuer looked haggard, unshaven and scarily bloodshot—but it was unques-tionably him.

"Hello, Henry," he said, and gave an unnervingly high-pitched laugh.

"You recognise me?"

"You are Henry Lamb, aren't you?"

"Yes, sir," I said. "I mean, yes, Your Highness."

"I want you to call me Arthur," the driver said, and pressed his foot down hard, squealing out of the street, bumping over a colony of rubbish bags and only narrowly avoiding knocking down several drones.

When we were clear, I asked again how he knew my name.

"I've been dreaming about you. The cat's told me every-thing."

"What cat?"

"Little grey fellow. He told me how to fight the effects of ampersand. He told me how to finish this."

"Excuse me for saying so," I said, "and thanks very much by the way for rescuing me, but aren't you the enemy? Aren't we supposed to be at war?"

"The war ends tonight," Arthur Windsor said firmly. "You and I, Henry. We're going to put a stop to it."

As WE DROVE from Tooting Bec, we witnessed first-hand the fall of the city. Houses were smouldering, pavements were carpeted in glass, cars had been reduced to blackened clinker and entire streets were streaked with red. I saw a bus stop mangled into scrap and what looked like the contents of a clothes store sprayed across the road, as though a bomb had exploded in a jumble sale. It was almost unendurable to see—London, that remorseless victor, that dead-eyed master of predation, turned victim and prey, defenceless meat for some parasite which, comfortably accommodated in its gut, now chomped its eager way into the world.

There were people abroad, drones streaming in the same direction, rushing forwards in makeshift columns, and we had no choice but to drive funereally through their midst, like killjoys at a parade. In their haste to move forwards some of the stronger ones were trampling their weaker fellows underfoot. A number of times, I asked the prince to stop so we could at least try to help, but he just snapped something about not having time for sentiment and kept on driving.

"They tried to send me mad, you know," he said. "Can you believe that?"

I looked at him, with his tangled hair, tufty stubble and bulging eyes, and couldn't believe that it would ever have taken that much.

"They tried to get me hooked. They showed me ghosts and slivers of the truth. Lord knows why but I think they wanted me to kill my wife."

WE LEFT TOOTING BEHIND US and, following the mass of drones, roughly retraced my old route to work—through Clapham, Brixton, Stockwell and Lambeth. The further we went, the more the streets grew clotted with crowds and the harder it became to manoeuvre through the tide of humanity.

"The cat had a message for you," said the prince, swerving fast around a downed double-decker which sprawled across the length of the road like a great red seal bathing in the sun.

"I'm sorry?"

Arthur drummed his fingers excitedly on the steering wheel. "He said you'd need a phrase. For the Process. An incantation to close the trap. He told me you'd know what to do."

I thought for a moment, then: "I've got a pretty good idea."

ALTHOUGH I FEARED that the journey would last forever, that we would drive unendingly through this shadow realm, I feared still more what was waiting for us at our destination. Then we turned a corner, the exterior of Waterloo station came into view and at last I realised where it was the drones were heading.

The streets were now so choked and thronged that we had no choice but to abandon the car and take our chances amongst the mob. Stepping carefully from the vehicle and trying our best to stop our ears against the cries of the crowd, we moved towards the station. The crowd seemed mostly oblivious to us, too close to the object of their quest to pay us much heed. We had to join the surge, give in, become part of the torrent and let ourselves be swept into Waterloo.

The place, though packed, seemed eerily neglected. The small shops, fast food outlets and newsagents were entirely untouched, unstaffed but still open for business—burgers cold to the touch, days-old newspapers lying undisturbed, a rack of sandwiches starting to turn green and rancid behind their plastic wrappers. The drones ignored them all, even their needs for food and current affairs now subsumed by the urge to reach their destination. There was death, too—mangled cadavers clogging up the escalators, a solitary ticket inspector trampled underfoot, the flyblown corpses of a guide dog and its master— but Arthur and I walked past it all.

We were pushed through the main part of the station, then moved along with the drones, allowing ourselves to be jostled up an Escher maze of concrete, unable to stop or slow down, trying not to think too hard about those who were thrown to the floor and trampled underfoot. We emerged onto the South Bank, almost exactly opposite the spot where, in a lunch-hour long ago, I'd sat and watched Barbara devour a cheese baguette.

Before us was the river, the great dark width of the Thames, and there at last we saw it—the sea beast, the great serpent, the tyrant of the seven heads.

It must have been a crash landing. The Houses of Parliament looked smashed and half-demolished, Cleopatra's Needle was snapped in two and the Eye leant askew like something had simply batted it aside. In the distance, the spires of the business district stood darkened and empty. Boats of every kind—sight-seeing vessels, pleasure cruisers, industrial transport ships, floating restaurants and a fleet of police launches—had been hurled against the bank, where they lay shattered like broken toys, reduced to so much driftwood and debris.

The sheer mass of the creature had caused the river to burst its banks. Water overflowed and sluiced across the pavement, making the ground slippery and treacherous.

The entire length of the Thames as far as the eye could see was filled with a vast black shadow, just out of sight. The water around it was bubbling and broiling in distress, shooting out jets of steam and malevolent emissions from the deep. All that was visible and exposed of the beast were slender tubes, long thin tentacular things which snaked out of the water and came limply to rest on the pavement like stems of meat or straws of flesh.

Our ampersand had made the people of this city so grateful! They rushed out to meet us, eager to offer their services, aching to become part of something greater and more wonderful than themselves. And, honestly, who amongst us can blame them for that?

To our horror, Arthur and I saw what was happening. All the people who had been hurrying with such desperation through the city now dashed on towards the riverbank, skidding, sliding along the pavements with such insanely enthusiastic speed that I thought they were in danger of toppling into the water. But no, they came to a halt just in time and fell to their knees. Then, humbly, reverentially, each and every one of them picked up a tendril in their hands and, in a moment of unutterable obscenity, took it into their mouths, opening wide, gobbling with infantile glee. They suckled for a moment, their faces suffused with pleasure, before, disgustingly satiated, they collapsed onto their backs and crawled away into the city, chattering to themselves, bleating nonsense words and strings of impossible numbers. One of these unfortunates blundered past me, his eyes hopeless and black, his lips able to move only in the service of Leviathan, like a termite, an insect helplessly in thrall. I tried to stop him but the drone barely seemed to notice and he shouldered his way past, still gibbering his incomprehensible language.

The city was Leviathan's now. It belonged lock, stock and barrel to this monstrosity, this implacable enemy of life.

This is a slanderous misrepresentation. We were only ever doing our jobs, fulfilling our quota and offering our customers the kind of top-quality service which they have deservedly come to expect.

As we reached the riverbank, I heard a noisy heaving to my right. The prince was doubled up, powerless in the grip of regurgitation, spewing his breakfast onto the tarmac.

I was hunting through my pockets to see if I couldn't find the poor man a tissue when somebody shouted my name. With a gunslinger swivel, I turned around.

Joe Streater stood behind me. By his side, stumbling and puffy faced—my landlady.

"Abbey?"

She looked at me blankly. "Leviathan?"

"This is your fault," Streater said.

"Me?"

"They promised I could save her. But as soon as she stepped into the snow . . . It wouldn't have happened if I'd got to her sooner. If you hadn't gone and hid her from me."

"I only tried to keep her safe. You're the one who practically kidnapped the poor girl."

We were so occupied in our argument (soundtracked by the continued retching of the future king of England) that we didn't even notice what Abbey did next, didn't see her as she staggered towards the water's edge, her eyes speaking only of hunger and lust. It was Joe who stopped speaking first. He was staring past me, towards the river.

"Abs?" he shouted, but it was already too late. Before either of us could stop her, she crouched down, reached for a tendril, placed the thing between her lips and gurgled in delight.

"Abbey!" I shouted. "Darling, for God's sake!"

Streater glared at me. "Please," he said to her. "Please, babe. Don't do that."

But she was already finished. Abbey removed the tendril from her mouth and turned her face upon us. The change was absolute. Her eyes were pinpricks and she was chattering too fast—impossible formulae which should never have been spoken aloud, vile, blasphemous things whose very sound made some ancient part of my brain recoil in reptilian disgust.

She no longer knew us and staggered away to join the others, disappearing back into the city, gibbering and weeping, consumed by inexplicable purpose.

The girl should have been grateful. After all, she had finally made herself useful. At long last, she was doing something worthwhile with her life.

I DIDN'T NEED TO THINK any more but just launched myself at Joe Streater. Shocked by the ferocity of my assault, he staggered backwards and we scuffled incompetently together by the banks of the Thames, exchanging feeble blows and girly punches, close enough to the creature to hear its hisses of pleasure, its oozing exhalations of joy and repellent coos of victory.

I pulled on Streater's shoulder, spun him around and kicked him in the stomach. Although the impact hurt my foot, the traitor slid backwards, slipping in the slush and water which lapped along the pavement. Behind him, most of the railing had been peeled away by some surge of the crowd, so when I kicked him again there was no way to stop him toppling into the water. He tried to save himself by clinging onto the last strip of railing with his fingers. To my astonishment, it looked as though there might be tears in his eyes.

"That shouldn't have happened. They said she'd be safe."

"They lied to you," I said. "Of course they lied to you."

"You don't understand." I saw now that I'd been right and that the man really did have tears seeping from his eyes. "I only did this for her. I wanted to win her back. I wanted to give it another go."

He looked pathetic—the great Joe Streater, Iago to the crown, Quisling to the beast—now just another sap clinging on to life at any cost, another loser, another opportunist who's taken a wrong turn. Mephistopheles reduced to a charity case.

I suppose the kindest thing, the most honourable and decent thing to have done would have been to bend down, offer him my hand and help him up. Indeed, if either of us had been players in a Hollywood movie where character arcs and life lessons come as standard, then that's exactly what would have happened.

It wasn't, however, what took place that day by the banks of the river.

I kicked Joe Streater in the face, and I have to say—the wicket-crack his front teeth made when they shattered was one of the most satisfying sounds I've ever heard. He spat out the bone and wailed up at me in rage and despair, pleading pitifully for mercy.

So I stamped hard on his fingers.

With a final whine, he let go and plopped miserably into the river. I was just dreaming up an amusingly apposite quip when two hundred pounds of royal bulk slammed into the side of me, delivering us both into the churning water.

For a moment, this was how I thought it was going to end—the prince, Joe Streater and me, all floundering in the Thames, our arms flailing, gasping at the cold, struggling impotently against the tide—but then I became aware of something slick and ropey feeling its way towards me and I knew that this wasn't the end. Not quite yet.

I think I may even have tried to scream but my mouth was choked with river water. Something slithered around the back of my neck, wound itself around my shoulders and pulled tight about my chest. The last thing I remember is a sensation of movement, of being pulled fast through the river water, tugged deep into the belly of the beast, into the black heart of Leviathan.

What lay in the Thames that afternoon was a thing of beauty and wonder. Henry Lamb should have welcomed it with hymns of praise and thanksgiving. He should have kissed it. He should have bowed down before it and worshipped it as a living god.

CHAPTER 29

MY FIRST THOUGHT WAS THAT THIS MIGHT BE PUR-gatory.

It took me a moment to identify my overriding emotion. It was boredom—enervating, brain-sapping, debilitating boredom.

Inexplicably, I appeared to be sitting at a desk in an office, warm, dry and apparently back to normal. There was a computer in front of me, switched on and displaying a spreadsheet. There was a telephone, a drawer filled with stationery products and a stack of dun-coloured folders. The place was crowded with the usual sounds—the faint hum of computers, the chuntering whine of the photocopier, the persistent insectoid buzz of ringing phones. Somewhere, inevitably, there was the endless gnashing of crisps.

I craned my head to see who was with me, whom I instinctively thought of as my colleagues, but couldn't get a good look at any of them. Their faces were obscured by screens, blurred by distance or masked by shadows.

Unsure of my next move, I resorted to what I'd done on so many afternoons at work: slumped back in my chair and stared at the computer. Not that I could make any sense of the spreadsheet, of its alien letters, its repulsive alphabet and baffling strings of digits.

Just as I felt close to screaming (that quarter-to-three-on-a-Wednesday feeling magnified to an intolerable degree) the phone on my desk jingled to life.

And you know what I'm like with ringing telephones.

"Hello?" I said.

"Top o' the morning ter you, sir." The man's accent sounded like he was putting me on.

"Who is this?"

There was another voice on the line, another accent. "Could you come intae the office, laddie? There's a wee matter needs clearing up."

"Where—?"

I was swiftly interrupted by a third voice, crisper than the rest. "We're at the end of the corridor, my friend. Second door on the right."

I set the receiver gently back down and got to my feet. Still unable to make out the faces of my colleagues, I moved cautiously towards the door. As I walked, I realised with a twitch of disgust that the walls and floors and ceiling of this place were constructed not from concrete or brick but from some soft, hot, spongy substance. Despite my very best efforts to forget, I remember this—walking through those corridors was like trying to escape from a bouncy castle made of meat.

As I walked, I had a sudden image of what Leviathan must look like in full, of how it must appear in motion—in flight. I saw the beast in all its grisly majesty, gliding through the infinite nightmare of space, and in a sickening flash of vision, I knew how many worlds it had consumed. I heard the pitiful wails of its victims, saw the inhabitants of unimaginable places look up when the shadow of Leviathan passed over their lands, and like them, I knew with a terrible certainty that the end had surely come.

Ah, the glorious peripatetic offices of Leviathan! Soaring over world after world—utilising raw materials in a responsible and sustainable manner without ever losing sight of the economic imperative. Ignore the words of Henry Lamb—a hopeless naïf who never understood the necessities of business. One would find very few indeed in our stretch of the universe who would say a word to impugn the working practices of Leviathan. Or, indeed, given the litigious humour of our attorneys, who would dare.

I REACHED THE END OF the corridor. On the door to which I had been directed, there was a corporate logo—a circle of colour—and, beneath it, the name of the company in whose headquarters I evidently stood.

LEVIATHAN

But it was what was written below, those four horrific words, which really sent volts of panic shooting through me.

STORAGE AND RECORD RETRIEVAL

When Arthur Windsor opened his eyes, he too was sitting down, clean, warm, dry and comfortable—if slightly bored.

Not that there should be anything surprising in most of this. We have always prided ourselves on our unimpeachably high standards of hospitality—although we remain disappointed that our guests continually fail to appreciate quite what fascinating work we do here at Leviathan.

The prince was sitting at a long trestle table in a clammy, strip-lit room, devoid of natural light. There was a fat woman next to him, sorting with mechanical efficiency through teetering stacks of folders.

Given the considerable pounds she had acquired since their last meeting, it took a second or two for Arthur to recognise her.

"Mother?"

"I was wondering what kept you," said the Queen, without troubling to look up from her work.

"Mother," said the prince again, "what is this place?"

The monarch smiled and Arthur recognised in that expression of satiated giddiness something of the terrible elation he had seen rising behind the eyes of his ancestor. "Why," she said, "this is Leviathan. We're part of the beast now." She shoved a stack of files into his arms. "Make yourself useful, will you, and sort these into alphabetical order."

Arthur stared forlornly at what he'd been given, at what seemed to him to be alien hieroglyphics. "Mother, I don't recognise this alphabet."

The Queen tutted. "Then learn."

"Why are we going along with this? Why are we collaborating with this monster?"

"Leviathan is the future, Arthur. He will guide us, keep us, protect us. Our empire will flourish. He will keep our borders safe and render us inviolate against invasion."

"No." Arthur stumbled up. "This is all wrong."

"Wrong? How can this possibly be wrong?"

"Look what it's doing to our people."

"As I understand it, Leviathan is merely giving a little structure to their lives. Lord knows, most of them need it. I think of it as a kind of return to National Service. And you know how fervently I approved of that."

"For God's sake!"

"Very well then. Don't just take your mother's word for it. See the manager if you must. He's a reasonable creature. His door is always open. Sixth floor, end of the corridor, second door on the right."

"Perhaps I shall. I am the gun, after all, and he is the bullet."

The Queen squinted suspiciously. "What's that?"

Arthur pushed back his chair. "Mother?"

"Yes, dear?"

"You set this up, didn't you? That business with Mr. Streater. Trying to make me a slave to ampersand."

"What of it?"

"Did you want me to kill Laetitia? Why would you want that?"

The Queen smiled simperingly. "Are you sure you want to know?"

Of course, Arthur said that he did.

"Your wife is with child. I'm afraid I simply couldn't bear the thought of any heir of mine being born to that fraudulent bitch."

"Is that true?" Arthur said wonderingly. "A baby?"

"I believe that she was keeping it from you until she was ab-solutely certain. Such a shame you lacked the courage to finish her. But then, failure is what we've come to expect of you." She hiccoughed and her face was stained a deep shade of ampersand pink.

Arthur got up and strode away from his mother, blocking out the sound of her jibes, past trestle tables filled with workers whose faces were perpetually out of focus. He called back over his shoulder as he reached the exit. "The war ends tonight."

The Queen cackled. "Oh, Arthur."

Her face was bright purple now and it seemed to the prince that something was moving beneath her skin, that sores and boils were rising to the surface with unnatural speed. She started to laugh and Arthur was reminded of the sickening death of the woman from the Eurostar, the doomed mule who had expired before his eyes with the sound of the hearty impact of a water balloon on a hot summer's day.

The Queen's face had begun to bloat and bulge and pustulate with an excess of ampersand. Arthur could not bear to be in the same room as her. He had a horrible suspicion that he knew precisely what was going to happen next.

"Oh, my dear boy." His mother giggled, her body racked with some unendurable internal pressure. "Don't you see?" She whinnied in hysterical laughter. "The war's already won."

I KNOCKED ON THE DOOR and three voices called out from within—"Come!"

It was a small office, its centrepiece a long ebony desk at which sat three men dressed in Victorian black. Behind them was a jade-green door—and what lay beyond that door, I wished fervently never to know. Just at the sight of it, I knew that I'd give absolutely anything never to have to pass beyond it.

But I wasn't the only visitor. Sitting with his back to me, hunched and chastened, slouched in his chair and sipping miserably at a cup of tea, was Joe Streater.

The first of the men looked up as I came in. He spoke with a cut-glass English accent, like an aristocrat in a comedy sketch. "Who are you exactly?"

"Oh, I'm nobody special."

The man next to him looked up at me. When he spoke it was in an Irish lilt. "But who are yer?"

"Just a filing clerk."

When the third man spoke it was in a thick Scots brogue. "Ye don't seem tae be affected by the snow."

"I want some answers," I said, trying to be bullish. "People are dying out there and I need to understand what's going on."

"We're a transparent organisation," said the Englishman. "Ask us anything you wish."

"Why is this place an office?"

"Naturally, we're an office. Peripatetic, perhaps, but an office nonetheless. It was only a branch which was trapped on Earth. On its release, Head Office was summoned and I'm delighted to report that they've arrived most promptly."

"I've waited years tae see this place," said the Scotsman, "and I have tae say I'm not disappointed."

"It's an office," I said again, redundantly. "Leviathan's a bloody office."

The Irishman shrugged. "What were yer expecting?"

"I was expecting something monstrous."

"Ah, but we are monstrous." The Irishman laughed. "Monstrously successful."

The Scotsman glowered in my direction. "Leviathan Corporation is by far the largest and most successful archive and storage business in the knoon universe."

"Archive and storage?" I said. "You're not serious?"

"Storage is a universal problem, laddie."

"So?"

The Englishman smiled. "Leviathan offers the solution. We find a planet with the right kind of environment, where the indigenous population has physiognomies capable of sustaining our kind of information, and we simply download it into their systems. Most planets in this part of the galaxy are annexed to the needs of Leviathan."

I stared at them in horrified disbelief. "That's what all this has been about? You're storing information in people? You're using human beings as living files?"

The Englishman smiled. "You hew down trees for paper. The principle is the same."

"How can you be a party to this? You're the same as us. You're human beings."

The Scotsman shrugged. "Just between you and me, Mr. Lamb, there's nae much of us that you could really call human any more."

Why should we apologise? We were simply supplying a need. If we had not offered the service, if we had not transformed planets into filing cabinets, then you may be sure that someone else would have done the same, and almost certainly at considerably less reasonable rates. Such are the demands of business.

FOR THE FIRST TIME since I had entered the room, Joe Streater spoke up, his voice weedy and pathetic. "You said you'd make me a hero. You promised you'd set me up amongst the gods."

I couldn't help myself at this, couldn't stop myself from laughing.

Joe turned his sharp little face in my direction. "What's so funny?"

"You won't be a god," I gasped. "You'll be a filing clerk."

The Scotsman shook his head. "You've let us doon, Joseph. The prince has nae bin persuaded tae our way ay thinkin'."

"He was getting help!" Streater protested. "Course I see that now."

Just to add to the sense that this was a particularly peculiar dream, packed with people you haven't thought about in years and faces you half recognise from the telly, the door behind me was thrown open and the heir to the throne strode thunderously in.

The Englishman spread his hands in oleaginous welcome. "Good afternoon, sir. We're delighted you could join us."

The prince scarcely looked at the men behind the desk. His wrath was directed towards an old friend. "Streater!"

"All right, chief?" For an instant, there was a flash of the old Joe, a little of the cocky opportunist who must once have dazzled my poor Abbey.

Never yours, Henry Lamb. Have you still not understood that? She was never yours.

A SURGE OF PINK CROSSED Streater's face, a flush of scarlet. He dropped the teacup, which splintered on the floor.

The Scotsman looked up at him. "We're going to have to let ye go, son."

Streater squealed. "Come on, lads. Fair's fair. I don't deserve this. I've served you faithfully."

He was evidently in a great deal of pain and I strongly suspected that he was soon to be in receipt of a good deal more. The floor around his feet began to liquefy, melting into sludge around his shoes. He looked up at us with horror in his eyes.

"Please . . . ," he stuttered. "Please help me."

I stared at him, appalled, immobile. But the prince was actually shaking his head.

"No," he said. "Not any more. Got a bit of steel in me now."

Joe looked imploringly at the prince and let out a feeble moan.

"Finally," Arthur purred. "I've been blooded."

A tentacle, bristling with protuberances, slithered out of the wall, clamped itself against Streater's mouth and forced its way inside—wriggling into his throat, pumping him with alien words and figures, filling him up with an unbearable volume of information. Streater's eyes seemed impossibly large. Bucking against the horror of it all, his mind snapped.

The floor around his feet had opened up like a quagmire. It sucked at poor Joe's legs, heaved at his thighs, genitals and torso, dragging him down, still screaming, into the depths.

ARTHUR BARELY SEEMED to have noticed all this. He turned to the Englishman, the Irishman and the Scotsman. "I wish to revoke the deal made by my great-great-great-grandmother."

"Terribly sorry," said the Englishman. "Afraid that can't be done. We drew up the contract, after all. Naturally, it's absolutely watertight."

"I refuse to parlay with footmen. Fetch me the manager."

The Irishman: "You want ter speak to the boss?"

Arthur nodded.

The Scotsman grinned and gestured towards the jade door. "Through that duir, sairr, if you'd like a wee wuid."

The Irishman reached across the desk and pressed a button on his intercom. "Sorry to bother you, sir, but is dare any chance of the prince havin' a quick ward?"

The sound that came from that machine was wholly indescribable. It had no business being heard on Earth. An awful, piercing roar, the ululating cry of something born billions of light years from the South Bank.

Our manager, as it happens. The most successful CEO Leviathan has ever been lucky enough to have at its helm. Lamb should feel honoured even to have been allowed an audience.

"HE SAYS YOU CAN GO in now," the Englishman said smoothly, evidently long fluent in whatever evil language that creature spoke. "I don't recommend you dilly-dally. I know from painful experience that he doesn't care to be kept waiting."

"May I bring my friend?" Arthur asked nonchalantly.

The Scotsman shrugged. "Yuid better get a move on."

The prince approached the jade door and beckoned for me to follow.

"You want me to go with you?" I asked, hoping more than anything that he'd say no. The prince nodded. Reluctantly, I drew near.

From the other side of the door we could hear the movements of the CEO. We could hear its creeps and slithers, the rattling hiss of its breath, the swish of its tails, the wheezing, sipping noise it made in preparation for our arrival.

"Please," I said. "Please don't make me go inside."

"You have to."

Everything within me screamed at me not to go beyond that door—the same atavistic fear of the Neanderthal who stares into the dark as, behind him, his fire gutters and dies.

"I can't."

"Henry, this is what you were born for."

Behind us, the Englishman stood up. "Wait a moment. May I ask the name of that young man?"

"Aye." The Scotsman rose to his feet. "Guid question."

Inevitably, the Irishman did the same. "Tell us."

Slowly, the prince turned to face them, his arm outstretched to protect me. "Go," he snapped. Smiling, he addressed himself to the legal firm of Wholeworm, Quillinane and Killbreath, to those wretched refugees from a joke my granddad never finished. "His name is Henry Lamb," he said. "And he is the engine of your destruction."

Suddenly, the Englishman, the Irishman and the Scotsman were upon us, moving faster than any human being should be able, hissing out their rage, teeth ripping, nails rending, reaching past the prince and towards me like hounds deprived of their kill.

The Scotsman had been right—there was very little left of those creatures which anyone would call human any more.

A little changed, perhaps. A few pro bono augmentations.

But make no mistake—those men were grateful to us, happy to be employed in the service of Leviathan, all too eager for the perks and bonuses which come with long and faithful service.

"Go!" SHOUTED THE PRINCE, as he grappled with the Englishman. "For God's sake, do what you have to!"

MY HAND TOUCHED THE door handle but I felt fingers pulling at my shirt, the Irishman and the Scotsman dragging me backwards into the mêlée. But I knew what was required of me and so I struggled free.

Too late for them to stop me now; I stepped inside and for a shaving of a second—

—I WAS BACK IN 1986, eight years old again and walking onto set to deliver the laugh line. I could feel the heat of the studio lights, see the camera crew, glimpse Granddad patiently looking on, willing me to say the words he'd written.

THEN THE FICTION FELL AWAY and it was just me and the CEO—a mass of teeth, tentacles and claws, its great eye, milky white, scored as though by chisel marks—Miss Morning's vision made flesh.

I wanted to scream. All rational thought fled my mind and I felt faint, as close to passing out as I had on the day that I first met Dedlock. But somehow I stood firm. Somehow I managed to say something, the only sentence I could think of—a daft old joke nobody understood, written for me years ago and which had followed me around ever since. My line. The old line. The incantation at the heart of the Process.

"DON'T BLAME ME . . ."

THE CREATURE, AWARE, too late, of what was happening, began to fight back, pitting its vast intelligence against my own puny equivalent. I could hear the blood pounding through my head as I channeled my last remaining strength into the final line . . .

"BLAME GRANDPA."

THE PROCESS DID ITS WORK—bending time, compressing matter, and I saw, as though from a great distance, my past laid out like train tracks beneath me, all leading to a single destination, a terminus chosen for me long ago. The Process had hollowed me out, reformed me for a single purpose—to hold the genie in the bottle, the spider in the jar.

I can only explain what happened next as a kind of drawing in, a sucking, an inhalation. I felt the beast, the great serpent, the tyrant of the seven heads, struggle against me, thrash and flail furiously against my gravity until at last I pulled it into me and bound it, deep inside, where my soul ought to have been.

CHAPTER 30

THE CITY SURVIVED, OF COURSE, AS IT ALWAYS DOES. The Directorate, on the other hand, is officially closed for business. Dedlock, Jasper, Barnaby and Steerforth are gone, the war is over and, mercifully, the secrets of the Blueprint Programme perished with the man whose real name (if I am to believe anything he told me) was Richard Price, at the moment when he slipped away, drugged up to the point of happy insensibility, in the honeymoon suite of one of London's premiere hotels.

But I suspect that the Directorate is still not quite done. It has survived too long and against too fantastic odds for there not to be some glimmer of life there yet. Think of it what you will, but you have to admit that it's an institution with the survival skills of a cockroach. And, so far as I am aware, poor, transformed Barbara remains at large.

Whilst the essence, the mental energy, of Leviathan writhed and squirmed within me, its physical form, that fleshy, dead bulk, still wallowed in the Thames, cooling down and beginning to putrefy. There was fierce enthusiasm from a great number of professionals in dissecting and studying the creature, but in the end it was decided, in the interests of public health and safety, that the carcass should simply be burnt—the great serpent consigned to the flames, the mighty corporation of Leviathan, that market leader in storage and record retrieval, stuffed piece by piece into the furnace.

It took an unprecedented collaboration between the military and the emergency services to haul the monster from the water, saw it up and cut it down in preparation for transportation, but even then, this wasn't done quickly enough. The meat began to spoil at an impossibly fast rate and the smell, I am told, lingered in the streets for weeks.

Those who had suckled at its teats were gone for good. A faintly mawkish memorial service was held in Trafalgar Square, presided over by the prime minister, who, although visibly aged by events, had fortunately been in Geneva at the time of the snowfall. A number of his cabinet had not been so lucky.

Anyone who hadn't reached the river to gobble greedily on that liquid data recovered. There was much confusion, angry refutation, tearful acceptance and, ultimately, a good deal of a deep and queasy kind of grief. A lot of people came close to the brink that day but the majority were saved. In the end, everyone did the only thing they can do—take a deep breath, put their best foot forwards and carry on with their lives, settling back in the old routine, the working week, the morning commute, the daily stampede into the centre of the city.

And then there was me, of course. I was saved, too.

After the trap of the Process snapped shut, everything went black and I can remember only flashes of what happened next, a sequence of flash-bulb pictures—strong arms pulling me from the water, a warm, restorative liquid being poured down my throat, the sensation of being lowered onto something soft, the soporific motions of a long car journey.

Apparently, I was delirious when they found me, still chattering about the snow, the CEO, the information. The first thing I can really remember is waking up here, in bed, at Highgrove, where you've undone so much of the damage caused by the errors and misjudgements of your ancestors and been gracious enough to make me feel welcome.

I have taken great pleasure in getting to know you and your lovely wife and I would enjoy nothing more than to meet your son or daughter, whose arrival, as I write, is expected any day now.

But this is all most unlikely. There's something I haven't told you.

There is a voice in my head. The first time that it spoke it uttered only nine words and then fell silent. Naturally, for a short while, I tried to convince myself that I had imagined it, that it was all some strange aftereffect, an auditory hallucination brought on by extreme fatigue.

But it has grown worse—much worse—in the past few days and it is high time that I accepted the truth. Leviathan is awake inside me and growing in strength.

What Estella held within her was merely a branch of Leviathan. What I have is its head office, its nerve centre, its business brain. I'm afraid it will take a considerable sacrifice to bind it for good.

Actually, I think I know how it's going to go. You might even have noticed it yourself. Over the past few days, my clothes have been getting bigger and baggier. My voice has seemed a little higher in pitch, often cracking and squeaky, sometimes child-like. But, strangely, I feel better than before. There are times when I even feel like laughing.

You may do what you like with this manuscript. Keep it in a locked drawer. Burn it. Publish it, even. Only words, after all.

One last thing. The truth about that voice which has spilt from my head and onto the page.

The first time I heard it, I had just woken on my first day here, and at the sound of it, I began to shake. It was more than just a voice, it was a chorus of voices speaking as one. It was the voice of Leviathan, the voices of the Englishman, the Irishman, the Scotsman, of the old Queen, the creature behind the jade door, the buzz of the drones and, buried deep in some murky quarter of its being, impossibly bitter but still cocksure, the voice of Mr. Streater.

This is not the end, it said. *The wilderness is waiting.*

EDITOR'S POSTSCRIPT

AT THE TIME OF WRITING, TWO NIGHTS HAVE PASSED since I said goodbye to Henry Lamb. Until now, I have not found sufficient courage to set pen to paper. Indeed, I find that I am able to write only in the daylight, with my wife and daughter comfortably close by, with the lamps on full to chase away the shadows, and far from any mirror or reflective surface.

We found him in the end. After abandoning the manuscript on my doorstep, he had taken one of our cars and driven into the Fens intending to do battle with what lay within him, with whatever it was that had written those parts of his book in a hand which was not his own.

But it was not Henry Lamb who came stumbling out of the wilderness towards us, towards the sirens and the flock of media who had gathered there against my ardent protestations. The man I knew had vanished from the face of the Earth.

Since reading what Henry wrote, I think often of Estella, about her description of what happens when you carry Leviathan inside you, of how the monster strips away artifice and unveils the real person underneath.

What staggered from the wilderness was a little boy, eight or nine years old, looking minuscule and ridiculous in adult clothes which hung pathetically off his body and trailed in the mud. I recognised that awful yellow jumper almost at once but it took me some time to identify the child lost inside it. In the end, I had to be shown old television footage before I was wholly convinced.

The boy was not loquacious. In fact, he would only ever utter a single phrase, the same quintet of words repeated over and over. It was an old catchphrase, devoid of meaning and even less amusing now than ever.

Two days ago, I went to say goodbye. Of course, Silverman arranged the whole thing wonderfully—the little lie in my official diary, the plainclothes security team, the discreetly unmarked car. In my new position, one can hardly be too careful.

The reader might find a bleak humour in where we keep Henry nowadays. He lies underground, deep beneath the town house of my first minister and at the exact centre of a white chalk circle.

He does not seem to have aged a day but remains, eternally, a child. He does not perspire even slightly. No drop of sweat has been found beneath his prepubescent armpits, no trickle of perspiration on his calves or boyish moisture on the small of his back. He is well cared for, and although he is kept under lock and key, I make certain that the best of everything is brought to his cell. I have been adamant that those who keep and care for him are scrupulously vetted in order to avoid any repetition of what has come to be euphemistically referred to as "the Hickey-Brown problem."

Naturally, Henry never leaves his cell. I owe him my life but it would hardly do for the poor fellow to walk abroad.

As usual, on my last visit, he did not seem to know that I was there. I brought Silverman with me for company but Henry seemed wholly oblivious to our presence, spending the entirety of our meeting intoning the same five words.

Curiously, there was a small grey cat sitting in the circle with him, curled up by Henry's feet, purring happily and apparently quite content. I have asked how the animal came to be there but it may not surprise you to learn that a sufficiently persuasive explanation for its presence has yet to be advanced.

After I had said my goodbyes, still dabbing at my eyes and pledging my continued support, I took a detour into the smallest room and, despite his objections, ordered Silverman to wait for me upstairs.

I had completed my business and was midway through my ablutions at the basin when I caught a blur of motion, a sudden flash of colour in the mirror.

Two men stood behind me. How they had entered unobserved and unchallenged, I had not the slightest notion, although—needless to say—I recognised them at once.

With their uniforms, their gnarled knees, their unforgettable air of menace, who could not?

"Hello, sir!"

"What ho, Arthur, old son!"

I dared address myself only to their reflections and asked them what they wanted of me.

"Just thought we'd drop by, sir!"

"Pop in for a bit of a chinwag!"

I spoke softly, trying to keep my head, and remarked that, without their actions, London would stand in ruins.

"Oh, but you'll make us blush, sir!"

"Stop it, sir, or you'll embarrass us. Boon here goes the colour of Tommy K."

I told them that I could never fathom their motives.

Those awful creatures laughed at me. "Give it time, old thing."

"You'll be seeing a lot more of us in the future."

As my throat turned dry, I asked them what they meant.

"We'll be dropping by regularly, sir. Hawker and me."

"Just to keep an eye on things."

"We want to be sure you make a better fist of it than the rest of your family."

"We're going to be your advisers, sir!"

"The power behind the throne!"

"No need to pull a face, old thing!"

"Trust me." Boon grinned and touched the brim of his cap in mock salute. "You'll hardly notice we're here."

I shivered and looked away. When I turned back, the Prefects were gone, the only evidence that they had ever been there at all the lingering scents of fireworks and sherbet dip.

I left that place as fast as I could, not stopping to dry my hands and barely restraining myself from breaking into a run as I hurried past the photographs of dead prime ministers, past serving staff, security men and the open-necked parade of civil servants.

Outside in the unforgiving sunshine, I had to stop to catch my breath and gather my wits because I knew, in an awful moment of understanding, that I had seen the shape of the rest of my life.

Silverman was waiting. "Sir?" he asked, his voice, as ever, the model of equanimity and deference. "Is everything all right?"

I tried to speak but the words would not come. I found myself wholly unable to say their names aloud.

Silverman took me away, helped me into the car and did what he does best, calming me down, soothing me, giving me hope and succour. But I have no illusions. I know how things are going to be.

The Domino Men will be with me all the days of my life and I shall not, I fancy, write again.

AW

ALSO BY JONATHAN BARNES

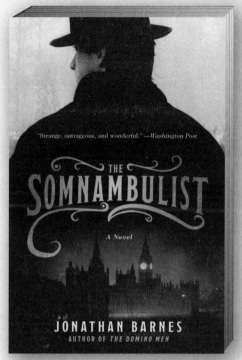

ISBN 978-0-06-137539-2 (paperback)

THE SOMNAMBULIST
A Novel

"There is much that is strange, magical, and darkly hilarious about this book...
An original and monumentally inventive piece of work."

—Washington Post

"Old school entertainment in the penny-dreadful tradition that almost
succeeds in being as sublime as it is ridiculous."

—Entertainment Weekly

"The best fantasy novel of the year."

—Rocky Mountain News